After-Life

Volume 1

By R. D. Davison

Acknowledgements

This book is dedicated to:

Averill Cooke, who I know, would have loved reading every chapter of it, had she have had the chance to see it come to light.

In further memory of Mabel Weaver and her fellow colleagues who were killed in a preventable factory explosion in Tipton, aged just 14 years old on the 6th March 1973.

Finally, this book is dedicated to anyone who has lost someone before their time. It is a written work that aims to make you smile, reflect, and work through the grief; as it did for me while I wrote it.

I would also like to thank the following individuals, without whom, this work would have taken much longer to be printed:

Samantha Lenton – for having the most faith in my writing from the get-go and encouraging me every step of the way.

Alexander Davison – for having the patience of a saint, while I became more and more of a social recluse to finish this work, and for being one of the first to buy a printed copy at full price.

Becki Bales – for continuing to inspire and encourage me with your enthusiasm throughout the After-Life drafted journey.

Graham & Susan Lenton – for always encouraging me to pursue my creative dreams.

Chapter 1. The Hall of Unlived Opportunities

It was a small gathering that attended Mabel Weaver's funeral. Somber faces shrouded by veils and painted with an array of grey, elongated, drawn expressions; their bodies cloaked and hooded in melancholy black, filled the pews. The dry, glazed eyes of the more senior guests, who had attended such circumstances one too many times; lazily turned to the podium where the vicar, his profession's uniform perfectly accentuating the theme of the room, stood to deliver his eulogy.

"We are all here today, to bear witness to and celebrate the life of Mabel Marionnette Weaver." Vicar Riddly had delivered innumerable sermons. So much so, that he knew his script's words by heart. The only ever-changing item in each instance was the dearly departed's name. There were a few snuffles and some choked sobs from those who had been close to Mabel, all bunched together on the front pew, uncomfortably. As the first part of his sermon ended, Riddly sat down and allowed the cheap speakers to crackle into life and play a rendition of *Those Were the Days My Friend,* the haunting voice of Mary Hopkins permeated through the room, falling flat on the jaded audience.

"Oh for...well, this is all rather macabre... Mary Hopkins? *Really?!*" Mabel puzzled, as she gazed around her assembled friends and family. Never before had she seen them as such! Even when her dad, Peter had left his mortal coil, there had been more laughter and joy. What had she done to warrant such a somber send-off?
The icily cracked tone of a disembodied voice tickled at her ear, "This is usually how funerals go... especially for one so young;" it said, in response to her musings.

Mabel froze and looked around. At least, she *tried* to look around. It was the funniest thing, really. She could see and observe those around her, but she had no sense of being physically present. Rather, she became more aware that she was a thought of her former self. Therefore, the act of looking around, was more in keeping with the idea that she *thought* of the concept of looking around, determined that this was more confusing than it should be, and asked out loud instead; "God?"

"If I had a penny for every time..." the sharp voice cackled, not cruelly; "no dear Mabel, I am your chaperone."

"My chaper'..." Mabel's voice drifted off as a vague sense of realisation dawned on her, "Oh! Will you be taking me on to heaven now?" She asked, somewhat intrigued and excited, she'd heard good things about heaven, after all. While she hadn't been a strict attendee of the church in her living days, she had always appreciated the architecture and soporific beauty that she had grown to attribute to the omnipotent teachings.

The cackle grew louder. Mabel shivered somewhat. Again, it wasn't that the sound was one of merciless cruelty. Instead, it seemed as though the owner of the voice was trying to convey a friendly chuckle but had long ago forgotten that such a jolly sound should caress and tickle one's ears, rather than mimic a magpie's call coming from a raven's throat.

"Alas, Mabel, only those who attended church regularly; only skipping days for ill health or personal matters, get the first-class pass to the golden gates." The chaperone explained, calmly; "For many, like yourself – there's a bit of a journey to take."

"Oh Lord..." Mabel muttered, "I've never been one for a hike." She chewed at her bottom lip nervously, (sorry) she *thought* of the motion of gnawing on her non-existent bottom lip.

The sound of a long robe softly dragging across a smooth surface approached Mabel from what she could only determine as being behind her. The delicate touch of a slender hand rested on her shoulder. Before she knew what was happening, Mabel looked down and could see her body materialise into being around her.

She was dressed in a plain white, summery dress. Her pale arms, slender and hairless in the ethereal hue that surrounded her, extended before her and reached out to display her small, delicate hands. She was surprised to find she could feel it! She patted her arms, then poked and prodded at her plump cheeks; combed her fingers through her straight hair, hoping to pull out a few strands so she could see what the ethereal hue was doing to its once chestnut brown colour – but alas, everything was stuck in perfect and pristine place.

"You cannot traverse the relative unknown, without your body in tow," the kind voice spoke. Mabel turned around and her eyes widened momentarily, before narrowing, questioningly. "I've seen you before!" She pointed her finger accusingly.

The figure sighed as he lowered his hood and allowed a cascade of long, silvery hair to spiral down either side of his pale, slender face. The silky strands lay to rest just on his shoulders. His eyes, a deep, pitch black with a faint glint of light in their centre, rolled, rather unsympathetically in response to her tone; as though he had received such an audience before.

"You came to take me away, after the explosion!" Mabel carried on, feeling a sense of injustice coursing through her.

"Indeed..." The being shrugged, almost lazily. The slight tap of a foot, from under his robe, indicated a vague hint of impatience. His voice had a slight accent that Mabel couldn't place, it sounded almost European.

"I told you to bugger off! That I wasn't ready!" Mabel snarled, "You said I was right, your mistake, you'd leave me be!"

The being's foot stopped tapping, and he tilted his head, a slight hint of uncertainty flitting across his face.

"I beg your pardon?" He managed to muster, after a prolonged pause.

Mabel glared fiercely at the figure; "I had just returned to the office after my lunch break," she forced an element of calmness into her voice.

"There was an explosion that permeated through

the building, I was thrown across the room – I was hurt, but not mortally! I saw you, flitting between my colleagues who had been centred directly over the blast zone, helping lift them and take them away, one by one. When you reached me, I told you to bugger off! That I..."

"Wasn't ready." The man interrupted, and scratched at the side of his face seemingly, nervously.

"Exactly" Mabel snapped, "so, please *Mr. Chaperone*, can you explain this?!" She thrust her hand angrily outward to the assembled mourners.

"Ah! Um." The man raised a delicate finger, then paused, resting it on his lips. He winced slightly, and bobbed his knees; before pointing to Mabel's coffin, which was hidden behind a plush velvety red curtain, *So Long, Farewell* chirruping out from the failing speaker.

Mabel watched the scene in mortified horror before spinning around, "Take me back!" She demanded.

"Excuse me?" The man scoffed; his crisp, frosty voice huskier now that it had a sense of flesh around it.

"You heard me!" Mabel snapped, "You've made a mistake, put me back in there... We can call it a Christmas miracle!"

"In Spring?" The man was puzzled, his voice sounding more and more perplexed.

"Well... when did God's son make *his* come back? We could say it was something similar!" Mabel sensed she was desperately clutching at straws.

"You want me, to return your soul and spirit to a prone corpse, that has been resting in state for several weeks; with a lack of blood and oxygen supply? You then want this to be deemed as the second coming of the Lord Christ, as you gurgle and moan in a vegetative state because your body has been deemed brain dead for (and I must stress this) *several weeks?*" The man raised a questioning eyebrow, "mistakes are rarely made – Mabel. You suffered intense internal bleeding and your order to 'bugger off' came over as garbled, incoherent sounds as you choked on your blood. My indifference to your command was an, admittedly unprofessional, attempt at sarcasm which might have been construed by yourself as a false advertisement – and for that I'm sorry. That being said Mabel, you are, I assure you, quite dead." The man calmly explained. "Now, if you don't mind, would you please take my arm?"

Mabel gaped, disbelievingly at the figure before her. Slowly, she turned back to observe the gathered group of mourners who were grimly shuffling out of the crematorium's doors; ushered on by the undertakers.
"But... I was only twenty-nine..." She weakly croaked.
Her chaperone slipped his arm around hers, "which is why you and I need to take a bit of a walk," He whispered by her ear, as he guided her down the steps of the podium and led her down the aisle toward the double doors which had closed behind her friends, her family, and her life. As they approached the beech wooden doors, however, the man led her toward a corridor to the left that took on a completely different hue to the rest of the room.

As they traversed down it, Mabel gaped at the array of empty gilded frames that adorned the walls on either side of them.

"What is this place?" Mabel whispered, cautiously.

"This? This is the hall of unlived opportunities. Moments in time that had been preordained for you but were not lived due to your life being cut short." The figure beside her explained.

Mabel nodded in agreement, before pausing and frowning; "no, I'm sorry – I don't follow."

The figure sighed. He was not meaning to come over as unfeeling, he lamented the loss of anyone who had passed before their time, but the questions! Every time, it seemed they were ready to fire off an argument about every part of the process he had painstakingly put in place to make their journey easier to bear. Once upon a time, it hadn't been too bad. However, as the living adapted their laws, rules, and societal norms to allow for the questioning of things they didn't altogether agree with, his job became a little bit more tiresome.

"What is it that you're struggling with?" He asked, calmly.

Mabel thought through her reasoning before carefully asking, "You said these opportunities were pre-ordained? Why, was my death not one of these opportunities?" She asked, feeling somewhat hopeful that she, Mabel, had found a loophole in the afterlife that might entitle her to a refund.

"Your death was pre-ordained, yet not set in stone;" The man shrugged, nonchalantly.

Mabel stopped walking, her brow almost set with a permanent frown of bewilderment, "nope. No. Sorry – I'm still lost."

The man masked another heavy sigh with the clearing of his throat, "Everyone who lives, has to die. Yes?"

Mabel nodded, yes, this was a perfectly reasonable and valid point.

"So," the man continued, "by proxy, your death was pre-ordained. How, where, when, and why, however, rests on you."

Mabel's eyes widened like saucers, and she opened her mouth to argue, however, the man raised his hand and silenced her. He pointed toward the frame behind her and as her attention focused on the blank canvas, an image came into view. As Mabel looked on, the image of her fifteenth birthday party materialised before her. She and a few of her school friends had gathered with her family at the local zoo and were entertaining themselves by mimicking the bored expressions of the enclosed animals.

"You were given the choice of attending the zoo on your fifteenth birthday or going on a trip to a theme park. You loved animals, so you opted to visit the zoo with your friends," The man explained, as Mabel nodded, smiling fondly at her younger self. So, innocent. She had no idea that she only had fourteen years left of life. Oblivious.

"It was one of the better birthdays I'd had. It was such a laugh!" Mabel smiled, "nothing went wrong – I think it's the first birthday I had where I didn't end up in tears;" She reasoned.

"Yes, well – on the same day, at the theme park your parents had considered taking you to, there was a freak accident on one of the rides. Some major injuries, but no deaths – *unless...*".
Mabel swallowed hard, "I'd have gone there, instead?" she whispered, hoarsely, concluding his point; as with a wave of his hand, the man changed the imagery on the canvas. There, was fifteen-year-old Mabel in the midst of a thrill ride, in a scene that had never happened. She was being thrown several feet in the air as a technical difficulty had resulted in the brakes of the ride failing, causing a horrendous and somewhat explosive crash in the main station.

Mabel gaped, wide-eyed at the scene, before turning to her chaperone; "so, our pre-ordained deaths walk hand in hand with us all our lives, and only take place, based on a two-way decision?"
"Not always two-way," the man explained, smiling faintly. Finally – some decent questions after a millennium of denial. "Sometimes there are multiple choices to make, and it just so happens

that one of those decisions results in a living being meeting an untimely demise. Ultimately, the decision comes down to where they have decided to be at a given time."

Mabel folded her arms and shook her head, "I'm sorry - but you cannot blame those who passed, as being the sole determiners of their demise!"
"Oh?" The man folded his arms, and smiled coyly, "why's that?"
"Well... what about mass shooters? Or rather, those who fall victim to the shootings. It's not *their* fault that some gun-toting fool decided to... Or victims of domestic abuse!" She hastily changed track, "How is it their fault when their partner..." She paused as her colleague raised his hand, again.
"You're coming into the morals of this. The premise of the shopper's decision to go shopping or the victim's decision to marry or be in union with their partner were all just that, decisions. Decisions that those individuals made. It's not a popular rule by proxy, but I wasn't the one who made it. It is agreed, however, that they were not

at fault and as such, they are not punished for their decisions in this world. They are instead met with the same path you and I are on, right now." The man calmly explained, with a smile and a knowing look that seemed to suggest he'd guided the conversation right to the point where he felt more in control.

"What path is that?" Mabel asked curiously.
"The path to deciding which of these decisions resting ahead of you – decisions that you did not get the chance to experience – would be the best choice to help you come to terms with your untimely end." He smiled, happily.
Mabel stared, open-mouthed. She'd just watched her physical body be sent off for cremation, how on earth could she be brought back to experience a wealth of potentially death-defying decisions before she was whipped back to this surreal afterlife?

"But my body?" Was all she could muster, jabbing her thumb over her shoulder.
The man grinned, "Ah you see, that's the fun bit

about this decision – you don't need one."

Mabel narrowed her eyes cautiously, "so I'd be..."

"A ghost, well – spirit really. Ghosts are usually those who choose to haunt the same place over and over without really opting to do much other than plague their family, friends, colleagues; etc. Spirits are free to interact with those around them, leaving very little trace of their having been about in the mindsets of those they engage with, once they *move on*." He grinned excitedly, a strange infantile impishness seemed to have replaced the broodier adolescent persona he'd sported earlier.

Mabel paused to consider out loud, "So, I can engage with folk and experience everything as if I were there in a physical sense? People would see and experience things with me – but after I'm gone, they'll have limited to no recollection of me?"

"Exactly! So, what do you think?" The man grinned, excitedly.

Chapter 2. A New Lease of Life

Mabel stood in quiet contemplation. As a secretary for a university, she'd learned that when dealing with individuals who were far more knowledgeable in their specific field; she was to be patient with their eccentricities. As her chaperone had indicated, life was made up of choices. In her last life, those choices had resulted in her dealing with academics who were exceptionally intelligent with all things research related maybe not so much when it came down to people skills.

Mabel had decided to pursue a career in administration, thinking it would lead to bigger and better things than the part-time store assistant work she'd undertaken, during her studies. The only lifestyle changes her choice had led her to, was a gas leak in the kitchen below her office suite and an untimely end. She wouldn't have minded so much, but had it needed to happen right after she'd returned from enjoying a bland tuna and sweetcorn sandwich that had cost over five pounds?

'Extortionate,' she'd thought at the time; 'this canteen is determined to bleed me dry of savings, one day!'

As this reflection highlighted the dullness of her past life, Mabel had a sudden thought.
She looked up at her chaperone and asked "What's your name?"
The chaperone blinked, confused. The question had thrown him off guard and for the first time since they'd met, he looked closer at his ward.
He paused for a moment, in deliberation; "in all my years, I don't recall anyone asking me my name. Least of all after I've presented them with the potentially endless array of possibilities ahead of them."

Mabel smiled weakly, "So, what is it then? I don't want to keep calling you, *my chaperone*. It seems almost degrading, don't you think?"
The man twisted his mouth in thought, folded his

arms, and closed his eyes. "It's difficult to pick one," he mused quietly; "I've had so many, you see. The joys of living an endless life, I suppose." "Okay," Mabel clasped her hands in front of her, patiently; she had all the time in the world, after all.

The man scratched at the faint stubble on his chin as he pondered over the question.
"The ancient Greeks would refer to me as Charon. Most of the Western cultures call me the Grim Reaper, some even call me Death but that's not really my true part. I was given a jackal's head and called Anubis by the Ancient Egyptians..." He then continued to list off many names that left Mabel gaping at the mullions of titles he'd tried and tested out throughout his time of *chaperoning* the deceased.
'Blimey...' she thought, as the droning of names went on; 'and there I was, grumbling about my *only* name.'

It was true, of course. Mabel's parents had been middle-aged when they brought her kicking and screaming into the world. As such, much of their social circle had not been too savvy with the more popular names of those in Mabel's generation. The result was the decision to name her after her mum's favourite grandma, Mabel; and her dad's favourite aunt, Marionnette. Throughout her drab existence, Mabel had silently cursed her name; it made her feel older than she was. The school ground teasing had been intense! Especially, when it transpired the headmistress's borderline feral cat had shared the same first name.

Her companion cleared his throat. The sound broke Mabel's reflection and he smiled at her proudly.

"I have decided to go with Thanatoscharonanubis Erebusyamabaldr Tartarus," he was positively beaming. Admittedly, it had taken a while, but he reasoned his more preferred sounding names seemed to work well together.

Mabel blinked dumbly for a moment as she slowly broke down the names. She wasn't completely ignorant; she'd studied the classics at university and recognised some of the titles that had been put together like a verbal representation of Frankenstein's monster.

"So... Death, ferryman, representative of funerary rites. Darkness, death (again); and justice, light, and beauty. Surname being torment and suffering?" She looked up quizzically at the inane grin of the man's face, in front of her. She didn't have the heart to tell him that this wasn't how names were made, largely because she didn't *know* how names were normally made. Instead, she shrugged, "very well," Mabel said; "although it might be difficult for me to recall *all* of that. So, what if I were to abbreviate it? Y'know, just like I'm Mabel, but my friends called me Mab."
"Very well, how about... Thet?" The man shrugged.
"Thet?" Mabel frowned.
"Yes! First two letters of the forename, first initial of the middle, and first initial of the surname, Thet;" there was that impish smile again.
Mabel smirked, bemused; "very well, Thet – it's

nice to meet you."

Thet beamed; it was nice to have a name of his choosing, for once. He looked kindly at Mabel, who smiled back hesitantly before he hastily added; "and it's a pleasure to meet you too, Mabel."

"Call me Mab!" Mabel shuddered, "I'm only Mabel on paper. Right, decision time."

Mabel swung her arms loosely by her side and looked around her for what felt like the hundredth time. Where was she supposed even to start? How many opportunities were open to her? Would they all lead to an untimely demise?

Cautiously, she approached the first of many small frames that hung to her left opposite the disastrous birthday theme park scene. She winced as the image, which appeared to be stuck in a nightmarish loop; illustrated a series of explosions, gore, and flying limbs. As she drew closer to the frame, Thet hurried up to her and made a sound that could have easily been construed as a terrified whimper.

"Maybe not that one," he offered with a smile that beamed as brightly as his brilliantly white teeth.

"Dare I ask?" Mabel mused, waving her hand in front of the frame, in mimicry of Thet's earlier party trick.

"Well..." Thet mused, "I suppose it's not *as bad* as some of the choices you could have made. You *were* famous."

"Oh?" Mabel tilted her head and pulled a pompous expression, "Do tell?"

Thet grimaced, "But your fame was gained from your death."

"Oh for God's sake," Mabel groaned, "how?"

"You decided to get drunk in London and went viral on social media, mimicking something called *The Ministry of Funny Walks*, behind a member of the Royal family, no less;" Thet quietly mumbled.

"How do you die from that?" Mabel asked, completely confused.

"Very easily, when one of the walks resulted in your foot accidentally colliding with the hind leg of the horse they were riding. The kick caused the creature to rear up and fall back, crushing you. I mean you just about survived that, but the security presence that dog-piled on you afterward, was the last straw;" Thet hastily explained. Mabel nodded, slowly, with a mortified expression before moving on to the next frame.

Again, Thet hurried over with another anxious sound.
"No?" Mabel asked, worriedly.
"Shark attack," Thet shook his head sadly.
"But, I can't swim!" Mabel exclaimed, "Why would I be anywhere near the ocean?"
Thet awkwardly grimaced and bobbed his knees, "Not the *ocean*. You were invited to visit an aquatic zoo-like attraction, with your sister who had guest passes to watch the sharks being fed. You agreed to go as you wanted to spend some quality time with your nephew – who kicked your legs from his pram and you just..." Thet mimicked a surreal swan dive and accentuated the action by adding "sploosh..."
Mabel stared numbly at Thet, who smiled sympathetically and encouragingly. Almost scared

to move on, she stepped over to the next frame and watched for Thet's reaction.

"Hmm." Thet mused.
"Third time's a charm?" Mabel asked, hopefully.
"Well..." Thet seemed to be weighing up an invisible set of scales.
"What?" Mabel asked, glumly.
"New diet trend – you became a successful ambassador for it. Bug eating. Plenty of protein to be had eating bugs. Not that I can see any attraction in it myself," Thet reasoned; "I mean, you lived well into your forties."
"Is that it?" Mabel asked although she could reluctantly understand. She couldn't imagine a diet consisting purely of bugs and insects would have seen her live a long and prosperous life.
"I think you'd have lived a lot longer, personally;" Thet reasoned. "Had the movement *Life for All Creatures Great & Small* not raided your Barcelonian villa, hauled you out to the cliffs, and thrown you into the ocean below;" Thet chewed nervously at the inside of his mouth.
"I suppose that'd do it," Mabel cocked her head.

"Not really," Thet couldn't help himself, "you miraculously survived the initial impact and somehow missed the rocks, but there had been reports of shark sightings and well." Thet bit loudly at the air, with an apologetic look.
"Shark attack? Again?!" Mabel raised an eyebrow, "Seriously?"

Thet stepped back and clicked his fingers and long lines of lights lit up the hallway. Disappearing off into the distance, an array of frames adorned the entire stretch. Mabel gaped, utterly transfixed at the potential host of opportunities.
"Okay," Thet surmised, "there were: five hundred shark attacks, nine hundred and seventy-five explosions; one hundred thousand instances of you walking through a live minefield. Fifty thousand of which saw you disregarding the screams of abject terror and horror from your friends, whom you were aiming to have a picnic with – your poor partner. Your left eye was always flung sky high and landed on his vegan spicy salad sandwich, every time..."

In total Thet listed off one million ways in which Mabel had met an untimely demise based on a series of poorly thought-out decisions. By the time he'd finished, Mabel felt what minimal colour had been left in her ethereal body, must have been completely drained!

"Was there *any* decision that I made," Mabel asked weakly; "where I had some modicum of success in life *and* a decent life span?"

Thet chewed on this question for some time, clicking his tongue against the roof of his mouth as he thought long and hard. On occasions, he would step back and count several of the frames before cringing and hastily shaking his head. He then started an annoyingly long deliberation that was accentuated with a series of 'hmms', 'umms', and 'ahhs'.

After what Mabel deduced must have been about several hours, Thet suddenly bounced up with an "Oh!" Hooking his arm out for her to take, he hurriedly strode down the hallway. Mabel desperately tried to keep up with his long strides. Thet was, after all, a mountain of a figure.

Finally, Thet applied his brakes in front of a frame that looked vaguely out of sorts from the rest of its kin. Its frame was dusty but a hint of gold leaf could be seen, barely shimmering in some of its intricate curves, in the dim light. Mabel looked at Thet questioningly, feeling as though she should be panting, and wondering why it felt odd to not be out of breath, or breathing at all!

"Here we go," Thet grinned, "this life sees you live to the oldest of *any* of your decisions."

"How old?" Mabel mumbled as she examined the frame. There was something about it that seemed to be instinctively calling her forward.

"Fifty," Thet's smile would have been contagious had Mabel allowed his energy to fill her with glee.

"My dad died at fifty," she sighed; "it was his last wish that I live at least a little longer than him. Still, if I can have a comfortable life for an extra thirty years, albeit in spirit form, I suppose there's no harm in giving it a go;" slowly, Mabel lifted her hand to touch the frame, but a sharp reprimanding tap on the wrist from Thet stalled her.

"Hold your horses!" Thet exclaimed, in shock; "I've not told you anything about this life, nor what is expected of you as a spirit!"

"Well, that's fine," Mabel responded, rubbing at her wrist which somehow seemed fleshier now than before; "you'll be with me, every step of the way!"

"Will I now?" Thet shook his head with an overly dramatic sigh. "No, I will be checking in on you every so often to ensure that you are on track. You will enter this life, just as the other versions of you have finished with choosing the wrong decisions – thus leaving the remaining right decision, for you. Now, as a spirit, there are some rules to adhere to."

Mabel rolled her eyes, "I suppose that's to be expected."

"Indeed," Thet nodded. "As indicated before, a spirit is someone who enters into a life and leaves very little to no trace of their having impacted on the lives of those around them."

"How does that lead to a successful life?" Mabel asked, confused.

"You will be living vicariously, through yourself," Thet casually explained, as if this should have been common knowledge.

"Oh! So, I *will* have a physical body, again?" Mabel allowed herself a moment of hope.

"In essence. You will be the mechanics behind the physical eyes. You will see the host of life decisions mapped out ahead of your physical vessel. Each path is colour-coded – red is imminent death, doom, and despondency; amber is a risky road that will lead to two choices of either death in peace or death by trauma – *usually.* Green, is the path you should *always* follow, as this is what leads you to the perfect conclusion of the life you allowed yourself to lead." Thet explained, happily, peacefully, and contentedly.

"But, if I'm to follow pre-ordained paths before me, I won't technically be *allowing* myself to..." Mabel started to argue as a light lit up above the frame. There was a large gust of air that blasted out of the ornate four sides, blowing away the dust and cobwebs; before a force of invisible energy started to pull her forward to the portal. "I WILL CHECK IN WITH YOU EVERY SO OFTEN! DO TAKE CARE! REMEMBER TO FOLLOW THE PATHS!" Thet yelled after her, over the vacuum-like sounds. Mabel only just had time to spot a series of intricately carved musical notes, raised hands, guitars, and drums, before she was pulled (rather unceremoniously) into a whirling mass of chaos.

She tried to scream, but her voice made no sound. Instead, she forced herself to focus on the cacophony around her. Were those cheers? Roars? Shrieks?

She jolted as a disembodied man's voice spoke into a microphone; "one, two. One, one, two, two. One, two, three... yup... Sounds good!"

Thud, thud, thud. SMASH! Whack, drrrrrrrr, da DUM! Tsch! BOOM, BOOM, BOOM. Screeches and whirls. Dips and dives of elongated notes as a guitarist went to town on their instrument.

Then... silence.

Mabel opened her eyes. The light shone on her face and warmed her skin to the core. She grinned, it felt so *incredibly* good!

Chapter 3. Kristoph Grayson

"I need a drink, you coming?"

Mabel blinked as her eyes adjusted to the sights and sounds surrounding her. She was in a stadium, and evidentially one of the first few attendees too. She was resting against the barrier in front of the stage and while there were a few members of crew and staff milling around, she and her friend were some of the only ones present who seemed to be there for the show, only. There was a slight prickling sensation around her neck and, lifting her hand cautiously to readjust the irritating item, she tugged gently at a lanyard that indicated she was a VIP for the event. Mabel smiled to herself, she'd never been a VIP for anything before, in her past life.

Mabel tilted her head back and admired the expanse of the room she was in. She couldn't help but feel a surreal sense of belonging, although, for the life of her, she couldn't place why. Everything seemed brand new yet dated too. It was like she was stuck in a surreal sense of déjà vu, where she knew none of this had ever happened before and yet it had – in another time, in another life. As she tried to come to terms with this new sensation, she felt a sharp jab to her side.

"Earth to Mab? I need a drink, you coming?" Mabel turned around a little sluggishly and stared, her eyes boggling. The woman standing next to her was her old school friend, Angel. Her full name was Angelica Rose Brown, however she abhorred it. It was the main reason they'd gotten along so well, having a shared loathing of their full names. In her last life, Mabel had lost all contact with Angel, yet in this life, they were still thick as thieves, apparently.

"You, okay?" Angel asked, suddenly concerned. "Sorry, must have phased out," Mabel shrugged, playing off the momentary lapse of concentration. She grinned and hated herself for how false the gesture felt. It was difficult for her to not feel more aware that the physical form of herself was simply playing host to her spirit.

'The question is,' Mabel thought to herself; 'am I

a skilled puppeteer or more of a parasite?'
It was a valid question too! Any time Mabel
thought of a movement to make, her host would
follow the thought process and move around,
albeit with a moment's hesitation. Even her voice
sounded different! It was as though there was a
delay in terms of what she wanted to say, how the
words formed; and in turn how they reverberated
back to her. In the grand scheme of things, it was
barely perceptible, however, Mabel was more
self-aware of her physical body now than she had
ever been in her previous life.

Angel raised a questioning brow before shrugging
off her friend's odd little turn. Angel was dressed
up to the nines! The show was going to be
somewhat gothic, judging by the artwork and
backdrop setup; not to mention Angel's
beautifully embroidered corset, which
accentuated her flawless curves. Her bottoms
were skintight, torn, and frayed black jeans. She'd
dyed streaks of electric blue in her jet-black hair,
which accentuated her piercing sky-blue eyes.
Mabel had always quietly envied the effortless
beauty of her friend.

Curiously, Mabel tried to make out what she, herself, had opted to wear and looked down to see wide, bell-bottom jeans with a studded belt wrapped around her waist. Mabel was mortified to spot splotches of dried paint and dust scattered around her knees. She was wearing an old t-shirt that had seen better days, the sleeves had tiny holes in them, and she wondered if her host's wardrobe might have an infestation of moths. Why was she wearing this? It was like she hadn't bothered to try, at all!

Mabel was so preoccupied with criticizing her outfit that she had completely forgotten Angel's question. She jumped as her friend cleared her throat.

"So, about that drink?" Angel enquired, "If we get to the bar now, we might be able to get a round in and return to our spot without having to rugby tackle anyone."

It was a somewhat fair assumption. Mabel had realised that Angel was also sporting the same VIP lanyard around her neck; so, they'd obviously been granted early access to the venue, to beat the crowds. Nodding dumbly, Mabel followed Angel to the bar, where a small group had already gathered. They were mostly men, all giants in comparison to them both, which wasn't hard. Mabel being five foot and a half, Angel maybe an inch or so taller; in their eyes, most of the populace who entered the six-foot range, automatically became almighty giants in comparison.

The bar had a mirror behind the myriad of spirit bottles hanging on display. Spotting her reflection, Mabel was horrified to note that her hair was in desperate need of an introduction to a hairbrush. She was certain there were even *more* traces of paint in the unruly nest of tangles on her head! Clearly, her new body was not one for putting in an effort when going out.

Turning her attention back to the bar, she noticed one of the men shifting his position to observe them both. His eyes seemed to hungrily devour Angel, from head to foot. He had dark brown hair, tied back tightly, a nose stud, and a pouty mouth. He smirked as he watched Angel excitedly place her order. Mabel watched as his tongue licked at his lower lip piercing. He smiled kindly at Mabel, but there was something about him that simply chilled her to the core. Angel took out her purse to pay for the drinks but was interrupted by the man who placed his hand on hers.

"No need, I'll get these;" His smile was sickly and more than a little unsettling.

"Oh!" Angel grinned, blushing slightly; "thank you so much!"

"You're more than welcome," The man casually wiped his card over the contactless reader and muttered "Put it on my tab;" to the bar person.

Mabel watched closely as Angel and the stranger started to chat away, happily. Angel was in full flirt mode, touching her hair and giggling politely while gushing over the band, Dark Omens, whom she couldn't wait to see perform. She jabbed her thumb back at Mabel;

"Of course, I wouldn't have been invited to be a VIP today, if it weren't for my amazingly talented friend, Mab! She's the brains behind all the artwork and theming here! The band offered her two VIP tickets to watch the show tonight. I've been a fan since they started, so naturally she picked me!"

Mabel couldn't help but feel her jaw drop slightly as she glanced back at the phenomenal backdrop display of the stage, 'I did that?' She thought to herself in wonder. It certainly explained the messy attire, if she'd been working hard all day to get the display so perfect. She looked down at her hands and noticed how messy they were. For the first time since she'd started observing this version of herself, Mabel couldn't help but feel an element of pride in her capabilities! She'd always been creative in some capacity and had spent much of her previous life yearning to pursue her talents. This version of herself had clearly stopped yearning and wishing for such opportunities and had instead gone out of her way to pursue them!

Allowing the warmth of these positive reflections to wrap around her, Mabel turned back to the conversation Angel was having with the stranger. She still couldn't shake the unsettled feeling she had around this man and it was only after a moment's observation that she worked out why.

His smiles and laughter never reached his eyes. There was something almost hollow in how they stared, unblinkingly at Angel.

Sensing it was probably best to steer her friend away from such a creep, Mabel cautiously ventured; "Angel? Shouldn't we get back to our spot?"

"Defo' Mab! Well... thank you, Aden!" Angel beamed at the man and, linking arms with Mabel, she hurried them both away, completely forgetting to pick up their drinks in the process. As they neared their original spot by the stage, Aden caught up to them both, holding two cups in his hands.

"You forgot these," He smirked.

Mabel mumbled her thanks and looked at Angel who seemed to be entertaining the idea of love at first sight as she gazed admiringly at him.

"I'm so sorry... thank you!" She whispered breathlessly, as she raised the cup to her lips.

In an instant, everything came to a crashing halt with what sounded like a prolonged, low, bass note rumbling around her head. Mabel staggered on the spot! The feeling was not unlike running into a brick wall after a downhill sprint. She stared, mesmerised at Angel who was frozen in time, her cup barely a moment away from her lips. The man, Aden, seemed to be leaning forward with an uncannily expectant expression on his face.

Mabel looked down at her cup and noticed that it was shrouded in red and amber hues. She looked back up and saw that Angel's whole being was drenched in the same aura. Thet had told her to expect shades of red and amber to appear when she was faced with risky decisions, however, he hadn't said *anything* about it branching out to those around her too! As she stared in horror at the scenario in front of her, a rush for survival kicked in. She could throw her cup on the floor and create a scene! No sooner had the thought crossed her mind, the ground took on a green hue and Angel's turned a deep amber. It wouldn't be enough to stop her old friend from taking a sip of her tainted drink.

Mabel desperately looked around her. There was a security person by the stage, shrouded in green.

She could flag that their drinks had been spiked to him, but then the question of 'how did you know?' would arise and somehow, Mabel didn't think that her excuse of being able to perceive the danger in certain choices, would settle as a suitable explanation. Furthermore, when toying with the idea, Angel's aura turned to a deep crimson. There'd be no way that she would be able to flag the security guard over before Angel consumed some of the awful drink!

As she berated herself for not thinking of something quicker, the sound of heavy footsteps broke through the low hum of energy clouding Mabel's mind. The pace of them was hurried, like someone was sprinting but at a pace barely human! With a sudden force, Mabel found herself grasping at air as the cup she had been holding was smacked out of her hands, along with Angel's.

"HEY!" Angel snapped, as the world around Mabel suddenly returned to a normal pace. It felt like she'd resurfaced from a deep-water dive and had rubbed her ears free of the excess water. All the surreal hues and tones had diminished.

Mabel looked dumbly down at the spilled cup on the floor, there was still a faint hint of maroon around the spilled puddles and an off-green to the dark wooden floorboards.

Hardly daring to believe her luck, Mabel turned to their saviour. There was a look of unbridled anger on his face. He was slight in stature and was certainly shorter than the large brute, Aden, who'd bought and spiked their drinks; but there was something about his mannerisms that suggested he was not to be crossed.

"Trust me, you'll thank me when you're not lying passed out or worse, in a layby!" He snapped at Angel, refusing to take his eyes off Aden; "I saw what you did! You have no place here! Get out!" He had a husky, deep tone to his voice that cut like a knife. His accent, Mabel thought, was not too dissimilar to that of Thet's; and she was surprised to find a sense of comfort in hearing it. "Hm," Aden sneered, "dunno what you're on about." He rippled his broad shoulders and wrinkled his nose in disgust at the man who had evidentially just spared Mabel and Angel from an unpleasant fate.

"Is there a problem, Kristoph?" The security guard that Mabel had spotted earlier had quietly approached the scene.

"Yes, Dean; there is," Kristoph responded, not daring to take his eyes off the now seething Aden in front of him; "we've barely opened the doors to fans and already our art manager and her friend have had their drinks spiked!"

"Righto, come on mate, time to go!" Dean, the security guard, grabbed Aden and dragged him effortlessly toward the emergency exit.

Mabel and Angel stared, bewildered at the retreating backs of the security guard and Aden. Kristoph turned his attention back to them both, his expression softening into one of quiet concern.

"Are you both okay?" He asked, calmly. His soft, husky voice was almost purring. "I'm sorry for reacting as such, but I had to do something! I saw him slip a powder of sorts, into your drinks and I... saw red." He shrugged feebly, looking apologetically at Angel's mortified face. He then turned to Mabel, "Mab, I'm so sorry you and your friend had to experience that. After

everything you've done for us here, too!"
Mabel started to stammer a feeble assurance,
completely blindsided by how his voice was
affecting her. She was interrupted by Angel,
however, who in an excited squeak, shouted out;
"Kristoph Grayson... the lead guitarist of Darm
Omens... just saved my life!" Her momentary
anger at his having spilled her drink over the floor
had immediately evaporated. Mabel couldn't help
but quietly thank Angel for having explained who
their knight in shining armour was.
Remembering herself, Mabel beamed at him;
"honestly, Kristoph, it's fine! Think nothing of it,
we're truly grateful for your having intervened!"
Kristoph however, frowned, puzzled; "why so
formal, Mab? I thought we'd agreed you could
call me Kris?" He chastised, jokingly. "Anyway,
I'd best join the rest backstage for a last-minute
warm-up. Should be a good show tonight." With
that, he made a slightly awkward bow before
pivoting on the spot and disappearing behind a
door marked 'Private'.

"Oh... My... Days!" Angel squeaked, breathlessly;
"Can you believe what just happened?!"

Mabel shook her head, quietly, "No, not at all."
"Kristoph Grayson. *The* Kristoph Grayson
looked out for *us*!" Angel was absolutely beside
herself with wanderlust. She clutched at her
lanyard, "I don't suppose our VIP lanyards will
allow us full backstage access?" As she continued
to bounce with excitement, Angel completely
disregarded the lack of enthusiasm from her
friend.

Mabel meanwhile was mithering over something
Kristoph had said: "I... saw red." The words
lingered in her mind, echoing around as though
on a loop. How had he been the only one
capable of breaking through that surreal pause in
time? How could he have intervened with such
lightning-quick reactions when even *she* had
realised certain responses wouldn't have allowed
enough time to prevent Angel from taking a sip of
her spiked drink? She stared at the door that
Kristoph had passed through and quietly
wondered to herself, was she the only spirit
pulling a host's strings, in this lifetime?

Chapter 4. Heavenly Figures

Thet quietly nodded his head in rhythm to the dull beat that could be heard thumping from the nearby arena. If he listened hard enough, he could just about make out Mabel entertaining herself by singing wholly and completely out of tune with the rest of the Dark Omens's fanbase. He grinned to himself; it was good to see a new lease of life being enjoyed. Especially Mab's!

He couldn't quite put his finger on it, but there was something about the stubborn ex-secretary that had struck a warm note with him. Maybe, it was because she'd been the first in however long to ask for his true name so that she could address him like an equal? Maybe, it was because she'd told him to bugger off when they'd first met? Whatever the reason, Thet couldn't help but feel a slight pang of connection with the young soul.

"You seem happy with yourself tonight, Charon." The voice cracked like a whip through the night sky. Thet had heard the owner of it approaching but had chosen to ignore the urge to look around. There was nothing worse than feeding the ego of a greater being, especially one who lived for such adoration and praise.

"Evening Azrael. What brings you here – of all places?" Thet greeted the angelic gatekeeper with a neutral coolness. It wasn't that he disliked the angel, far from it. It was more so that the angel did very little to endear himself to those he deemed beneath him in the afterlife.

As Thet had reviewed Mab's life before greeting her, he'd observed how she had withheld from snapping at multiple personalities in her workplace, owing to their ignorance of the more administrative elements of her professional role. She, like Thet, had provided a service that she was proud of. It wasn't her fault that someone had failed to sign and date a form that could not be approved without such conditions being met – much like in Thet's role. It wasn't *his* fault that some souls didn't make it up the pearly steps due to the constant changes in goalposts being advertised by the almighty.

Once upon a time, there had been ten commandments to go by and that had been all one needed to follow to ensure a path to heaven. Nowadays, it seemed that a soul had to dive through hoop after hoop and spend crippling amounts on charities and churches of choice to ensure they even got to *meet* Azrael face to face! So, it had become custom for the angel to regularly scorn Thet for *slacking* on the job and not *finding* the right souls, fit for heaven. While Mabel might have labeled the culprits of her vexations as "bloody academics!" Thet had taken to cussing the "Holier than thou, angels!"

Azrael looked around their setting, unimpressed; "our targets are low again, Charon."
"That's a shame," Thet shrugged, not in the mood to enter a dialogue with the angel.
"I was under the impression I'd be joining you to accompany two souls to heaven, this evening," The angel sniffed; "either I'm early, *or...*" he cast a callous sideways glance at Thet; "you're dragging your proverbial heels... *again!*" He smirked smugly.
Thet sighed and made a physical effort to extend

his arms and turned about on the spot. With a dry and cutting tone he responded, "I hadn't realised Heaven's numbers were so low, Azrael. I imagine the pressure you're under from your superior is rather tiresome. Especially, if it's resulted in your forgetting that to lift souls to heaven, one needs to extract them from their physical host, and – as you can see – we are somewhat lacking in those right now."

The angel's smirk faltered, fleetingly; "then hurry them along, Charon – we don't have all night."

Thet cocked his head, "don't we? I was under the impression you had nothing else better to do, seeing as you've decided to loiter in this abandoned parking zone, with yours truly."

Azrael wrinkled his perfectly sculpted nose, unimpressed with the chaperone's tone. He opened his mouth to retaliate with a cutting remark but was interrupted by raised voices and staggered footsteps, indicating a struggle.

"How many times are we going to do this dance tonight, Aden?" Echoed the Bristolian accent of Dean the Security Guard's voice, from across the empty parking space. "That's the third time you've somehow gained entry to the venue. Third time you've been caught out, tampering with a girl's drink. Maybe if you were more of a charmer, you wouldn't have to resort to such tactics to win some affection?"

"Gerroff me!" Aden yelled back, as the two men came into view, shoving and lashing out at each other.

Dean shoved Aden down to the ground and stood over him, panting from the exertion of having dragged the drink spiker several streets away from the Dark Omens performance.

"ARGH!" Aden yelled out in pain, as he landed heavily on the sharp stones, the unforgiving edged gravel scratched his hands and arms with their course embrace.

"Now then... you... will... stay... away..." Dean panted, as a cold sweat started to run down his face.

Something was up. He attended the gym regularly, ate healthily, and prided himself in not filling his body with unhealthy chemicals – yet his breathing was unnaturally laboured. Dean grabbed at the stitch that ached sharply in his side and winced. Pulling his hand away, he breathed out raggedly at the red sheen that glistened over his palm.

"Yeah!" Aden jeered, as Dean slumped heavily to his knees, "not so big *now*, are ya!" He jumped up and kicked some of the loose gravel in the dying security guard's face, while he pocketed the incriminating blade into an inside jacket pocket. He knelt, next to Dean who was now on all fours and desperately rummaging in his inside jacket for his phone.

"Now then, I'm going to go back to that show, and do what I've been *trying* to do for the last few *hours,* WITHOUT your interference!" He spat, cruelly, in Dean's hair and kicked the security guard's phone out of his hand, before starting to saunter off.

"You utter FILTH!" The security guard staggered to his feet, and with all the strength he had left, Dean launched himself after Aden, throwing him hard, up against a large dumpster container.

The angel, Azrael, and Thet watched on. With each passing moment, they drew closer to the men. Azrael looked utterly mortified at the display of violence being illustrated, tugging at his neatly curled and permed hair, while Thet seemed mildly amused.

"Should we, *do* something?" Azrael asked as Aden gasped out in pain.

"Hm?" Thet cocked his head, watching Dean stagger backward, smiling grimly at his actions. Aden crumpled forward in a weird suspension, having been impaled on a long, jagged piece of lead piping that was jutting out of the lip of the bin.

"I suppose we could start with introductions," mused Thet as he casually strode up to Aden's now prone form. With a wave of his hand, he detached the man's spirit from his body.

The ethereal figure of Aden blanched in horror at the sight of Thet and Azrael, "bloody 'ell!" He whimpered.

"How charming..." Azrael physically recoiled from Aden, as though he were a boil ready to burst.

With another wave of his hand, Thet released Dean's spirit from its physical form; as the guard fell back limp, exhausted, but with a look of grim satisfaction on his face.

The haunting form of Dean shimmered into life and stared at Aden, Thet, and Azrael, then groaned; "I suppose I should have expected some form of judge and jury to be watching that spectacle."

Aden glared viciously at Dean, "You killed me!" Dean shrugged, "eye for an eye."

"Gentlemen," Thet interrupted them both, pre-emptively anticipating a continued argument in the afterlife; "you have joined us at an opportune moment. Weren't you just saying Azrael that you were expecting to gather two souls, tonight?"

"Well... I... um..." The angel spluttered, helplessly; "Charon, these two cannot possibly enter heaven!"

"I see. Well then, I suppose Heaven's targets must remain below par in comparison to the *alternative...*" Thet smothered a smirk, poorly, as Azrael squirmed uncomfortably.

"Not that I suppose it helps," Dean interjected; "but I donated a proportion of my monthly salary to guide dogs for the blind, without fail. I attended church every Sunday as a kid, although I admit to having fallen by the wayside as life and other commitments took over. I always intended to pick the habit back up though;" Dean hastily reflected, with a hint of melancholy in his voice. Thet turned to Azrael, "I see. Azrael, does this make things that little bit easier, for you? Here we have Dean, who aside from comparing the act of attending church as being a *habit*, has only conducted one, truly foul deed – which was to react rather aggressively to Aden's threat. Which was to do what, exactly?"

Before Aden could answer, Dean piped up; "this leech attempted to spike two VIP girls, and several others throughout the night, failing on three accounts; courtesy of myself." He puffed his chest out proudly, yet Thet's features had turned fixed. His eyes, normally a pure black with a green-blue flame glowing centrally, but far back; turned into a fierce red.

"I do beg your pardon?" He turned, sharply, to face Aden.

"It was just going to be for a bit of fun..." Aden shrugged, suddenly a lot less boastful and thuggish when faced with the threatening vision of Thet.

"Erm, Charon?" Azrael looked utterly bewildered at the chaperone's display of character, "I do believe you're shaking."

"Pray tell... Aden... John... Taylor..." Thet spat each part of the man's name out with such venom, that the three others in his company winced, defensively; "what did these **VIP** *girls* look like?"

Aden couldn't respond. His voice cracked, feebly as he began to shiver in fright. Dean was helpful as always, however, managed to answer on his behalf.

"Two girls, one with electric blue in her hair, *gorgeous* blue eyes; pure stunner I must say. The other one was the stage art design manager – lovely girl, that Mab, although she did seem a bit spaced out, earlier! I put it down to this dolt 'ere." He jabbed his thumb in the direction of Aden.

"Very... helpful, Dean Andrew Hunter." Thet responded in a forced calm tone, "You intervened, I presume?"

"I spotted Kris confronting *this* ass and escorted him out for the first time. It was about an hour or so before the support act came on." Dean nodded, glaring viciously at Aden. If he was going to the *alternative* place, he was determined to make damned sure he'd take Aden with him.

"I say, Charon?" Azrael asked again, cautiously; "I really must ask why all of this questioning is necessary."

Thet snapped angrily at the angel, "It's *Thet*, Azrael. Not Charon, *not* chaperone, *NOT* reaper being. Thet! The questioning is necessary because it transpires there is *ONE* soul you will be taking with you tonight. No more, no less!" The angel opened his mouth to argue, paused; considered the options before him, and nodded; "very well. Mr Dean Andrew Hunter, please – follow me," Azrael grumbled through a clenched jaw.

As the angel and security guard disappeared from mind and sight, Aden was left babbling on his knees, weakly; in front of a livid Thet.

"I'm sorry, okay!" Aden finally managed to express; "had I known you were sweet on those girls; I'd have steered clear!"

"You weren't to know," Thet nodded, his eyes still burning a fierce red, betraying the suppressed rage that his voice hid so well; "that being said, one of those girls had just entered into a new lease of life and barely five minutes in you attempted to harm her!"

"But, it didn't work, did it? Like that guard said, that Kris guy, he called me out! I ended up booted out, and she came to no harm."

Thet considered this for a moment, "What did this Kris look like?"

"I'unno, typical metalhead," Aden shrugged. "Hair longer than it should be allowed and straighter than a ruler. Skinny bloke – a gust of wind could have blown him over. Oh, he had an odd tattoo, on his arm, 'ere." He gestured roughly to his wrist, as he tried to roll up his ghostly sleeve.

Thet's fiery red eyes suddenly extinguished into an icy blue, "the design?"

"Buggered if I know." Aden held up his hands, defensively; "some horned devil thing with three heads. The dude's in a metal band, they're all into devil's n' stuff like that, aren't they?"

Thet tilted his head and observed the personal style choices of Aden John Taylor. Hair longer than it had any reason being and tied back so tightly one could see the thinned-out patches where his scalp shone through. His ghostly form had also kept the nose, and lip piercing which trembled on his miserable, pouty bottom lip. Thet was also aware of the feebly designed snake wrapped around an apple tattoo, on the man's ankle.

"Not all of them are *into* Satanism, Aden." Thet rolled his eyes, exasperatedly and flicked the top of the man's ghostly head. Aden yelped as he disappeared through the ground in an instant. Turning his attention toward the arena's venue, Thet mused to himself, "Some of them wear their demons on their sleeves."

Preparing for another one-to-one meeting with a greater being, Thet made his way to the heavy kick drum beat that filled the air like ripples of thunder. Two deities in one night, he considered,

as he approached the venue's main entrance,
'Aren't I lucky' he thought, morosely.

Chapter 5. Genius, really!

The Dark Omens performance had been just what Mabel had needed! As the band had smoothly transitioned through their setlist, Mabel had been surprised to experience an occasional flashback. The recollections and insights were brief, yet they were enough to leave her marvelling at what her physical form had been up to, before serving as her host.

Through such snapshots, Mabel had come to recognise that Kristoph Grayson was the lead guitarist for Dark Omens. From her host's perspective, the man had always stood somewhat aloof from anyone, outside of his fellow band members. As she watched the guitarist initiate a riff off with the rhythm guitarist, Mabel concluded that it must have pushed him uncomfortably out of his comfort zone, to intervene when Aden had spiked their drinks.

The rhythm guitarist threw his pick mockingly at Kristoph's face, at losing the riff-off, much to the humour of the crowd. Mabel joined in with the innocent jeering. According to her host's memories, Eric Payne provided backing vocals, rhythm guitar, *and* sneaky on-stage cigarettes to the rest of the smokers in the band; above all though, he was one of her closest friends. Mabel quickly noticed that each time she looked over at him, he was already watching her and Angel keenly. There was no doubt in her mind that Kristoph had shared the details of the earlier altercation.

As the players drew out the last few notes of the final song, the lead singer Adrian Smyth bid the crowd a safe journey home. Mabel felt her host's body tense, Ade did have a habit of dragging out his farewells, however, he kept this one short and simple:
"From the bottom of our cold, cruel hearts; we thank you all for being the best friends a band could ever ask for!"
As much as the majority of the crowd started to file out of the assigned exits, Mabel rolled her eyes at the few hopeful stragglers who lingered near the barrier with herself and Angel, in the hopes of meeting a band member or two.

Courtesy of her new insights, Mabel knew better. Dark Omens tended to loiter backstage while the main crew started to take apart the elaborate drum set and sweep up the main stage area. Only when it was crew and catering staff left in the main foyer, did they come out and attempt to wind down after a show. As VIP members, Mabel knew that Angel (who had been a fan of the band since their first show in the mid-noughties), would be able to meet and greet her idols, albeit briefly. Casually, Mabel linked arms with her giddy friend and guided her to the bar. The bar staff had shut up shop just before the encore but had graciously left a few of the bar seats out, which Mabel and Angel both clambered onto wearily, grateful to sit down and rest their aching feet.

Angel sighed and leaned her elbows back on the edge of the bar while watching the last of the crowds trickle out of the doors. Lazily, she nudged Mabel, who was mirroring her friend's stance, easing the tension off her lower back; while also scrutinizing the set and considering the most effective way to break it down without it falling to pieces.

"Mab?" Angel's voice croaked, sore and fatigued from its strenuous use throughout the night; "you're the best, y'know?"

Mabel waved away the compliment, "What are friends for?" She grinned, "I just hope you don't walk away with regrets – you know what some say, never meet your heroes."

Angel laughed, the normally chirrupy sound now flat, with exhaustion; "they're not my heroes, Mab. We've been over this. Kristoph is my soon-to-be husband, Eric is my baritone rhythmic best man. Adrian is my uncle-in-law, Jésús is my bass guitar-playing pet dog; aaaand Pete is my drum tutor." She yawned widely, as Mabel rolled her eyes in mock exasperation.

"Of course, how could I forget? I'm sure the guys have all agreed to this arrangement?" Mabel asked, mockingly.

Angel shrugged, "they've not got a choice on the matter. They're dealing with Angel Brown, after all!"

"They haven't a hope in hell." Mabel laughed tiredly.

Mabel tilted her head back and allowed some of the tiredness to creep down her neck and into her shoulders. As she wiggled her toes in the air on the high stool perch, a thought crossed her mind. If this new lease of life provided choices for her to make, would that entail having a family of her *own?* She cast her mind back to her previous life. Failed attempt after failed attempt at relationships since her mid-teenage years had left her with a somewhat jaded opinion of romance.

Mabel turned to face Angel, intent on playfully mocking her friend's interesting choice of a husband, only to see her friend staring with a perplexed expression at something across the hall from them. Following Angel's gaze, Mabel was shocked to see a random figure standing stock still in the centre of the venue, dressed in a smart three-piece suit and staring straight toward the stage. His silvery hair was iridescent in the neutral lighting.

"I get that feeling sometimes," Angel leaned over to Mabel, conspiratorially, "y'know the one, when you show up for a meeting and realise you got the wrong date, time... *venue?*"

Mabel stifled a giggle, as she replayed the memories of her host. No, there was no evidence that this figure had *ever* attended a Dark Omens concert while she'd served as the Art Manager. Sighing, Mabel slipped down from her perch on the stool. The band refused to run the risk of being accosted by *any* lingering fan (unless they were VIPs), after a particularly volatile incident, involving Kristoph several months back. If they *had* seen the figure standing there, Angel would be left waiting all night to meet her future family and humanoid pet dog.

Cautiously approaching the still figure, Mabel cleared her throat, "Hello, is everything okay? The show's over, now;" politeness was always the best route to take, she'd found.
"Good evening, Mab, I trust you've had a good night?" The figure spoke in an all too familiar tone.
Mabel froze, "Thet?" She whispered, conscious that Angel was watching with intrigue.
"In the flesh... in a manner. Do you like the suit?" While Thet spoke, he barely moved a muscle, remaining rigid in place and staring

unblinkingly toward the stage.

"Very dashing, but completely out of place here." Mabel quietly appraised, "Thet, is everything okay? Why are you here? Did I do something wrong?"

For the first time, Thet moved his head. Mabel's eyes widened in horror, Thet clearly wasn't used to portraying a human. His eyes were still as black as night and his body moved unnaturally, like the Tin Man in the Wizard of Oz, before he'd applied some oil to his joints. If Angel were to approach them, there was no doubt in Mabel's mind that questions would be asked as to how on earth an acquaintanceship had been founded between them both!

"You have done nothing wrong at all Mab. I'm just here to see an old friend, or two," He smiled broadly at her, in what Mabel could only assume was meant to be a reassuring gesture but came over as quite haunting.

"Oh!" Mabel looked about her, "who do you know here? I thought this was a new lease of life for *me* and no one else?"

Now it was Thet's turn to look a tad uneasy, his

smile had become rather fixed, and he was conscious of the fact that he might now be deemed as being leery; "yes, about that...". He saw Mabel's eyes narrow questioningly and hastily waved his hand, pausing time. There'd be enough of it to explain, later.

"Charon?" Kristoph's soft voice broke the quiet hall. "I didn't think it was time for our check-in. Asmo and I only saw you the other month," as he spoke, Kristoph rubbed a towel roughly over his face while apprehensively approaching the figure who had begrudgingly granted him access to a *new lease of life*, on the proviso that he steered clear of trouble. As he drew closer, he spotted the stalled figure of Mabel; suspicion etched across her features.

Kristoph paused for a moment, before slumping his shoulders with a groan, "There's been a cock up, hasn't there?"

Thet held up his hands, "I wouldn't say that, per se."

"Really?" Kristoph stared, mesmerised at Mabel; "because that looks an awful lot like our set manager? She looks like she's familiar with you!

One spirit per lifetime, you *both* said. This is a sandbox realm, one where I can continue improving myself to ensure wherever I end up, will be good."

Thet nodded, "Yes, but..."

"And you threw our *set manager* into this world ... again, I stress, a *singular* world, *for me*!" Kristoph interrupted him. "Look, I'm just about being a good boy here. I already intervened with some asshat who tried to off her *and* her friend! They were *shrouded* in red; you should have seen it. Incidentally, you've not seen the security guard, Dean, have you? I saw him head outside partway through the night, he shouldn't have let you in, especially when you look like you're about to sue us."

"Ah! Yes, about that..." Thet tried to regain control of the conversation, yet Kristoph ranted on, relentlessly.

"*Keep out of folk's ways and just play your music.* Those were *your* words! That was all I had to do in this world. It was all I *wanted* to do in my last life and, were it not for circumstances, I would have done too!"

Thet folded his arms, "Circumstances being getting yourself bound to a demon? And not just any demon at that, either... Asmodeus!" Kristoph's mouth shut tight, and he closed his eyes, muttering; "it was out of my control, you both know that!"

"It was, just like it was well within your control to refuse his help," Thet smirked, as Kristoph pouted. "Now to reiterate, Kristoph. Yes, this is a *mostly* sandbox realm, The figures featured here, however, still count as souls to those above and below. Yes, it has been brought to my attention this evening, that two spirits are sharing a new existence in the same lifetime – yours and Mab's. I grant it's a rare phenomenon, but it can happen – I believe the humans call such instances *kindred spirits.*" Thet pinched the bridge of his nose, "the issue here, however, is that kindred spirits only come about when a lifetime is tampered with by a someone outside of the more *human* spectrum. So, as I only know of one other such individual who is familiar with this world, I was wondering if you might be persuaded to invite your demon friend to join us for a little chat?"

"What makes you think this might involve him, Charon?" Kristoph asked, dragging his gaze away from Mabel, where it had been since the term kindred spirit had been divulged.

"Long story..." Thet sighed, "Oh, and it's Thet now. I've grown somewhat tired of the name Charon."

"Huh," Kristoph grunted, before closing his eyes and pressing down hard on the whitened scar tissue that had been scorched deeply into the skin, just above his wrist.

Kristoph hated the sensation of summoning Asmodeus. He shuddered as pins and needles rippled up and down his body and his head started to throb. To think, just one fateful encounter with a surreal Satan-worshipping fan, and he'd found himself living the most messed up nightmare that he couldn't seem to escape from.

The discoloured patterning and design on his arm rippled as a demonic figure with great bat-like wings; four heads – a cow's joined with that of a twisted goblin creature's that dribbled bile, which in turn was connected to a ram's head, and finally, a salivating beast at the end of a long neck – came to life on his arm. Each of the four mouths yawned widely, before scuttling under and over his skin like a four-legged spider. It scratched up his arm, cackling maniacally just below his ear, before digging its pin-like claws into Kristoph's spine and scraping every inch of skin down his back as it made its way down to the floor.

Thet watched on, unphased, as Asmodeus crawled out from inside Kristoph's trouser leg and proceeded to grow to a more accommodating height to match that of his summoner.

"Six years already? My how the time flies. How y' doing Cha-cha?" Asmodeus flickered a serpentine tongue flirtatiously at Thet, who continued to stare on, unimpressed.

Kristoph cleared his throat, "it's Thet, now." Why he felt the need to correct the demon, he had no idea. He felt no warmth to either deity, but of the two, at least Thet had always been moderately pleasant and polite.

"Thet? THET?! Where did *Thet* come from?"
Asmodeus spat out droplets of bile in the
pronunciation of Thet's newly honed name;
"what kind of name is Thet, anyway?" he cackled,
maliciously.
"An abbreviated one" Thet answered, "thank you
for joining us, Asmodeus. I was wondering if
you..."
"Ah, da, da, dab, dab, der, duh, duh..."
Asmodeus waved away Thet's conversational
tone as his attention turned to the ever-
scrutinizing expression of Mabel. "I say... she's an
apple I'd happily pluck." He stroked the side of
her cheek and nuzzled her neck, seducingly.
"ENOUGH, Asmodeus!" Kristoph snapped,
surprising himself for once again feeling a sudden
uncanny sense of protectiveness over the set
design manager.

The demon chuckled maliciously and snapped
his fingers, in response, three ornate armchairs
materialised behind each of them. Thet sat down
on the edge of his seat with an unrelenting straight
back, Kristoph cautiously perched on the edge of
his seat; while Asmodeus practically flung himself

into his own, like a king on a throne; morphing his physique to that of a horned demonic being in a toga, his whip-like tail flicking playfully, like a cat's.

"You're no fun anymore, Kris – this new lease of life is making you more *holier than thou* than you have any right to be" Asmodeus sniffed with mock hurt and stuck his nose in the air like an infant throwing a tantrum.

Thet and Kristoph exchanged a glance of uncomfortable alliance.

Clearing his throat, Thet calmly picked up where he had been cut off before; "Asmodeus, would you care to explain how Kristoph's frame materialised at the very end of the Hall of Unlived Opportunities, just as I was looking for a new lease of life for Miss Mabel Marionnette Weaver?"

"Phew! What a name!" Asmodeus laughed, mirthlessly; "her parents didn't give her a chance in hell with that ensemble, did they?" He grinned widely at the other two, who remained silent and unyielding in their unimpressed frowns.

With an overly dramatic sigh, Asmodeus expelled

"Why do you think it was me? Angels can stoop to lows too – as we *all* know!"

Thet crossed his left leg over his right and leaned back calmly in his chair, before offering the demon a stern glance; "they can. However, not many of them are aware of this pocket of existence's *purpose*. Nor are any of your counterparts downstairs. They know of its existence and their numbers fill nicely with the souls they receive from it; however, they do not necessarily know that Kristoph is living out the life he was forcibly stripped of," Thet's jaw clenched with ill-disguised aggravation before he pressed on. "We, Asmodeus, that is you and I – agreed to provide this life as a sandbox mode for Kristoph's spirit to flourish and live out the rest of his days. Now, the frame was completely changed and mangled when it appeared in the hall, otherwise I would have spotted it a mile off. As such, it would have prevented me from allowing Mab's spirit to join in this world – yet here we are, with two souls that are clearly triggering some bookkeeping issues upstairs, and no doubt downstairs too.

Asmodeus furrowed his brow, "how'd you figure that?"

"Azrael..." Thet sighed, "he joined me this evening complaining of heaven's figures not reaching their desired targets."

Asmodeus scoffed, "They need to stop moving the goalposts then."

"Hm," Thet stroked the back of his hand, "he was also of the opinion that he would be taking away two souls – Miss Mabel here and her friend at the bar, over there. Instead, he took away a security guard and hell received a malicious individual by the name of Aden."

Kristoph suddenly leaned forward, "Hold on, Dean's dead?!"

"Ah, yes – sorry, meant to mention that earlier," Thet apologised hastily. "It was quick and relatively painless, and he took out Aden in the process who had dealt Dean's final blow in turn. So, really, they took themselves out... I digress; however," Thet shook his head and opted to ignore Kristoph's strangled sounds of disbelief; "you have jeopardised this world Asmodeus, and for what?"

Asmodeus lounged lazily in his chair, before groaning and leaping up, "Right, *fine*! Yes, I tweaked things a bit. Figures aren't great either way and there are more souls stuck in limbus patrum than those up top or down below would truly like to admit; so much so, the residents have made a cosy little sanctuary there, have you been? I've heard it's nice in the wintertime but questionable in Summer" He grinned again, but seeing the impatient looks on the faces of his audience he pressed on with an exasperated groan.

"No one appreciates true genius these days! Really! I devised that our figures on *both* sides need to start growing and as no one's checking in on the land of limbo these days, I thought kindred spirits representing each end of the pole was the perfect solution! Where one protects the other from a fatal decision, two souls will pay the price – that way heaven's count goes up and hell does too. Life continues. Genius."

Chapter 6. A Plan Revised

There was a brief moment of bewildered silence as both Thet and Kristoph processed Asmodeus's sadistic scheme. The demon in question had an air of proud smugness about him that only seemed to swell the more he congratulated himself on the plan he'd concocted. As Kristoph mouthed soundlessly like a goldfish to the hall in general, Asmodeus conjured up a small chalice of claret and proceeded to breathe in the strong fumes, deeply; he then exhaled with joy before knocking the entire contents back in one. As he pulled the cup back from his mouth, there was a deep, dark, crimson moisture painted around his lips, giving him an almost nightmarish clown look.

Thet had heard and seen enough; "your genius, Asmodeus;" he snarled viciously, making the demon jump and stare wide-eyed at the reaper. "Your genius plan has undermined *everything* I vowed and promised both Kristoph and Mab!"

"Pray tell, how?" Asmodeus sat forward, intrigued.

"I promised both these spirits a new lease of life, somewhere safe..." Thet paused as Asmodeus scoffed loudly; "*safe enough* – where they could live out a healthier lifestyle, only faced with a few choices that would always be highlighted before them to ensure they took the right path. You have bastardised that *entire* premise!" Thet was beside himself. He had always prided his word as being one of honour and truth, neither of which were what people wanted to hear sometimes; but it offered a small modicum of comfort in a realm where very little made sense to the newly departed.

"Oo, those are fighting words, Thet!" Asmodeus chuckled, devilishly; "bastardised? Really? You can talk. Isn't this whole realm your bastardisation of purgatory?"

"You demons and angels are more alike than any of you ever care to admit," spat Thet; "so embroiled and wrapped up in your schemes, you never stop to think of those your actions impact!

No, you leave it to the chaperones to clean up the confusion and mess you leave behind in your wake."

"Demons are fallen angels', mate," Asmodeus retorted, coolly; "we might have lost our heavenly privileges, but we never forget our roots and old behaviours."

Thet narrowed his eyes, angrily; "indeed, you all share the same opinion that humans are pawns to be shuffled across a chess board to suit your macabre games. Tell me, how often have you engaged with Kristoph on a one-to-one level *without* allowing your agenda to manipulate matters?"

Asmodeus glanced over at Kristoph who had resumed his scrutinization of Mabel, while he and Thet had been arguing. The demon reflected on the night he'd been summoned to attach himself to the guitarist. By rights, it had been a surreal night for all involved.

Kristoph had been the unwilling victim and Asmodeus had needed a laugh, so he'd agreed to it. It wasn't a bad agreement, in his eyes. Kristoph suffered crippling stage fright before each performance. Prior to their arrangement, each warmup had involved Eric and Adrian finding their guitarist slumped weakly over the toilet, bringing up a week's worth of food as his nerves wreaked havoc on his insides. It had been Adrian's idea to post a cryptic post online to the multitude of fans, enquiring about permanent cures for stage fright. Admittedly, he'd not considered for one moment that some of those fans might be unnaturally obsessed enough to read into such a post. Nor that the same fan had spent much of the previous month stalking Kristoph's every move and had witnessed the vomiting, in secret, before each show, from a neighbouring cubicle. There hadn't been a single moment when Adrian believed that *anyone* would resort to mopping up residual stomach acid and collecting strands of Kristoph's long hair from a hair band, left on the side of a bathroom sink by accident; after Adrian and Eric had helped mop down their friend's sweat covered brow, one night.

Charles Valentine, however, had been that one fan. Out of the goodness of his misled heart, he voluntarily followed each of those steps. Sure, many had called him obsessed. Charles however, deemed himself the one true lookout for his idol, Kristoph Greyson.

In one ill-advised fan meet-up session, Charles had rugby tackled the guitarist in what was later deemed by the judge to be a callous and planned-out act, branding Kristoph's wrist with a horrific image depicting Asmodeus's crude caricature. How he had slipped a branding utensil by security and successfully heated it to burning temperatures, no one quite knew.

All Kristoph knew, was that when he arrived at the hospital, he had a scorched branding on his right wrist, and a demonic being leering over him on his left side, assuring him that his stage fright would forever be a thing of the past but only if he allowed the deity to possess him before each show. It had seemed a good idea at the time, until the night things went too far, and Kristoph had found himself being introduced to Thet. At that point, the jig was up. Asmodeus sighed glumly, Thet had a point. Any interaction with the human had only been because his demonic ego had required inflating in some capacity – but he wasn't about to admit that now.

Asmodeus folded his arms in a sulk, "how dare you assume I don't have Kris's best intentions at heart!" he expressed defensively. Dramatically, Asmodeus clasped his clawed, scaly hands to his chest.

"You don't have a heart, Asmodeus; quit with the act," Thet sighed, with frustration; "the fact remains that we have Kristoph who is just one (maybe two) sins away from a first-class ticket to spend eternity alongside *your* boss. Then we have Mab who..."

"Ah yes, the set manager!" Asmodeus surveyed Mabel, as though she were a Grecian marble statue in a museum, "you seem rather smitten with her, Thetty-Poo."

Thet shifted uncomfortably at the comment, the action wasn't missed by either the demon or Kristoph; "I'm not" Thet mumbled, like a schoolboy denying having feelings for his schoolyard crush.

"What's *her* spirit's story?" Kristoph asked, out of morbid curiosity. He hadn't intended to speak out, but it was all beginning to make sense, this idea of kindred spirits. Mab had always been there behind the scenes in this world, just like everyone else. Admittedly, he'd paid her more attention than he was proud to confess. With Asmodeus's influence, however, being ever present, Kristoph decided to distance himself from her and remain aloof. The intensity of his sudden urge to protect her and inability to take his eyes off her through the show must have been when her spirit was placed in her host! He'd been attracted to her before; now, he felt uncannily tied to her in a surreal and unfathomable way.

Thet folded his arms and chewed his bottom lip, evidentially uncomfortable with speaking on Mabel's behalf. Finally, he sighed loudly and raised his arm, bringing the set manager out of her frozen state.
"Don't you wave that magic hand at *me*, Thet..." Mabel blurted out. Evidentially she'd been anticipating the reaper's earlier actions. The sudden change of atmosphere in the room

however, caused Mabel to choke back her anger as she stared at the maniacally grinning face of Asmodeus; the guilty expression on Thet; and the politely curious features of Kristoph.

"What have I missed?" She faltered, hastily changing her tone, as she recoiled from Asmodeus's lecherous leaning, Mabel added "And who is *this*?"

Thet stood up and guided Mabel to his seat, "my humble apologies, Mab;" Thet sighed, dejectedly. "It would appear there's been a slight change to our pre-conceived plans."

"That figures," Mabel looked questioningly between the three faces. Aside from the delinquent features of what was clearly a demon, there was an air of sheepishness hanging around them. "I suggest someone bring me up to speed on things, sooner rather than later."

Thet cleared his throat, "of course, Mab."

As meticulously as he could, he briefly introduced Asmodeus to her and detailed how he was connected to Kristoph. Cautiously, he then detailed Asmodeus's deranged plan. By the time he'd reached the part about their being kindred spirits, Mabel's face had taken on a whiter shade of pale.

"So," Mabel leaned forward, her hands pressed together; "in summary, Hell and Heaven are screwed because the powers that be keep shifting goalposts. This has resulted in limbo becoming so overrun that there's hardly any space for any more souls?"

"Yes," both Thet and Asmodeus nodded in unison.

Mabel continued, "And Asmodeus's plan sees Kristoph as the hell side of this paradoxical world's scale, and me as heaven's side. If either one of us has to protect the other, two souls in this world die and are commandeered by either an angel or demon – pending their actions in this world?"

"That's about the sum of it," Thet grumbled, dejectedly.

"Meanwhile," Mabel frowned, desperately trying to piece things together in her mind; "those in limbo remain stuck in limbo, and no one is doing anything about them."

"Um..." Asmodeus's smug look faltered.

"So, limbo continues to grow, while this world will eventually run out of souls;" Mabel persisted, as Thet and Kristoph smothered their amusement as Asmodeus's smugness continued to slip away with each word. "Kristoph and I will be the only ones left. Once we die here, we then join where? If I know I have condemned a soul to die by protecting Kristoph, doesn't that make me a sinner and worthy of a place in hell, instead of heaven? In turn, if Kristoph has gone out of his way to protect me, doesn't that eradicate any sin from his past life and make him worthy of heaven?"

Asmodeus sank, defeated into his chair; "well, of course, I hadn't ironed out *every* kink in the genius plan!"

"It's not genius, Asmodeus;" Mabel glared at him, fiercely; "it's lunacy on a grand scale! Two men died this evening, and they needn't have. Were Kristoph and I assigned our rightful afterlives in the first place, they would still be alive. So, really – take Kristoph and me out of the picture, life can go on as normal. Unfortunately, however, you can't do that because limbo is currently overrun because of poor management. So, no one can get from one end of the spectrum to the other without resorting to extremes in their living days, which they are unable to relive because that would mean *no one* could ever truly die!" She paused to catch her breath, "does that about sum up this idiot's '*genius*'?" Mabel asked Thet and Kristoph, feeling like her head was spinning in circles.

"I see why you both like her," Asmodeus snarled from his seat, disgruntled and begrudgingly feeling a sense of admiration for Mabel, himself. "I rarely allow a woman to label me an idiot, without smiting her mercilessly;" He growled, threateningly.
"Oh please," Mabel rolled her eyes, surprising herself with this newfound confidence; "I remember learning about your story, Asmodeus. You're the demon of lust, your fatal flaw was one of possessively loving another. You were so *powerful* that you were overcome by a *human* and were cast down to hell to toy with sexual desires. If anything, you're the omnipotent fiend of adult films, worldwide. Hardly the smiting

type. Unless you enjoy whips and chains."
Kristoph snorted loudly and involuntarily. As he
caught sight of the thunderous glare Asmodeus
cast in his direction, he hastily smothered his
mouth.

"You're smart, Mab – I'll grant you that."
Asmodeus snarled, "But in these realms, being
clever doesn't always serve you well, just ask
him!" He jabbed his whip-like tail in Thet's
direction.

Thet waved away the comment, "Thankfully, we
can put a stop to this now. I can extract one of
you from this lifetime and move you to an
alternative realm which...".

"No, you can't!" Both Kristoph and Mabel
jumped up, defensively.

Thet stared at them both in shock, "I can't?"

Mabel's eyes were wide with horror; "Neither of
us a dead! I mean, well, we are – theoretically but
right here and now, we're alive and kicking!"

Thet considered her arguments and folded his
arms, "But to keep you both here means that
Asmodeus's ridiculous plan continues to take
effect."

The group paused in troubled contemplation. Thet was right, of course. There was no denying that remaining together in the realm would keep Asmodeus's plan working like a well-oiled engine, set to run off a long line of tracks into disaster. "Who's in charge of limbo?" Mabel asked cautiously.

Asmodeus scoffed and in a camp voice he snidely responded with; "your lord and saviour." Although he shared a subtle look with Thet, that seemed to suggest there was more to it than what he was letting on.

"So, what's he doing while limbo is overcrowding?" Kristoph asked, vexed.

Thet and Asmodeus exchanged a disconcerting look, "stuff," Asmodeus shrugged.

"Stuff?" Kristoph frowned, "what stuff?"

"Stuff, stuff!" Asmodeus emphasised, "Stuff that you needn't worry your perfect little cranium over." He patted Kristoph's head, patronisingly.

Mabel and Kristoph looked at each other. It was clear that something was going on but the two supernatural beings in their company were not willing to divulge more than was necessary.

Limbo was overrun with souls who needed to move on and the one person who had the power to determine one path or another was otherwise engaged. The infancy of a new plan came to Mabel's mind, and as she worked on putting flesh on its bones, she smiled inwardly at the possibilities it might offer her and Kristoph.

"I have an idea," Mabel announced to the group, "but it will need some meticulous care and attention to detail, to pull it off successfully. If done properly, I think it should be enough to ensure that Kristoph and I get to stay here, and Asmodeus's plan can continue to work. The figures in both heaven and hell will continue to rise healthily without jeopardising the peace of this or any other realm. All's well that ends well." Thet offered out his hand, "Please, indulge us Mab."

"Make this world the new limbo. Thet, you could relocate an even number of souls from limbo to this realm. Ensure the number isn't too large that it'll be noticed, or too small that it won't make a difference. Kristoph and I will enter ourselves into scenarios that will require a right or wrong choice with each soul you bring about. The decision will be taken out of our hands and put into theirs, instead" Mabel paused as Thet frowned.

"But Mab," Thet shook his head, "that takes your choices away! What if they make a decision that results in you or Kristoph dying?"

"That's the beauty of the plan, Thet." Kristoph smiled, weakly; "you're aware of it and know how to return us to this, what did you call it Asmodeus? Bastardised purgatory! If we die here, we're sent to limbo, you simply bring us back. Asmodeus's plan comes back into effect, and we continue helping souls move on."

Asmodeus and Thet both looked at each other ponderously.

"The idea holds merit," Asmodeus acknowledged.

Thet frowned, "it's not exactly the most subtle of plans, Asmodeus," he murmured.

But the demon waved his hand as if shooing the hesitancy of the reaper away. "I propose," Asmodeus held a thoughtful stance, "just until things become more manageable in limbo – that you and I Thet, create a bit of a miracle."

Thet narrowed his eyes, "what kind of miracle?"

"I propose that we make Kris and Mab here, temporarily immortal;" Asmodeus grinned, impishly.

"HA! And you expect *none* of our superiors to notice that, how?" Thet asked, aghast.

"Easy, we make these two our familiars!" Asmodeus folded his arms with a confident nod.

Chapter 7. Lilith

It is a truth universally acknowledged, that many will encounter a moment in their living years, which will inspire them to consider what sounds will accompany them down to the lower echelons of Hell. Some like to believe it is a song that they loathe, being played on a loop. Others like to consider the prospect of torturous scenes, screams of agony, the groans and moaning of the maimed haunting their every move deeper down. Few realise that the sound is universal. It is the sound of a steady and constant clicking, like that of someone tap-tap-tapping on a typewriter. For you see, as one descends to the abyss, the walls of its entrance are lined with drab and dull offices, filled with hosts of grey-faced dictators forced into a life of administrative servitude; no longer able to rise above their ranks and speak out loud enough to rally the masses. Their punishment is to remain mute and serve no other purpose but to fill in the same questions on a questionnaire over, and over until their fingers start to shrink and blister into minuscule stumps.

It was a subtle form of torture, but one that Lilith enjoyed watching; not least because most of the dictators surrounding her, reminded her of the same men that had once scrutinized and ostracized her. If the dictators served as the administrative team, Lilith was their taskmaster; sat quite comfortably on a plush cushioned swivel, office chair.

Times had changed since she'd been cast out of Eden for not abiding by Adam's rule. Once upon a time, she'd had a throne. Thrones were grand, extravagant pieces of furniture that symbolised power and dominion. Lilith had hated her throne. How can one illustrate their power as their arse goes numb on a harsh slab of carved alabaster? She'd argued the point with Lucifer on multiple occasions.

It had cropped up in a staff meeting several months before Mabel's untimely passing, as to whether the managerial staff of Hell would like to make any changes to their office suites. Lilith's first and only request had been for the best office chair Hell could provide – and *boy* did they provide.

Memory foam seating that molded around her perfectly sculpted derriere. Controlled recline that ensured one could lean back languidly and not feel as though they were likely to be catapulted to the next dimension. One supportive, yet cushy headrest that ensured her meticulous posture would never run the risk of hunching. In short, the chair was just shy of perfection. There was only one flaw with the design, in Lilith's eyes. The seat would occasionally creak as she sat on it, causing a momentary lapse of self-confidence in her weight.

As Lilith surveyed her team of disheveled, diminished, and overall depressed dictators, Lilith sighed and leaned back languidly in her office chair throne. In the grand scheme of things, her life in this other realm wasn't too bad. It was on very rare occasions she felt compelled to intervene with the lives of humans in the world above, but, watching the misery play out on the faces of the men who had spent much of their lives using and abusing their power; was all the tonic she needed to ensure a happy and content life, ruling the entrance to Hell.

"How are you, this evening, my Queen?" The deep and harmonious voice of Samael, her partner, caressed Lilith's ears.

Lilith did not look like the rest of the demonic presence. In fact, many of the mortals entering Hell regularly overlooked her and considered her to be another human, like them; until she cracked a whip and they found themselves chastised for such thoughts. Lilith prided herself on looking every bit as human as she could, with raven black hair, and silken skin that shimmered and rippled in the dim light of Hellfire. Admittedly, she did like to flaunt her assets, but as far as she was concerned, she demanded such respect in her realm, that she could do so with the safety of knowing that if anyone so much as glanced at her with a salacious thought in mind, they would soon find themselves in a fate worse than that which they were already bound to, courtesy of Samael.

Lilith twitched the corner of her mouth in

response to her lover, "I am well, my love. Must you test me with such trivial questions?" She sighed, already bored of the niceties.

Samael smiled dotingly at her, although his face betrayed a sense of unease that did not miss his lover's attention.

"Tell me..." Lilith stared deeply into her lover's eyes.

Like all his progeny, Samael's eyes were as black as pitch with a hint of light glowing deep in their recesses. Depending on their owner's mood, the light could alternate between cool blue, to fiery red in a matter of seconds. In the blink of an eye, the flames could hop from a simmering spark to a raging inferno. He wore a long tunic, wrapped loosely around his torso which could morph into the most magnificent wings that arguably outshone Lucifer's own.

Samael was the angel of Death, with Lilith by his side, they had sired a small army of offspring who had been allocated a range of roles; most of which consisted of escorting souls to the afterlife for judgment. Just like any decent parents,

Samael and Lilith doted on their brood, however, there was one of their own who never seemed to follow the correct path.

Samael's lips pursed as he gazed, with fatigue at his wife; "it would appear that one of our children has become embroiled in a convoluted agreement."

Lilith leaned back in her chair, tensing with frustration as an uncomplimentary creak issued from the stem beneath her seat. She didn't need to ask which of their offspring Samael was referring to.

"What kind of agreement?" Lilith sighed with the frustration only a mother, whose child had once again been caught feasting at night on the treats that were supposed to be kept for the week, could mimic.

"I cannot see," Samael frowned, with frustration; "it would appear it is a shrouded agreement that he has entered into, as I cannot perceive from above, nor can I determine its origins from below."

Lilith leaned forward, "So it is with one of my brethren?" She mused, a slight lift to the corner

of her mouth; "only they can shroud such dealings from the sight of greater beings."
"That is what I fear," Samael grimaced, "you know these fiends better than anyone else, my love. Can you think of anyone who would have such close connections with our son?"

Lilith chewed on the idea. There were many of her colleagues and those deeper down in the echelons of Hell who would happily make deals with her army of reapers, yet few deals were successful and fewer yet were conducted in secret outside of hers or Samael's ever-watchful gaze. She narrowed her hauntingly dark eyes and surveyed her administrative team, before snapping her fingers at a particularly short man with a ridiculous pencil moustache.
"You!" She sneered, "Bring me a list of demonic possessions," she commanded, before lounging back in her seat.

The tiny man looked like he'd rather do anything *but* a personal task for the Queen of Hell, however, his punishment demanded he obey her every whim; and he scuttled off, with sweat leaking through his clothes and beading around his forehead.

"Demonic possessions, my dear?" Samael queried, intrigued.

Lilith nodded, curtly; "our son has an avid infatuation with the living. If a deal has been struck with one of my brethren, there is every likelihood that there is a possession involved."

Samael considered this thought process, before frowning and shaking his head; "I'm sorry my dear, but I do not follow."

"I don't expect you to," Lilith yawned widely and shrugged, as the little man hurried up the steps to her office chair and knelt rather unceremoniously at her feet. With great care, he lifted a large tower of paperwork above his greasy, pristinely combed, black hair.

Lilith leaned forward and started to run her long, slender, index finger down the list of possessions that had taken place over the last few years. She smiled as a favoured name or two appeared on the list. Occasionally, she would pick up one sheet of paper, and rifle through several others, before tossing the held piece of paper aside. All the while, the small man remained bent on one (shaking) knee, desperately trying to keep the paperwork held aloft. The mountainous list of possessions had been printed on half of the fallen trees of the Amazon and weighed a small tonne.

Finally, Lilith emitted a slight 'hm!' of recognition. She clicked her fingers impatiently, to the man holding up the paperwork and pointed to a discarded sheet to his left. Desperately, the little human reached for the discarded sheet, his other hand gripped tightly the side of the precariously balanced mountain of papers held above his head. As he successfully grabbed at the sheet and held it up, Lilith snatched it angrily and cross-referenced the piece with another list.

"Interesting..." she mused, under her breath. Samael edged a little closer to look over her shoulder, but she tore the pages asunder, before he could review them, and stood up suddenly. The movement startled the tiny man at her feet to flinch backward, lose balance, and tumble down the steps in a cascade of muted yelps and flurries of paperwork.

"I will be taking a trip up top;" Lilith sighed, lazily. "Be a dear and don't wait up."

Samael knew better than to argue. Instead, he watched on in admiration as Lilith gracefully descended the steps, treading over the whimpering human being as an added insult. Looking up toward the entryway above her, Lilith smoothed out her starlit dress and with one graceful leap, took flight. Her wings manifested from her back like a bat's and scraped at the walls of the cavernous space; the beat of them sounding like an almighty clap of thunder, that caused the wide mouth of Hell to shudder in trepidation.

* *

Kristoph and Mabel were standing with matching dumbfounded expressions feeling completely ill at ease, as both Thet and Asmodeus had linked arms, bowed heads, and started whispering in tongues. It all seemed rather complicated. As she watched the two supernatural beings hash out the secret miraculous deal that would ensure their handy work would bypass their superior's notice,

Mabel couldn't help but consider the repercussions of a contract with a demon and a reaper.

There was a heavy-hitting feeling in the base of her chest that told her the life she had been looking forward to exploring and getting to know more of, was now just another pipe dream that had been cruelly ripped away from her. Mabel sighed inwardly; she should have known it was all too good to be true. After all, she'd already heard over a million similar alternative scenarios; as well as having lived through one prior timeline where her life had been cut ridiculously short, all supposedly based on her independent decision-making, but none of it seemed fair!

Kristoph meanwhile could feel a ball of anger bubbling up inside him. It churned from the pit of his stomach and rose to his throat. As the muttering and hissed whispering continued, he found himself using what limited self-control he had to bite back from screaming 'What on EARTH are you guys playing at?' Curiously, he cast a glance over at Mabel. She looked both determined and terrified all at once, and quietly he admired her ability to remain calm throughout the whole ordeal.

When he'd first encountered Asmodeus and came to learn that he was under a strictly bound contract; the fear and self-loathing he'd experienced, had been overwhelming! Admittedly, he'd soon gotten used to some of the more pleasing aspects of being connected to a demon – especially one as fun-loving as Asmodeus, but it did have its setbacks. The worst attribute of the demonic persona was Asmodeus's inability to rest. The creature *fed* off the crowd's energy, as though each attendee was a delicate morsel at an all-you-can-eat buffet; the issue being, that his appetite was never satiated!

Kristoph had lost count of the number of times he'd found himself in situations where he'd had to barricade himself in the back recesses of the Dark Omen's tour bus, simply to remind his demonic hitchhiker of who the boss of his body was! After all, it was never any fun waking up next to a stranger who insisted that he had promised her the world, only to once again allow the demon to regain its unholy control, purely to let her down gently enough, in a way that avoided too many unwanted lawsuits.

As he continued his subtle appraisal of Mab, Kristoph couldn't help but wonder how she fitted into all of this. Why had Asmodeus chosen *her* to be his kindred spirit? The two of them had never really spoken much, before her new spirit joining her physical host. Even when they *had* spoken, Kristoph had gained the distinct feeling that she hadn't liked him from the offset. He supposed it hadn't helped when Eric had introduced him to her as 'the womaniser of the band, the heart-break kid' – if only he knew, Kristoph thought bitterly!

As the conversation between Asmodeus and Thet continued, Mabel shuffled closer to Kristoph. "Is it still too late to run as far away from these two as we feasibly can?" She whispered. Kristoph sighed glumly, "Trust me, it can't be done - I tried it. Until I can find a way of removing the binding curse that bloody fan scorched into my skin, Asmodeus there will know our every move from now, through to when our physical body dies," he murmured, sullenly.

"Oh," Mabel said, glumly. She folded her arms and casually looked back at the stage's set design that her team was no doubt gathered behind, paused in time, unaware of their manager's current indisposed dealings. It really wasn't fair, Mabel clenched her jaw; she'd been looking forward to embarking on this new life, too.

Kristoph frowned as an idea crossed his mind, "I suppose if we are immortal, would that mean we are immortal for the duration of our agreed sentence with Thet? Or, until the end of time?" He pondered out loud.

Mabel chewed on her bottom lip while she considered his point. Could she live eternally in this new world? What would be the repercussions of that? The questions were endless. Her internal monologue of ponderings was cut short, however, by a delicate '*ahem*' from the rear of the room making everyone, including Asmodeus and Thet, jump.

"My dear child, I don't suppose you would like to introduce me to your friends?"

Thet, whose complexion was naturally a ghostly pale, seemed to take on a sickly sheen of phantom green.

"Mother?" he croaked, uncertainly.

"I think this is my cue to bid farewell," Asmodeus said nervously, as he took several steps closer to Kristoph.

"You will stay put, Asmodeus;" the stern, maternal voice spoke from the dark recesses of the hall.

Mabel and Kristoph looked around desperately, but no matter how hard they strained their eyes, they could not see the owner of the voice that held such power over a demon *and* a reaper. Instead, an intense chill descended over the group. Dressed in her ragged short-sleeved top, Mabel hugged herself tightly to maintain some semblance of warmth. Even Kristoph, who rarely felt the cold, struggled to disguise the disquieting cold feeling of dread that ran down his spine.

"So," the woman's voice possessed such authority that everyone stood to attention as she spoke;

"your father was right. Tell me, Asmodeus, how long have you been coercing my son into agreeing to your terms and conditions?" There was a swish of a silken skirt and a very attractive and intensely stern-looking woman materialised, in the seat that Asmodeus had enjoyed not long ago.

Mabel and Kristoph gaped, open-mouthed, barely able to contain the intrinsic sense of awe at the woman. She looked barely middle-aged, and yet she was mother to Thet? Thet looked older than *her*!
Asmodeus knelt on his knee and kissed the woman's foot, which was adorned with rings, anklets, and a multitude of jewels.
"Dear, Lilith," he purred, as he stroked her ankle. His tone dripped with charm; "I assure you, there has been no coercion. I would not be fool enough to even *attempt* to coerce any of your spawn into a deal."

Lilith smiled pleasantly, yet Mabel couldn't help but feel it was the smile a cat would bestow on a rat before it sliced and diced it to pieces. As the image came to her mind, Lilith looked directly at

her, and Mabel felt her blood run cold. Those eyes! They pierced straight through her!
Mabel felt herself involuntarily choke on air, as Lilith lifted Mabel with a casual wave of her hand, an invisible force gripped firmly around her throat.

"I know this one," Lilith whispered, as she crossed the space between Asmodeus's chair and where Mabel now hovered, in one single stride. She gazed closely into Mabel's eyes, peering deep into their auburn warmth with her blackened knife-like glare. With an unnatural speed, Lilith snapped her attention to Kristoph and mimicked her earlier motions, causing him to choke loudly and struggle helplessly in the air, too.
"This one too, is familiar;" she mused, as her features became livid.

Lilith turned to both Thet and Asmodeus, all pretenses of calmness and pleasantries diminished; "explain yourselves!" She snapped, viciously.
Asmodeus whimpered tentatively, "I didn't think any harm could happen if they didn't *know* each

other."

Lilith glared dangerously at the demon, who shrank away from the group.

"This is *your* doing?" She snarled, maliciously at the demon.

"And mine, mother!" Thet stood firmly in between the demon and his mother, his voice betraying a hint of uncertainty; "please, I'll explain if you let them go – please, Mab's turning blue!"

Lilith cast a cursory glance at the two beings, before flicking her wrist, sending them both sprawling down to the ground, coughing, and choking, while rubbing their necks. Instinctively, Kristoph hurried to Mabel's side, once again driven with an impulse to protect her. Cautiously he held her hand, and the two of them watched on in first surprise then bemused confusion as Asmodeus turned to them both and with a feeble smile asked, "So, how much do you two know about Adam and Eve?"

Chapter 8. Revelations

"Adam and Eve?" Mabel croaked, her throat still sore from Lilith's display of anger. "As in, Garden of Eden, original sin, Adam and Eve?" Lilith 'hmphed' humourlessly, under her breath; "briefest overview, ever."

Asmodeus shook his head with frustration and hurriedly pressed on, "Well, yes anyone who's anyone knows those crucial parts of the story. Okay, well..." Asmodeus stopped, sighed, and slumped forward, defeated. From behind him, Lilith clicked her tongue against the roof of her mouth and glowered loathingly at him. The demon grinned, sheepishly in response.

"My son," Lilith pinched the bridge of her nose as she turned to face Thet; "how many times have I warned you about the potential ramifications of being too lenient with the mortals?" She softly chastised; "I told you once that complications are bound to arise. Now, even I will admit that this is a rare case, but this just happens to be one *massive* complication that has been brought about because of your reluctance to let humans move on, and your demonic friend over there, taking full advantage of your leniency!" She jerked her head sharply back at Asmodeus.

Lilith took a steadying breath and turned to address Mabel and Kristoph. She refused to kneel to their level, preferring instead to stand at her tallest and glower down at them with a cold expression. She sucked noisily at her teeth before using her telekinetic powers to drag Asmodeus's chair closer to her. Sitting down gracefully, she crossed her right leg over her left and wrinkled her nose at the two beings, hunched on the ground, before her.

"Do you know what happens to those, who don't adhere to the laws of the Almighty?" She asked with a quiet calmness that betrayed a hint of venom.

Kristoph glowered angrily at the woman, what on earth gave her the right to treat them so appallingly?

"I can't imagine it would be good;" He responded sternly, through gritted teeth.

Lilith smirked, "understatement of a lifetime.

There are laws, *humans*, that must be adhered to in life. at least that was the consensus, once upon a time, anyway. Women adhered to their men, men adhered to their maker, and so on;" calmly, she twisted a ring around one of her slender fingers.

"I was Adam's first wife, would you believe?" Lilith smirked, "I refused to adhere to *him*, the sniveling wretch. As a result, I found myself cast out of Eden. I found some comfort in the arms of the angel of Death, siring many heirs and dominating the entrance to Hell as recompense for *daring* to establish my own free will." She held her head high and stroked the back of her hand delicately, before continuing. "While it was not the life I would have wanted to lead, I feel I got off fairly lightly in comparison to Adam and Eve," she smiled cruelly. "They were condemned, you see. Cast out of Paradise for eating the forbidden fruit and disregarding the rules set in place by the almighty. Those who illustrated the first sin of the human race were left to experience all the luxuries that a human life without healthcare, shelter, and comfort can afford."

Lilith rested her hands calmly on her lap and smiled, sweetly at Kristoph; "Adam died first, at the ripe old age of forty," slowly she steadied an almost sympathetic look at Mabel. "Eve followed suit not long after. Their physical bodies were buried yet their souls were not welcome in heaven – they were the source of original sin, after all. Heaven forbid they enter Hell! Especially, after they had spent the rest of their meager existences repenting for their wrongdoing. So, here's the rub – what do you do with two souls who belong in neither heaven nor hell?"

Mabel narrowed her eyes, questioningly, and looked enquiringly at Thet; "limbo?"
Lilith laughed a singular bark like 'HA' and clapped her hands with mock delight; "oh you are *precious*!" She tilted Mabel's face upward with the tip of her toes; "my dear, limbo only came about after the almighty had his little miracle child. No, my dear, they enter purgatory. Doomed to live a drab life in darkness with no beginning or end, unable to find rest and peace. Their ultimate punishment was to never again cross paths – that is until now." She smiled

grimly, and for the first time, there was a hint of uncertainty that flitted across her features.

Mabel's eyes widened as realisation dawned on her and she cautiously glanced over at Kristoph. She didn't dare believe what she was hearing. Slowly, she returned her gaze to Lilith's and was surprised to see the demon queen's normal, cold expression, soften into a knowing look of recognition.
"You cannot possibly mean, that I... that Kris ... that *we* are..." Mabel fumbled over her words. Kristoph snapped out of his anger momentarily and looked at Mabel, "That we are what?"
Mabel swallowed hard, "If I've understood what Lilith's said – I think she's trying to imply that you are Adam and I am Eve, reincarnate!"
Kristoph's eyes widened in disbelief before he snorted loudly. His shoulders rocked violently as his body spasmed into a contagious fit of laughter; "you cannot be serious!" He cried out in disbelief.

Lilith raised an eyebrow as both Thet and Asmodeus ventured to step closer to the trio.

Kristoph was laughing so hard he had to grip his sides, he even had tears welling in his eyes. Mabel frowned and groaned.

"I fail to see the funny side in all of this," She murmured with an unimpressed tone.

"Well, think about it!" Kristoph wheezed, "I'm bound to a *demon*! If I'm Adam – why on earth did the powers that be, allow that to happen? Why do I not remember *Paradise*?" He asked in a mock, pompous voice; "and finally, and this is the biggest crux, you say Adam and Eve spent their lives repenting? Well, this version of Adam *certainly* gave up, as he plays lead guitar in a Satanic band!" He let the ripples of laughter wash over him again, as Mabel shook her head slowly, in frustration.

Hesitantly, Mabel glanced up at Thet, "Is all of this true, Thet?" She asked.

"Thet?" Lilith interrupted her, "You changed your name, *again*, to... Thet? Why can't you just be happy with the name we bestowed on you at birth?"

Thet shuffled his feet, "Because you sired hundreds of us in one moment and named us all reapers in order of birth. The humans granted us familial names, I just combined a host of my favoured ones and for Mab's ease, abbreviated them;" He smiled affectionately at Mabel, who returned the look with a smile of comfort.

Thet stepped around his mother and held his hands out to both Kristoph and Mabel, who took them and stood up, brushing off the dust and grub from their jeans.

With a saddened expression, he looked at Mabel, "I'm afraid mother is correct. Had I been aware of your origins; this would never have happened. Asmodeus has well and truly hoodwinked me, this time. Yes, Mab, you and Adam have been reincarnated so many times now that you have all but forgotten your original lives. It can happen with souls who spend a prolonged time being reincarnated. Please believe me though, I had no idea of your origins."

"In my defense..." Asmodeus piped up from behind Lilith's seat; "I didn't know Kris was Adam until I spent some time chilling out in that ridiculously old memory of his."

"The point remains, you *knew*, Asmodeus."

Lilith snapped, silencing the lustful demon; "yet you *persisted* in uniting the two representatives of original sin. Why?"

Asmodeus looked surprisingly weak and miniscule in comparison to Lilith. Even by Kristoph's standards, the belittling of the fiend who had in some ways helped him through some of the more troublesome moments of his musical career, was a little much. With more courage than he felt he had, Kristoph spoke up and found himself defending the demon.

"I'm just offering this out there, based on what we've learned tonight. He was only doing what the rest of *you* have failed to do."

Lilith swooped closer to Kristoph and towered over him. It was evident to all in the room that there was no love lost between the two figures, even if the one could barely recall his former self, let alone his first arranged marriage with the now Queen of Hell.

"Pray tell, little Adam, *what* have we failed to do?" Lilith snarled, menacingly.

Kristoph shrugged, "Try to fix the numbers and figures for Heaven and Hell."

It was clear that whatever Lilith had been anticipating as a response, Kristoph's reply was not one she had expected.

"The figures are off?" She asked, over her shoulder.

"Terribly," Asmodeus groaned, "many of my kin haven't fed off a deplorable human soul for a few centuries now, they're more than a tad hangry."

"Heaven, too?" Lilith turned to Thet.

"It would appear so, mother." Thet nodded.

Lilith nodded, subtly, "your informant from up top?"

"Azrael," Thet and Asmodeus answered, in unison.

Lilith groaned loudly, "That pompous ass? How he got to be the guardian of the gates, I will never know. So," she rested her hands on her hips, suddenly with a managerial head on her shoulders; "Asmodeus unites Adam and Eve to rectify the numbers in Heaven and Hell, how exactly?"

Hastily, Thet and Asmodeus offered a brief overview of the demon's original plan which Mabel and Kristoph had improved upon in theory. By the time they'd finished, Lilith was quietly chuckling to herself while pinching the bridge of her nose.

"Well, this is all rather intriguing. So, the son of the Almighty, has vanished?" She asked.

"Not vanished, just busy doing... stuff, if the rumours are to be believed;" Asmodeus nervously corrected her.

"Hm," Lilith glared suspiciously up to the rafters of the hall, as though she could see up to the heavens; "very well, doing *stuff.* Adam and Eve are reunited, until now, unknowingly and determined to put their lives on the line to rectify the failings of the Sunspot. Their award being, no doubt, original sin forgiven and a chance to *finally* move on?" She smiled, slyly; "are you both *sure* the conniving minds of your original souls aren't still flourishingly active?"

Lilith shook her head, "Very well, I will allow for this surreal deal to go by. I will turn a blind eye to whatever business you conduct in Limbo. I will also, be keeping a closer eye on what's happening up top through my contacts. It might surprise no one at all to know that much of this arrangement isn't sitting quite right with me;" before anyone could say anything further, Lilith stood up and with a final disapproving glance around the assembled group, disappeared on the spot.

It was some time before anyone spoke again. Unable to maintain the awkward silence any longer, however, Asmodeus cleared his throat; "right, well, I think we all got off rather lightly there."

Thet straightened his three-piece suit and took a moment to compose himself, "Right, well; I will bid you all adieux. Asmodeus, I will select a few souls at random from limbo over the coming weeks. Mab, Kris? Look out for me, come the next full moon; I will introduce you to the souls due to move on then. Asmodeus," he turned to the demon, "I'd like to say it's been a pleasure..." He shrugged, before walking off into the darker recesses of the hall, as Asmodeus cackled in response, shrank into his original minuscule creature form; and scuttled back through Kristoph's being.

No sooner had he disappeared, than a squeal from the bar made both Mabel and Kristoph jump. "Kristoph Grayson, I am a *huge* fan!" Angel had come bounding over from the bar, breathless, with excitement.

Kristoph grinned helplessly, "call me Kris," he shrugged. With a subtle turn to Mabel he muttered, "At this stage, I don't think it matters what I'm called, anymore."

Mabel sighed and smirked, "I'll leave you both to it and send the rest of the guys out. Angel, if you need me, I'll be backstage bringing down all those religious icons." She chuckled humourlessly and winked at Kristoph who couldn't help but smile back.

Chapter 9. Bo

It had been a week since Kristoph and Mabel had learned of their unique origin stories and had begrudgingly taken on the mantel of rectifying the overcrowding problems in Limbo. In just a few days, they were both on more familial terms, than they had been before! After a couple of shows, Mabel learned from Kristoph that Dark Omens were in the midst of a European tour and were set to wrap up their UK leg of the journey, in York.

Aside from Mabel and Eric Payne, no other member of Dark Omens came from the UK. As a result, Mabel found herself being bombarded regularly by Kristoph, who had taken to requesting titbits of historical information about the various towns and cities the tour bus journeyed through. One evening, as the two of them enjoyed a quiet bite to eat at a roadside café, their conversation turned to their remembered upbringings. Mabel couldn't help but envy Kristoph's unique ability to recall elements of his more distant reincarnations, courtesy of his demonic bond providing regular reminders. As Kristoph considered how best to bite into a particularly messy burger, he casually detailed living in various countries around the globe, before finally detailing his more recent structured childhood, in Sweden.

"Apparently my current reincarnation must have got his fill of different cultures and beliefs and decided to return to an ever so slightly Christian rebirth in Sweden. I think it might have had something to do with some of the country's impressive churches," Kristoph said; "I mean the architecture is phenomenal and I can appreciate the desire to worship in any of them. I just... I dunno, I used to roll my eyes at the prospect of someone *other* listening in. Now, though..." He looked down thoughtfully at the burnished scar on his wrist and fell quiet.

As the band's tour bus finally pulled up at York's Hotel Muriel, close to midnight, Mabel couldn't help but grin. She loved the city of York. In her last life, it had been a place that had provided no end of happiness for her. Whether it was the history the streets were steeped in or the morbid fascination it had in being the most haunted city in the UK, Mabel couldn't tell. All she knew, was that whenever she passed the signs saying 'Welcome to York' she felt at home.

Adrien Smyth, the Dark Omens lead singer, had been bullied by his friends to check in a day early to their hotel, purely to enjoy a rare day of leisure. Upon hearing the news, Mabel felt her chest soar with excitement. Within moments, she had compiled a detailed itinerary of shops she aimed to visit, sights she was desperate to see; and places she was determined to eat in. Overall, it was a list of locations where she could enjoy her own company, in peace.

As Mabel sat down for breakfast the following morning and started reading a tourist pamphlet for a nearby museum, the chair opposite was pulled noisily away from the table, and, looking up, Mabel was surprised to see Kristoph looking rather worse for wear and nursing a cup of black coffee.

"Rough night?" She asked, folding away the leaflet.

"Somewhat," Kristoph yawned, widely. "Asmodeus is restless, he hates leisure days."

"How come?" Mabel glanced at the clock on the restaurant's wall. She sympathised with Kristoph's plight, but she was also conscious of the time. She'd woken up at seven to be full of breakfast by eight, after which point, she aimed to grab a taxi into the main city centre to beat the queue for her favourite shop, the Phantom Sellers in the Shambles.

"It means there's no outlet for him," Kristoph explained. "He's the demon of lust. Adoring fans are like an intoxicating drug for him;" Kristoph sighed, "without that, he goes into a funk and gets restless, and angsty. It's exhausting for me, as it's all I can do to keep him contained and not run riot."

Mabel chewed absently on some toast as she mulled over Kristoph's predicament; "you know what you need, Kris? Some retail therapy, why not come with me into the city, I'm certain you'll love it!"

Kristoph yawned widely, "Ready when you are,

Mab;" he winked as he downed the rest of his coffee.

The taxi dropped them off right by the base of York Minster. Even though the shops weren't due to open for another couple of hours, the crowds were already starting to gather, evidentially sharing the same idea as Mabel, to beat the queues. It was Kristoph's first time seeing the city from a tourist's perspective and he couldn't help but get swept up with the first wave of visitors to the city as he craned his neck back to admire the full majesty of its cathedral. He looked around him and marvelled at the cobbled streets, so far removed from any other town or city he'd visited in the UK.

"It's like I'm in a different country," he marvelled.

"Welcome to York," Mabel grinned, "it has that effect on you."

The two of them ventured deeper into the city, the narrow streets encouraged them to walk closer, side by side. They'd barely taken a few steps away from the minster's towering turrets when they found themselves in the main square. The smell of food from the artisan bakeries filled the air, so much so that even Mabel, who'd gorged herself at the all-you-can-eat breakfast, felt compelled to grab a pork pie for a brunch snack later; insisting that Kristoph share it with her. Slipping down a side street, Mabel sighed as she saw the already impressive queue to the Phantom Sellers shop, trailing further back from its front door than she'd have liked.

"So much for beating the queue," she said, glumly.

Kristoph looked up and down the medieval, narrow passageway; marvelling at how close the top floors of the shops were to their opposing neighbours.

"I'm happy to wait if you are!" He grinned, barely able to contain this sense of enjoyment that he'd not experienced in a long time.

It wasn't that much of a wait either, Mabel had to admit. Once the store merchants opened the shop door and started letting in small groups of shoppers at a time, they found themselves walking out with two bags full of unique clay ornaments in the shape of ghosts. Mabel had coveted a rustic clay and fiery red glazed ghost whom she insisted on calling Victor. Kristoph meanwhile was busy stroking the smooth contours of his own soothing ice blue and white ghost, who he'd dubbed Hugo in compliment to Mabel's choice of name. They'd also grabbed a few smaller ghosts for their band members. Mabel was certain that Eric was bound to love his little white ghost who sported the running mascara gothic look and went by the name of Boo. Kristoph, meanwhile, had grabbed a stormy and broody-coloured ghost for Adrian and named him Lesmes, following on from their Victor Hugo inspiration.

As they continued down the narrow, cobbled street of The Shambles, they were both accosted by a man in a dark, ominous undertaker's attire. "Would a lovely couple, such as yourselves, be interested in a ghostly encounter, tonight?" He winked, conspiratorially, before thrusting a small flyer for a ghost tour around York into Kristoph's hands.

"They're really punting the ghosts here, aren't

they?" Kristoph casually reviewed the flyer, before slipping it into his pocket.

Mabel shrugged, "it *is* the most haunted city in the UK, apparently;" she explained. "It's only right that they should feel the need to jump on such a selling point."

Kristoph shrugged, "Y'know, I have yet to find a populace outside of America and Britain, that matches both of your enthusiastic obsessions with ghosts and spirits. Don't get me wrong, I get that it's everywhere, but you guys and the Americans really get off on all of this," He giggled.

"Hm," Mabel pondered on it, "what can I say? We're just a morbid populace."

Kristoph laughed, and playfully draped his arm over Mabel's shoulders, casually squeezing her in a brief hug; "all things considered Mab, you are the least morbid person I know;" He grinned at the flush of rose that coloured Mabel's cheeks at the sudden hug, then pointed ahead; "what do you think that guy's advertising?"

Mabel shook off the sudden rush of confused feelings before following Kristoph's pointing finger. Ahead of them, stood a man, looking lost in the middle of the pathway. He carried a wooden, circular shield, cradled in his left arm and a small axe in his right. Every which way he turned, tourists would admire his attire of an aged cotton tunic and worn woolen trousers tucked into thick, hide-skin boots.

"Huh," Mabel shrugged, "must be a pundit for the Viking Museum. Although..." She frowned as they slowly drew closer; "he looks lost!"

Sure enough, the man seemed to be in a complete state of desperation. If anyone came too close to him, he would grunt under his breath and raise his shield defensively, clattering the axe on its edge in the hope of warding them off. Sadly, it wasn't having the desired effect. If anything, it had started to attract a small crowd of tourists who had started to take photos.

The man turned about on the spot wildly, his eyes wide and alert. When his gaze met Kristoph's and he took in the guitarist's long, fair hair and piercing blue eyes, he whimpered; "bregðr við!"

Kristoph stopped dead and grabbed Mabel's arm, not daring to move his eyes away from the man who continued to repeat the phrase "bregðr við!" while slowly moving closer to them.

"Kris? What's he saying?" Mabel murmured.

"It's old Norse," Kristoph frowned, "my understanding of it is a little rusty, I think it either means 'leave' or..." Before Kristoph could say anymore, the man had shakily reached out his hand and rested it on Kristoph's arm.

"Ah! There you are!" The world around the three of them came to a pause as a familiar albeit somewhat distressed voice appeared from behind them.

"Thet!" Mabel jumped, "I didn't think we were to expect you for another couple of weeks!"

Thet waved her frustrations aside and held out his hand, invitingly; "I see you have met Bo."

Bo turned in response to his name and pointed at his chest, with a confused expression.

"Bo?" Mabel and Kristoph repeated, with some trepidation.

Bo turned to face them both and started to smile weakly, again pointing at himself.

"Indeed," Thet nodded, "now then, Bo and his kin are your first group to help move on."

"I'm sorry – his *kin*?" Kristoph frowned, "Also is he... um, that is to say," he cleared his throat and with a voice drenched in uncertainty he asked, "Bo? Um...þinn vinkingr?"

Bo's face frowned, before breaking into a wide grin and he started to pat Kristoph's arm, rather aggressively, chanting "já, vinkingr!"

Mabel slowly looked between Thet's beaming face and Kristoph's pale look of abject horror, "So, Bo is a Viking, and his *kin* are..."

"Also Vikings, and um, missing, for the moment;" Thet finished her sentence for her, looking about him. "I mean, they shouldn't be too hard to find, they're all dressed in similar attire and..." Thet paused and frowned as he gazed over Mabel's shoulder, "I do believe that's one of them riding a bike!"

Both Mabel and Kristoph nearly cricked their necks from the speed with which they span around, only for Mabel to groan loudly; "no Thet, that is a pundit advertising a Viking Museum. They do that here, they dress up and promote around the streets."

"Oh dear," Thet murmured, as Bo yelled out

'VIKINGR' and charged toward the cyclist who was frozen in a state of stasis. Mabel and Kristoph shared a desperate glance, before racing after him.

Thet waved his hand and the Viking named Bo stopped on the spot, giving Mabel and Kristoph a chance to catch up with him, breathless and bewildered. As he joined the duo, Thet had an apologetic look on his face.

"I am sorry both, I had no idea that dressing up as Vikings was a regular pastime with the living," Thet explained, dejectedly.

"It's not so much a pastime," Mabel panted, "it's a form of living for some. We're humans Thet, we enjoy learning about our ancestry and heritage – well, some of us do. Others struggle to comprehend the value of how our lives have evolved unless there is a visual representation that they can compare their current lifestyles against;" She laughed, exasperatedly. "What you have inadvertently done Thet is unleash a small army of *true* Vikings into a city which prides itself on its heathen heritage. I thought you only intended to bring a couple of souls out of Limbo at a time?"

Mabel added with some uncertainty.

"Ah, yes – how are we defining 'a couple' these days?" Thet asked, barely disguising the guilty amusement he was finding in this new dilemma.

"The same as I presume it has always been, Thet," Kristoph chimed in, "two!"

"Right;" Thet bowed his head, "I might have gotten a little confused on that point."

"Y'think?" Mabel stared at her reaper friend, dumbfounded.

"Well, you see;" Thet reasoned, "Limbo is more overrun than I wanted to believe. After visiting there, the other night, I reasoned we could start moving souls on a little quicker, if I brought out a couple of larger groups," His voice rose, nervously.

Kristoph sighed, "And you thought Vikings would be the easiest starting point for us. Thet, they don't even adhere to most modern-day religions! They have Odin, Thor, Freya, and Hela – their own stories of creation. Thet, they are the masters of storytelling, they are going to know if we are mis-selling them paradise and, need I remind you – Valhalla is their paradise, a realm they can only enter if they *die in battle*!" Kristoph shook his head, "Thet, these guys can only truly move on if they go down swinging! They crave fame! They desire a battle worth fighting. Now, I don't know about you Mab. But I've never really swung a battle axe before."

The group fell silent as they pondered on the situation at hand. Finally, Mabel hesitantly cleared her throat.
"You said you brought Bo's kin, but Thet, you also mention you got confused with the terminology concerning 'couple'. You didn't just bring Bo's kin out of Limbo, did you?"
Thet shook his head, "No, there was one other clan."
"Oh for the love of..." Kristoph groaned.
Mabel frowned, "do you know why they ended up stuck in limbo?"
Thet breathed in deeply with a saddened expression, "They were both *reserve* clans, you see. Bo and his kin were based here in York and the other group I've brought out of Limbo were from further south in what was then termed Mercia. There was an all-out war in 1066

between..."

"Hardrada and King Godwinson," Mabel nodded; "I remember vague details about it from uni. So, two small clans, but – Godwinson was the English King at the time, and a Saxon. If both clans are Vikings, they need to be pitted against an army of Saxons, they won't fight each other."

Thet grinned, "Ah, you see, that is why I thought I would help you out. The other group from Mercia is a small spattering of Saxons. They fell out of favour with Godwinson by not raising their banners and fighting for their King, hence their being stuck in Limbo. Bo's kin never received the memo to fight, thus dying dismally of old age and never really finding peace (in Viking theoretics, at least)."

"So, we find a common ground for these two clans to hash it out, and they move on?" Kristoph reasoned.

Thet nodded, "I'm inclined to believe that this would be the case, yes."

Kristoph turned to Mabel, "I don't suppose you would know of anywhere discrete where a deadly battle would go by unnoticed, here, in York?"

Mabel's mind entered into hyperdrive as it desperately tried to concoct a scheme that might work to their advantage, "I can think of somewhere, but Thet – you *need* to rally these beings together somehow, or at least bring them to the same location. We cannot have true-to-life Vikings and Saxons running amok in modern-day England, it's going to create chaos and carnage! It's also going to attract a wealth of attention from higher and lower beings, which you and Asmodeus both want to avoid. Also, we're going to need your powers to stop time!"

Thet nodded, "Very well, I can rally up the clans. It's going to be hard to bring them all together without their going for each other's throats from the offset, though."

Mabel grinned, "you won't have to. Get Bo and his kin to the Dark Omen's tour bus at the Hotel Muriel, then gather the Saxons. The Moors are as good a place as any for a battle, just look out for the band's tour bus. That will be our maker, I'm inclined to think that Bo and the Saxons will do the rest."

Thet nodded and in the blink of an eye, he and Bo vanished. Kristoph grabbed Mabel's arm with a look of severe concern, "I did hear you right, didn't I? The Dark Omen's tour bus?"

Mabel nodded, as she started to weave between the crowds that had come out of their paused state.

"Mab, think about this – our equipment is still on that coach, and you are expecting a small army of Vikings to sit amiably on said moving vehicle, without reacting to the modernity?" Kristoph could feel the panic rising inside of him, not least because of the envisioned rage of Adrian Smyth; "Mab, if Adrian figures out what's happening, I'll be sacked, heads will roll! He's a lenient guy, but he has his limits and I'm inclined to think that the grand theft auto of a coach full of supplies, might be the proverbial final straw!"

Mabel chewed on her lip, without breaking her stride; "so, what do you propose?"

Kristoph fell into step by her side, accidentally bouncing into several tourists in the process; "alternative transport?" He suggested, feebly.

Mabel shook her head, "Kris, Thet has dealt us a

tough card here. Either we help these two ancient groups to move on, or they return to Limbo – which is impossible. Or they remain here in the world of the living – again, not an option. You and I both know that getting a vehicle large enough for a small army is not going to be easy, not least because it'll draw questions from any designated driver. I'm sorry Kris, but the tour bus is the only option we have!"

Kristoph grimaced, "Adrian's gonna kill us," he groaned, weakly.
"Not unless we ask him," Mabel thought out loud, as she stopped on the spot and looked at Kristoph's perplexed face; "Vikings lived for their battles to be sung in sagas, it was how they secured their everlasting fame. If we sell this as a favour to an old, *very old* friend, with no questions asked; we can ensure that we get full use of the coach and Dark Omens gets a new random single to add to their repertoire. The rest of the band and us, get to witness a once-in-a-lifetime battle that should have taken place centuries ago. Both Saxons and Vikings move on, and we have helped clear Limbo of two large

groups;" Mabel hated the slight sound of deranged panic in her voice, but she had to believe that this would work. Lilith's mocking had hit a sore nerve with her back at that fateful after show meeting. If Limbo's populace could start to reduce, based on their help, maybe she and Kristoph could finally rest in peace once their times came to a natural end.

Kristoph shook his head, "At a push, I can see Adrian agreeing to this – but I think even *he'd* be more than a little unnerved when this battle gets bloodier than anticipated!"

"Well," Mabel winked, "it's a good thing we know a demon and a reaper who can manipulate what people perceive, isn't it!"

Chapter 10. Setting the Scene

The taxi journey back to the hotel went by in a bit of a blur. Kristoph couldn't shake the nervous knot in his stomach as he struggled to envision an outcome of this scenario which didn't see Adrian and the rest of the band kicking him out of the line-up, for collaborating with the idiocy that made up Mabel's plan. As they got to the hotel's carpark, the first sight that Kristoph saw was a highly confused Adrian Smyth desperately trying to converse with Bo and his "kin". Kristoph stopped short, the colour draining from his face.

"I thought kin meant family," he groaned as he dragged his hands down his face, causing his features to look even more drawn and exhausted. "In Thet's defense, kin can mean like-minded individuals. Also, he *did* say that Bo and his kin were set to enter battle, once upon a time;" try as she might, even Mabel couldn't hide the slight rise in tone to her voice, betraying the growing levels of disbelief in Thet's decision-making capabilities.

Kristoph shook his head, "I thought a handful meant like, ten people? Mab, there's got to be at *least* fifty Vikings here!"

Mabel was too busy chewing on her bottom lip, nervously, to respond. They needed to have a long chat with Thet to determine realistic numbers in the future, *if* they miraculously pulled this stunt off. She cast a quick glance over at Kristoph and could see the nerves on his face, 'Come on Kris, keep your composure, you need to sell this concept to Adrian!' She thought, desperately.

They both dived out of the taxi and raced toward the ensemble of confused bandmates and temporarily reincarnated Vikings. As soon as he spotted Kristoph and Mabel's mortified faces, Adrian's expression switched from confused, to one of suspicion and (Kristoph couldn't help but think) fury. Swallowing back his nerves, Kristoph charged ahead of Mabel, he'd be damned if she was going to suffer Adrian's anger at point blank range.

"Kris," Adrian's voice was a forced calm, his Scandinavian accent coming through strongly; "funny thing. I came outside for a smoke, and to admire the view, and I see our tour bus is being raided by a hoard of Vikings," He tilted his head questioningly at Kristoph, as Bo and his brethren started to chant 'Vikingr' in response to his use of the term.

"Adrian, I..." Kristoph began, but Adrian waved his hand, dismissively.

"I've come to accept that since you've joined our group, strange *stuff* seems to just happen;" Adrian pinched the bridge of his nose, "I accept it as a Kris quirk – so, please, if these lot are anything to do with you, or... Mab?" He extended his arm out to Mabel, who poked her head out from around Kristoph's torso with a sheepish grin, "can you tell them that any damage to the bus will be coming out of both of your earnings from this tour? Also, please, could you perhaps tell them to piss off... as they are vaguely annoying;" Adrian murmured under his breath, leaning closer to Kristoph.

"See, this is the thing, Adrian," Kristoph hastily explained the concocted story he'd hurriedly assembled in the taxi ride over to the hotel; "yes, they're to do with me, *kind of.* Mab and I went into the city and encountered Bo here..." he rushed to Bo's side and draped his arm around the confused Viking's shoulders and patted him comradely on the chest; "I admit, there's a bit of a language barrier and I think that's what's caused the confusion. Bo and his... uh, *friends* are actors. They are committed to their art and live as Vikingr, even perfecting the language," He laughed (almost maniacally) as Bo and his "friends" picked up the 'Vikingr' chant, again.

Adrian cast a brief sideways glance at Mabel, who grimaced and tried to convey a look that suggested this wasn't a completely fabricated story and that Kristoph wasn't ad-libbing on the spot. "Anyway," Kristoph loosened his grip on Bo and hurried over to Mabel and Adrian. "From what I could make out, they have an arranged reenactment battle scheduled for this afternoon, in the middle of the um..." He glared at Mabel for assistance.

"Moors," Mabel added, feeling somewhat superfluous.

"Yes, in the middle of the Moors!" Kristoph snapped his fingers gleefully, in relief. "It's against their foe army... the Saxons," Kristoph whispered under his breath to Adrian. He didn't want to see the reaction fifty Vikings would have to the word Saxon.

"Uh-huh," Adrian raised an unconvinced brow, "and you thought, why not offer them the tour bus?"

Kristoph made a small whimpering noise and looked hopelessly at the lead singer. Before Adrian could say anymore, Mabel jumped to Kristoph's aid.

"Look, Adrian; this is a once-in-a-lifetime battle that they've been rehearsing for... for years. They've not had a chance to enact this event due to a host of timing restraints and, in the instance of today, their chaperone has dropped them in it *big* time," She grumbled the last part, with a certain Reaper in mind. "I admit, I think I might have allowed my creative inspiration to get the better of me. *I* suggested we get you all on board with this, as I know Vikings love nothing more than their sagas being sung. Kristoph suggested it might offer you, Adrian, the chance to think of some lyrics outside of your normal repertoire that might get your creative juices going. I mean think about it, if we can get some cameras set up, we could have a free video shoot. You could write out a suitable song that could go viral..." Mabel could see Kristoph's shoulders drooping with defeat out the corner of her eye and she couldn't help but feel she was grasping at straws until Adrian did something that neither of them had anticipated.

"Ah hell..." He flung his arms in the air, "Who told *you* I was a sucker for medieval re-enactments, Mab?" Before Mabel could respond, Adrian twirled gracefully on his foot and turned to the rest of the confused band members, "Guys! It's gonna be a cosy ride to the Moors, with fifty Vikingr; but we're gonna write a saga fit for Odin!"

No sooner had he said this, Adrian and the rest of Dark Omens and the few set technicians who'd gathered outside to see what was happening, all charged toward the tour bus, graciously inviting Bo and his brethren to clamber on board.

Mabel and Kristoph remained rooted to the spot, hardly daring to believe their luck. Mabel noted the mildly guilty expression on Kristoph's face, as he rubbed at his wrist.

"Righto folks," an all too familiar voice erupted from the Hotel's foyer, "we've got a lot to do and a limited time frame, but by Job (sorry) Jove, we're going to do it!" Mabel stared wide-eyed as a fiery, red-headed man in a loose Hawaiian shirt and cargo shorts, sashayed out into the carpark.

"Asmodeus?" Mabel whispered, gobsmacked.

"Call me Mo," the demon in disguise winked, jovially; "I was summoned to pull a rod out of a Smyth's arse" He chuckled mischievously, "Don't worry – I'll be on my best behaviour. So, are you ready m'dears?"

"Won't the others get suspicious?" Kristoph mithered.

"Not at all," Asmodeus reassured them both, "as far as they're all concerned, I've been with you since day one;" having said that, the demon hooked his arms around the necks of both Mabel and Kristoph and dragged them unceremoniously to the coach.

The journey to the Moors was the most uncomfortable experience all parties involved had ever partaken in. Even Asmodeus showed signs of weariness as with every turn in the road, Bo or a member of his army would suddenly jump up and yell some unintelligible obscenity at a landmark, or a church, or in (one instance) a herd of sheep. Adrian's nose was close to touching the limited space of the table as his hands scribbled lyrics furiously into a notepad. Eric and Kristoph, meanwhile, were desperately attempting to establish a melody that would be befitting of a Viking's battle saga.

Mabel felt utterly useless. Sat on the tiniest edge of seating left available on the smart, leather settee; she'd switched on the plasma screen television in the hopes of relieving the tension, only to hastily switch it off again as one of Bo's kin started to yell viciously at the contraption. The saving grace was that Asmodeus had somehow managed to cast a charm that helped to translate much of the Old Norse Bo and his brethren spoke. Mabel was surprised to discover just how relatively calm the Vikings were; especially, considering they all knew they were about to enter a deathly battle where not even one of them would survive. Quietly, she wondered if Thet was having an easier time with the army of Saxons that were (hopefully) awaiting their arrival in the middle of the Moors.

As she considered this, she cautiously reached out and patted Asmodeus's arm. The demon had taken to flirting with one of the few shield maidens in the coach and was laying it on so thickly that the poor woman was looking around uncomfortably for an escape route. Asmodeus looked down at Mabel, reluctantly; "yes?" He asked, rather disgruntled.

"I don't suppose you have a sketch pad?" Mabel asked, cautiously.

The demon frowned, puzzled, before pulling one seemingly from out of nowhere. He handed this to her along with a set of smart, high-end, graphite sketch pencils.

"Thank you," Mabel murmured, as she set to

work, hastily sketching the faces around her. Asmodeus crouched down next to her and watched her work on the shading of Bo's impressively long, braided hair and beard; and snorted. "You do realise these people will all be dead in a matter of moments? Is there any point in drawing their portraits? They're not exactly going to have the time to frame them."

Mabel shrugged, "I saw a group of people die in my last life, Asmodeus;" she murmured under her breath, quietly hoping that no one else could hear her. "And do you know, I can't recall a single face of any of them;" She looked up with a saddened expression that caught the demon off guard. "Just because they're going to leave this world and move on, doesn't mean I have to forget them too. I mean, you have seen countless mortals come and go, I cannot remember a single face from *any* of the lifetimes I have lived, and apparently, there have been a multitude of those. Today, I'm going to help orchestrate the deaths of all these people, to help them move on. These people built their lives around being remembered for their acts of bravery and heroism. Sure, they will have a song written about this day, but I will have their faces etched onto paper. That, to me, shares more than any bloody-themed song ever could."

"How so?" Asmodeus asked, genuinely curious. Mabel showed the rough sketch of the Vikings she'd put together, "look at their hands, their clothes, their faces. See how some smile, how others look worn? See how this one's hands have a few digits missing, the scars on their faces, the intricate braiding of their hair. These people had lives, long ones at that, by all accounts, both in life and in Limbo. Today is their final day, full stop; and this is how they looked."

Asmodeus shrugged, "they just look like a bunch of barbaric mortals to me," he said, before standing up and craning his neck to get a better view through the window.

"And I suppose we all look the same to you, Asmodeus;" Mabel sighed, "I wonder, what set Sarah apart from the rest of us *barbaric mortals?*" She cast a disapproving glance up at the demon who stood tensely with a pursed mouth, opting to ignore her. Clearly, the conversation was over.

Presently, Happi the coach driver, brought the large tour bus to a standstill by tucking it away into a surprisingly accommodating layby. Asmodeus was the first to take charge, calling all to attention and ordering first Vikings and then band members to vacate the vehicle safely and orderly and to gather on the heathery outcrops on the other side of the road. Evidently, his translation charm worked both ways, as the army of Vikings nodded and (somewhat unsteadily) clambered down the steps of the coach and assembled across the road accordingly.

Mabel followed the rest of the band and breathed in the fresh, earthy scents the Yorkshire Moors had to offer. They couldn't have picked a more scenic spot for such an event. Mabel gazed lovingly out across the rolling landscape, painted lush and green with regular patches of purple where lavender and heathery outcrops grew in clusters, scattering across the landscape. It was early afternoon, and the setting was sparse of any other people, aside from themselves.
Kristoph hurried over to Mabel's side; "I don't see Thet *or* any Saxons, do you?" He murmured

in her ear.

It was true. The Moors offered very little in terms of tree line. Standing in one place, one could see for miles in any direction. It would be exceptionally hard for a couple of hikers to go by unseen, let alone a small army of Saxons. Mabel nervously clasped her hands, this had to work; for the sake of everyone involved, she had to have faith that Thet would be on time. As Kristoph continued to mither, Mabel had a sudden burst of inspiration.

"Kris!" She hissed, breaking him out of his mutterings; "is the Dark Omen's set still tucked away in the bus?"

Kristoph stared at her, numb; "you've got to be kidding? That whole set? Crammed into the cargo hold with our amps, guitars – and Pete's drum kit? Do you *really* think we would risk harming any of your displays? We normally tuck it into the spare coach that the rest of the tech crew manage!"

Mabel's shoulders slumped. Of course, she should have known that! While she had spent the last week erecting and disassembling the set display, she'd left it up to her crew of artisans to store it away; at no point had she thought to consider which coach the display was stored in.

Seeing the brief look of disappointment on her face, Kristoph grimaced; "hold on, let me take a look and see if there's *anything* of the set stored there."

As he hurried away, Eric Payne, the multi-talented member of Dark Omens slunk over, and nudged her with a mocking look; "you two seem to be getting on better than before. I was under the impression you thought him a two-faced womanizer. Just one stereotypical lead guitarist diva?"

Mabel rolled her eyes, mockingly; "I never said those things, Eric – you did. I just merely nodded on occasion."

Eric chuckled, "he seems to have calmed down a lot since you both started becoming thick as thieves. It's a relief, truly. It's about time he started behaving more human and less like... Kristoph Grayson."

Mabel giggled quietly. Eric meant well. For all the teasing, he and Kristoph were close friends. When Kristoph had been attacked by Charles Valentine, Eric had been the one to single-handedly lift the deranged Satanist off his friend with a well-aimed rugby tackle. With his stature towering over most of the other band members, at six and a half feet; his actions earned him the nickname Eric the Great.

Eric looked over Mabel's shoulder at Kristoph who had practically disappeared inside the underbelly of the tour bus, and frowned; "what's he lost now, Mab? His marbles were scattered to the wind years ago."

Mabel snorted, "he's looking to see if any of the set display is kicking about in there. He's doubtful, but I think he's humouring me."

Eric raised an eyebrow, "since when does Kris do anything chivalrous and charming for a woman? Also, are you mad? You think we'd be able to cram the set in there with all our kit – without damaging it?"

Mabel sighed, "Yes, yes, I *know* it's usually stored in the other *identical* coach. I just wondered, was all. I just thought, Saxons being religious and Vikings being part of the heathen army – it might be somewhat fitting to have some element of religious iconography as a backdrop to this um... video;" She finished, weakly.

No sooner had she said this, than a muffled 'whoop' came from the base of the coach. As Mabel and Eric watched on, Kristoph slowly started to crawl backward, out of the cargo holder, grunting with exertion as he dragged out a large and battered, wooden cross. Mabel swallowed hard, as Eric hurried over to help his friend drag the prop out of the coach. She'd *never* made a cross of such magnitude for the set before! Where on *earth* had it come from? As she watched on, Asmodeus' smug drawl tickled her ear, "You can thank me later. I believe there's a certain *sunspot* who'll be wanting his claim to fame back; once this little debacle is over."

Chapter 11. The Battle that never Was

The scene was set. As is its want in England, the clouds started to roll in as Bo and his brethren gathered with the few tools and weapons, they had brought with them, from Limbo. Asmodeus's conjuring skills were working overtime; so much so, that both Mabel and Kristoph shared some concern that his actions would no doubt be noticed by a greater being of some form.

Any time someone complained of a vital item being missing, "Mo" would be called into action and would happen to have just the very thing that was needed to make things right in the world once more. The sight of the crucifix had inspired a wealth of pent-up aggression from the small heathen army, as they clattered axes and swords against their shields. Someone had assembled a small campfire and a group of twenty men were gathered around it smoking and eating items that seemed to be stoking up a blind rage, some were even biting the edges of their shields with crazed and deranged eyes, staring in every direction; they sniffed at the air like predatory creatures, half-starved.

"Berserkers," Asmodeus explained, under his breath to Mabel, as she stared transfixed at their mannerisms. "Do yourself a favour and steer well clear of them, from this point onward."
Steer clear. It was a simple instruction but one that Mabel struggled to do as her role in this scenario required her to be in the thick of things, helping with the coordination. She quietly envied Kristoph who, along with his bandmates, had set up shop on a small stage that had been erected just out of harm's way but close enough so that the events could be seen by all.

As the first few peels of thunder sounded overhead, the dull tread of marching feet and the rumbling of galloping hooves could be heard approaching from the opposite westerly direction. In the weak sunlight that broke through from the bruised sky, flashes of dazzling light could be seen as the rays glinted off metal helms in the distance.

In the grand scheme of things, Bo's gathering was miniscule! Fifty Vikings hardly made up an army, yet the cacophony they made in response to seeing their enemy slowly approaching over the horizon, was deafening.

Heavy deep drumbeats from behind her caused Mabel to yelp out in surprise. Pete, the drummer of Dark Omens had struck up an intensely heavy beat on the kick and tom drums. With each blow to the drum skins, Bo and his fellow soldiers would grunt in response. Hammers, battle axes, swords, and spears would clatter against shields. The screeches from the shield maidens wailed in accompaniment to Kristoph's guitar melody. Finally, as Adrian's vocals cut through the unforgiving cloudburst that had started, Thet materialised by Mabel's side with an exhausted but somewhat impressed look on his face.

He beamed at Mabel, "a perfect send-off;" he folded his arms as he surveyed the surroundings. "I have paused time, for those outside of our gathering here. This event will go undisrupted – nice touch with the crucifix, how long did it take

to erect that?" His positive demeanour
diminished when he glanced at Mabel's face,
"you didn't put it together, did you?"
Mabel shook her head and pointed to Asmodeus,
who was busy throwing himself into the role of
videographer.
"Damn your eyes," Thet murmured; "we'd best
get this over with swiftly before a certain someone
notices it's missing."

Adrian's voice rang out across the haunting scene:

"The Gods of men wakened hounds from Hel
Washed their homes with crimson blood.
Doomed those lives they once wished well.
Laid down laws, lost to the flood."

Thet blinked with a curious expression, "rather
morbid lyrics" he appraised, as Bo rallied his
berserkers to charge toward the oncoming
enemy.

The Saxon army would no doubt have shrouded
the sky in a volley of arrows, were it not for the
fact that their numbers were more closely
matched with the Vikings. As the first of Bo's kin

staggered back from the initial ranged attack, Mabel looked back hesitantly at Kristoph, his eyes wide with morbid fascination, yet with a sickly hint of green around the edges of his face. The band played on relentlessly and as more and more of the warriors fell in battle, no longer moving; Mabel gawped at the thrill and excitement on Adrian's face, as he powered through the most morbid and strangely empowering lyrically-filled song she'd ever heard.

Cautiously, she tugged at Thet's arm, "what exactly are the rest of the band seeing right now?" She asked, her voice barely more than a hoarse croak.

"They're mostly seeing the same as you, me, *Mo*, and Kris," Thet shrugged, nodding his head in time with the heavy crash of the snare and toms.

"Mostly?" Mabel repeated.

"Well, admittedly they don't see the blood and the more... ooosh!! *Gory* elements:" He explained, as Bo swung his axe down heavily on a de-helmed Saxon, who sank to his knees with a vacant stare up to the heavens.

Mabel felt her knees begin to buckle and a sudden urge to bring up her breakfast started to creep into her gut. Unsteadily, she staggered on the spot and bumped against Thet, who looked down at her with a look of embarrassed realisation.

"Of course, sorry – you're not used to such sights. I forget sometimes," He linked arms with her and practically dragged her to a more covered space around the back of the tour bus where much of the action was hidden from view; "is this any better?" He asked as the death cry of a fallen soldier echoed around them.

Mabel shuddered, "Barely," She shook her head, "This is awful, Thet!" She brought her knees up to her chest and wrapped her hands around her head to dull down the sounds of the battle.

Thet watched Mabel with a sympathetic curiosity, "Maybe it would be better to choose a different life for you, Mab," He affectionately rubbed her arm, full of compassion; "you shouldn't have to bear witness to any of this."

"I can't leave Kris to do this on his own!" Mabel shook her head, once again turning her attention to the lead guitarist, whose eyes looked surprisingly bloodshot. She couldn't help but feel a sense of peace when she looked up at him. Her mindset shifted from mithering over the mortifying events happening on the other side of the coach and instead focused on how they could both work together to overcome such a traumatic event.

Thet followed her gaze and smiled softly, "You have both been through and seen so much, in your various lives. It would be wonderful to see you both finally rest in peace and move on;" He sighed, sadly.

"Do you agree with the punishment we received?" Mabel asked, curious to hear Thet's take on the matter.

"It's not my place, Mab," Thet answered, clearing his throat nervously.

"Not your place?" Mabel frowned, "Thet, you're a reaper! If anyone has an entitlement to share their thoughts on the outcomes of those in the afterlife; surely it would be you?"

Thet shook his head, "It doesn't work like that. There are rules, hierarchies, and institutions. In the grand scheme of things, I am just the chaperone. I move souls on to their next destination before addressing the next soul to pass on. That's it! Truthfully, this is the most involved I have *ever* been with a soul – two souls in fact," He added, as he nodded up toward Kristoph, who had just strummed his final power chord.

Mabel lowered her hands from her ears and swallowed hard. It was deathly silent. The smell of wet metal, sweat, and blood filled her senses and as she stood up, she found herself grappling at the side of the tour bus to prevent herself from collapsing in a sickly heap. Shakily, she followed Thet to peer around the rear of the coach. The scene before her made her choke!

Not a single person was left standing. There were no cries for help, no long-drawn-out moans of anguish; it was all silent as the grave. Kristoph staggered to join her, looking about the scene with a haunted expression. Whether it was through a combined sense of grief or horror, they didn't know, but their hands linked tightly and refused to loosen as they joined Thet, who was standing over the prone form of Bo. The Viking's once golden hair was now darkened with mud and blood.

Behind them, the rest of the Dark Omens were busy cheering and whooping with Asmodeus as they celebrated a job well done. Kristoph, however, couldn't stop staring into the lifeless, steel-blue eyes of the Norseman at his feet.
"Kris?" Mabel sniffed, "Are you okay?" She asked, tentatively.
Kristoph cleared his throat and looked upward. The darkened clouds had ironically started to clear away to show a baby blue sky. He could feel the tears in his eyes, and he felt ridiculous! He'd barely known these people, *why* did he feel this way?
He shook his head slowly, "when we first met Bo, he kept saying bregðr við."
Mabel nodded, "he did, you said that meant leave? Didn't you?"
Kristoph nodded, "I also said my understanding of old Norse is limited. I looked it up while we were on our way here," He sniffed and hastily

wiped his eyes, "it loosely translates to – one is afraid. He was scared, Mab. He was in a world unlike any he'd ever known, one that *we* both find pleasure and comfort and *happiness* in. All he could feel was fear. And yet, look at his face now."

Mabel reluctantly looked down and drew in a sharp intake of breath, "he's... smiling."
She turned to look at Thet, who shrugged; "where else would he have felt at home, other than on a battlefield against an enemy? Many are stuck in limbo and have no comprehension of what it's like to feel at peace. Many are unsettled with the call for war and conflict clamouring at their bosom. I admit, this has been a trial by fire for you both" Thet sighed, as he rested his hand on the heads of the immediate group of bodies around them. "For what it's worth, I cannot see a single soul here who is struggling with their passing."
"Y-you can see them?" Kristoph stammered.
Thet nodded, "Every one of them. Bo is beaming at you both. Just take a moment to consider how long these souls have been stuck, unable to rest.

Now they're..." he gracefully waved his hand, "moving on. Now then," Thet stepped over a few more bodies; "I'm afraid I have a bit of tidying up to do, so, you might want to check in with Asmodeus. I think he's had a little too much fun, for one day;" He smirked as they all turned round to see Adrian and the demon of lust hugging each other and dancing on the spot, laughing as though they were old friends.

Still holding tightly to each other's hands, Kristoph and Mabel made their way back to the rest of the band. The energy in front of them was in stark contrast to that which rested behind them; so much so, that it was difficult for them not to feel some small sense of relief at being with present-day company. While there was the hustle and bustle from the tech crew, who were hurriedly disassembling the stage and drum kit; the rest of the band were bunched together and looking fresh and rejuvenated.

Adrian hurried over to them with a beaming face, "Quite possibly the *best* experience I have ever had! We should do this more often!" He beamed from ear to ear, "Kris, you might be deranged, mad, downright *infuriating* sometimes – but when you have an idea... Wow!" He mimicked the sound of a small explosion coming out of his head and laughed loudly, before turning to Mabel; "and you! To think of this setting, to put together that crucifix, in so short a space of time – where is it, by the way?"

Mabel stuttered as she looked about her, but Asmodeus came to her rescue; "I think in the excitement it's been trampled on and now resembles a charring heap of ash," He winked at Mabel out of the corner of his eye and muttered in her ear; "it's back in pride of place. No one will be any the wiser, cheer up – I think we got lucky, kiddo. Hey! Have you seen the video I recorded?"

Before either Kristoph or Mabel could say anything otherwise, Asmodeus thrust a smartphone under their noses and puffed his chest out proudly, "What do you think of that?" As they watched the clip unravel, their jaws dropped. Nothing in the video revealed the horrors they had witnessed unfolding on the battlefield. Aside from Bo and his soldiers racing in to meet the oncoming group of Saxons who, Mabel realised, had been nameless to them both; most of the video centered on the band, with a few surprisingly close shots of the berserkers as they had pumped themselves up full of rage.

"How on earth did you record this, so well..." Mabel gawped, "on a smartphone?"
Asmodeus cackled, "I'm a Jack of all trades and master of many! You alright there Krissy babe, you're looking rather haggard?"
Kristoph shook his head, "I'm fine, I... I just need a lie-down, I think. Mo are you good to take care of Mab while I help clear things up here?"
The demon nodded, somewhat perplexed before jovially nudging Mabel in the ribs, "So, my delightful cherubim, one hundred souls now sent over to their next destination. No longer doomed to live in a state of limbo. I mean in the grand scheme of things, it barely makes a dent in the numbers, but *what a start*! I wonder, I know we had some Romans tucked away in there, do you think we could do something similar?"
"I bloody hope not!" Mabel shuddered, her response coming out louder than anticipated

causing Asmodeus's grinning face to falter and a few heads from the tech crew and band to turn, in the process.

The demon narrowed his eyes and drew closer to Mabel, "y'know – *Eve* – a little gratitude wouldn't hurt!" he snarled, threateningly.
Mabel glared viciously back, "You forget your place, *Mo,*" she hissed back. "Just remember, it is *your* fault we're in this situation. Kris and I were entitled to a life of...".
"Purgatory, everlasting!" Asmodeus snapped back viciously. "You are both the original creators of human sin, *remember?* The sooner you recall that and accept that you are no better than the likes of me, or my kind – the *better.*"
"What's that supposed to mean?" Mabel asked, fighting to keep her voice at a lower volume.

The demon chuckled manically and tickled her ear with his tongue, making her cringe, as he whispered; "Demons and devils, we all have our dark attributes, Mon Cherie. Think through all the lives you've both led, why do you think you haven't endeared yourself to your creator yet?

Could it be..." He mockingly gasped, before poking her on the nose, "You both belong in the bowels of Hell with the likes of me?"

Mabel shook her head with a furious expression, "We weren't welcome in either realm, by your accounts."

"Indeed?" The demon chuckled. "Tell me, my dear Mab, when did it become common practice to believe *all* the words that spill from a demon's mouth? Tut, tut... In all your lives, you've still not learned to ignore the pearls of wisdom from the lower echelons. History looks set to repeat itself and you my dear, will *never* move on if you continue to take everything as gospel."

Chapter 12. The Failings of the Heavens

"Next stop: Hannover, Germany;" Eric flopped down on the settee next to Mabel after they had all clambered onto the bus from a phenomenal nighttime show in York. Stretching out his full frame languorously; he sighed happily, "Best country in the world!"

He hummed languidly as he rested his head on Mabel's shoulder. "Say, that sketch is coming along nicely! Shame we couldn't bring Bo and his mates with us, I reckon the Germans would have loved seeing that re-enactment."

Mabel closed her eyes and shook her head. It had been hard enough turning her back on the deceased warriors on the grounds of the Moors, but to know that Asmodeus had charmed the band to perceive each of the 'historical actors' as jovially waving them off afterward had not sat right with her at all. If anything, her little te-et-te with the demon had convinced her to have as little to do with the being as she feasibly could.

Some good had come from the previous day's events however, she could now sketch away to her heart's content with the sketch pad Asmodeus had given her. Also, she and Kristoph were now closer than they had ever been before, and (most surprisingly), the band had taken on a whole new appreciation for her. Adrian had insisted she keep them company on their tour bus. Room was made in one of the bunks at the rear of the bus, which had previously played host to Jésús's collection of magazines he'd deemed "unfit for a delicate lady's eyes".

They now had a couple of days ahead of them to take a steady and leisurely journey by coach and ferry across the channel to Germany. It was granted that flying was only acceptable for tours in the States, as Pete the Australian drummer, suffered from crippling aerophobia, citing "being in a tin box, several thousand feet in the air, is much closer to my maker than I'd like to be." As the American aspect of the tour wasn't due to take place for another month, the band had agreed to travel by bus for the UK and European leg. It had proven to be an insightful experience for all involved. Mabel especially, enjoyed learning about the array of quirks that hindered them at various points of the journey.

She'd been surprised to learn that the outgoing Jésús, the bass guitar player, suffered from a surreal form of claustrophobia. When she had hesitantly agreed to join the band on their bus, he had nearly cracked several of her ribs in a bone-breaking hug.
"Thank you *so* much, for agreeing to this!" He'd beamed. Stemming from Barcelona, Jésús's strong Spanish accent was thick, as he excitedly explained; "I have been desperately littering my bed with adult revistas – no, magazines, sorry. I hoped these guys would prefer such a *unique* library instead of my snoring, and I thought they maybe wouldn't mind my sleeping on the settee in the wider area of the bus if they had some *light* reading to *enjoy*. It's worth the price of a few Sharpie face tattoos," He grinned sheepishly, as

he hurriedly shared his vulnerabilities under his breath to her.

"Are you absolutely sure you don't mind?" Mabel had asked him, somewhat unconvinced. Waving away her concerns, Jésús had simply laughed; "sí, please, by all means! Mabby, I can cope with ascensors – no eh, no um el-e-va-tors? Um, how do you say? Er, also cable cars, aeroplanes – but ah, put me in a little litera, erm, bunk-a-bed? Nope!" He shuddered, shaking his head; his dark oaky thick hair swaying luxuriously from left to right.

His hair was his pride and joy. It rested softly on his shoulders and always smelt like roses. Jésús was easily the most stylish member of the band, with his preferred style of clothing being torn jeans and plain white designer t-shirts that molded complimentary around his physique. Many of the younger female fanbase of Dark Omens saw Jésús as their future partner. Eric, ever the joker, would laugh off such comments; by insisting, "If they heard him in the bathroom after a bowl of paella, they'd say different!"

As the bus rolled on into the darkness down toward the southern coast of England, Mabel rested her head against Eric's. There was no need to worry about mixed feelings or emotions, Eric was generally perceived as being the most affectionate member of the band, hugging just about anyone and everyone. In Mabel's mind, he was the papa bear who held everyone together; even though he was the second youngest member of the band, next to Kristoph.

Almost absent-mindedly, Mabel started to finalise the rough sketch of Bo and his group of warriors, just as Kristoph emerged from the back of the bus, grabbed a bottle of water from the mini-fridge that was tucked into the side of the settee; and perched on the arm of the seat, next to her, to watch her intently.

"Hm, I see you've made him smile," He appraised, "it's a beautiful picture Mab. You'll have to do a group portrait of all of *us* next." Mabel chuckled under her breath, "If you all felt inclined to stay still long enough, I could." Adrian smirked, "what are you trying to say?" In a burst of energy, he suddenly hopped up as though something had bitten his behind, "we're a fairly docile band, Mab;" he shrugged, as he swirled on the spot and grabbed the unopened bottle of water from Kristoph's hand, "just because you're not quick enough with the pencil..." In a move that caused Eric to laugh out loud, Adrian performed a poor moonwalk back to his seat, which Jésús had opportunistically stolen.

Adrian paused and looked Jésús up and down, before shrugging and flopping down on his bass guitarist, shimmying his back end into Jésús's lap, gaining an outburst of laughter from the group. Jésús grunted as he pushed the lead singer up, but Adrian leaned back, completely relaxed. "Eugh, you did not need to go dead weight, Ade" Jésús strained and giggled, before giving up and letting Adrian flop back onto him.

Eric yawned loudly, "Well folks, I think it's well passed my bedtime. Pete?"

Pete jumped up from the table where he'd been slumped, half asleep, "huh?" He snorted loudly, as Eric's voice jolted him awake.

"Care to read me a bedtime story?" Eric mocked,

patting the drummer's shoulder affectionately, "Come on mate, you did well tonight, but you're knackered! Bedtime."

One by one the members of Dark Omens sidled out of the community area and to their designated bunks. Very soon, it was just Kristoph, Mabel, and Jésús left lounging in the communal space. Kristoph rested his head on Mabel's shoulder and closed his eyes, listening to the soft scratch of her pencil's nib on the thick paper. It had been an exhausting twenty-four hours, but somehow Mabel's company had been all that was needed to pull him through it all.

He felt Mabel rest her head against his, and a feeling of warmth and comfort that he hadn't felt in a very long time rushed over him.

Remembering they had company, Kristoph opened his eyes and glanced over at Jésús who smiled sweetly back at him and placed his hand over his heart. Kristoph smiled contentedly and closed his eyes, only to open them again at the sound of a small clatter.

Sitting up, he realised Mabel had dropped her pencil and her head was leaning forward, its owner having fallen asleep at the helm. Jésús snorted quietly and ushered them both to the back bunks. As gently as he could, Kristoph lifted Mabel into his arms, and with extreme care on a moving tour bus, he carried her to her bed and tucked her in. She barely opened her eyes, but as he turned away, her hand reached out and grabbed him in a firm but soft hold. Not wanting to disturb her any more than he had already, Kristoph softly kissed her hand, before resting it down on the small pillow. With a vague feeling of reluctance, he turned his back on the sleeping set manager and headed to his bunk, just outside the doorway.

* * *

Thet stood appraising the situation, through the portrait frame in the Hall of Unlived Opportunities. He couldn't explain it, but there was something about this reincarnation of Adam and Eve that he felt connected to. Could this be the one lifetime, that would see them finally move on?

Dressed in his normal work robe attire, and his usual deathly appearance, he sighed inwardly. The kids had done well with their first assignment. Every member of the Saxon army had been hand-delivered to Azrael, while each of Bo's army had been assigned their more traditional gateway to Valhalla. He watched as Kristoph kissed Mabel's hand and sighed contentedly, there was something about the idea of a budding kinship that made Thet's surprisingly natural romantic tendencies bloom.

"You're getting attached," came Asmodeus's lazy drawl from the darkened corner behind him. Thet shrugged as he watched Kristoph shimmy into his bunk, twisting his body so he could gain a last view of Mabel before his eyes shut with fatigue.

"Is that so wrong?" Thet asked, "You seem rather taken with Kris, after all."

"His lifestyle, perhaps;" The demon shrugged, approaching Thet's right side and casting a disparaging glance towards Kristoph, "I don't think much about how he's feeling right now, though."

Thet looked over at the demon, quizzically; "whatever do you mean?"

"He means," the pompous tone of Azrael made them both turn suddenly on the spot. Thet hastily tried to clear the image from the frame, however, the angel snapped his fingers and Thet's hand was stalled and left to hang in the air, useless; "that as a demon of *lust,* he's only interested in the more physical elements of attraction, not the deeper and more emotional elements."

Asmodeus glowered at the angel, "Coming to mingle with the commoners from up high, brother?"

Azrael sniffed and cast an unimpressed glance at the demon. "I heard a rumour, I had to see for myself. So, these are the two humans who are supposedly the source of all sin?" He leaned closer to the frame to get a better view of Kristoph and wrinkled his nose, "they still look about as pathetic as they did when Father plonked them in his back garden, all those years ago."

Thet and Asmodeus glared furiously at the angel, who continued ignorantly; "I suppose I should thank you both for the random influx of repentant Saxons?" He sneered as he watched Kristoph turn over in his bunk with a relaxed smile on his face. "I don't doubt you'll also be pleased to know that the heathen army has settled in well at their ostentatious tree house."
Thet's eyes narrowed, "you can thank the two humans you've just labeled as pathetic, for that." Azrael turned his attention back to the reaper and the demon and stalled at the livid expressions on their faces; "I say, have I touched a nerve?" Asmodeus glowered at him; "not at all. I would say however, that you have five seconds to get to your point before I show you some of my more lustful moves that are deemed as a bit too unfavourable by even Beelzebub's standards." He snarled, menacingly
"Tch, such a temper;" Azrael scoffed. "I came down to offer you both a heads up. As much as it pains me to say... you and those humans have

helped take a few of the more insistent hordes off my back with your actions. I know how long those souls had been lingering in Limbo."

"Happy to oblige," Thet stepped in before Asmodeus could say anything.

"Yes, well;" Azrael smoothed down his silken, heavenly garb and ran a finger over a few loose strands of his eyebrows; "I have it on good authority that this little troupe in the frame is headed to Germany, next?"

"How could you possibly..." Asmodeus snapped before Thet covered his mouth.

"Your sources might be on to something," Thet hastily chimed in.

Azrael's mouth curved, slyly; "in the recesses of Limbo, I hear there is a gang of street urchins who have been running amok since the thirteenth century. They call themselves the Piper's Friends."

The reaction to Azrael's comment caused Asmodeus to shudder, "I know of them," he grumbled.

"Yes, we all have;" The angel grimaced, "they are the epitome of lost souls. Their number started at one hundred and thirty originally. During their stay in Limbo, they have been steadily recruiting any young soul who finds their way there. I like to imagine they're fairly harmless."

Asmodeus scoffed, "You keep imagining Azrael! If it helps you sleep at night. You and your holier-than-thou kinship up top are all the same, preferring to imagine the best rather than seeing what your lackluster efforts have caused! You forget how close to Hell, Limbo is. We see more than you. We know more than you. You just turn a blind eye, while we watch on, helplessly." Azrael laughed, mockingly, "helplessly? You could have taken a few of the Piper's friends down to your lower echelons decades ago."

The angel had gone too far. In a burst of anger, Asmodeus drew out a whip of immense length. Its rat-like rope was swathed in barbs and ended in a spiked tip. In retaliation to Azrael's taunt, he lashed it, threateningly. The sound cracked like lightning and temporarily deafened both the angel and Thet, while the spiked tip slashed at a hung frame, causing irreparable damage.

"Those souls were *pure* when they entered Limbo, Az!" The livid Asmodeus hissed, his voice a venomous rasp; "their time spent in that God-forsaken state is purely a failing on *your* part, *NOT* ours!" He growled viciously, and stalked, as a lion does its prey, closer to the balking form of Azrael.

Azrael cleared his throat, a hint of regret betraying itself across his features; "be that as it may, their behaviour since entering Limbo, only seems to indicate that their souls were quick to be tainted and as such... their ah, um... destination, would naturally be more fitting for a more um..." His words started to fail him as Thet, finally breaking free from the angel's charm rushed forward and stood between the angel and the demon.

"Settle down, Mo'" He rested his hand gently on the demon's heaving chest; "Azrael, you forget your place! One more word and I will allow my companion here to chase you to the ends of the heavens with his weapon of choice."

The angel stared wildly at Thet, "I beg your pardon? Who on *earth* do you think you are?"

"I am a *reaper*, Azrael. I chaperone souls from one destination to the next. I hand deliver them based on the auror of their souls, full of confidence that their heavenly or demonic hosts will address them accordingly. If you were to venture into Limbo now, you would see more souls who had been destined for *your* gates, than Hell's. Face it, you either got lazy, or you recognised that the goalposts have been shifting for far too long. Either way, the Piper's Friends were innocent children when they entered the realm. Scared. Lonely. Desperate. You cast them away, *why?*" The small blue flames in Thet's eyes burnt a hot red as his anger and curiosity grew.

Azrael looked practically defeated as he babbled helplessly, before dejectedly muttering "Their behaviour... they were to listen to and respect their elders. They opted not to. They put their faith, blindly, in a stranger who played a happy tune."
Asmodeus growled a deep, guttural, and feral snarl; "why does that sound so familiar, angel? Tell me, how many miracles have our father's prodigy conducted recently? Don't think we are

ignorant of his current actions. We know of the ascension!"

Azrael's eyes widened in shock, "how..."
"Our father is sick," the demon spat; "his son is set to take over. While the two alpha cats are away, the angelic horde apparently gets lazy and fat. No, Az! The Piper's Friends are destined for heaven, *NOT* Hell. I will gladly rest my own condemned and damnable soul on the line to ensure it happens!"
Azrael looked between the demon and the reaper, before hanging his head, defeated; "very well" He sighed, "Thet, arrange for the urchins to find their way to your human pets, they'll figure out the rest!"

"On two provisos," Thet's voice was calm but there was a hint of danger to it that caused Azrael to pause his retreat with a hesitantly questioning glance.
Thet stood tall and proud next to Asmodeus, "First, you come to Limbo with me, *now*. Second, you will from now on refer to our friends on Earth as Kris and Mab! *Not* pets!"

Utterly defeated and dejected, Azrael nodded glumly and reached out his hand. Thet snatched it in a firm hold and, before Asmodeus could tuck away his whip, Thet had whisked the angel off to Limbo.

Chapter 13. Limbo

Limbo was a land of chaos. Upon entering the realm, Thet and Azrael paused on the top step of a spiral staircase that had no railings and was crumbling from an unmeasurable time of abuse. Its final step rested somewhere far below them; lost in the sea of buildings, townscapes, and mulling crowds. Even from so far up, Azrael felt the need to cover his ears with his hands as the collective moaning and sighing from the realm's inhabitants was deafening.

"What on *earth* is that awful sound?" He groaned, miserably.

Thet cocked his head, rather non-plussed; "ah, that would be the sound of the choir of Repentance and Satanism," He said; "I grant, it's a rather morbid sound to those unfamiliar to it. Personally, I rather like it. I find it incredibly impressive how they have incorporated the frantic cry of rebel yells; the pure sound of gospel; and a series of phenomenal guitar solos, from a host of musicians - who passed *far* too soon in their professional capacity; into a eulogy, dedicated to their chosen deity."

Azrael slowly turned on the spot to gawp at Thet, "There are Satanists down here?" He gulped, "Do they not *know* what rests in store for them?"
"Oh yes," Thet nodded, casually. "You see that tent over there?" He pointed towards a plush red tent that looked more in keeping with the Renaissance period of travelling entertainers. "The one that's resting on the head of... my goodness, what in all that's holy *is* that thing?" The angel blanched, shuddering at the sight.
"Hm," Thet shook his head disappointedly at Azrael's reaction. "You recall the artist Jheronimus van Aken, more familiarly known as Hieronymus Bosch?"
Azrael cast a guilty, blank look of ignorance at Thet.
"Of course you wouldn't," Thet sighed. "Hieronymus Bosch was a Dutch painter who spent much of his living years traditionally painting religious concepts in oil on wood. Beautiful work, you should check some of it out should you ever feel inclined to descend from on

high. Much of Limbo's architecture and planning is based on his imaginings. The surreal and bizarre themes seemed to fit the scene better than anything too regal or majestic. You wouldn't know him, I suppose, as he was sent here many centuries ago by you or whoever was standing by the heavenly gates at the time."

"Why was he sent here?" Azrael mused, "If he was devoutly religious and spent his time depicting the various stories of the scriptures..." "We may never know the full truth of it," Thet interrupted him, impatiently. "All I can assume though is that his piece titled Krist in Limbo, hit a bit too close to home with someone from upstairs and he was booted down to Limbo. During his time here, he helped manage the construction of much of what you see before you. That tent hosts regular talks from Hell's representatives or even some of my brothers and sisters. The fleshy giant it rests on top of, spews out all the souls you send down here from heaven, he's affectionately dubbed Gape;" at the angel's mystified expression, Thet added; "as a nod towards his gaping mouth." The reaper grinned, as Azrael issued a slight whimper.

"Thet, I don't understand;" the angel mustered as he tried with all his might to absorb the disorder and monstrous elements of Limbo before him, "you say the reapers and demons from Hell offer talks here, who speaks on behalf of heaven?" Thet snorted loudly, "no one."
As Azrael blustered and flushed a rosy, red in embarrassment, Thet started to descend the steps confidently, "suffice it to say," he called over his shoulder at his mortified angelic companion, "there are few who maintain their love for the heavenly host, down here."

Azrael fell into step behind Thet, feeling exceptionally conscious of the sheer drops on either side of the stairwell, "so... whatever happened to Hieronymus Bosch?" He asked as casually as he could, trying to make light conversation, "Maybe I could strike up a deal with him and find a place upstairs, more suited for his talents and convictions?"
Thet stopped so suddenly, that Azrael nearly

collided with him and had to sit heavily on the
sandstone steps to prevent himself from toppling
over the edge.

"You don't get it, do you?" Thet shook his head,
pityingly. "Every soul you will encounter here has
given up on *ever* reaching a higher place."

"But... the Choir of Repentance?" Azrael
persisted.

"... and Satanism – it is one whole title. Their
members are repentant of having spent their lives
worshipping a deity who barely heeded their calls,
and they instead clamour to the Lord of Hell.
Incidentally," Thet cleared his throat as he
continued his journey further down,
"Hieronymus Bosch made a deal with
Baphomet, centuries ago."

"The *GOAT*?" Azrael blurted out, louder than
he'd anticipated.

Once again, Thet sighed heavily stopped his
descent, and turned to face Azrael, who had
hardly moved from his seating place, his knees
knocking together with uncharacteristic
nervousness. "Baphomet has many guises. Just
because their natural preference incorporates a

more caprae appearance doesn't mean that they always present themselves as such," Thet rolled his eyes, before turning around.

"I'm sorry," Azrael frowned, "*they*? Baphomet has always been one being, now there are more of him?"

Thet groaned with exasperation. "He changed his pronouns to they, them, and their several centuries ago. Now Azrael, you can either follow me down here so we can address the Head of the Piper's Friends directly, or you can continue mithering on this step making an arse of yourself further. Either way, nothing will change the fact that the angelic host has successfully alienated *everyone* in Limbo against their cause! Your being ignorant of pronoun preferences, the head architect's status here, and downright judgmental attitude toward anything or anyone that doesn't have a halo in their back pocket; is honestly, very disrespectful. So, with all due respect, I will do the talking for the both of us – you just stand behind me and (as Asmodeus would say), look pretty."

It was an arduous descent, but thankfully Azrael recognised good advice when it was received and took on the role of a rosy-cheeked and blonde-haired mute. Discretely, he cast a charm to hide his more angelic attributes from the suspicious looks from many of the hordes of Limbodians, and somewhat reluctantly took to observing the surreal elements of the environment around him. In contrast, Thet seemed completely at home, and the angel was surprised to learn that many of the populace treated the reaper with far more respect and reverence than he, as an angel, had ever experienced even when he *had* admitted souls through the heavenly gates. As they crossed a bridge that rested over a river running with pitch and tar; child-like laughter echoed out from below them.

Thet held his finger to his lips and quietly approached the wall of the bridge and invited the angel to watch and listen to two young children, who were busy dipping their toes into the thick, sludge-like water. The youngest child had marks of soot on her cheeks and her once sky-blue dress was now frayed and smudged with the grub from the greasy cobbles of the Limbodian streets. Her dark, russet hair was matted and hung lankly around her face, which in contrast, shone with pure joy as she cast stones into the centre of the liquid. Her older companion was busy combing the petrified dirty blonde hair of a porcelain doll, the shade matching her mop of greasy hair that had been chopped unevenly short by what must have been a rather crude pair of sheers. She rested her back against her younger friend while she sang sweetly:

"Ein Kleiner Mensch stirbt nur zeum Schein,
wollte ganz allein sein.
Das Kleine Herz stand still für Stunden
Man hat es für tot befunden.
Es wird verscharrt in nassem Sand
Mit einer Spieluhe in der Hand.
Nur der Regen weint am Grab
eine Melodie im Wind
und aus der Erde singt das Kind."

Both reaper and angel were spellbound by the soft, angelic voice that seemed so ill at odds with the world in which it found itself.

Unable to resist, Azrael cautiously approached the children who froze on the spot as he knelt beside the older girl and, stroking the doll's head, returned its locks to the shimmering strands of pure blonde that had once cascaded down its back.

"Such a beautiful song," he smiled softly. It had been so long since a child had graced the steps of heaven. He'd almost forgotten just how pure and innocent they could be; "what is it called?" He asked.

"It's called Spieluhr." Thet answered from his perch on the bridge.

"Ah, yes – I recall the song," Azrael mused. "It's about a young child with a music box, yes?"

Thet lowered his head and gave the older girl an apologetic look, "close. It's about a child being buried *alive* with a music box... I apologise for my friend's ignorance, young one." He smiled grimly.

The girl grinned, "I was wondering if we might see you down here, Mr Grim." She smiled graciously at the reaper.

"Wait," Azrael blinked, suddenly uncertain; "you're familiar, with him?"

"Of course," the girl smiled sweetly, yet there was a hint of mania behind the eyes which caught the angel off guard. "He brought me and my friends here many years ago and told us to wait until we were called to attention by an angel. The call never came," she lamented, "but Mr Grim regularly visited us, bringing a collection of toys and trinkets in the process. Annabelle here, being my favourite." She held the doll up in the air. To Azrael's horror, the angelic porcelain head of Annabelle twisted one hundred and eighty degrees, independent of its holder, to stare unblinkingly at the angel.

Thet forced himself to stop enjoying the discomfort of his companion and decided to intervene; "Azrael, I would like to introduce you to Helga Schneider. Ringleader and Mastermind of the Piper's friends. Helga, this is Azrael, he's an... acquaintance of mine, who might be able to assist with your plight in Limbo."
Azrael stared, still rooted to the spot with fear from the deranged doll, "Yes, well... 'might be able to' being the overarching phrase of such a statement," He smiled, weakly.

"Are you an angel?" The youngest girl, who'd been throwing stones into the river asked, as she tugged at the hemline of the trench coat Azrael had guised his angelic robes as.

"No! Well, that is to say, um – I might be. I might not be! I could be... I..." Azrael stammered and stuttered, unable to tear his eyes away from the haunting doll's expression.

"Mr Grim," Helga mused, "you brought us a schwachsinnig."

The insult stoked Azrael's typically haughty demeanour and, shaking himself free of his uncertainties, he scoffed; "I am most certainly not an imbecile! I am just erm... a little... er... out of my comfort zone. I'm sorry, could you get her to stop?" He asked Helga, as her younger companion had taken to wrapping herself up in his long coat and peering around the fastenings with a cheeky face.

"Why?" Helga asked, sweetly; "does it make you uncomfortable?" Her doleful blue eyes widened and expressed intense sorrow. She tucked her top lip behind her bottom lip and forced her jaw to tremble with sadness.

"It is rather," Azrael struggled, as Thet smothered his amusement behind his hand.

"Well GOOD!" Helga snapped; "my group of friends have been left to feel uncomfortable by you and your host of angels since 1284!"

Azrael folded his arms and glared sternly at Helga, "I *assure* you; I would recognise such a young face. It was *certainly* not *me* who sent you down here!"

"Whatever," Helga sighed with a bored tone, as she turned her back on the angel. "Mr Grim; Bo and his army have gone. The only believers in those above, the Saxons, they've gone too. I'm not stupid. They've moved on, haven't they?"

"They have," Thet nodded, resting his elbows on the wall of the bridge. "I have a couple of friends in the living world who were able to help them. They did so well, that I wondered if you and your allies here, would like to have a chance to meet them and perhaps, move on too?"

"Pending good behaviour!" Azrael hastily interjected.

Helga mused on the idea for a little while before pursing her lips and whistling a strange tune. The melody reverberated all around them and cut through the throngs of crowds who continued to shuffle about, listlessly. Multiple whistles in response to her summons echoed around the expanse of Limbo as from drain ways, chimney stacks, course hedgerows; behind the craning necks of gargoyles on the taller towers or dangling from the streetlights; Hundreds of street children responded to their leader, eagerly. As a collective, they gathered in a large group by the riverside, much to Azrael's chagrin; jostling, poking, and prodding each other. All of them ignorant to Azrael's discomfort, as they closed in tightly around him.

"Friends of the Piper," Helga called out to the assembled children, "our time has finally come to decide, do we want to move on from our home in Limbo?"

There was a momentary pause before an almighty cheer erupted from the gang of children. Helga looked up with a mischievous grin at Thet, "I think that's an affirmative."

Thet nodded back, "Very well, I will head back up top to inform my friends."

"Hold on... Mr Grim..." Azrael called out, desperately, "Wait for me!" he cried as he awkwardly tried to move around the tight group of children.

"Oh no, Azrael," Thet grinned; "you're my assurance! It's an agreement Helga and I made decades ago. If I ever get delayed with a promise to return, I leave behind a toy or a trinket as an assurance of an apology for my prolonged absence. You said yourself, you're not an angel; and you've served as such a delightful hiding place for young Esther there, that I thought you would make a perfect assurance of my promised return, what do you think Helga?"

"He'll suffice," Helga surmised, "although he does complain, a lot."

"You don't know the half of it," Thet muttered by her ear. "Right, I must be off. Have fun all, until I return. Oh, and Helga? If there's a talk going on in Gape's tent? Maybe take my friend there? It might prove to be *enlightening.*" Before Azrael could utter a single word of protest, he'd been swarmed by the children of Limbo who massed together to carry him further into the streets. Thet returned to the spiral stairwell, laughing a maniacal laugh that would have made even the bravest of souls shudder.

* *

The Dark Omens tour bus rolled onto the ferry slowly, after having been subjected to an intensely unpleasant customs search.
"I wouldn't mind so much if they just tidied up after themselves;" Pete grumbled as he stacked up Jésús's unique library of magazines. "I mean it's clear we're not harbouring anything illicit."
"I dunno," Eric snorted, as he flicked casually through one of the magazines, "I'm fairly certain some of the antics detailed here are illegal in several states," He turned the magazine and made a show of appearing intensely intrigued by what it detailed, before hastily tucking it away in to the pile of reading materials.

Jésús glared sullenly at Pete, "Maybe they wouldn't feel compelled to strip search the bus, if you did not insist on using a black sharpie to draw *this* all across my cheek, in my sleep!" he jabbed angrily at a comically large, infantile depiction of a penis dripping tear drops into the corner of his mouth.

"Hey... Zeus" Peter giggled, "clues in the sound of your name. Zeus would have been proud to have been blessed with such a member."

"My mother named me Jésús, pronounced heyseus, not Hey-Zeus, you Pagano!" Jésús pursed his lips, as Peter snorted.

"Ah, give over Zeus," the drummer smirked, "we've always said, sleep on the communal couch at your own risk. We all know, sharpies were only designed for such a job as that;" He grinned like a Cheshire cat at the bassist, whose expression remained unchanged.

Pete sighed melodramatically, "Look if it bothers you that much, I'm sure Mab might have some wet wipes in her toiletries that you could steal. Where is Mab, anyway?"

His question wiped the unimpressed look off Jésús's face, as he smirked knowingly; "I believe she's in the back room, with our lead guitarist." The rest of the assembled group turned to the bass player with questioning looks. Eric was the first to drape a friendly arm around Jésús's shoulder, "Tell you what, Hey-hey. I will get you the wet wipes if you drag your smutty head out of the gutter and do not imply through tones, that our set manager and lead guitarist are getting up to secret antics. Yes?"

Jésús groaned, "but they..."

"Yes?" Eric tightened his grip around Jésús's shoulders.

"Very well;" Jésús hung his graffitied head, his shock of hair flopping around his face, hiding the smirk that refused to budge.

"That's better," Eric let go of Jésús and moved toward the back of the bus, "I'll ask Mab about those wet wipes for you. Maybe you could shove one in your gob and wash your mouth out with it? I'd say it was your potty mouth shouting that drew the customs lot to our bus," he laughed.

As he approached the door, he heard excited muffled voices from within. Suddenly feeling a hint of discomfort; Eric hesitated, 'I sincerely *hope* I'm not disturbing anything' he mithered. "Thet, you cannot be serious! Children? The Vikings and Saxons were one thing, but *children*?" Mabel sounded frantic.

"This is getting completely out of hand!" Kristoph's voice chimed, "I thought we agreed that the number you gave us last time was far too high. The more people you bring up from Limbo, the more likely those more *senior* in your world, or closer to us - in ours - are going to notice. We cannot keep relying on Asmodeus to blindside the band into going along with this, he's a demon after all! The guy's a loose cannon!"

"Speak for yourself," the voice of the cameraman from the Viking video shoot suddenly pitched up, "incidentally, you might want to check the door, I don't think our conversation is as private as you might think."

"Oh bugger!" Came a strange, cool, and unnerving voice, "I forgot to freeze time!"

Eric barely had a chance to back away from the door before it suddenly and quietly swung open, and a pair of strong, clawed hands dragged him rather unceremoniously into the back room, where Kristoph and Mabel looked at him guiltily. They were accompanied by a terrifyingly demonic deity and a skeletal being, in an ominous robe. Eric blanched. He gulped. He whimpered. He looked at Kristoph and Mabel, shook his head; huskily ventured "nope", and fainted.

Chapter 14.
Indoctrinated

"Have you frozen time?"

"Yes Mab, no one else is going to hear us."

"He landed heavily. Kris, do you think he's okay?"

"He's a big boy, isn't he? I wouldn't say no to a bit of rough and tumble with..."

"Shut up! And yeah, Eric's taken worse falls before now."

"I'm just saying; give me half an hour, an hour max; maybe throw in a few bales of hay, I could play the innocent farmer's daughter, he the stable boy..."

"Do you have an off switch? Is there *anyone* that you don't feel the need to screw around with?"

"I'm the Demon of lust Mab, it's what I do. Anyone and anything are fair game in my world."

"Hey guys, I think he's coming round! No, scratch that, just a hypnic jerk."

"Bloody hell, what are we going to tell him?"

"Mab, babe, chill."

"Shut *up*! Seriously, Mab's made a good point, what are we going to tell him?"

"What do you mean, Krissy-poo?"

"What do you *mean*, what do I mean? He saw you in full demon form! He saw Thet in his reaper form! Can't you charm him like you did with the Viking situation?"

"No can do my sweet little baboon. Charms only work on those who have not perceived the full picture before. He's seen us both, there's no charming that image out of a simple mortal's head. Nope, there's nothing else for it, he's got to be indoctrinated into our little social circle."

"Oh for..."

"Although I think it's more of a social square..."

"Mo, just *stop*, PLEASE! Okay, Eric? Can you hear me? Are you alright?"

Eric kept his eyes shut tight. Desperately, he fought to keep his breathing steady; 'if they don't suspect I've come to, they'll all go away.'

"Aww, that's cute, he's practicing mind over matter with delusion!" The patting sound of a bare foot came closer to Eric's face, and he breathed in the scent of spiced wine and

swallowed hard. He felt his body tense as the
same foot poked a toe on his face, turning it from
side to side; "trust me, Eric Payne, you are
dealing with the master of delusion, you're only
prolonging the inevitable. Sooner you open those
puppy dog peepers, the sooner we can get
introductions out the way;"
Eric struggled to find his voice as he croaked out,
"I don't want to be a stable boy."

There was some muffled laughter and a soft and
caring pair of hands rested on his shoulder as
Mabel's soothing voice sounded close to his ear;
"Eric, I'm so sorry about all of this. You weren't
supposed to witness it. No one was *ever* supposed
to witness us all together, like this."
Eric opened his eyes. Slowly, the room started to
come into focus. Kristoph was stood by his feet,
looking down at him with a mix of humiliation
and concern. Mabel was beside him with nothing
but sympathy and care in her eyes. Then there
were the other two figures.
Eric refused to spend too long looking at them, as
his brain wasn't quite ready to process their being
present just yet. Slowly, he turned his head and

looked at Mab, "So, it's my lucky day then? Kris, do me a solid? Help me up?"

Together, Kristoph and Mabel helped Eric up and guided him toward Mabel's bunk, where he sat down heavily. The springs creaked under the sudden weight of a body nearly twice the size of its usual guest. Kristoph cautiously peered around the doorway to double-check check time was definitely frozen before slipping out and returning with a bottle of chilled water from the mini-fridge. Perching on the bed next to his friend, he handed over the bottle, hardly daring to make eye contact.
Eric glugged down half its contents, before breathing out a steadying breath.
"Okay, I'm just about ready, "he sighed. "Kris, Mab – what the actual Hell is going on here?" She shouted in his thick Welsh accent.

As steadily, calmly, and clearly as they could, Mabel and Kristoph detailed every aspect of their adventures with Thet and Asmodeus. Eric remained silent throughout. Only his eyes betrayed any sense of reaction as they widened at various intervals. When Mabel shared the revelation of her being Eve and Kristoph being Adam reincarnated, Eric's brow contorted into a quizzical expression; however, his features relaxed when he noted Thet's shrug and nod of acknowledgment. As Kristoph detailed the truth behind Bo's final fight, however, Eric's extended rope of patience started to fray.

"Hold on. You mean to say – we abetted, encouraged, and even *serenaded*... a MASS murder... in the middle of the Moors. With the actual crucifix as a backdrop? And you both feel *no* remorse for any of it?" Eric gaped, incredulously.

"Of course, we feel regret," Kristoph sighed; "but for us to rest with a clear conscience, we have to remind ourselves that it was the only way they could move out of Limbo."

"Right," Eric looked like he was desperately trying to decide if his two friends required sectioning or not. "And you are now going to off a bunch of *children*? H-HOW are you going to sleep at night after THAT?"

Mabel shook her head sadly, "We were in the

midst of discussing this when you were um, that is when Asmodeus here, dragged you in."

"Huh," Eric finally turned his attention angrily toward the demon, who wiggled his fingers in a flirtatious wave at the rhythm guitarist; "and *you're...*"

"Asmodeus, Demon Lord of Lust, *huge* fan! At your service, if you ever need servicing that is," He grinned charmingly, as he bolted over to shake Eric's hand vigorously. Eric grimaced as the calloused, clawed hands wrapped around his own. Why did they feel uncomfortably cold, clammy, and fiery hot all at once?

"So, you're the demon that was branded into Kris's wrist by that deranged fan?" Eric rubbed his hands together for comfort, as Asmodeus released his grip.

"Deranged fan? Charles Valentine was a doting, albeit weak-minded soul. Still, you gotta admit, I help wooden Kris sell the sex appeal on stage!" Asmodeus winked happily and stood proudly. Eric shook his head weakly as he turned to Kristoph, "You allow this muppet to possess you before every performance?"

Kristoph shrugged, "it beats the stage fright," he sighed, sadly.

Eric blinked with complete fascination, before suddenly pointing at his friend; "all those girls who you took to your bed after the shows and had to be reluctantly turned away..." Slowly he turned his pointing hand towards Asmodeus who again wiggled his fingers in a flirty wave and offered a little bow.

"Yeah, that would have been me. Don't worry – Kris and I have something of an agreement in place, *now,*" The demon's smile suddenly became quite fixed.

"Which is?" Eric asked, feeling somewhat uncertain, addressing a demonic deity.

"All girls have to be over consenting age, there's to be nothing more than a kiss; and if he can't keep me in my trousers, then he's to allow me to return to full control," Kris groaned, holding his face in his hands as even Mabel blanched at the news of such an agreement.

Asmodeus casually leaned his back against the wall, "and they say sex, drugs, and rock n' roll is dead," he quipped, sarcastically.

"Uh-huh," Eric eyed the demon and Kristoph with growing concern. "Returning to my original question though... children? Mab! Please, tell me you're not *really* considering this?"

Mabel looked sadly between Eric and Thet before reasoning; "it's not as clear-cut a case as all that. Eric, these children have already passed, but due to a divine mess-up, they've been stuck in Limbo since... When, exactly, Thet?" She asked.

"Since the thirteenth century," Thet stepped forward, extending his hand to Eric.

Eric nervously looked at the skeletal hand reaching out to him, "Is it safe to even touch that? I read somewhere that the reaper only needs to make contact with someone and they drop dead."

Thet chuckled, "I assure you if it were that easy, my siblings and I would have successfully wiped out the human populace by now. Eric, you are safe to shake my hand. Also, it's Thet, not Reaper."

Eric nodded, "well, at least you seem vaguely more *normal* than the demon."

"Indeed," Thet nodded, "we *can* change form if our natural presentation unnerves you."

"Nah, you're good," Eric sighed, already weighing up the pros and cons of therapy.

"Very well," Thet bowed and backed away. "As Mab was saying, these souls have been trapped in Limbo for centuries, if not longer. Mab and Kris are both taking on a task that should have been managed by beings higher in authority than both Asmodeus and I. The powers that be, however, have failed these souls and they have been enduring no end of torment, trapped in a land where there is no end in sight; no rest, no salvation, no peace. The souls I aim to bring up from Limbo now may appear childlike, but they are older than any living mortal in this world. Do not let their appearances deceive you."

Eric shook his head, "I'm sorry, but I can't get behind this. What happens to the physical body? What happened to Bo and his army? What happened to the Saxons? We just drove off!" He ran his hands desperately through his ebony shock of hair as the realisation of their actions sank in.

Asmodeus laughed, "You think we'd leave a hoard of bodies scattered around the place?"

Mabel frowned, "I did wonder. Neither of you mentioned what happened to the physical, fleshy aspects of these bodies."

Thet smiled, "It's one of the few things I pride my genetics on. I can create bodies, or rather, the mirror image of a body. It's what you and Kris both reside in. Those husks, if you'll excuse the crude term, are not your true physical forms. They are creations of my own. Imagine, if you will, a sculptor with his clay. He breathes life into his art, but the life happens to stick, and he animates his creations before he puts them in the kiln. Once he's finished with the clay formations, he can fold it back into its original pile and create something else."

Eric scoffed loudly, "You mean to say Kris and Mab are just fleshy lumps of clay that will disintegrate when their time is done?"

"I believe that sums it all up, yes." Thet nodded.

Eric blanched, "What if someone were to witness that?"

Thet looked knowingly at Kristoph and Mabel. Mabel frowned before piecing this information together; "that's why you said no one would remember our being in their lives. The clay you use is charmed. Once it's gone, the charm's broken and any memory of us is erased from a living being's mind."

Thet nodded serenely, but Eric jumped up in anger; "NO!" He shouted, "No! You can't do that!"

"Eugh!" Asmodeus made a retching sound, "human sentimental emotions, it's sickening."

"For you who have no friends, *demon*!" Eric snapped, his sharp retort taking Asmodeus aback. "Kris and Mab are dear, *dear* friends to me. You cannot expect me to forget them when they leave this realm. That's not how life works! Why do you think Mab sketched Bo and his friends? It was so we could all *remember* them! They were Vikings, obsessed with leaving sagas and legacies. What you're threatening to do with these two, strips them of *all* of that! You take away any right to their leaving behind a lasting memory."

Asmodeus laughed, mockingly; "I'd have thought original sin was a tough legacy to beat, personally."

Eric waved his mocking away, "That was then, I'm talking about the lifetimes they've lived since! You cannot tell me that they made no impact on the lives they touched in each reincarnation? I mean their births, for one! You want to strip a parent of the memory they had of having held their child for the first time?"

Asmodeus snickered and turned to Thet, jabbing his thumb at Eric, but stopped when he saw the reaper looking about as troubled as a skeleton in a robe could.

"You can't seriously be taking all of this into account?" The demon scoffed.

Thet folded his arms, "Eric makes a very valid point. Both Kris and Mab have made many impacts in the lives that they have lived, I can see each one now when I look back through my archival mind. The latest one of Mab's ensured someone survived, while she did not."

"I beg your pardon?" Mabel suddenly snapped out of her admiration for Eric and turned sharply to face Thet, "You kept that quiet!"

"On the contrary, you refer to it often. You told me to bugger off, that you weren't ready – I admit

I tweaked your memory somewhat to believe that when we first met; you seemed rather reluctant to leave your funeral, you see," Thet kicked nervously at the floor, "you did tell me to bugger off, but you said *she* wasn't ready! You knew you had gone."

Mabel's jaw dropped, "I... what?"

Thet sighed, "The explosion in your office hit a couple of areas. You were always so kind to the cleaners, having worked your way up from being one originally. When the first explosion happened, you saw it, and the following ones, blazing a trail in your direction. There was a cleaner, with her headset on, surprisingly oblivious. You flung yourself into her! The blast threw you both across the room, but you received the full force of it. When you saw me, you automatically assumed I was there for you both – it was just you. That woman held you in such high regard from that moment forward and yet..." He cocked his head, his flickering blue flame eyes turning a soft green hue in his musings; "she cannot recall your name or face, only the knowledge that she miraculously survived where others did not."

"EXACTLY!" Eric erupted, "How is that *fair*? On that woman? On Mab? On me, when these two go? On the guys out there?" He jabbed his finger toward the closed door, where the rest of the Dark Omens band members remained, frozen in time. "Y'know, we only gained success when Kris joined our group, his skills with the guitar are unmatched in my opinion!"
"Well... I wouldn't go as far as to say that" Kristoph flushed crimson, thinking of the multitude of guitarists he'd admired through the ages.
"Quiet!" Eric snapped, but with a smile that took the edge off; "when Mab created our set designs, she made our show light up in ways that no other has, in my memory! The backdrop is incredibly realistic. When they go, all I'm going to recall is a guitar melody that comes from a haunting ghost of a memory and an unknown set member who happened to be skilled enough to make things look spectacular. Now, you want to do that with... how many children are we talking about here?"

"About one hundred and thirty (give or take a few thousand)," Asmodeus mumbled.

"HA!" Eric laughed out humourlessly and collapsed back onto the bunk, "I'm sorry, but unless you can find a way in which innocent children (clay bodies or not) can be moved on without suffering a mortifying demise, I cannot get on board with this arrangement. Nor will I allow you to remove the memory of these two from my mind when the time eventually comes around."

Thet and Asmodeus looked from Eric to Kristoph and Mabel, who both held up their hands helplessly. Incredulous, Asmodeus took a step closer to Eric.

"I could silence him by reaching out to some of my kin?" He mused.

"And what would you say?" Thet shook his head, "You didn't want any of them knowing about this plan in the first place, yet now you'd happily consider detailing all, in the hopes that one of them will work their way into Eric's mindset? No. More to the point, I won't allow it."

"Oh?" Asmodeus mocked, "And a cweepy, ghoulish weaper is weally going to fwighten me?"

Thet's eyes smoldered and an acrid-smelling smoke issued from the empty sockets, hissing violently as their flames turned a deep red and grew; "do you know what happens when a demon dies?" He asked, sinisterly in a voice that rippled through the small, enclosed space. The sound of it caused Mabel, Kristoph, and Eric to huddle closer together for protection.

Asmodeus swallowed unnerved, "It's not something we demons like to discuss."

Thet's skeletal grin looked truly menacing, "let me place a little image in your head to ponder on," he snarled, as he tapped the temple of the demon, who shakily breathed in and crumpled to the floor; "now then;" Thet continued, as Asmodeus shuddered in the corner. "Should you consider harming *any* human with your kin to make ends meet, you have seen a taste of what I am capable of doing to ensure you will *never* bring your brethren into this agreement to suit your devilish purposes, understood?"

Asmodeus, uncharacteristically humbled, nodded meekly.

"To address your concerns, Eric;" Thet addressed the rhythm guitarist who practically jumped out of his skin at the sound of his name. "I believe there might be a way in which we could help the souls of these children move on, *without* their being any gory aspects. You see, the children in question are a mystery. They vanished when following a piper…".

"The pied piper?" Eric interrupted, "As in the children's story?" All nervousness seemed to have evaporated.

"Well, yes," Thet sounded confused, "humans read this story to children?"

Eric laughed, "It's a grand-scale mystery that was never solved. They just vanished. Some say they were abducted; others say it was a plague that caused death by dancing. I'd always wondered. I have a degree in English Literature you see, and we addressed such things. I love delving into the historical contexts of texts." He grinned wildly at Kristoph and Mabel, who weakly smiled back.

Thet appraised Eric quietly, "If it were to become popular knowledge how these children passed, I believe it just might address the mystery surrounding their demise. As such, they may just find peace."

Kristoph frowned, "but, surely, they already know how they passed?"

Thet nodded, "indeed, they do. But it's no good conveying that to the predisposed in Limbo. The *living* have to know, so that it can be registered with those above that these were innocent souls. Like Eric said, they need to be remembered. Hm;" He mused for a moment, "You know, I do believe you and I are going to get on *very* well, Mr. Eric Payne."

For the first time since entering the back room, Eric beamed; "right, where do we start?"

Thet pushed his hands together as if in prayer, "all in due time. Mab, Kris?" He addressed Mabel who was still trying to comprehend the revelation of her passing, "I will head to Limbo right away and inform them of my plans, expect to see a sign from the other side when this coach reaches its destination; oh, and Asmodeus?" He turned to face the demon who was slowly standing up again, "either change into a more suitable form or return to your mental home in Kris's head, you will be summoned when needed."

Chapter. 15 A Frühlingsfest Carole

The Dark Omen's tour bus finally applied its breaks in the early evening hours near the Hotel Muriel in Hannover. By way of ensuring costs were kept strictly to a minimum throughout the journey, Adrian had sat with his management and bookkeepers to discuss the budget assigned to accommodation between shows. As Adrian was always keen to keep costs somewhat low but maintain a modicum of luxury wherever he laid his head, the Muriel franchise had been a no-brainer to the organisers. Mostly located on the outskirts of more historical city centres, the Muriel prided itself on fusing historical architecture with modern-day comfort. The result was, beds large enough for a King, Queen, and all their offspring to sleep together in one; and glamorous bathrooms that made even Kristoph feel vaguely regal with a fresh, Egyptian Cotton gown hung on the door and slip-on slippers tucked away in the cupboard, all to make one feel royally fancy.

The mood of the band members descending from the bus was mixed. Adrian, Jésús, and Peter were all eager to set up their kit later in the day, for the night's Frühlingsfest event in the city centre. As such, they practically skipped off the bus, checked in, and disappeared to their rooms for a brief wash before their work truly began. Mabel, Kristoph, and Eric, however, trailed slowly behind them.

Since the conversation between Thet and Asmodeus, Eric had lost some of his more jovial persona and seemed to be constantly on the verge of asking a question, yet never getting there. As Mabel headed into the foyer to check herself and the men in, Kristoph pulled Eric back and pointed to the quaint patio seating area where he offered him a cigarette. Eric gladly accepted, and the two sat quietly enjoying a peaceful social smoke while looking out over a darkening park across the road.

Eric took a slow drag and breathed out a steady stream of smoke through his nose, closing his eyes and reveling in the momentary feeling of serenity. Finally, he turned to Kristoph, meeting his eyesight firmly for the first time since the conversation on the bus. In one breath he asked the question he had evidentially been bursting to ask for so long:

"So, you and Mab being the reincarnation of Adam and Eve; have you both, y'know... *reconciled?*" Eric hated how his voice had inadvertently reached a new octave in his question, however he was morbidly curious. Kristoph choked on the inhale of his cigarette and laughed out incredulously, " *That's* what you've been bottling up all this time?"

"Well, yes! I mean, when you think of it all – Kris, you and Mab are *parents!*" The recollection of his early Sunday school years suddenly flashed into Eric's mind, "do you think Abel and Cain were reincarnated too?"

Kristoph swallowed hard. The two infamous sons of Adam and Eve hadn't crossed his mind once since he'd found out about his reincarnation;

"bloody hell," he stubbed out his cigarette and pulled another one out of the pack, offering the packet to Eric in turn who graciously accepted.

"You should not smoke those, they're nicht so gut for you!"
Kristoph and Eric froze at the childish voice and slowly looked at each other, wide-eyed.
Hesitantly, they both shifted in their seats to face the owner of the voice. There, in the single seat between them, sat a young girl with a doll. She couldn't have been any older than thirteen, her features were not too dissimilar from those of a traditional porcelain doll. As she sat smiling broadly at them both, her feet dangling inches from the ground; the men couldn't help but think she looked serene and angelic. The only things that made her appear somewhat inhuman, were her ethereal hue and translucency.

The two men stared, speechless. Eric inadvertently started to make a strangled scratching sound that might have been a scream had his throat not instantly dried out upon seeing the apparition in front of him. Kristoph's newly lit cigarette was now quickly burning to a stub between his fingers as he gawped, with a look of frozen terror.

Mabel yawned loudly as she appeared through the main entrance, jangling two sets of keys with a drained expression on her face. "Right guys, I've got the keys. Eric, you're in room 330. Kris, I dunno why, but Adrian's arranged for us to *share* a room. It was going to be a king bed in a *special* room; however, I've managed to downgrade us to... a... twin..." her explanation stalled to an unsteady halt as she took in the scene before her.

"Guten abend, Frau Weaver," the ghostly girl beamed widely at Mabel.

"Hallo..." Mabel croaked weakly, as she desperately fumbled for a spare chair to collapse in.

The girl turned her attention back to the two frozen men, "so," her German accent was so delicate, as she slipped between English and her natural language; "Mr. Grim told me he had two freunden originally, but now it is three? Which of you is Herr Greyson?"

Kristoph's cigarette hissed angrily at its user for

being so rude and singed his fingertips, jolting him back into a more awakened state; "Um... I... I am, Miss?" He couldn't help himself. Formalities were important to her, so he felt compelled to respect them.

"Meine name ist Helga Schneider, wie gehts?" She instinctively held out her hand, before hastily tucking it away with the glimmer of sadness flickering across her features.

Eric cleared his throat and waved, nervously; "how do you do? I'm sorry, my German is not brilliant, Miss Schneider."

Helga grinned happily, "Not a problem! Mr. Grim said it would be worth speaking in English, as he said two of the three are from England and as such," she cleared her throat and offered a surprisingly convincing imitation of Thet, "' might be ignorant of any language outside of their own'. I just wanted to test you, to see how true that might be. Apparently, very."

Eric looked utterly mortified, "I am so sorry!" He blustered, making the girl giggle.

"Oh, you are lovely!" Helga covered her mouth to hide her laughter, as it pealed around them, sounding both melodic and utterly haunting at the same time.

Mabel cautiously drew her chair closer to her friend's table and hesitantly asked, "Mr Grim? Do you mean Thet? Are you here from Limbo?" Helga frowned, "I did not know Mr. Grim had a new name. I like it!" She smiled, simply; "and no, I am not *here* from Limbo, I am *in* Limbo. Mr. Thet left an assurance who has kindly helped to establish a means through which I can communicate with you from here. Limbo is rather hard to leave, you see, and there are so many of us," She shrugged apologetically. Mabel nodded, "I understand. So, you and your friends are looking to move on? Thet indicated that the truth needs to be shared with the living for that to happen. Can you recommend a starting point? We have a performance later today; however, we can make a start as soon as we...".

Helga's laughter cut Mabel off, "how can you begin to start investigating something that had no clear end?"

Kristoph groaned quietly and covered his face

with his hands, "You're going to make us work for this, aren't you?"

Helga hummed pleasantly, as she tucked a few stray hairs from her doll back into place, "Have you read any Charles Dickens?" She asked, excitedly.

"Some," both Mabel and Eric nodded.

"He is somewhat of a celebrity here in Limbo" Helga continued, "my favourite story of his is a Christmas Carole."

"Oh... no." Kristoph hunched further forward, sliding his slender fingers through his hair.

"Oh... yes, Herr Greyson!" Helga laughed, the sound now coming over as more maniacal than innocent. "On the stroke of midnight tonight, all three of you will be greeted by some of my Piper's Friends. They will each share an element of our journey with the Piper from Hamelin. After that, you should have all the information you need to share with the world!" Helga held her hands wide in her excitement, showing off the doll in turn.

At the sight of her Annabelle doll, Eric cried out in terror, while Mabel jolted so far back in her seat that she nearly toppled backward. Kristoph, meanwhile, laughed so loudly that he had to wipe a tear or two from his eyes. No sooner had she said this, Helga disappeared, and Kristoph, Mabel, and Eric turned to face each other with a look of mounting disbelief.

The Frühlingsfest performance was one of the more funnier and entertaining shows Dark Omens had performed in a while. Asmodeus had taken over Kristoph at the build-up to their appearance and had flirted with many in the crowd from a distance, yet the guitarist's performance was different. Instead of feeling pushed back into the recesses of his mind, Asmodeus had quietly encouraged Kristoph to be more present; to enjoy the thrill of the show more, while he handled the nerves. The screams of excitement from the crowd were intoxicating and Kristoph couldn't recall the last time he'd felt more alive and at home on the stage in his own skin!

Eric was back to being as hilarious as ever. As he leered over the crowd, he was gifted a stick of candyfloss from a young fan which he took a chunk from and tossed toward Kristoph. The sticky treat landed thickly in Kristoph's hair. The briefest of food fights had then started on stage between the two guitarists and had only eased when Mabel had been forced to hurry on set to clear up some of the mess after Jésús slipped rather compromisingly, on a half-eaten hot dog.

Some of the fans were wearing comical Viking helmets, clamouring for the band's latest viral song to be played, which Adrian was only too happy to oblige. After the show had come to an end and the set packed away; Adrian, Jésús, and Peter decided to rejoin the festivities and enjoy some of the carnival attractions. Mabel, Kristoph, and Eric, however, reluctantly returned to the hotel, claiming to be exhausted from the journey and the show. All three had agreed to sleep in Eric's room for the night, as it was the largest of the two with its grand King-size bed.

It was half an hour before midnight when Eric invited Mabel into his room. She was dressed in a plain black vest with the Dark Omen lounge trousers Kristoph had allowed her to borrow while she crashed on the bus. Kristoph, meanwhile, had followed Eric back to his room to enjoy the lavish bathroom that the small twin Mabel had secured for them, didn't allow. As such, when Mabel entered, feeling fresher after a brief shower; she was subjected to the sight of Kristoph walking out of the bathroom with just a towel wrapped around his waist, water droplets beading down his chest, and his cheeks looking flushed from the sauna-like conditions.

Mabel couldn't help but feel a tickling rush of butterflies in her stomach as she took in the brief sight of his surprisingly muscular, yet slender torso. His left pectoral was covered in dark Celtic knots that linked in with a sleeve of various pagan deities he had spent days in the tattooist's chair, enduring. Asmodeus's branding on his right wrist stood out as a whiter shade of pale in contrast to his natural fair skin tone. As Kristoph finished towel-drying his hair, it hung, fluffy, messy, and matted around his face, and Mabel felt a sudden urge to comb her fingers through it. Quietly embarrassed for her moment of weakness, she shook her head and perched on the ottoman at the end of the bed to watch the news reporter on the television detailing the continuing celebrations that were scheduled to last well into the early morning hours.

"So, how are we going to do this?" Eric asked, jokingly.
"What do you mean?" Mabel blinked, as she drew her attention away from the television.
Eric grinned wickedly, "Well, you know. Getting into bed as a threesome?"
"Really?" Kristoph sighed, exasperatedly, as he stole a spare pair of Eric's pyjama bottoms from his friend's duffel bag; "I have enough of that kind of chit-chat from Asmo."
"Oi!" Eric called after Kristoph's giggling, retreating figure; as the lead guitarist disappeared back into the bathroom to dry off and change.
Mabel snorted, "Something tells me you're relishing this."
"Well," Eric stretched, "the way I see it, it was only a matter of time before you two got together. Even without the whole biblical connections."
"How so?" Mabel puzzled, "You said yourself, I

hated Kristoph."

Eric winked, "you did, but he was *mad* about you. Besides, having the demon of lust on his side, chances are those feelings were a lot more intense than he let on. Yeah, I reckon you'd have succumbed to his charms in the end."

Mabel shook her head, "yeah, right. His charms? Or Asmodeus's?"

Eric was about to answer when the room's lights went out. The television screen went black, and the temperature dramatically dropped. From the bathroom, there was a bump, a bang, and Kristoph's voice cursing loudly as he staggered in the darkness to rejoin his friends. Together, the three of them huddled closely on the bed; all joviality disappearing in a single moment. All was silent as Eric's wristwatch beeped discretely to inform him that the time was now midnight.

Kristoph's sharp intake of breath from their left, caused Mabel and Eric to whirl around and face the doorway leading to the bathroom, where a faint, formless, white glow had started to develop. Presently, a young child's voice started to sing

innocently:
"Hamelin Town's in Brunswick.
By famous Hanover city;
The river Weser, deep and wide,
Washes its wall on the southern side;
A pleasanter spot you never spied;
But, when begins my ditty,
Over seven hundred years ago,
To see the townsfolk suffer so
From vermin, was a pity."

"Why are ghost children so terrifying?" Eric whispered shakily into Mabel's ear.
There was a rush of cold air from behind them, causing Mabel to yelp as they each span around again. There, on the pillows at the head of the bed, sat two identical boys. Both were barely older than five, their faces were white as sheets and their eyes darkened as though from years of sleep deprivation. Slowly the young figures started to crawl closer, their voices now a sinister whisper:
"Rats!
They fought the dogs and killed the cats,
And bit the babies in the cradles,

And ate the cheeses out of the vats.
And licked the soup from the cook's own ladles,
Split open the kegs of salted sprats,
Made nests inside men's Sunday hats,
And even spoiled the women's chats,
By drowning their speaking
With shrieking and squeaking
In fifty different sharps and flats."

The boys were barely a hair's breadth from Eric's face before they both grinned impishly and sat back on the bed, cross-legged.

"Güten nacht! I am Sven," said the twin on the left.

"Und I am Claus" said the twin on the right.

In unison, they both held out their hands, "Come, dance with us!"

Mabel felt both Kristoph's and Eric's hands grip her arms tightly, with fear. She turned her head to look at both the men and nodded encouragingly. Looking like they would rather stroke and befriend a bunch of rats than hold the ghostly hands of the boys, both Kristoph and Eric, (keeping their grip on Mabel's arms), reached out and took hold of Sven and Claus's hands.

Chapter 16. The Rats of Hamelin

Eric's hotel room swirled around in a thick, viscous spiral of vapor, moisture, and gloop. By the time everything had stopped spinning; Mabel, Eric, and Kristoph found themselves on their hands and knees, gasping for air and patting down their pyjamas. Surprisingly, their clothes were bone dry; yet, each of them felt certain they were dripping with an indescribably soggy moisture, which chilled them to the core.

"W-wh-wha-what the *hell* was th-tha-that?" Eric struggled, through chattering teeth, letting go of Sven's hand quickly. The ghostly twins looked at each other with an expression that appeared to indicate this was a regular reaction to such an irregular event.

"We have taken you all back to the day the Piper came to town," Claus explained, he pointed ahead of him toward the town of Hamelin in the distance. The cobbled path before them merged in with an ornate bridge, leading into the town centre.

Eric and Mabel stared wide-eyed at the scene, both struggling to believe what their senses were telling them. Kristoph wrinkled his nose and glanced at his two friends, somewhat envious of their awe and fascination. He didn't want to break the spell they both seemed to be under, but their faces seemed to suggest that they'd entered a magical land of wonder when all he could pick up on was:

"Rat piss. Guys, the place stinks of rat piss!" Kristoph pulled his t-shirt up over his nose, as the acrid smell stung at his sinuses.

Mabel pulled her vest over her nose in turn as her mystified senses gave way to clarity, and the stench stemming from the city reached her nasal passages too. "I suppose it's to be expected," her muffled voice reasoned, "there is a rat infestation here, after all."

Eric looked at them both and shrugged, "Can't smell a thing."

Mabel and Kristoph's eyes bulged widely, both watering from the intensity of the stench.

"Seriously?" Kristoph choked, "You're not fazed by it? Eric, it is *so* powerful!" He choked as he breathed in; the rich aroma struck the back of his throat, like a knife.

"Nope," Eric beamed, "not a thing. These passages have been able to detect smell for several years now, *finally*, it's come into use. All those years of smoking!" He chuckled non-plussed as his two friends expressed their concerns silently in a stolen glance, between each other.

The twins, Sven and Claus, had watched this brief discussion with growing impatience. Finally, Sven called out in a rather aggrieved tone, "Come, follow us!" and not bothering to wait for the adults to stall them further, he and his twin brother, skipped ahead.

As they crossed over the bridge, the signs of the plague of rats became even more apparent as they gawped at the build-up of rodent faeces piled up in nooks and crannies, with a couple of the whiskery culprits gnawing at indistinguishable scraps. Upon entering the eerie town centre, the first thing that hit them was the silence. The stillness of the epicentre of Hamelin was such that Mabel, Kristoph, and Eric stopped in unison and looked around, puzzled.

"But... where *is* everyone?" Kristoph frowned, turning around in confusion to look about the town.

Claus pointed ahead to a large structure before them. The front façade was adorned with windows facing out toward them with ornate décor around the rooftop; the building stood out as one of the more grandiose designed constructs in the town. The third and fourth-floor walls displayed a host of cast iron bells that hummed quietly, as though they had not long ceased their clamour for attention.

"That is the town hall," Claus nodded, "Mama und Papa are in there, with many of our friend's parents too."

"Will they be able to see us, if we enter?" Mabel asked uncertainly, suddenly very much aware of their attire which would not conform to the societal norms of 1284 AD.

"You will not be seen," Sven answered, in his sing-song voice.

"You are all ghosts, in this world," Claus smiled sweetly, as he and his brother raced toward the town hall doors together.

Eric shuddered quietly, "ghostly children. You guys get Vikings as your first soirees with the afterlife, I get ghostly children. How's that fair? Still, this is summat else! The history, I mean breathe in the heritage around you!"

"I'd rather not!" Kristoph winced, "Can we *please* get to the town hall, this smell is *insane!*"

Hurrying their pace, the trio walked up to the large oak doors of the town hall. Mabel reached out to pull them open, only to fall directly through. She shivered as she regained her composure, while Eric and Kristoph merged through the doors behind her, smirking.

"You must send us a postcard on your next trip," Eric muttered, chuckling at his joke.

"Hush!" Mabel rolled her eyes, "it's the infamous town meeting. Listen!"

Still unaccustomed to being ghostly apparitions themselves, they carefully navigated their way around the crowded hall. As they approached the stage, they both inhaled sharply as there, full of life, with gleaming golden hair, an inquisitive yet cautious expression on her face, was:

"Helga!" Kristoph blinked.

"Of course," Eric breathed. "In the story of the Pied Piper, it was said that one hundred and thirty children in total, disappeared from Hamelin. The oldest was the thirteen-year-old daughter of the mayor! I suppose it makes sense that she's a voice of authority for the youngsters in Limbo if her dad was of such a political persuasion. I just hope she does a better job at keeping her promises, than her dad did."

Kristoph sighed, "Okay. You guys are going to have to fill me in, I have no idea what this tale is all about;" He blushed, embarrassed at his lack of knowledge.

"Seriously? You've never heard of this story before?" Eric gawped, flabbergasted.

"Don't worry Kris," Mabel reached out to hold his hand, affectionately; "you'll pick up the gist of things, pretty soon."

No sooner had she said this, than the grumbling and mumbling in the hall subsided as the purposeful steps of a large, ruddy-faced man with a plumed white wig approached the podium on the stage. He looked tiredly over the assembled crowd and stifled a yawn, before drawling lazily: "Court is in session to discuss the topics of the day. Herr und Frau Spiel. Trade, butchers. Taxes overdue. Frau Friedeburg. Trade, baker. Taxes, overdue; reports of delayed orders, prolonged leave of business absence. Herr und Frau Spitz. Trade, candlestick makers. Missing orders, overdue taxes..." The drone of the mayor's speech to the townsfolk and their list of assigned issues seemed to drag on for hours. Mabel found herself considering that while it might be a once-in-a-lifetime opportunity to witness history in the making, some aspects would be better suited unwritten, for fear of deterring any interest in the topic for future generations.

The list of grievances was cut short by a disgruntled man, waving a rolling pin.
"Of course, my business has been shut!" He thundered, "In case it had escaped your attention, we've had a rat infestation for the last few months. I cannot keep up with the demand of orders both in and out of the town when my supplies have all

but been befouled by the vermin that litters our streets!" There was a general murmur of agreement from the crowd at this outburst. The man, emboldened by this modicum of support, rallied on; "I, and I am certain a number of us here, want to know what the Mayor of Hamelin intends to *do* about the rats!"

Numerous heads were nodding with a few louder voices expressing their agreement with the small baker. The mayor, however, looked unphased, as he pushed his half-moon spectacles further up his nose and surveyed the man closely.

Sighing with excessive boredom, the mayor leaned over his podium and blandly explained; "I will have order! All queries and concerns are to be sent in writing to the mayor's office, where they will be handled with..."

"NONSENSE!" The voice of a frustrated woman from the back of the hall shouted, "My baby was bitten multiple times by the rats! My husband has been unable to convey his harvest to the mill as it's all been spoiled by the loathsome devils! Our livelihood is smelling fouler than the odour of the town!" She shrieked.

"At least they're aware of the smell," Kristoph muttered under his breath, conspiratorially to his friends.

"Order!" The mayor issued sternly, "as I was saying, before being rudely interrupted. All queries and concerns will be handled swiftly if submitted in writing to the mayor's office."

"Well, that's no use" Mabel scoffed, turning to glare at the pompous mayor on the stage.

"Why's that?" Eric and Kristoph asked, in unison; grinning at each other before Eric hissed, "Jinx!"

Mabel shook her head, but suppressed a smile at the infantile jibe, "Half if not most of this townsfolk are humble traders. They'll know some level of literacy or numeracy to get by, but not enough to write a strongly worded letter, least of all anything to be taken seriously by *that* buffoon," She jabbed her thumb over her shoulder at the mayor; "note his attire? He's not affected at all by the infestation."

Kristoph and Eric looked closer at the mayor who was wearing a sky blue, crisp, tailored suit. His attire was immaculate. The buckles on his shoes glimmered in the light that seeped through the single-paned windows. Even Helga seemed to be shifting uncomfortably in her seat, glaring at her father while she casually rubbed some dust from the underside of her chair onto the skirt of her dress.

"Poor thing," Eric mumbled, "she's embarrassed."
While the three of them watched on, the crowded hall became more and more rowdier, as each newly raised voice of aggrievance inspired another citizen to join in with their frustrations.
"ENOUGH!" The mayor finally shouted, slamming his hand down heavily on the podium, causing the hubbub to die down, instantly. "What would you propose I do?" He asked, with a snide smirk; "do any of you know the ways to charm a rat? Do any of you *know* of anyone who can charm a rat? No! As far as I am concerned, the problem with the rats rests on the cleanliness of your stores and homes. Maybe if you paid more time honing your homely skills, your hovels would not be serving as nests for the creatures."
"How *dare* you!" This stern response came from

a rather respectable-looking woman who had managed to secure a cushioned seat by the window; "my husband, Rudolf, passed just last week after a bite from one of those creatures turned putrid. The little beast bit his leg, while he slept in our freshly made bed. While he wore freshly cleaned robes. While he rested in a room that had been swept, polished, dusted, and varnished to within an *inch* by our serving staff's capable hands! Mayor Schneider, our families have been close and firm friends for many a year, do you mean to insult my housekeeping as such? This is a problem that you have left to get out of hand, as your home is based on the outskirts of the town, far removed from the epicentre of this hell! I *implore* you. See reason! Do not let your ignorance blind you from what is truly happening!" The woman sniffed dramatically and dabbed at her eyes with a silken handkerchief.

The mayor seemed to chew on the inside of his cheek as his eyes narrowed at the woman, while her attention was taken up with putting her handkerchief away.
"Papa?" Helga stood up hesitantly, "Please.

Cousins Sven and Claus passed from a fever caused by the fleas of the rats just last week. Please papa, help!"

"Children should be seen and not heard!" Mayor Schneider scolded Helga, who snapped her mouth shut and bent her head low, her cheeks a deep crimson.

"Röv!" Kristoph cursed under his breath, as he glared at the mayor, suddenly feeling an urge to comfort the girl whom they had only just met in her ghostly form.

"Hm?" Eric frowned, "did... did you say something?"

"He's an arse!" Kristoph snarled, "These people are suffering and the man's claiming ignorance and projecting blame. Typical authoritarian dolt! He's allowed his power and comfort to go to his head."

Eric and Mabel nodded, quietly amused at how invested their friend was becoming in the Hamelin plight.

As the anger in the room started to rise again, there was a sudden burst of energy as the oak doors flew open. There, dressed in a colourful ensemble with a pipe, stood a tall and handsome man. He looked around smugly at the assembled crowd, who had fallen deathly silent with looks of repulsion directed toward him. The figure slowly and purposefully approached the stage, as the sea of people parted to allow him space. Not one face showed signs of recognition or polite intrigue. If anything, the hall had turned their hostilities from the mayor to the piper.

As the man came closer, Kristoph smelt the air and swallowed hard. Instinctively, he pulled both Eric and Mabel out of the way, standing as tall as he could in front of them, defensively.

"Kris, what on earth?" Mabel gasped, stunned at the sudden display of strength.

"He's possessed!" Kristoph murmured cautiously, "This is a supernatural scenario we're in. I've no idea if the entity that's possessed this guy has any inclination that we're here – but I don't want to risk the chance of him discovering us. We need to blend in with the crowd, *now*!" He snapped quietly, as the three of them hurriedly merged behind groups of the gathered townsfolk, desperately averting their eyes while trying to look as inconspicuous as possible in their modern-day attire.

"I see your town is as welcoming as any other," The figure smiled, charmingly at the crowd and winked mischievously at Helga.
"State your case and begone, piper!" grumbled the mayor.
"Oh, tut, tut! There I was playing my pipe along the Wesser River banks when I heard the town bells of Hamelin a-calling. A summoning, I thought! Well, who am I to deny a summons?" The piper's voice was soft, melodic, and soothing. Mabel noted that some of the younger women in the hall had softened their stoic gazes and were relaxing their stances.
"The summoning was for the townsfolk, *only*!" The mayor snipped.
"Indeed," the piper stroked at his flute, "my humblest of apologies. You see, as I traversed through your delightful town, I noted that you're under the tyrannical rule of a plague of rats. Forgive me," the Piper swiped off his feathered cap and bowed low, clearly a showman; "I thought what luck. I happen to have a tune in

mind that would rid you all of such a curse, which I would gladly do – for a small price..." He bowed his head low again, but Kristoph could still see the villainous grin on the man's face.

"Don't fall for it; don't fall for it; don't fall for it..." Kristoph implored under his breath.
"What price?" The woman who'd lost her husband Rudolf stood up before the mayor could respond.
"Just enough to see me carry on with my journey across this fine country in comfort and security," The piper tipped his hat to the woman and winked at her, with hungry eyes. His gaze glazed over briefly as his focus moved closer to Mabel who had slipped behind a couple to the right of the widow, however, he shook his head and returned his attention to the mayor; "simply two ducats will cover all fees."
"Done!" The widow shouted out, as the mayor blustered in dumbfounded anger.
"Jolly good," The piper grinned maliciously, "I'll return tomorrow for my payment."
No sooner said than done, he swirled around and strode confidently toward the exit. He paused as

he passed close to Eric and inhaled deeply, before rippling his shoulders and continuing on his way.

As the doors slammed shut behind the piper, the town hall of Hamelin began to shimmer and shake, as Sven and Claus picked up their unnerving poem, singing harmoniously together. First Claus latched on to Kristoph's hand, while his brother intertwined his delicate fingers with Eric's calloused and long digits; Mabel hurried forward and completed the small circle by linking arms with the two men. When she opened her eyes and lifted her head, she realised her physical body had slumped over Kristoph's chest, while she'd been in her trance. The last whispered words she heard from the boys lingered in her mind; "help us, please!"

"Oh, this is *not* good!" Kristoph stood up shakily from the bed, lost his balance; and collapsed back heavily, before resting on his back and covering his face.
"How so?" Eric asked, desperately trying to process all that he'd witnessed, while also

readjusting to being back in the waking world. "The piper is possessed! That's *not* good! We're not dealing with a sound-of-mind musician. Imagine me out of control with Asmodeus at the reigns and loving every minute!" Kristoph groaned. His head felt like it was splitting in two, "I think I'm going to be sick;" he shuddered. Mabel chewed her bottom lip, "The piper seemed ever so flirty, you don't suppose it *was* Asmodeus?"

"Nah," Kristoph shook his head. "Asmodeus is many things, but he has a surreal soft spot for kids. It's not in his nature to see them come to harm. No, there was something else about that guy and I don't think it was necessarily demonic."

Mabel sighed and steadily got up to grab three bottles of water from the hotel room's fridge. She yawned widely as she said, "I suppose. I only asked as Asmodeus does have a penchant for being the centre of attention, especially with women. It was hard not to notice the sex appeal that guy exuded over the women in that hall." Eric and Kristoph couldn't help but snort loudly. "What?" Mabel giggled, innocently.

"Do I *exude* sex appeal in *your* eyes, Mabel?"
Kristoph smiled weakly, as he reached out for
one of the bottles she held.
Mabel rolled her eyes and scoffed, "In the eyes of
the women in the hall you idjiot, not in *my* eyes."
She shuddered inwardly, as she recalled the
piper's roaming gaze; before jokingly tapping the
bottle on the top of Kristoph's head.
Eric smiled as he accepted his drink bottle from
Mabel and muttered softly: "The lady doth
protest too much."

Chapter 17. Beloved Deities

Sipping quietly at their water, the trio sat on the bed gathering their thoughts after the surreal experience of having travelled through a ghostly time vortex. Eric was still shuddering over the apparitions of Sven and Claus. To ease the uncertainty in the room, Mabel turned the TV back on. They were surprised to find out that barely any time had passed since their visit to medieval Hamelin. To calm his overthinking, Kristoph picked up Eric's acoustic guitar and started to idly play a range of melodies that barely linked together.

"It's no good," Eric groaned loudly, after a while "I need a smoke! Care to join me, Kris?"
Kris looked up blankly, his mind having been lost to his melodic strumming. Cautiously, he looked at his own watch before sheepishly glancing over at Mabel, "will you be, okay? We shouldn't be too long."

Mabel snorted, "I'll be fine. We're not due another apparition for another forty-five minutes, by Helga's reckoning."

She paused to consider how ridiculous such a statement sounded in her own head. "You two go ahead, I'm going to see if I can spot Adrian, Peter, or Jésús in one of these news reports," She grinned, hoping she sounded more aloof and relaxed than how she truly felt. Kristoph narrowed his eyes suspiciously, unconvinced; but reluctantly took her word for it. Carefully, he rested the guitar against the wall, and headed outside with Eric.

Mabel sighed and headed to the bathroom. The warmth from the hotel room was stifling in comparison to the clinging chill that she'd experienced in Hamelin. Looking at her reflection in the mirror, Mabel was surprised to see beads of sweat building up on her forehead. As the sweat began to drip, she noticed the colour in her face drop to an ashen pallor with a green hue around her cheeks. The fine hairs on her arms stood on edge as a wave of nausea overwhelmed her. Unable to hold back, she bent over the toilet and proceeded to heave and dry-retch over the basin.

"Rough night?" Thet's soft voice asked.

Mabel couldn't answer. While hearing his voice had made her jump, she was more concerned with feeling her stomach pressing against her spine as she gasped before violently retching again, her hair slipping down in front of her face.

She felt the soothing strokes of a hand on her back, while another hand deftly and gently held her hair back as finally, she brought up the few sips of water she'd had earlier. Mabel took several steadying, gulping breaths while massaging her sore ribs. Calmly, she closed the lid to the toilet and turned around. She was surprised to see Thet in human form, dressed in his usual smart three-piece suit, offering her the flannel from the bathroom's counter, with an apologetic expression.

"Are you alright, Mab?" The concern in his voice was calming and comforting.

Mabel nodded and hastily washed away the sheen of cold sweat, before grabbing a fresh toothbrush the hotel had provided and, stealing some of

Eric's toothpaste, started to brush away the acrid taste of bile.

After spitting out the minty wash, and drying her face on a plush, soft towel; Mabel felt a little better, if not somewhat shaky and wobbly on her feet. She smiled weakly at Thet and went to take a step toward the bathroom door, but her knee buckled beneath her. Deftly, Thet reached out a hand and, with more strength than she'd ever have given him credit for, caught her before she fell. With ease, Thet lifted her up into his arms and carried her into the main hotel room.

She was relieved to see that Kristoph and Eric had not yet returned from their cigarette break. Quietly, she shakily uttered, "thank you Thet, I dunno what came over me."
Thet smiled and tucked a dampened strand of Mabel's hair behind her ear. He was being so affectionate that Mabel felt her cheeks flush with a sudden blood rush.
"You have just astral hopped without any prior experience. The sensation can be exceptionally overwhelming for *anyone* who's never done it

before. It takes a strong stomach to handle such an experience without being poorly," He knelt beside her and with more concern, he cautiously asked. "Are you *sure* you want to continue with tonight's events? I can always ask Helga if she can break the ghostly traversing into separate nights, rather than just hours," He smiled warmly, and Mabel couldn't help but feel an alarming and confusing mix of emotions as she looked into his friendly features.

Blinking her eyes rapidly, and shaking her head, Mabel reached out her hand and held Thet's. She enjoyed the feel of it when he was in his human form, it wasn't as cold as one would have thought.

"I'm fine, Thet;" she smiled. "The guys will be back soon, and we'll be good to go."

Thet stroked the back of Mabel's hand, his brow creasing subtly as a myriad of confusing thoughts crossed his always working mind, "very well," he murmured. "Were you able to glean anything from the first meeting tonight, with Sven and Claus."

Mabel nodded, "Kris seems to think the Piper

was possessed."

Thet's features hardened slightly, "possessed? Why? Did he see an entity by the Piper's side?"

"No," Mabel shook her head, uncertainly; "honestly, I'm not sure how he knew;" Mabel described the surreal event as best as she could, while Thet quietly stood by her side continuing to stroke her hand softly.

"You say you think the entity sensed you were there?" Thet asked, cautiously.

"I can't be sure," Mabel sighed. "It was like it knew something was amiss, but the memory of the Piper didn't recall us being there. So, I think we just about evaded its gaze. That said, it picked up on a scent around Eric. Its eyes also glazed over as it tried to tune its focus toward me. It seemed to ignore Kris, though;" She reflected, ponderously.

Thet opened his mouth to respond, just as Kristoph and Eric returned.

"Oh! Thet!" Eric grinned, "good to see you, I think?"

Kristoph took one step into the room, and his gaze fell on Thet stroking Mabel's hand.

Instantly, his lips pulled into a tight thin line, "Thet." He muttered, by way of a cold greeting. He turned to Mabel and raised his eyebrows in surprise. "Mab, you look..." His expression softened as he took in the pale and washed-out colour of her face, "what happened?" Kristoph hurried to her other side and crouched down. Swiftly he grabbed her free hand, in a warm and tight hold. The smell of cigarette smoke spilled from his lips and clothes; the scent seemed to fill the room and it made Mabel's head spin. Feeling another wave of nausea, she desperately snatched her hands back and hastily rushed to the bathroom.

"Was it something I did?" Kristoph mithered, as he looked sadly at his empty hand.
Thet flexed and relaxed his own fingers and shook his head, "Mab is having some trouble overcoming the effects of astral hopping, it can happen. She'll be alright. Just... keep her hydrated, for me?" Thet turned to walk away before stopping abruptly, "Kris? Mab said you seem to be of the opinion that the Piper was possessed. How could you possibly know?"

Kristoph glared at Thet. He couldn't quite explain it, but he felt a sudden urge to tell the reaper to 'go, do one' and 'leave them alone'. Forcing such intrusive thoughts to the recess of his mind however, he tapped the side of his nose and said, simply "the smell. Asmodeus has a similar scent. It fills my senses when he takes over. I recognised it immediately."

Thet narrowed his eyes, there was something about Kristoph that he still didn't quite trust; "what did it smell of?"

Kristoph shrugged, nonchalantly; "sweet. Like honey or syrup."

Thet's eyes widened in surprise, "Asmodeus smells of honey?" In response to Kristoph's nod of confirmation, Thet turned around again slowly; but paused. "You know, it's rare for a demon to smell of anything other than sulphur. I will check with my contacts in the after realms to determine where one might find a deity aside from Asmodeus, who has a characteristically sweet scent. In the meantime, please, take care of Mab," He issued again, before disappearing.

Kristoph glowered menacingly at the spot where the reaper had disappeared and bunched his hands into fists; "take care of Mab, for me!" He mimicked in a comedically shrill voice, "the idiot seems to have forgotten it's because of him and the freak linked to *me*, that she's here in the first place! Twat!" He snarled under his breath. He snatched his abandoned bottle of water and took an angry gulp from it. He turned to look at Eric for support and was met with a knowing smirk. "What?" Kristoph snapped, angrily.

Eric snorted, "you're only pissed at him because you're jealous. Although, for the life of me, I can't think why."

"*Jealous?*" Kristoph scoffed, "of Thet? Are you sure it was a normal roll up you just smoked?"

"Listen," Eric lowered his voice, as the sound of retching in the bathroom diminished; "I saw the same thing as you. It's evident the guy's got a strange thing for your Eve. It's only natural you should feel a hint of jealousy."

"She's not *my* anything!" Kristoph hated how defensive he sounded, yet he couldn't help but agree with his friend.

There was no denying the fact that when he closed his eyes each night, his lingering thoughts rested on Mabel and how wonderful it would be to hold her close at night; to listen to her soft breathing, feel her body rise in his arms with each breath; both simply enjoying the (potentially) limited time they had left together in this life. Kristoph shook the idle thoughts from his head as Mabel reappeared from the bathroom, looking exhausted. Automatically, he reached out to her and helped her back to the bed where she rested her head on the pillows. Softly, he stroked her forehead, smiling concernedly down at her.

Mabel looked up and smiled back, weakly; "I think I might take a power nap," she said, sleepily. "Are you going to watch over me, while I sleep? I don't want to miss the next haunting;" She chuckled, dopily.
Kristoph snorted softly, and whispered, "I'm not going anywhere, without you."
Mabel smiled serenely before closing her eyes. In next to no time, she was in a deep sleep. Kristoph pulled a chair up to the side of the bed and stroked her hand softly, enjoying the feeling of

the silken skin of her palm. He glanced over at
Eric, who was stood in the centre of the room,
watching them with a smug look on his face.
"Shut up," Kristoph grumbled, struggling to hide
a vague hint of a smile.
"I didn't say a thing," Eric held his hands up in
mock defence, before miming a beating heart
against his chest.

* *

Mabel awoke, just as Eric's watch started to sound
the hour. Kristoph had fallen asleep in the chair
beside her, still holding her hand; while Eric had
been channel surfing, lying on his front with his
feet propped up on the pillows next to her head.
The tinny sound of his watch caused him to
switch off the television and jolt backwards, so
that he was sat at the head of the bed.
Gently, Mabel shook Kristoph's shoulders,
"Kris? It's time;" she quietly whispered.
Kristoph quietly groaned as he came around,
rubbing his eyes sleepily. Mabel shuffled closer to
Eric and patted at the space she'd made, inviting
him to join them.

"I'm going to sleep well after all of this" Kristoph mumbled, as he flopped heavily next to her, yawning widely. "Not to mention undergo a wealth of therapy."

The three of them waited patiently for the next ghost like child to join them, but nothing happened. The room remained warm. The lights stayed on. To all intents and purposes, there was no sign of a haunting happening around them, at all.

Kristoph rested his head back on the pillow with a contented sigh, "Thet must have told them not to bother, on account of your being ill," He affectionately rubbed Mabel's back.

Mabel shook her head, "I told him not to do that! They'll be here."

"Quiet," Eric hissed; "can you hear that?"

Mabel and Kristoph sat upright and listened carefully. The sound of a cheerful melody had started to play. Faintly at first but growing in volume.

"I don't recognise that tune," Kristoph frowned. He looked at both of his friends, who also shook their heads with regrettable ignorance to the playful melody which was coming from across the room.

"It's coming from the landing, outside!" Mabel pointed to the door.

Reluctantly, the three of them got off the bed and quietly crept toward the hotel door. They were barely a few steps away from the entryway when the door slipped from its latch and slowly swung open before them. The hallway had changed, completely. Ahead of them lay the slight incline leading out of Hamelin town square, the sound of the melody was chirruping sweetly from there.

"Goodbye piper goodbye..." An excitable voice sang, sweetly, by the side of the door.

Mabel peered around the doorframe as Kristoph held on to her waist, "I can't see anyone," She whispered, concerned.

"Goodbye piper, goodbye!" The voice repeated in a whisper close to her left. With a sudden rush, Mabel felt a ghostly hand haul her back into the streets of Hamelin. The cries of fear and surprise told her that Kristoph and Eric weren't far behind her.

Once the flurry of the exertion had stopped, the three of them brushed the dust off their pyjamas and drew closer to each other and retreated to the pavements of the town square. There was a celebration taking place. The colour of the celebratory bunting, the cacophony of music, and the smell of freshly baked goods served as a stark contrast to the demoralising scene they'd witnessed during their first visit. Even the acrid smell of rat droppings had gone! The populace was dancing, milling together, cheering, and exulting their relief at the lack of rodents.

"I'll see you again, but I don't know when – goodbye piper, goodbye!" The delicate voice sang close to Mabel's shoulder. As Mabel turned her head, she was surprised to see a young girl no older than ten waving to someone in the distance.

Mabel cleared her throat and reached out to pat the girl's shoulder, "hello? Are you one of the Piper's friends?" She asked.

The girl turned her rosy cheeked face toward the sound of Mabel's voice, "I wanted to see the celebrations again, it was such a wonderful day" The girl sighed.

The town started to pick up the sing-song chant that the girl had been singing. Kristoph frowned, there was something about the lyrics that didn't settle right with him, "I'm sorry, what stage of the story is this?" He enquired, apprehensively.

"Why, the stage where the Piper returned to claim what he was owed, of course." The girl smiled sweetly at Kristoph, yet there was a hint of something ill at ease he couldn't shake off.

"And... what was *your* part in all of this?" He asked, curiously.

"Oh, I was the one that invited my beloved Piper friend here in the first place. I was also the one who helped him claim his debt." The girl's smile turned hideously fixed as her warm, chestnut eyes turned into two, menacing, black holes.

Chapter 18. The Piper Returns

The girl returned her gaze to the celebrations taking place in the square and breathed in the aromatic scents of the freshly baked goods that the bakers were displaying on a host of tables. Eloquently, she opened her arms wide and started to dance in a circle, following the memory of townsfolk around the square; all the while, the melody from the entertainers grew louder and more excitable. The trio stood uncertainly to the side, watching the performance with a growing sense of trepidation.

Finally, Eric leaned closer to his friends, "I'm not the only one who thinks our tour guide is a little... y'know... unhinged?" he whispered, uncertainly. Kristoph and Mabel nodded, slowly; as the young girl laughed out loud, with her empty eye sockets creating a negatively haunting element to what should have otherwise been a joyous event.
Eric shook his head in disbelief, "she let the piper

in? So, she *knew* the guy! How does a child her age, know a guy of *his* age?"

Mabel chewed at her bottom lip, "I'm not sure, although – Kris? How did you know the piper was possessed?"

Kristoph explained his reasoning, "you see, Asmodeus has a scent. It's not your typical sulphur, rotten egg smell that you would naturally associate with a demon from Hell. His is sickly sweet, like honey. I suppose it's a better way of gaining the interest of someone you like, smelling nice," He shrugged, "I smelt it straight away from the Piper, but it was more potent. It was so strong! Almost like he should have been dripping in honey and syrup from head to foot. I'm surprised you guys couldn't smell it?"

For anyone who has a passion of a subject matter, there comes a moment in their lives where a mere word or description can trigger the memory of a torrent of pointless information on a related matter. As Kristoph detailed the scents of honey and syrup, with the background music playing so sweetly and the townsfolk dancing around; Mabel found herself traversing down a mental rabbit hole of mythology. Slowly, but surely, the pieces started to add up in her mind and as the realisation hit her like a brick to the face, her eyes widened in horror.

"This is not going to be pleasant," she frantically whispered.

While their tour guide continued to laugh and dance, Mabel grabbed hold of Eric and Kristoph's arms and dragged them to a quieter area of the town square. It was a spot that offered a vantage point from all angles, to avoid any unwanted attention from the deity whom she quietly hoped was out of sight and mind.

"Mabel, what's going on?" Kristoph murmured, holding her shaking hand tightly, "what do you know?"

Mabel swallowed hard, "how much Greek mythology do either of you know?" She asked cautiously.

Kristoph sighed, "little to none, there was a battle in Troy? I think? Some guy with a weak ankle?"

Eric snorted, "his name was Achilles, and it was his heel" He elaborated, before turning to Mabel; "I know some, why?"

"Well," Mabel wrung her hands, "this is medieval Germany. Religions are shifting from the more pagan beliefs to the more institutional. I'm struggling to believe this could be the case, but it all adds up that the deity who is possessing the piper, might be an early pagan god from Greek mythology."

"Which one?" Eric frowned, "there were hundreds!"

Mabel grimaced, "out of all the Greek Gods, there's only one that comes to mind who could shepherd wild creatures; flirt with anyone and everyone as he represented fertility. He also had a penchant for playing the pipes."

Eric's eyes widened in horror as his mind caught up with Mabel's. Kristoph however, looked completely lost at sea and stared wildly at them both, "who?!" He asked, exasperatedly.

"Pan." Eric croaked, "of course it would be Pan;" he groaned weakly as he slumped forward and rested his head heavily in his hands.

"I don't understand, who's Pan? What's wrong with him?" Kristoph asked, his concern growing. Slowly, Mabel started to explain. "Pan is a demigod from ancient Greece. His father was Hermes, the messenger God, his mother was Penelope, a human – also the wife to Odysseus, but that's a whole herd of pigs I won't go near!" Eric's snort was muffled as he rubbed his face, but he pointed at Mabel, "I see what you did there."

"Anyway," Mabel continued. "He was born part human, part goat. When his mother saw him, she ran away in fear, supposedly. The Gods loved him though, and he became the link between humanity and wild wilderness. He could also be vicious when provoked and terrifying too! His call to battle was said to instil fear and panic in to the enemy, hence the term panic deriving from his name."

Kristoph stared blankly at Mabel, "I mean, this is fascinating, but I don't see how he could be causing any harm to the children?"

Mabel looked around at the people dancing and her eyes rested on their tour guide, who had returned to her spot by the side of the square and was staring, listlessly toward the incline out of the town.

Mabel shook her head sadly, "I desperately hope I'm wrong;" she murmured, as she started to chew on her nails. "But seeing our guide, I can't help but wonder. Remember the term she used? Her *beloved* piper?"

Kristoph nodded, and Eric finally dropped his hands from his face; "you don't suppose?" Eric's face was pale, but no longer with fear. His eyes narrowed as he looked at the young girl. She was gazing longingly towards the exit of the town, "you don't suppose he *did* anything, to her?"

Mabel grimaced as she shrugged, "he was the god of fertility and sex. He was a satyr or fawn like creature. He unashamedly had relations with nymphs. One young girl, playing too close to the woodlands. One tune played the right way, a few well-chosen words; I mean look at her – she's besotted," she gestured to the girl.

"Hold on," Kristoph snapped. "Are you suggested that by *doing* something to her, you're saying he...". Kristoph couldn't even finish the sentence as the repulsion of what was being discussed took the wind out of him.

"I don't know whether he did anything

physically," Mabel tried her best to soothe the rising anger in the men, "but I wouldn't be surprised if he's groomed her. If she let him in, and then helped him to return in order to collect his debt; she's proving that her devotion is to *him* and no one else."

"We've got to stop him!" Eric snapped, "I can't, in good conscience, allow a town's populace of children be groomed and kidnapped by someone who... I mean, what would he do with so many children, anyway?"
Mabel shook her head, "the number of believers in his existence as a pagan deity might be dwindling. What better way to keep his way of life going if he has a small flock of his own lambs following him?"
"But, the children are going to perish at some point, in the next twenty-four hours!" Eric snapped, "how is that going to benefit him?"
Mabel looked sorrowfully at her friend, "it would serve as a reminder to the adults; never to forget the old ways, or else."

Kristoph had heard enough. Before Eric or Mabel could stop him, he stormed over to the young girl with the blackened eyes. With more strength that he'd anticipated, he spun the girl around by her shoulders so he could stare in to the two black voids in her face.

"Your *beloved* piper. Where is he?" He snapped.

The girl smiled simply, completely unphased with being manhandled by him; "ah, ah, ah!" She wiggled her finger in his face, "that's not how this works. You will have to wait and see!" She trilled. "Ah!" She turned her head over her shoulder and pointed in the distance. "Look, my beloved approaches, victorious!" So, saying, without another word spoken, the girl gathered up her skirts and raced toward the lone figure who had appeared over the crest of the incline, playing a merry tune on his pipe that accompanied the rapturous melodies from the town.

Eric and Mabel grabbed Kristoph and pulled him into a side street, as he went to launch after the girl.

"We can't interfere with this!" Mabel hissed, "I'm

not happy about any of it either but the story has to play out, otherwise these kids will *never* find true peace!"

Kristoph looked sharply at Eric and was relieved to see the same level of anger on his friend's face; "Mab," Kristoph shook his head, "please..." Shakily he inhaled a steadying breath, "I cannot allow these children to be lead on defencelessly."

"I don't see any other way, Kris;" Mabel sighed, "I'm sorry!" She bowed her head, "I know I sound callous, but all of this is a memory, it's already happened – we're just here to put the pieces together and spread the word."

"So, that's it then?" Kristoph snapped. "Pan gets away with his lesson of tough pagan love, a bunch of kids are killed in the process and, what? He stops what he's doing? If he's truly that vengeful Mab, he's not going to stop! He will continue this. Think of all the children in the world who go missing on a regular basis, if we allow this to go by unchallenged, who's to say that it's not Pan whisking them away for his own sordid reasons?"

Mabel wrung her hands, panicked, "I don't *know*!" She shook her head, "I don't want any of this to happen the way that it is! I just wanted to help these children find peace!" Her shoulders slumped, defeatedly.

Kristoph looked at Mabel, his anger shifting slightly to regret, for having snapped at her. "Hey," he forced a grim smile and pulled her into a comforting hug, "we'll figure something out. We all will. One thing's for sure though; Pan will not be getting any of the recognition *he* hoped for, regardless of the outcome of these events." Mabel breathed in the scent of Kristoph's cologne, as she cautiously wrapped her arms around him. Even through the midst of the tumultuous music, she could hear his heartbeat pounding fiercely in his chest. Slowly, she pulled back and smiled up into his sea blue eyes, which looked down at her with such comfort and encouragement that she couldn't help but feel inspired.

"I think I have an idea, but it's going against the rules of the story somewhat" she mused, "I want to try and get our tour guide on board, but something tells me she'd be unwilling to see her charming beloved for who he really is. Unless..."

Mabel gave Kristoph a long, hard stare; "there were another deity who could help her see things from a different perspective?" She stepped back and drew her hands back from around his waist, stroking down his arms, before resting on his wrists.

"You think it wise to get *him* involved in this?" Kristoph murmured, looking down at the mark of Asmodeus that Mabel's hand rested against.

Eric cleared his throat, "from what you said, he loathes the thoughts of kiddies coming into any harm. If nothing else, it wouldn't hurt to hear what he has to say on this matter."

* *

The scene from the street had changed in a matter of moments. The music had come to a shaky end as the piper returned, victoriously and zeroed in on the mayor who was busy devouring a rather large slice of black forest gateaux. Mabel watched the muted argument between them transpire from the safety of an upstairs window, in the upper floor of one of the town's bakeries.

"If we're going to do this, we need to do it now,

so there's enough time to formulate a plan of action," she mithered to the men.

Kristoph took a deep breath, closed his eyes and pressed firmly on the scorched mark on his wrist, "Asmodeus?" he murmured, "we might need your help with this. Things aren't as straight forward as we'd hoped."

As the branding on his wrist came to life with a maniacal laugh, Eric watched on in awe, as Asmodeus appeared from Kristoph's ankle. "When are they ever straight forward, Kristobelle?" Asmodeus chuckled. "Right, what have we got here then?" In a single stride, Asmodeus joined Mabel by the window and looked out; "ahhh, Hamelin. You know, I had a pet rat in Hell who stemmed from here. Lovely fella, called him Jim."

Asmodeus grinned at the group, who looked at him grimly, "sheesh, tough crowd you lot are."

"Asmodeus?" Mabel sighed, "we've worked out what happened to Helga and her friends. That is to say, we have a strong feeling."

"Marvellous!" The demon grinned, broadly; "you know, I always did wonder. It was so hush, hush when they appeared in Limbo. None of them wanted to talk about it. I blame the angels personally,"

"Angels?" Eric asked, "angels are real, too?"

"You catch on quick, Mr. Payne!" Asmodeus winked, "bodes well for all future endeavours."

Eric sat down heavily on a sack of flour, "why didn't they intervene?" He asked the room, in disbelief.

"Intervene?" Asmodeus looked between the strained faces of the three humans and felt the surreal sense of uncertainty seep into his mind. "Krissy-poo, I don't suppose you could bring an old, fragile, and delicate demon up to speed?"

It took a little time and some clarification from Mabel and Eric, but very soon Asmodeus had been brought up to date with the state of affairs in Hamelin. Within moments, he was hopping with rage at the window.

"That conniving bastard! The son of a... Out of all the *ungodly* things... I... Once upon a time, it was a done thing, but... his interests were in *nymphs*, not *children*!" Asmodeus spluttered, his demonic presence grew, and his eyes burned like fiery lumps of coal. He stormed about the upper floor of the bakers in a rage unlike any they had witnessed him in before.

"Exactly what we thought!" Mabel agreed. "Asmodeus, you see that girl behind the piper's back?"

The demon stood so close to Mabel she could feel the heat from his rage, radiating around him like a rippling aura; "the black-eyed child?" He snarled, "definitely the after-effects of having seen a deity in their full form. The childlike innocence is burned away from their eyes, it's the only way we know in the afterlife, that a human has been in close contact with an otherworldly being."

Eric swore quietly, under his breath, shuddering at the myriad of disturbing thoughts of how such an encounter might have transpired.

"She's besotted," Mabel explained. "We need her to see Pan for who he really is. In this state, she'll never truly find peace, even if we do bring to light what took place here. We need her to be on our side. She was the one who granted him access to return to collect the children, you see."

Asmodeus clicked his fingers with a stern

expression. As Mabel watched on, the girl vanished from the town square altogether; "leave her with me, there are ways in which we can return her ability to see the smoke through the trees. Sadly, the innocence in her eyes will be all but gone, that doesn't mean to say reason is not unattainable. One thing's for sure," the demon hissed, "Pan needs to be stopped!"

"How though?" Eric asked, "we're only human, after all. He's a bleedin' goat god!"

"Demigod," Asmodeus snarled, "they're the worst. God complexes, the lot of 'em. They're tricky, but not impossible to reign in."

He tapped his long claws off his fanged teeth, "you still have one astral voyage left of this venture, yes?"

Mabel nodded in response, "yes, that's when he comes to take the children away."

Asmodeus growled a low, guttural rumble. It was almost like that of a feral beast, readying itself for a fight, "very well. I need to check on a few matters with Thet's *assurance* in Limbo. Kris?"

Kristoph jumped at being addressed with his natural name, with no flirtatious add on.

Asmodeus offered a fleeting smile, "when the final haunting takes place tonight, let me take control of you. Demigod verses a demon is never a pretty sight. Demigod possessing a human, verses a demon possessing a human however, well – the odds seem more in your favour, don't you think? There are more children in Limbo than I would like to admit. Not *one* of them has been truly open with how they got there! I need to be sure of all our suspicions before the start of the next haunting. I won't be long. Stay strong, all of you."

No sooner had he said this, Asmodeus vanished; leaving Kristoph with a burning sensation on his wrist as the branding swelled on his skin, furiously red. Once again, the world around them warped as they were slowly pulled back to the waking world. Mabel's eyes widened as, before the mists of the ghostly vortex clouded her view, the Piper looked directly up at the window she'd been spying on him from, and grinned the most unnatural, malicious, and terrifying smile she had ever seen!

Chapter 19. Eric's Loss

Kristoph, Mabel, and Eric fell back and landed in a heap in the middle of the hotel room. Eric and Kris barely had a moment to process any of what had just taken place, before Mabel jumped up and began to anxiously pace around them, muttering. They watched on, puzzled, as she started to tug nervously at her hair, chew at her nails and jump each time a door shut further down the corridor from their room.

"Um, Mab?" Eric asked, cautiously. "Is everything alright?"

Mabel shook her head, her eyes wide with terror, "he knows, he knows, he knows!" Her voice shook with emotion and her breathing had become erratic.

Kristoph jumped up and stalled her pacing, "easy now, Mab. Who knows what?" He asked, softly. Mabel shook her head; her eyes were stinging, and her head was swimming with sensations. Everything was overwhelming and chaotic! With a groan she slumped forward into a heap on the floor and grasped at her head, "it hurts," she whispered faintly, shutting her eyes tightly; "why does my head hurt so much?"

"Maybe it's the astral hopping?" Eric suggested, his voice thick with concern as he cautiously approached them.

Kris shook his head, "I dunno – she seems to be in a lot of pain. I don't think it's just the astral hopping that's doing it."

Mabel looked up through strained eyes. The room around her shimmered before her, as a deep red hue descended over her vision.

"Everything is *red*!" She yelped out, in panic.

Eric crouched down in front of Mabel and looked into her eyes, "there's nothing wrong with your eyes Mab, you're not bleeding. There are no burst blood vessels..."

Mabel shook her head, "NO!" She turned to look up at Kris with a wild expression on her face, before shouting out in desperation, "Kris! *EVERYTHING* is *RED*!"

The colour in Kristoph's face drained completely, and he sank slowly down to the ground beside her. Eric however, looked lost, "I don't understand," he said, helplessly.

Kristoph shook his head, "it's part of the deal that was made with Thet but;" he paused, "I thought the traffic light system went out of action when we agreed to go under Thet and Asmodeus's employment?"

Eric still looked completely baffled, "traffic lights?"

Mabel took a steadying breath, "the sole purpose of being reincarnated into this world, was so that I could live as full a life as I could, without it being cut short. Any decisions or encounters that I made would offer a traffic light system. If I always opted for the green light, my life would continue safely. Amber, my life would be in jeopardy. Red, I've made a wrong choice, and my life is forfeit," she explained with a forced calm.

Eric stared, petrified; "but how?"

"He knows," Mabel choked. "The last thing I saw before we returned to the here and now... was the piper, Pan; he looked up at the window, and smiled at me. It was unlike any other smile. It was wicked, vicious. He knows."

"I don't get it," Kris's voice croaked; "why is it

affecting *you* and not me?"

Mabel took another deep and steadying breath, "I think... it has something to do with you playing host to Asmodeus," she spoke slowly, as her mind worked overtime. "I noticed him ignore you in the hall, during the first memory. He sniffed around Eric, he tried to scope me out – but he ignored you. When you mentioned his scent and that Asmodeus smelled similar, it makes sense. He doesn't know you're there Kris; he can't see or smell you as you are another possessed being. It just so happens that the being you're possessed by has a similar odour. As such, I'm certain he cannot discern between his own scent and that of a similar supernatural entity, who has a similar smell, that is."

Eric frowned, "so, why am I not seeing red?" He asked, nervously.

Mabel sighed, "Because you're not a reincarnated being, Eric. You're a living, breathing, never been dead before human."

Kristoph stood up, his face flushed with anger, "I'm calling this off! Thet and Asmodeus want to get Limbo sorted? They can do it themselves! I cannot and *will* not see you die Mab. I don't want to lose you! I can't..." he slumped down on to the bed heavily, "I can't lose you Mab."

He heaved a sigh that was weighted with raw emotions as Mabel stared up at him, her eyes wide in shock at this sudden outburst of emotion. Eric cleared his throat awkwardly, "and I think that's my cue to step outside for a cigarette," he mumbled, before slowly backing out of the doorway.

The room fell silent as Mabel continued to massage her temples. Kris sat on the bed, uncertain of how to act after having opened up to her.

"Kris, I..." Mabel didn't know what to say.

"Forget it," Kristoph shook his head; "forget what I said, I just got...".

"Don't," Mabel pulled herself up on to the bed beside him and rested her hand gently on his mouth, "don't start playing off that episode as one of those '*I got caught up in the moment*' things," she said.

"If you feel anything for me, I'd much rather you be honest with me and not play it off."

Kristoph couldn't help but feel lost in Mabel's eyes; so bright and so warm, with their dark chocolate brown hue and bursts of black diamonds in her irises. Her dark lashes were so long and fluttered naturally, like they wanted to hide such precious gems from the cruelties of the world.

His gaze slowly dropped down to her lips, parted ever so slightly and so inviting. There were so many thoughts racing around his head; begging, pleading, *screaming* at him to make the first move - yet the smallest whisper in his ear sounded the loudest; "if she dies, it will destroy you."

Kristoph's heart felt like it would burst out of his chest if it could, and he could feel himself leaning closer as her hand fell from his lips. Her eyelids started to close as their faces drew closer together. He could feel her delicate breath brush against his lips. Kristoph's head felt caught up in a haze as he brushed a strand of hair away from her face, they were mere moments apart.

"Ahem," Thet's voice broke the spell that had enveloped them. His usual soft undertones cut through the room cold and sharply; "I don't mean to intrude."

Thet was dressed in a more relaxed attire of chino trousers and a figure flattering short sleeved shirt, displaying a myriad of otherworldly designs that rippled up and down his arms. It was clear to Kristoph and Mabel, that Thet had noticed the various tattoo designs that adorned the skin of their friends and had tried to mimic them, but with his own other-worldly flair. Mabel couldn't help but be impressed with how the Celtic knots moved like cogs in a machine, slowly and intricately passing over and under the interlocking lines.

Thet's eyes shone a cold icy flame, as he took in the scene of Kristoph and Mabel's closeness.

"Thet," Mabel gasped, her voice husky.

Thet's gaze softened somewhat at her voice, "indeed."

He nodded, trying to ignore the burning sensation that seemed to be stemming from somewhere beneath his sternum; "I thought I would stop by to see how the latest astral hop was treating you, and to provide you with an update on my findings in Hell. Apparently, the hop has treated you both very well. I'm sorry to have interrupted whatever *this* was! Kristoph, Mab – I will come back at a more convenient time," he grumbled, through clenched teeth.

"No! WAIT!" Mabel and Kristoph both cried out, as Thet turned his back on them. Slowly, the reaper turned around, with a questioning expression on his face.

"Thet, I'm seeing red. Everywhere!" Mabel couldn't hide the sob that forced its way out as she felt the despair of losing everything around her.

Thet's eyes widened in horror as he automatically reached out to hold her. He spotted Kristoph's cautionary stare however and faltered. Calming the urge to swipe the guitarist off to the afterlife, Thet folded his arms; "that's not possible. Asmodeus and I stalled the colour system, to ensure you both remained immortal during this process, as we didn't know how long the clear up of Limbo would take. You shouldn't be seeing any red, amber, or even *green* aurors, at all. Kristoph? What about you?"

Kristoph shook his head, not daring to tear his eyes away from Mabel. He wanted to absorb every physical movement she made, hear every lilt to her voice. He didn't want to miss a single moment, not if she were living on borrowed time.

Thet slowly paced around the room as he mused on the news, "this is very concerning. Only an individual further up in the echelons could even come remotely close to..." slowly, he looked up at them both and widened his eyes with worry; "of course!" Thet's voice was barely a whisper, "I managed to narrow the scent you described, Kristoph, to a small group of deities who predominantly reside in a small haven that was abandoned by the ancient Greek gods centuries ago. The place *reeks* of ambrosia."
Kristoph frowned, "ambrosia being?"
Thet waved his hands, "unimportant. The fact remains that the sweet, honey like scent you assign to Asmodeus stems from there, as he tends to have a bit of fun with the nymphs the realm's nymphs."
"What about Pan?" Mabel asked, hesitantly.
Thet's jaw dropped, and he fell silent before

staggering back and slumping in the lone armchair that resided by the door; just as Eric cautiously poked his head around the entrance with his eyes closed.

"Are you both decent?" He asked, almost apologetically; "I only ask as the corridor is swarming with ghost children, and I'm freaking out!"

Thet leapt up and swung the door wide open and ushered Eric and (what must have been) most of Limbo's young populace through the door. Mabel and Kristoph found themselves having to stand in the doorway to the bathroom as the room's large expanse was quickly consumed by the mass of children who swarmed in, buzzing with chatter and excitement. Eric desperately hopped, skipped, and skirted around the ghostly figures with a mix of yelps, whimpers and hums of apology and darted between his friends, using them like human shields. The combined group barely had time to introduce themselves to each other, when the lights began to flicker and, seemingly pulling themselves up through the floor; Asmodeus and a figure Mabel had never met before appeared, huffing, puffing, and jostling each other rudely.

"When you said 'you're to return up top, Azrael' I rather thought you meant further north than here. Eugh! Crawling through the floorboards is so *demeaning*!" The stranger moaned.

"Get over yourself, Az!" Asmodeus hissed, "you said you wanted to help, I thought some field work would do you good. Now then, where's my host?" The demon looked around wildly, and his gaze fell on Thet; "ah, good of you to join us. I suppose the humans brought you up to speed?" Thet shook his head, "not quite. Asmodeus, what in all that is dead, are you doing?"

The rest of the room seemed just as curious to hear the demon's response, however Mabel quietly stepped forward, "um, hello – everyone. I am so pleased you have all been brave enough to come forward. I believe I am right in thinking you all know of Mr. Grim?" She held her hand out to Thet who smiled weakly at the children, before morphing back into his standard reaper attire. This simple change encouraged the children to smile broadly, with recognition.

Mabel cleared her throat and, feeling a hint of confidence diminish the anxiety caused by the obscuring mist of red across her vision, continued. "Mr. Grim has arranged for his friends and us three," she pointed to herself, Eric, and Kristoph, "to help you move on. Through our time in Hamelin, we've come to learn that there was a figure who... wasn't kind to you." Cautiously, she chewed at her lip as she considered the right words to use; "however, we've only been aware of a relatively smaller number of children in comparison to how many of you are here now. Would I be right to assume that you are *all* in Limbo, because of the same if not, a similar figure?" She asked, uncertain of the reception such a question would receive.

The room fell gravely quiet, uncomfortably so. The adults in the room observed the children eagerly, awaiting some confirmation or response; sadly, all they received was a nervous silence. Determined, Mabel doggedly pushed forward. "Okay, you're all nervous of speaking up, yes?" She asked.

There were a few weak nods of the head and

some uncomfortable shuffling of feet, as a few of the children looked over their shoulders, anxiously.

"It's perfectly normal to be scared, but I can assure you, this is a safe room. Mr. Grim will *never* let anyone here come to any harm" she smiled warmly at Thet, who nodded slowly in confirmation.

"We have Asmodeus here too, who, well... yes, he's a demon. However, he will fight *anyone* who would try to hurt any one of you!" She cast a hesitant glance over at the demon, who nodded sternly, his face set – all his usual bravado set aside for the seriousness of the situation at hand.

"Then we have... um... Azrael?" She asked, hesitantly. "I'm sorry, I don't really know who you are." She shrugged helplessly at the stunned angel, "but, if Asmodeus and Mr. Grim vouch for you, then I'm sure you're here to help too." Mabel cast a quick look at Thet, whose shoulders shook as if with quiet laughter.

"Finally," she swallowed, "you have the three of us. I'm Mab, this is Kris, and this is Eric. We want to get to the bottom of all of this, and we think we're close. We just need you all to be incredibly brave and just nod or shake your heads to a couple of questions, is that okay?"

There were a few hushed conversations which hissed around the room. Finally, Helga Schneider stepped forward. Holding her head high, she offered a single nod; "I will speak on behalf of my young friends, I do not fear repercussions."

Mabel's heart filled with awe at the young girl's confidence.

Slowly, she sat down to be at eye level with Helga; "we have seen the piper that took you all. We know he was not alone. He had a figure from another world using him like a puppet, did you ever see that figure?" Mabel asked.

Helga nodded her head, a few of her friends gathered around and nervously nodded their heads in agreement too.

"This figure, did he have the appearance of a fawn, that is, part man, part goat, outside of the piper guise?" Mabel queried, hesitantly.

Helga and a larger number of the children dressed in apparel like her own, nodded their heads.

Mabel nodded, "thank you."

Slowly she stood up and surveyed the room of ghostly children. They were of all years, some in their infancy, others in their mid to later teenage years by sight. All of them were dressed in a wide array of styles from the different eras, some even looked unnervingly modern.

Clearing her throat Mabel addressed the group, "I can see that not all of you stem from the streets of Medieval Hamelin, I can see you span from across the globe and across the decades and eras. I doubt you all met this figure as a piper, however, would I be right to assume you all encountered this faun figure?"

As one, the room full of children nodded their heads, some had ghostly tears welling in their eyes.

Mabel swallowed hard, "this figure hurt you; and I can see he has continued his vile scheme through the centuries, we need to stop him. He knows that we are on to him, we just need to gain some ground on him to be a step ahead. We have met the twin ghosts of this figure's past. The second ghost we met brought us to our present meeting," Mabel grinned at Helga, who positively beamed back; "we need the ghost of his future! Would his latest victim please be brave enough to step forward?"

Cautiously a teenage boy shuffled his way to the front of the crowd. He looked to be about sixteen. His dark black hair fell delicately over his left eye, and he wore a denim jacket with sewn band patches adorning every spare space of fabric. Mabel heard Eric gasp, before the gentle giant jumped down from his hiding space behind Kristoph. Desperately, he reached out to the boy, his eyes brimming with tears, "Tom?" He choked, "not you, too!"
The boy named Tom looked sadly at Eric and nodded slowly while reaching out his ghostly hand to Eric, who tried in vain to hold the delicate haunting image in his own large palms. Eric sniffed and turned to Mabel, shaking; "I think I need to speak to my sister," he struggled, breathlessly, "Tom's my nephew!"

"Eric," Kristoph whispered, in shock; "I had no idea."

Eric bowed his head, "Tom went missing the other day. He was out on an end of school celebratory camping trip with his friends in Snowdonia. Missy called me to say he'd not come home. I told her not to worry, that he'd be back soon with all his friends and gear, ready to make a mess."

No sooner had he said this, the rest of Tom's friends shuffled forward, sadly.

Tom looked glumly at his uncle, "Uncle Eric, you've got to stop him. Jack's still alive, but the devil's hunting him. He's terrifying. His eyes are black, his yell chills you to the bone. H-he said that I was just another lamb for his flock, he insisted on taking us to his farm. We tried to run, but he caught us off guard! He has a pipe that he plays. He started to play it and we couldn't help ourselves. It was like the pipe had a voice. It controlled us. It guided us, to this clifftop. It ordered us to..." Tom's head hung low, "we couldn't fight it, Uncle."

Eric crawled on his knees toward his nephew, his shoulders shaking with grief as he reached out and as delicately as he could, wrapped his long arms around the ghostly figure of the boy. Through his barely controlled emotions, Eric asked, "are you able to take us to him?"

Asmodeus and Thet slowly moved around the crowd and knelt next to Eric, their faces taught with constrained emotions, "we can get you there" Thet assured him, before turning to the group of children; "you have all been phenomenally brave. Because of you, no child will ever fall victim to this being, ever again!" Cautiously he turned to Mabel. "Mab, you have been incredible, but I must insist that you sit this one out. Until I can be sure that Pan has been dealt with, we cannot risk you coming to any harm. You will stay here with the children until we return, no questions asked."
Mabel nodded slowly, wiping her eyes. She rested her hand on Eric's shaking shoulder, "Eric? Will you be alright?"
The gentle giant, who'd allowed his arms to fall by his side turned to Mabel with a fierce look in his face, "I don't know how, but I will not rest until this goat is dead!" He snapped.
Asmodeus chuckled wickedly, as Eric stood up

and joined the rest of the men, "that's my stable boy." In the blink of an eye, the group of men vanished, leaving Mabel behind.

"Miss Weaver?" Helga bent down so that her hauntingly sweet face was so close, that Mabel felt like her nose was being tickled by cobwebs; "Mr. Grim says you are good at portraits. Can I have one, with Annabelle?"

Mabel smiled weakly, "with pleasure, Miss Schneider. If I have time, I will do a group portrait of you all!"

Chapter 20. A Fight for Survival

Even at the start of Summertime, the Welsh wilderness had a chill to the air. Kristoph shivered and wrapped his arms around himself, suddenly wishing he'd grabbed a hoodie before they had ventured out. It would come as no surprise to anyone, that a vest top and pyjama bottoms lacked a great deal of comfort and security from the raw Welsh elements.

Eric, too, was chilly; however, the adrenaline of seeing the ghostly form of his nephew seemed to have eradicated any sense of discomfort. He looked around them, desperately, his ears straining for any sign or sound of trouble. All seemed unnaturally serene and peaceful, however. It almost felt as though someone had anticipated their appearance and had hastily put on a display of calm to mask the chaos that resided beneath.

The group of men stood tensely and silently for a while, listening. The chatter of a couple of territorial squirrels cut through the air sharply, but the normality of the sound didn't deter the gathering. There was a soft breeze, rippling through the leaves, gently caressing the bare skin on each member.

Finally, Eric turned to Thet and asked, "how do you normally do this?"

Thet frowned, questioningly, "do what, Eric?"

"Find the dead, of course!" Eric snapped. He had it in his mind that if he were to locate the body of Tom and his friends, Pan wouldn't be too far away.

Thet frowned, "I am truly sorry for your nephew, Eric; however, I was not there to move him along. It must have been one of my many siblings. As such, with their soul not emitting a lost aura, I'm just as in the dark as you, I'm afraid," he sighed and rested a comforting hand on the broad shoulder of the Welshman.

"That said..." Thet mused, "I recall Tom mentioning a cliff? Perhaps we could start looking out toward the sharper precipices, as opposed to in the middle of a woodland, Azrael?" He turned to the angel, who appeared to be surprisingly at peace with their current setting.

Azrael turned his attention from admiring the intricate veins in an oak tree leaf, and nodded his head, "yes Reap... uh... I mean, Thet?" He blustered, apologetically.

Thet sighed, quietly; "could you take to the skies and follow the cliff lines? Keep an eye out for the prone forms of a few young men," he cast a quick glance over at Eric who sniffed loudly, "once you have found them, send one of your *signs.*"

Azrael opened his mouth to argue that as an angel, it was *his* job to issue orders; however, a stern glance from Asmodeus shut him up, immediately. With a curt nod of his head, the angel turned his back and with a flex of his shoulders, the most magnificent display of wings shimmered down his back.

Even Eric, who was still struggling with crippling grief, could not ignore the majesty of the display. They were like no wings he or Kristoph had ever imagined. They looked like delicate silken swathes of fibrous lights. They certainly didn't look strong enough to carry the weight of a fully grown man, yet when Azrael fanned them out, they stood firm and assured, glistening almost transparently, like the wings of an insect. Azrael caught the wide eyed, impressed look on Kristoph's face and smiled smugly.

"It's rare we angels reveal our identity to humans. When we do however, they seem to think our wings should appear feathery and downier, like a swan's. Just imagine the cumbersome weight, however!" He beamed proudly, as his wings glistened in the weak moonlight.

"If they've always looked like *that*, where did we get downy impressions from?" Kristoph asked, as Azrael took flight with one heavy beat of his resplendent wings.

Asmodeus scoffed, "that would be down to good ol' Gabriel."

At Kristoph's puzzled expression, he elaborated further. "When our father impregnated the human vessel with his sunspot, they had a right ol' time trying to secure a place in which she could give birth. I suppose you know the story?"

Kristoph nodded, conscious of Eric's teeth grinding with disinterest; Asmodeus continued regardless. "Well, Gabriel was sent to oversee the birth. Y'know, what with our father being a somewhat absentee dad. So, down goes ol' Gabriel, not too familiar with the more gruesome aspects of human life. He tried to assist with knocking on the inn doors too, only to have one woman upturn her toilet bowl on him, from an upstairs window. Suffice it to say, his wings got rather sticky and gathered up no end of dust, feathers and down from the stable they eventually had to settle for. Hence, feathery wings. Apparently, feathery faecal covered primaries and secondaries are all it took for a bunch of shepherds to think angels flew with glorious swan like feathers. Suffice it to say, Gabriel returned up top, quite literally stinking to high heaven!" He chuckled maliciously at the memory.

Kristoph couldn't help but grin, despite the sombre circumstances they were in. He turned to Eric who was glaring into the darkening woods with a look of fierce anger in his eyes. Kristoph's smile disappeared at once and he cautiously approached his friend. What could he say? There was no collection of words in his vocabulary that would make any of this situation better for Eric, so, quietly; he rested a comforting hand on Erics broad back before opening his arms wide to instigate a comforting hug.

Eric smiled weakly, "cheers mate, but not now. Until that angel returns, and I have Tom in my arms, I'm not going to relax."
He patted Kristoph's shoulder and breathed out heavily, "how long does it take for an angel to fly the expanse of the Snowdonia cliffsides, anyway" he grumbled to the group as a whole.
"Most angels?" Thet ignored the rhetorical aspect of Eric's question, "about a couple of hours. Azrael is one of the quickest of the bunch, wouldn't you say As?" He turned to the demon who looked sour at the thought of having to say something complimentary about the angel.
"Next to Luci, he's pretty quick, I s'pose" he begrudgingly admitted.
"Indeed," Thet nodded, "so, I wouldn't have thought it would take him too much longer... ah! Here he is now."

The hasty beating of the angel's wings sounded more akin to a few sharp gusts of wind. When he landed however, his face was not beaming with victory. Nor was it pale with grief or concern. Instead, it was rather confused.

"Well, I found the boys" Azrael gritted his teeth and mimicked Thet's nervous knee bob, "but they seem to be in the peak of health singing rather poorly to a beaten-up acoustic guitar."
"WHAT?!" Eric shouted out, his knees nearly collapsing in shock, as he hardly dared to believe it.
Azrael held out his hand and as the group of men held on to him, the enclosed woodland disappeared around them and they found themselves clustered together on a clifftop, looking down on to a custom-made camp. There below them, a group of boys could be seen singing, rather drunkenly, around a weak looking campfire, strumming on an untuned guitar. The loudest of the group was Tom. His dark hair swinging lazily in the breeze; he was mimicking one of Dark Omen's hit songs, while dancing in a surprisingly accurate manner befitting his uncle.

Eric frowned, "I don't get it... if Tom and his mates are alive, who were those kids we saw in the hotel room?"

Kristoph's blood ran cold as he turned to Thet, who slowly turned to look at him in turn. The reaper's eyes were royally ablaze.

"We need to get back to the hotel room, *NOW!*" Thet snapped.

* *

Barely, a moment after the men had left and Helga had suggested she create a portrait of them all; Mabel had hurried to her original hotel room and gathered up her sketch pad and pencils and had returned to the room full of ghostly children. Each one of them looked at her, expectantly. She smiled weakly and looked at Helga, "it will only be a rough sketch, I'm afraid. I'm not a perfect artist but I have a decent photographic memory, so I'll be able to add the finishing details later – once you've all..." She couldn't finish the sentence, instead she shrugged, helplessly.

Helga grinned, "it's not a problem, Miss Weaver."

She bobbed up on to her tiptoes, "I know it will be perfect. Can I have a look at the picture you did of Bo?" She beamed, "simple Bo was lovely, albeit a little too angry, sometimes."

Mabel grinned, "he was rather excitable, wasn't he?"
She tore out the page she had finished of Bo and his group of Viking warriors and passed it on to Helga, who stroked the course paper, tracing the pencil lines with her ghostly fingers.
"I used to love drawing," Helga mumbled as she admired the detail and shading Mabel had applied to Bo's plaited hair braids; "but father thought it a fad. He preferred me to embroider instead" she sniffed, "or play an instrument. He never really favoured my artwork."
"Why was that?" Mabel asked, absently, as she started to sketch out the group of children around her as hastily and accurately as she could.
Helga giggled, "because I loved drawing the ugly and unseemly. I drew rotting fruit and vegetables. I thought they had so much more texture than in their fresh form. I didn't like the rats, but there was something ghastly adorable about their sharp

front teeth and the way they gathered. It was like a small community."

Mabel snorted, "there's nothing wrong with displaying the darker sides of life. Some folks just don't like to see what's happening around them being depicted in art. The messages in a piece of artwork can sometimes say more than words ever could. It might have been that your artwork was so good Miss Schneider, it made your father question his own actions as Mayor."

Helga mused on this before shrugging, "Maybe so, but I don't think he was a fair man, Miss Weaver. If he were, he would have paid the piper and we would not have been sent on to live our afterlives in Limbo."

Mabel turned her attention to Helga, who was sat cross-legged on the ground, stroking her Annabelle doll's hair, and smiling at the picture of Bo.

"Where did the piper take you?" Mabel asked, hesitantly; hoping that by focusing on the paper and her craft, it would hide the sheer curiosity that she knew she was barely containing.

Helga sighed, "For many of us in Hamelin, he took us to a cave. We heard our parents racing close behind us, but the sound of the music from his pipe was too hypnotic, so we didn't stop. There was a large boulder which he pulled across the entryway. I remember wondering how slight a man could move so large a rock, then it was darkness and silence. I do not recall too much, it all happened so quickly. I just remember a deep voice whisper by my ear...".

"For you my dear, something a little more special, I think" Mabel looked up with a jolt. Helga and the other children were staring, wide eyed over her shoulder. Swallowing her own fear, to avoid it showing in front of the infants, Mabel turned her head.

Tom and his friends stood uncomfortably close and were leering over her shoulder, however they were changed. They no longer looked weak, scared, frail and timid. They stood close together, their eyes sunken in. Cruel smiles spread widely across their faces as they bent their heads toward the ground but tilted their gaze upward. Closer, and closer, they moved together; until it started to look like they were merging into one being. H-Helga," Mabel fumbled, as she jumped up, her sketchbook slipping to the floor, "you and the rest of the children stand back!" She ordered, as she positioned herself in front of the young girl like a barrier.

The figure of Tom and his friends shimmered together. The sound it made was otherworldly, like a swirl of force was shuddering around the room, with a faint hint of bird song accompanying the performance. All the while, Mabel and the children stepped further back. The red that had been shrouding Mabel's vision darkened into a deeper crimson.

The anger she felt was unparalleled. It wasn't so much the fact that she was about to die, imminently, that riled Mabel. It was the fact that it would happen in front of a host of children! Children, who had already seen and experienced more horror in their short lives, than *anyone* should be forced to experience.
'This is good' Mabel rationalised to herself. 'If I focus on the anger, it should diminish the fear. If

I'm going to go out tonight, it'll be swinging, not timid and scared.'

Bunching her fists, Mabel stood firm as the figure before her grew in height and morphed into the form that had been haunting her imagination since the mention of his name.

Pan's hooves took a few steadying steps forward as his thickly furred goat legs took on a more physical form. His lean yet muscular torso stemmed upward, shredding through the denim jacket. His long arms swung down lazily and hooked around so they rested on his hips, in a smug stance. Finally, the dark locks of the ghostly boys shimmered into a shock of wild and untidily curly hair, sculpting around an ageless face into a smart beard. Goatish ears, just about poked out of Pan's mane, while a pair of thick, strong, and vicious looking horns pierced through the bare skin of the demigod's forehead. The horns creaked like unoiled hinges on a door, as they looped around to form an impressive helm.

"Miss Mabel Weaver," Pan poke calmly with a sickeningly sweet smile, his voice was a deep baritone. While his persona oozed with polite control, Mabel sensed it was all a façade. There was a hint of demonic danger to the deity's mannerisms. It was as though all sense of goodness had been stripped away over the years and had been steadily corrupted as he'd ventured out on his path of vengeance. As Mabel stared up at the wide smile that played on his face, the tune: 'Never smile at a crocodile' suddenly came to her mind.

"Pan," Mabel forced herself to address the deity in a voice that sounded braver than she felt. The creature's smile broadened, showing two large rows of iridescent pearl like teeth. He took a step forward and leaned over her; his large frame nearly filling the room, his face inches from hers. "I've never encountered such a vision as you, my dear," he mused, stroking the side of her face. Mabel grimaced at his touch however, she glared defiantly back at him, undeterred. There was something about him that reminded her of the man from bar who had tried to spike the drinks that Angel had ordered for them, just a few short months ago.

"You have no right to touch me," she hissed, viciously.

Pan laughed. It was a loud, belly laugh, that filled the room with the smell of honey and sugar; from his breath.

"Oh, Miss Mabel. I have every right to touch whomever I wish. I am the God of fertility, after all; and you, my little lamb, are just too enticing to ignore!" He leaned closer to her so that his intoxicating breath filled her senses, the smell was too much. Mabel fought the urge to gag on how strong his scent was, there was no escaping it!

Refusing to allow the discomfort to overwhelm her, Mabel forced herself to focus on her anger with the deity. It wasn't hard. Whether it was the way he had casually claimed to have full right to her body, or the smug look of glee on his face at her discomfort; or even the audacity he had to behave in such a way in front of the children... Mabel couldn't quite place what impulse drove her to do it. As Pan's lips puckered and he leaned in closely; with all her weight behind it, Mabel drove the base of her palm upwards, smashing Pan's nose completely out of place.

The demigod reeled back in pain with a deafening roar. He snarled viciously and stamped his hooves as his nose corrected itself miraculously and, wiping away a golden moisture from the top of his lip, he growled menacingly.

"Feisty, for a mortal;" Pan sneered.
With a feral cry, he leapt forward and grabbed Mabel with such a ferocious display of speed and force that it took her completely off guard. He threw her onto the floor, violently, in retaliation. Desperately, Mabel tried to claw toward the space under the bed; however, Pan was far too quick for her. With an iron-like grip, he grabbed her ankle and swung her through the air so high, Mabel felt the top of her head brush the ceiling. Her stomach lurched to her throat as she was flung down heavily on to the bed. Mabel gasped as the wind was knocked completely out of her.

"MISS WEAVER!" Helga screamed, along with many of her friends.
Mabel desperately kicked out as Pan continued to pursue his game of leering menacingly over her, but she could barely catch her breath to

scream as he applied all his weight onto her shoulders, pinning her down. Mabel could feel and hear her shoulder bones creak and ache under the sheer pressure.

Pan laughed, mirthlessly. While the terror she felt was overwhelming, Mabel couldn't help but be transfixed by his stare. Pan's eyes had turned to a deep ebony black, void of anything other than pure devilish glee. As she turned to look away from Pan's sheer joy at her discomfort, her gaze rested on the furious expressions that were imprinted on the faces of Sven and Claus, who were rooted in the corner of the room. The boys had passed at such a young age; too soon to have born witness to what occurred to their cousin Helga, yet also, both indirect victims themselves, to Pan's vendetta.

Seeing their anger in the face of such brutality instilled Mabel's urge to keep fighting. Viciously, she kicked out at Pan's groin, relishing at the sight of him wincing in pain as her feet collided with the more sensitive area between his goat shanks. As she fought with all her might, Mabel couldn't help but envision what Pan could have done to Helga and potentially to so many others in the room around her. The envisioned imagery only served to fuel her resentment; and the anger and hatred she felt toward the creature grew tenfold. It burned inside her like a raging inferno; and yet, even with the adrenaline coursing through her, Mabel could still feel the fight within her start to deplete, as the physical exertions Pan displayed, greatly outmatched her own.

Chapter 21. A Race for Life

Pan's head leered closer to Mabel's with a
Cheshire-cat grin spread widely across his face.
Mabel could feel his hot breath blowing out of his
mouth over her skin and she recoiled at it.
"Please, Pan! Not in front of the children!" She
heard herself feebly whisper, as a final desperate
plea.
"MISS WEAVER, NO!" Helga's cry echoed
around Mabel's head as with a flurry, Pan leapt
up with a triumphant cry and, grabbing Mabel's
leg, flung her across the room.

Mabel landed heavily, but it was not on a plush
carpet. Standing up shakily, she was surprised to
discover that she was stood on a dusty path. She
shivered as the cool moonlit air softly caressed
her skin. She was outdoors, yet none of the
environment she was in, was recognisable! One
thing was certain however, Pan had disappeared.
The only sound Mabel could hear was that of her

heart pounding in her head, as she hastily she tried to steady her breathing, all the while straining her ears for the slightest sound. Where on earth had Pan taken her?

"How's this for privacy?" Pan's voice echoed all around her, menacingly close and distant all at once.

Mabel jumped up and looked around; "where are you? Coward!" She could hear the ill-hidden fear in her voice and hated herself for being so weak.

"That would spoil the fun, don't you think?" Pan's voice cackled, wickedly. "I've always enjoyed spectating a good hunt. Maybe it's time I partook in one, myself."

Mabel was relieved to feel a sense of frustration touch her inner core, "are you a cat, Pan? Toying with your game, before finishing it off? I'm not biting. You either address me now or return us both to the hotel room. My friends will find you regardless! There's nothing you can do to me that they won't do to you, tenfold!"

Pan laughed, heartily; "this one has spirit!" He cooed, his voice rippled on the leaves and through the trees; "however, I have a little bargain for you."

"MISS WEAVER!" The gut-wrenching scream of a young girl shattered the serenity of the woodland.

Mabel's stomach somersaulted, "HELGA?!" She called out.

Pan's laughter was manic, "Here's a deal for you *Miss Weaver*, come find the young Mayor's daughter; and I will return you both to the waking world."

Mabel looked around her. There was nothing to indicate in what direction Helga or Pan were based, "I'll need some clues as to where you are!" She called out into the glade.

Pan's chuckle sounded almost like a sinister growl, "not a problem. I will take you to her, myself – you will just have to outrun me, Weaver!"

Mabel barely had time to register his words when the thunderous sound of hooves gathered to her left. Spinning in the opposite direction, instinctively; Mabel burst into a fast sprint. As she gained ground away from the galloping hooves, she felt her attire change around her. Looking down, she gasped as her pyjama trousers and vest changed into a chiffon gown, tied with a rope around her waist. As she continued to race forwards, she felt the dirt, stones, and twigs stab at her feet, and swiftly realised she was now running bare foot through the woods. Pan's laughter sounded to her right, and hastily, Mabel swirled immediately to her left, darting off the path and between the trees, her mind a blur of sheer panic.

"MISS WEAVER! HEAD TO THE RIVER!" Helga's voice rang out in the distance, but Mabel couldn't see a river! She could barely see a thing before her. The world Pan had taken her to was indescribably dark. Even the moonlight struggled to break through the thick canopy of tree branches in full bloom. Bracken and brambles lashed out at her ankles and legs, snatching, and tearing at the chiffon robe.

Mabel's chest was burning from the exertion, and she could feel herself tiring. Just as she thought she could go on no more, the rumbling of hooves gathered speed behind her and Mabel's adrenaline coursed through her blood, pumping as much energy into her legs. Pan's demonic cry rang out almost directly to her left and Mabel cried out in terror as she dodged a vicious swipe from a muscular arm, as it reached out from behind a tree.

"HELGA!" Mabel cried out desperately, "I SEE NO RIVER!" She called, as she burst out into an open expanse, and looked around her.
There was a small, abandoned church that had seen better days, standing dilapidated and pitiful ahead of her to the right. Gathering her composure and gulping greedily at the citrusy air around her, she tried to think straight. Pan was a deity from an ancient religion, she reasoned, why would there be a church here? As she crept cautiously toward it, the bright light of something shining on the ground to her left, caused her to stop in her tracks. Hardly daring to believe her eyes, she hurried toward it and despite everything, she grinned. It was a small trickle of water, reflecting the weak moonlight, leading back into the forest to the left, away from the church.

Mabel barely had time to call out to Helga when heavy panting and the pawing of hooves, scraping at the ground sounded, behind her. Spinning around, Mabel gulped, as she took in the fiery glare of Pan; his body slick with sweat, glistening in the beams of moonlight. He looked tired, but almost victorious, as he eyed her up and down. "Such a pretty gown, don't you think?" He panted heavily, "I thought it rather befitting of such a nymph, as you."

He growled, as he crouched down and leapt with an impressive display of agility, toward her. Mabel screamed and once again put on a burst of speed and splashed through the weak trail of water, barely having time to appreciate the coolness of the fluid, easing the sores gained from the earlier pursuit.

Desperately, Mabel hoped that the source of water, would lead her to a river. The hooves splashed behind her as the small babbling brook started to widen to a stream. Forcing herself to ignore her burning chest and limbs, Mabel plunged further on. It's just a monstrous sprint to the finish line now, she reasoned, in her

exhausted mind; as the water started to gain in speed, tumbling down a few small rapids.
The ground she ran on had started to change in texture too. Her bare feet no longer padded through sharp, unfriendly stones and stabbing thorns, but slapped against the smooth and slippery surface of a riverbank. The hooves continued to thunder behind her as finally, in the distance, Mabel spied the children.

They were all strung up, like marionette dolls around yet another church-like monument made of red stone. The children must have seen her too as they all started to cry out her name, rallying her forward, encouraging her. Helga's voice screamed her name the loudest as Mabel raced forward, blindly. Tears started to cascade down her face, as she extended her arms before her; anticipating a free-fall into the rushing river below her, but then the ground shifted again. Suddenly, Mabel found herself tumbling down a sharp decline! Over and over, she fell. Rocks, stones, bracken, and twigs lacerated her arms and legs until finally, she landed heavily in a hole in the ground.

Barely allowing herself time to register the pain in her limbs, Mabel stood up and desperately jumped up, clinging onto the lip of the hole, but it was no use. With a victorious cry, Pan leapt deftly over the gap in the ground, and landed heavily on her fingers; the rim of his hooves treading down forcefully on her nails, causing her to cry out in pain.

"So close, and yet, so far!" He jeered, as with a flurry, he jumped into the hole, pinning Mabel down.

With all the power in her lungs, Mabel screamed out, desperately. She scratched. She bit. She flailed her arms and fought with every ounce of her being. Pan growled as each attempt to paw at her gown was swatted away.

In sheer desperation she called out "KRIS! ERIC! THET! ASMODEUS! GET THE CHILDREN!" She had no belief that the men in her life would or could hear her, but she clung to a desperate hope that wherever they were; they would make it to the children in time to rescue them. Even if it was too late for her.

The struggle seemed to go on for an eternity, until out of the darkness a voice filled Mabel's head.

"ENOUGH, PAN!" The bark of Helga Schneider filled the moonlit air, her voice elevated in a way that drowned out the river's torrent. Pan stopped his onslaught immediately and glared murderously at Mabel, before leaping up, out of the earth. Before, Mabel could fathom what was happening, a familiar arm, decorated in inkwork reached over the edge, and she looked up into Kristoph's wide and concerned eyes. She could barely restrain her cry of relief as she weakly raised her arms. Slowly, Kristoph, with the aid of Eric, pulled her out of the ground and sat with her. Together, the three of them watched on in a murderous rage as Helga's ghostly form shuddered and took on a dark energy. Mabel dared to turn her head away from Kristoph's chest and gasped as the reddened hue, she'd been surveying the world in, started to turn ochre.

As she watched Helga, she was reminded of all the haunted children in the horror films she'd seen in her last life. The lush, blonde hair that shimmered with a beautiful auror, suddenly looked wretched and messy. The blonde an ashen grey. Her innocent eyes that had always betrayed a sense of knowing, now glowered, venomously.

"You've gone too far Pan," Helga hissed viciously at the fawn, who was being restrained by Thet.

"No where near as far as I could have gone," he cackled wickedly, "*you* would know!" For the first time, Pan addressed the children who had been cut free of their bonds by Asmodeus and Azrael. The demigod sneered at each of the young faces; "I see so many of my flock here, have I not treated you as well as I should have? Maybe not. But, to grow one's farm; one must regularly add to the herd."

"We were *never* yours to take!" Snapped a tall girl from the back of the crowd. Mabel recognised her instantly as the one who had taken them to Hamelin in the last memory.

Pan tilted his head, "Penelope Schmidt!" He tried to take a step toward her, yet Thet wrenched him back.

Penelope's eyes were a piercing blue and glowered at Pan with loathing, instead of adoration.

"I trusted you," she hissed. "You promised to rid the town of the rats! You promised this and your future assurance that no more harm would befall our people!"

Mabel was entranced! The children were gathering around Pan, seeing him struggle uncomfortably against Thet's strong hold. Their eyes no longer blackened out with the charm he'd cast over them. Even the demigod, himself, betrayed signs of discomfort as the children closed in on him.

"Children, settle down!" Pan grumbled, "you will force my hand otherwise," he smirked wickedly, yet the children continued their encroachment.

"Try it," Penelope snapped, "we see you for who you really are Pan" she spat his name out; "the unwanted love child who was never loved himself!" She laughed, but it was a hollow and cruel sound.

Pan bared his teeth at her, shaking violently against Thet's relentless grip.

"Oh, very dear, Pan." Asmodeus's voice was thick with venom, as he drew closer to the fawn, "it seems you're in a spot of bother."

Mabel turned to Eric, a sudden thought breaking through her fatigued mind. "Eric, the ghost boys weren't Tom and his friends, they were all Pan! He was there all along. The children, they're..."

"No longer afraid of him," Thet spoke calmly next to Pan's ear, "as such Pan; your powers are superfluous against them," The reaper glowered, with a malicious glee.

Pan roared maniacally. None of the night had gone quite the way he had anticipated; "and who do you think *you* are Charon? You have no right to speak to a God, like me! Let alone restrain him in such a manner!"

Asmodeus snickered, "*demi*-god, Pan – even your own astral figures preferred to watch you loiter on earth, rather than on their great space above Mt. Olympus!"

"Demon!" Pan spat, "do not think I haven't seen you loitering around here, with my nymphs!"

"*Your* nymphs?" Azrael scoffed, "dear me! My understanding was that they were created to be free creatures and as such under no one's possessive rule. Much like the children here, that you have ruthlessly claimed as your own through the ages."

The angel looked thunderous in his polite rage. Pan laughed, "and where were the angels, when I took them, hm?" He grinned wildly, "where were the angels and the higher powers when the belief in my ways and the ways of my kin fell by the wayside?"

Azrael frowned, "your religion did not have angels, Pan; so, none of us came to your aid. None of your kin came to your aid because they were reliant on belief to survive. As the belief in your ancient lives has all but depleted, you have no one left to answer to, from your *own* heritage."

Pan's eyes flared ferociously, "then I will continue to take every last, lonely, forgotten, abandoned child until the last believer goes! It is through their belief in me that I live on! You see before you, my flock? They all know of me and believe in me! Through them, I live!"

Thet tightened his grip around Pan's arms with a ferocious strength, causing the fawn to wince in pain. Asmodeus, struck Pan across the face and with a dangerous calmness, placed his hand around the demigod's throat, tightening his grip. The children all smiled broadly with a hunger Mabel could only sympathise with. They wanted to see Pan hurt in ways no human could even begin to imagine.

The demon cooed close to Pan's face, "look around you, goat! All these eyes see you as the rat that you truly are! You are no more a righteous being than I am. These children will move on to their rightful host and will find peace, their belief in humanity restored by Mab. Their belief in all things good, restored by a range of heavenly hosts more in keeping with a faith you have no right to!"

Pan struggled against Asmodeus's grip on his throat, and Mabel was pleased to see that the demon was applying just as much force to prevent the demi-god from moving freely, as Pan had applied to her.

"Now, now, Asmodeus;" Azrael soothed, "I'm sure Thet can handle Pan from here."

"*We* could teach him a lesson!" Helga sulked,

her bottom lip pouting. It would have been comical were it not nightmarish for Mabel to consider how an army of ghostly children could undermine and break down an other-worldly being.

Thet smiled kindly at Helga, "I quite agree, Miss Schneider. He will be taught a lesson, but it will not be by yourselves. You beautiful children have done more than enough."

His gaze hardened as he turned his attention toward Pan, "I, however, will see to Pan from here."

Pan scoffed, "you, Charon? What could you possibly..." Thet's eyes turned black as Thet rested his right hand against Pan's temple. In an instant, Pan's eyes widened in fear and horror. His once terrifyingly bold cry became one of muted horror as Thet moved his hand over Pan's mouth; "incidentally Pan, my name, is Thet!" He snapped, as in the blink of an eye, the two vanished.

Chapter 22. No Mere Mortal

The world fell quiet as the assembled figures left behind; looked around, lost.

"Righto," Azrael stepped forward, breaking the uncomfortable silence. "I believe we've had enough of Pan's little playroom; don't you think?"

With a wave of his hand, the scenery around them all changed as they all staggered and slumped to the ground in Eric's hotel room. Mabel glanced down and was relieved to see she was back in her normal attire; even if her arms were still scratched and torn, covered in bleeding welts.

"Now then," Azrael continued, serenely. "I have some work to do with you all, don't I?" He beamed at the children who all looked up at him, uncertainly.

"Our story needs to be told," Helga frowned. "Without the world knowing what happened to us, how can we move on?"

"Leave that to us, Helga," Mabel spoke softly, her voice thick with fatigue. "We know what happened to you, all of you."

She addressed the rest of the children; "we will retell your story as best as we can, with Asmodeus and Mr. Grim's help of course."

"Ahem!" Azrael glanced over to her and raised his eyebrows in anticipation.

"...and Azrael's?" Mabel added, uncertainly.

"Of course!" Azrael nodded, excitedly. "It is an angel's job to spread the word, after all. However, we might have to reinvent the story ever so slightly, for it to be more palatable for modern-day ears."

"A-and you will continue with the portrait, Miss Weaver?" Helga held her doll closely to her breast.

"Of course," Mabel assured her; "I will perfect the portrait."

"You won't forget me? Or us?" Helga asked, her eyes wide. Mabel was surprised to spy a trace of nervousness and fear dance across Helga's features.

Eric stepped forward and crouched down next to the young girl's spirit, "Miss Schneider, there is no need to be afraid. Azrael will take good care of you, and I *assure* you that I will not let up on Mab until she has perfected that portrait. Nor will any of us forget you, or what you have all been through. If anyone deserves peace, it's all of you."

"Couldn't have put it better myself," Azrael beamed; "right, um, shall we?"

With another fanciful wave of his arm, Azrael opened the door to the hotel room. What lay beyond however, was not the usual hallway, but a bright, blinding, and dazzling light. One by one, each of the children thanked Mabel, Kristoph, Eric, and Asmodeus as they cautiously approached the doorway and passed through. Finally, only Helga remained, still hesitant.

"It's okay, Helga" Mabel assured her, "you'll be safe and secure there, in a better place."

Helga turned to Mabel and slowly approached her, before looking up at Asmodeus, imploringly. "You restored the vision for my friends, could I ask if you could do one final thing?"

The demon knelt down, "anything, little one"

Asmodeus acknowledged, kindly.

Helga whispered into his ear and while he did furrow his brow in confusion, he nodded, and fished into his robes and drew out a small pouch. He dipped his hand into it pulled out a small pinch of dust from inside and blew it over Helga, who giggled.

"It tickles," she grinned, as she held out her arms which slowly took on a more solid form, along with the rest of her figure.

"Quickly now," Asmodeus warned, "life essence doesn't last long!"

Helga nodded and before Mabel could even question what had just transpired, Helga's arms had wrapped tightly around her shoulders as in a warm embrace.

"Thank you, Miss Weaver, for being so fearless against Pan. Without your energy, we wouldn't have been able to stand up to him the way we did. You've saved us all," She smiled with genuine sincerity as she pulled back, the solidity of her body fading away. As she slowly approached Azrael, Helga glanced back over her shoulder with one final look, before stepping through the doorway and out of sight. Azrael closed the door fast behind her and turned to the rest of the group, his expression changing to a more businesslike front.

"I will be back once I have opened the gate to all those children. I am determined to get to the bottom of who sent them to Limbo in the first place, as it was certainly not me! Something about all of this is not adding up and I need to figure it out, I will keep you updated of my findings." He turned to walk away; however, Asmodeus pulled him back.

"Just... be careful," Asmodeus shrugged, nonchalantly. "It's one thing for a demon to ask questions in Hell, freedom of speech is welcome, after all. However, we all know how well investigations and queries up top tend to work out... angel," he smirked, casually.

Azrael raised a brow and nodded, "duly noted... demon;" he smiled back and disappeared.

No sooner had he gone, Eric yawned, loudly and flopped back onto the bed, exhausted; "I dunno about you, but I think that all went rather well." Mabel's jaw dropped in disbelief at the comment, "speak for yourself!" She snapped and hopped off the bed in anger.

"Hey! Mab! I didn't mean..." Eric blustered, mortified, as she stormed out of the room.

Kristoph stood up slowly, "It's alright," he smiled tiredly at his friend, "I'll sort it."

Hurriedly pausing the hotel door before it slammed shut, Kristoph disappeared after her, shutting the door softly behind him.

Eric groaned and ran his hands over his tired face. "Well, I feel marvellous now. That nephew! The idjiot. I must call my sister, Missy, and tell her where he is;" Eric picked up his phone, but Asmodeus plucked it out of his hands.

"No you won't," Asmodeus chuckled. "You are in the middle of Germany, how on earth could you *possibly* know where Tom and his friends are? No, stable boy, you are going to get some rest while *I* pay a visit to your nephew and his friends and scare them into returning home, capiche?"

Eric was too tired to argue, "fine – whatever. So long as he gets back safe, I'm happy."

"He will," Asmodeus assured him, "as for those

two..." he turned to where Mabel and Kristoph had disappeared a moment ago.

Eric chuckled sleepily, "yeah, I wouldn't advise that you see them just yet. The whole 'we just survived a thing' energy might be all over them."

"Huh," Asmodeus looked toward the doorway, "well, I know when I'm not wanted."

"Do you though?" Eric asked through a yawn, "I mean, I'm trying to sleep and you're still here, talking."

Asmodeus rolled his eyes and skulked out of the room, following Kristoph's scent through the hallways down to the ground floor where he slipped through the hotel door which led to where Kristoph was desperately trying to soothe Mabel; who was sobbing, uncontrollably.

"What in the world?" He asked but Kristoph shook his head.

"I don't know," he murmured helplessly. "We got to the room, I asked her to talk to me and she just broke down!"

Kristoph rubbed his hand over Mabel's shoulder, the simple show of affection however caused Mabel to recoil.

"I'm sorry!" Kristoph held his hands up, panicked.

Mabel shook her head, and noisily swallowed back a suppressed sob, "no, *I'm* sorry." Wracked with shame, Mabel turned her head away from Kristoph; "it's just that..." Wincing from the pain caused by the movement, she pulled up the short sleeves of her shirt to reveal two impressive, dark purple handprints that Pan had brutally pressed into her skin when he's had her pinned to the bed. Gingerly, Mabel stroked down her torn, scratched, and scarred arms; closing her eyes in pain as she held up her blackened nails, still bloody from where Pan's hooves had landed on them. Finally, she carefully rolled up her trouser legs to reveal the savage gashes that had swollen angrily down her shins. The battle scars off Pan's assault.

Asmodeus slowly approached her, sat down on the spare twin bed and issued a low whistle. "Pan did a right ol' number on you, didn't he?" While Asmodeus had thankfully diminished his more demonic features to appear as a more humanistic being, his features were still heavily pronounced. Mabel couldn't tell if the frown that left deep furrows across his brow were part of his standard look, or a disapproving response to the sores across her body.

Asmodeus nodded his head indicatively toward Mabel's lap, "he didn't, y'know?"
Mabel hastily shook her head in response, "no. You all got there just in time and Helga's cry distracted him; but As... I have never felt so helpless! He made me race him!" Mabel wiped away a fresh wave of tears that had started to course a trail down her cheeks.
"I managed to outrun him but then I fell into that hole. He then pinned me down and... to think of what he did to those children... to Helga! I mean I broke his nose at one point, before he even took us to that world... but even then!"
Asmodeus's eyes widened in shock, "sorry, you *outran* Pan and broke his nose? How?"
Mabel wiped her eyes and patted the base of her palm, "I just slammed my palm upward into his face. I've never had to do it before, but it's done in films all the time. I just figured; how hard can it

be? I have never felt so angry." The memory of Pan's vile justifications drenched Mabel in a fresh wave of grief.

"Kris, he made out that he had every right to my body, and I felt so utterly disgusted and filled with rage that I..." she mimicked the punch. "I knew it was broken because I heard the crunch. He staggered back and there was this golden liquid, which I guess is demigod blood? As for outrunning him, I don't know what came over me, I think it must have been pure terror, or adrenaline."

Asmodeus gaped in utter disbelief at her reflection, "but... how?!" he gasped, incredulously.

"She just said, mate!" Kristoph exclaimed, tiredly; he could feel his body shaking with suppressed hatred and intense guilt.

"I know what she *said*," Asmodeus sighed, "I'm just struggling to comprehend it. Guys, no mortal should *ever* be able to make a deity of *any* kind bleed! Let alone be able to match pace with them!"

"That's because Mab is no mere mortal," Thet

spoke softly from the corner of the room, making them jump.

"Apologies," Thet smiled, "I returned to Eric's room, and saw he was out cold, so I followed the scent of honey and syrup to this room; it's amazing really. Until Kris mentioned it earlier this evening, I'd not noticed the smell before. Asmodeus, you smell so sweet."

In a few steps, Thet had crossed the room and perched on the edge of the bed next to Asmodeus and gently rested a comforting hand on Mabel's knee.

"Pan's been... dealt with," he said, awkwardly. "Mab, I saw what he did to you in his memories. Are you alright?" He brushed the top of her head and taking her hands in his, he gently stroked his thumbs over her broken and bloodied nails. With meticulous care, Thet started to focus on soothing the open wounds on her arms and legs.

"I'm alright Thet," Mabel reassured him. "What do you mean I'm no mere mortal?"

"Precisely that," Thet said. "You and Kris are Adam and Eve reincarnated. As such, the power of the almighty runs through both of you. If you come under the attack of any being of immense power, you could certainly cause some damage; admittedly it wouldn't be much in the grand scheme of things, but it would certainly be more harmful than anything dealt by an average human," he explained calmly.

"So, why couldn't I fight off Charles Valentine?" Kristoph asked, confused.
Asmodeus rubbed the back of his neck, uncomfortably; "yeah, I had a feeling you were going to ask that."
The Demon sighed, "truth is Kris, I saw it the instant I entered your mind. You'd given up with your life and had no fight left."
Kristoph lowered his head, as shame swept over him.
"That being said," Asmodeus glanced over at Mabel who had started to drift off on Kristoph's shoulder, now that the pain from her wounds had all but gone, courtesy of Thet. "I can't begin to imagine what it could be, but something's given you a new lease of life, recently."

Kristoph offered the demon a crooked smile as he delicately kissed the top of Mabel's brow.

"I think..." Thet breathed out shakily, as Mabel lifted her head and gazed softly into Kristoph's eyes; "that we had best leave you both to get some rest. Asmodeus, shall we?"

The two beings stood up and turned away.

"Wait!" Kristoph turned to Asmodeus, "don't I need to summon you back?"

Asmodeus chuckled, not unkindly; "kiddo – I can come and go as I please. I'll be back with you by morning. I have a stable's boy's nephew to chase home."

The Lord of Lust winked knowingly and disappearing with Thet, leaving Mabel and Kristoph alone.

In the silence of their own company, a surreal feeling of uncertainty descended on them both.

"Some night, huh?" Kristoph smirked, awkwardly.

Mabel smiled, "Yeah, some night."

She stood up and staggered, her legs ached so much from all of running in Pan's world.

"Thet has a point though, all I can smell is honey

and syrup!" Mabel shuddered as she sniffed at
her arms; "I'll never be able to touch the stuff
again!" She groaned loudly, as she sat down on
her own bed.

Kristopher grimaced and looked at her,
apologetically.

"I suppose I should keep my distance then," he
sighed, dramatically.

"Why?" Mabel asked, her sleepy gaze lifting to
look at him.

There was something about the way his soft voice
danced around every word with his thick Swedish
accent that offered a distinct melody and betrayed
any emotion the man was feeling at any given
moment.

Kristoph laughed, "because I assume that's how I
smell on a daily basis, with Asmo' possessing
me."

"Huh," Mabel's voice mused, "funny, I never
noticed it with you."

"Really?" Kristoph frowned, "it's quite intense."

Mabel frowned and moved back to where she'd
been resting against him before. Without
warning, she leaned over and breathed in deeply

by the crook of Kristoph's neck. She smiled and hummed contentedly as she smelt his cologne, the faint perfume from the conditioner he'd used earlier that night, and a hint of mint from his breath. The sudden closeness and feel of her breath so close to him made Kristoph close his eyes and involuntarily sigh loudly. Shocking himself with the sound, he opened his eyes wide with embarrassment. Mabel chuckled in turn, close his ear. The sound was like music to his ears! Barely containing the hope that she might feel the same way, Kristoph turned to face her, and his nose brushed softly against hers, making her jump.

"Sorry," he mumbled sheepishly.

"It's alright," Mabel whispered softly, her mind whirling.

Cautiously, she leaned closer to him. As Kristoph rested his hand against her arm however, the sound of Pan's maniacal laugh filled her mind in a cruel flashback. Mabel froze instinctively and sucked in a sharp intake of air.

Kristoph dropped his arm immediately and slowly he took a step back.

"I- I'm sorry;" he faltered, "I didn't mean to scare..."

"No," Mabel shook her head, "you didn't scare me. I've just had an intense night."

Kristoph nodded, "I agree. Maybe we shouldn't pursue anything too risqué tonight?"

Reluctantly, he stood up and helped Mabel up and gestured toward her bed.

Mabel followed his hand with her eyes and stared at the crisp white sheets and the soft plump pillow and sighed.

Feeling a surreal surge of confidence return to her as she looked up into the soft and caring features of the man, who had offered her nothing but care and support since their first true introduction to each other; Mabel smiled.

His deep ocean blue eyes looked down at her with an enveloping calmness and only seemed to entice her to be nearer to him.

"Perhaps, a goodnight kiss, wouldn't harm?" She said, somewhat breathlessly

Kristoph didn't need to hear any further hints, as a rush of adrenaline surged through him. In one fluid movement he'd gathered Mabel into his arms and sighed contentedly as he felt her lips rest against his. The thrill that coursed through him made him melt into her own embrace, as he felt her fingers run hungrily through his hair. Mabel felt her heart might burst with joy and felt a pang of regret as she felt him pull back from her. In turn, Kristoph didn't open his eyes, as the ghost of Mabel's kiss lingered on his lips.

It was her laughter that forced him to slowly open his eyes and look at her. His mouth fell open in shock and he staggered back and looked around in amazement.

"You see it too?" Mabel laughed; her voice full of joy.

Kristoph could barely speak. Ever since his possession with Asmodeus he had lived in a haze of amber and ochre. As he gazed into Mabel's face however, and saw her expressions of joy, his world suddenly glowed emerald, green.

Chapter 23. Pardoning a Sinner

The rest of the European leg of the tour went by drama free. Asmodeus had made it his mission to become a regular among the band's entourage. To avoid raising suspicion, he had taken on a multitude of guises: a photographer one day, an interviewer another, and at one point a long-lost cousin of Eric's. Mabel couldn't help but feel his decision to loiter close to them, stemmed from either a secret pact of protection made between the demon and Thet; or a surreal fondness he had developed by being incorporated into their group. It hadn't escaped her attention that Asmodeus had somewhat softened in his demeanour toward her and wasn't as bothersome for Kristoph, like he used to be.

Whatever Asmodeus's reasons, one thing was certain; aside from their demonic friend staying close by, all other communication with Thet and Limbo seemed to have fallen quiet. Not that any of them would admit it out loud; but Eric, Mabel, and Kristoph were all quietly relieved. After the ordeal with Pan, it was a silent agreement between the three of them, that they had earned a reprieve from moving souls on from Limbo, for the time being at least.

Besides, Kristoph and three of his fellow band members had found themselves taking on the somewhat cumbersome act, of being Pete Campbell's counsellors. The Dark Omen's drummer, Pete Campbell, had regularly stressed that a cruise to the States would be far more relaxing than an intensive flight. Much to his chagrin however, his suggestions had fallen on deaf ears. As the US stretch of the tour loomed closer, the thought of getting on to an airplane and flying, had filled him with no end of dread.

Even Asmodeus had groaned loudly, while in the guise of one of Kristoph's personal guitar technicians. Pete had started to act out. One of his more regular tactics if his complaints fell on deaf ears was to start throwing drumsticks at each of the band members, purely for the satisfaction of having aggravated them as recompense for their making him suffer in silence.

As Kristoph and Eric focused on carefully packing away their gear after the final European show, in preparation for their trip to the States in just a few short hours; Pete had started to wield his drumsticks like a baton. He smartly tapped Jésús and Adrian over the head in a steady four-beat rhythm, while singing:

"5 band members sat on a plane in the air, 5 band members sat on a plane. One passenger freaks and opens the door... 4 band members sat on a plane in the air..."

"Y'know, I have a host of kin, *down south*, who might be able to sway Mr. Campbell's mind. Just say the word!" Asmodeus slyly suggested to Kristoph and Eric as he shook his head at the small scuffle that had ensued from one too many taps on the head by a drumstick.

"Why are you so eager to help Pete out?" Eric asked as Adrian desperately tried to grab one of the drumsticks out of Pete's hands, only to have it jab him sharply in the ribs.

Asmodeus shrugged, "who said anything about

helping the guy? I've been touring with you guys for how long now? If I hear *one more* whimper about the dangers of flying, I might be forced to take over Kris and open the emergency exit, mid-flight."

Kris and Eric gaped at him open-mouthed, "why on *earth* would you do that?" Kris hissed, angrily. "Peace in our time? Less drumstick related injuries? Offering Pete, the chance to actually *have* something to complain about as he spirals down to earth..." Asmodeus smiled wistfully at the thought.

Finally, the day of the flight to Orlando, Florida arrived. Eric and Adrian had been forced to drag a heavily sedated Pete, through to customs, while Mabel and Kristoph headed the remainder of their band's entourage into the duty-free lounge. Since their moment of closeness in Germany, the two were inseparable and had been eagerly anticipating the chance to skirt around the airport's delights and seemingly conduct themselves as a new couple.

There was something about the way cosmetic displays looked in the duty-free stores that made Mabel want to part with her hard-earned money quicker than if she were held at gun point. Dousing themselves in a range of perfumes and colognes, like misbehaving school children, they dipped and dived between the other early morning travellers and snuck out of view of their colleagues, stealing kisses behind the corners of stores. It was the most enjoyment either of them had experienced in any lifetime they could recall. Finally, they slipped into a newsagent and bought a large bag of sweets and puzzle books to work through while on the flight and flopped down in the private lounge's plush armchairs. Quietly, they started to work through a series of codeword puzzles, while keeping an eye on the boarding monitor.

As the rest of the band members finally joined them, the nearest café finally noted the potential for custom outside of just two loved up travellers and decided to switch on their television to entice the group to spend a few notes on an overpriced bagel.

Mabel and Kristoph's heads were bent so low over the codeword puzzle book that they didn't notice Adrian's features freeze in terror as he glanced up at the café's television set. It was Eric who drew their attention however.

"Ade? What's occurring?" Eric frowned.

"Um," Adrian's voice cracked, nervously. Hesitantly, he pointed toward the monitor and cautiously glanced at Kristoph, "um... Kris?" He grimaced.

Sighing and leaning back in his chair, Kristoph cast his eyes over the main headlines which were being detailed in muted silence on the screen. The brief snippet of a mug shot flashed up and Mabel watched in shock as the colour drained from his face completely.

Hurriedly, Kristoph raced toward the café counter, "can you turn that up, please?" He asked in a panicked voice.

Mabel could only observe the scene with mounting concern. Slowly, she rose to join him, but with a sudden cry of anger, Kristoph stormed off towards the toilets.

"They can't be serious?" He shouted to himself,

as his retreating back disappeared.

"Kris?" Mabel called after him.

"Okay, what just happened?" She asked the rest of the band.

Adrian groaned and stood up; "Valentine's been pardoned, according to that headline," he groaned, with exasperation. "I've got to go talk to him. Eric – are you okay to bring Mabel up to speed?"

Eric whistled slowly, as Adrian hurried after his lead guitarist.

Mabel looked at Eric, in horror "Valentine? The crazed satanic follower, Valentine? The guy who branded Kris? He's been pardoned?" Her voice wavered, "they can't do that!... Can they?"

Eric and Jésus shook their heads, they both looked just as stunned at the news.

"This has to be a joke!" Jésus mithered and leaned forward. Slowly, he shook his head in disbelief.

Eric shook his head and snorted, "yeah, right. Because news reporters regularly like to troll their audience;" he said sarcastically.

"Hush," Mabel waved at them both, to quieten

down "they're talking about it more now!"
Hurriedly, the three of them dashed to the café
bar, leaving Pete slumped in a deep stupor on his
own, dribbling on to his chest.

The American anchor man looked haggard as he
shared the details behind Valentine's pardoning:
"News just in: Charles Valentine, of Tampa Bay,
Florida; is due to be pardoned of the part he
played in the assault of Kristoph Grayson, lead
guitarist of the heavy metal band Dark Omens.
Valentine, was charged for viciously assaulting
Grayson with a branding iron in a meet & greet
with fans on the 31st of October 2021. His
pardon comes after new evidence has come
through to suggest Valentine acted compulsively
in a bid to *help* the guitarist."
The reporter raised a judgmental eyebrow to the
camera before saying, "Sandy Moore, our Florida
correspondent, has more... so, Sandy, what's the
latest on this?"

The stern face of Sandy Moore stared blankly at
the camera as the feed delay played its role to
perfection. "Thank you, Gerry. Yes, Judge

Harold Dickson from the County court of Orlando, ruled earlier today that while Valentine's actions were misguided, they were not done with malicious intent. Grayson is due to perform with the Dark Omens band in their US tour, which is scheduled to start this week. It's unknown whether he has been informed of this revelation, however, we will endeavour to reach out to representatives of the band to secure his thoughts on this matter."

Eric breathed out another long, low whistle and pinched the bridge of his nose, "new evidence?" He looked hard at Mabel.

Jésus shook his head, "Valentine is an amenaza!" In response to Eric's confused expression, he tutted; "he is a menace! Because of him, we had to tighten our security tenfold, readdress our meet and greets; we have become so far removed from our fanbase because of that estúpido! Kris has *finally* started to behave more *human* in the last few weeks. This is enough to tip him right back to the deprimido husk he was before!" Eric shook his head, "deprimido? Kris is no longer depressed, I agree; but I think that is more

so down to a certain someone here," he nodded
to Mabel, who flushed. "I have to say though, it
seems like this has all fallen into place a little too
timely to be classed as a coincidence."

Jésús shook his head, "so, you blame an act of
God then, huh? Tch!" He ruffled his silky brown
locks, looking around him. "I'm going to help
Adrian find Kris, we need to think up an
estrategia! Pete? Will you come?" He shouted at
the drummer, who simply grunted and issued a
loud snore indicating his indifference to the
ensuing drama.

"pfft!" Jésús scoffed in response and stormed
after his friends, uttering obscenities in Spanish.

Eric and Mabel slowly returned to the lounge,
feeling numb. As they flopped heavily down in
the leather chairs, Eric leaned closer to Mabel
and under his breath uttered again, "new
evidence. Right before we land in the States, near
that madman's hometown. Mab, would it be
worth a chat with our *friends*?"

Mabel chewed at the inside of her cheek, before
snapping her fingers loudly in front of Pete who
didn't flinch. Mabel smirked, one perk of Pete

being unconscious on strong sedatives, there'd be no way he'd believe anything overheard about demons, angels and reapers.

"Thet and Asmodeus *could* help," Mabel whispered back to Eric. "I don't doubt Asmodeus will already know all about it by now, from his connection with Kris's thoughts. As for Thet though, I've not seen or heard from him since that night at the Muriel. Y'know, I've started to wonder if he's avoiding me." She sighed, glumly.

"Why's that?" Eric asked.

Mabel blushed; how could she explain her reasoning without it sounding like she was bragging?

"Well... I can't be sure, but I *think* Thet might have tried to display some form of affection toward me, while we were in Germany;" she grimaced as she said it out loud and lowered her head, not wanting to see Eric's judgemental expression. "You see, the thing is... that same night, Kris and I... well, we um..."

"Go on," Eric leaned forward, with a wide grin on his face.

Mabel couldn't help herself as she smiled fondly

at the memory, "we kissed," she mumbled.

"HA!" Eric clapped his hands, triumphantly. "I knew it! I *knew* summat happened that night! The whole tension between you both was off the charts." His laughter soon eased as Eric considered Mabel's suspicions.

"As for Thet, I don't think you're far off the mark. I would go so far as to say the reaper's been hit by Cupid... Blimey, you don't suppose there's an actual Cupid? That's all we need, a baby with wings and ranged weaponry" Eric violently shook his head, as he tried to shake the image from his mind. His untidy mess of dark locks seemed to shroud his head like a black cloud.

Looking up at Mabel his brow furrowed, "you didn't kiss in front of Thet, did you?"

"What? No!" Mabel blanched. "We did start to get kinda close in front of him though and he did sound a bit 'put out' when he left us." Mabel sighed, "do you suppose he's hurting?"

"Well," Eric relaxed back in his seat. "We've all felt the sting of unrequited love. Look, I think you need to rectify things with the reaper sooner rather than later; as right now, I don't doubt your hot blooded lover Kris is seeing a whole lotta *red* right now; if you catch my drift."

Mabel nodded absently at Eric's words, "give me a moment" she said finally and slipped away to the far side of the lounge, which remained vacant and empty.

Leaning against the railing by the large window, Mabel looked out over the runway. She watched as a plane emblazoned with red, white, and blue colouring, swooped down to land. With a silent groan she rested her forehead against the cool glass window, she chastised herself quietly.

'I should have known the lull of events would never have lasted!'

As the plane on the runway started to crawl slowly to its assigned unloading bay, Mabel closed her eyes and focused on conjuring her friend from beyond the waking realm. Would he even hear her? She had to give it a shot, regardless of his feelings toward her, he was their ally in this surreal existence. If anyone would be able to offer any sound advice, it would be him!

"Thet?" Mabel whispered quietly, feeling more than a little self-conscious at the idea of talking to herself in the corner of a public lounge.

"Thet, if you can hear me, something's happened. I could really do with some of your sound advice, right now;" she closed her eyes and envisioned Thet's friendly features. The way he had managed to tame his smile from a skull's grimace to that was a subtle upward curve at just about anything she said, the warm amber glow that lit up his eyes whenever he turned to her. Mabel smiled inwardly at the warmth her reaper friend exuded around her, it was strange. For obvious reasons, she'd never considered Thet to be anything more than her friend and yet... an uncomfortable fluttery tickle in her stomach caused her to open her eyes wide. She'd felt it before, in the Muriel hotel room; as Mabel focused her mind back on the issue at hand, she couldn't ignore the small voice testing her in the back of her mind: 'maybe Thet isn't the only one with conflicting feelings.'

"You called?" The sound of Thet's voice by her ear, made her jump violently out of her bizarre musings.

"Thet!" Mabel yelped.

Spinning around, she looked up into the impossibly dark eyes of her friend, the two hollow spaces in the top of his head glowed with the dim ochre light she had imagined. Apparently, he'd taken to the chino and flattering tshirt style, with animated tribal tattoo designs. Mabel had to admit, it was a good look on him.

"I didn't think you'd come," she managed, as the shock of his appearance eased into quiet relief. Hastily she waved for Eric to join them, but her friend continued to stare listlessly at her with a perplexed expression frozen in state.

"*You* called," Thet smirked, following her gaze; "I thought you wanted a quiet chat, so I've paused time."

"Oh," Mabel blinked, suddenly uncertain.

Privacy for the two of them once again. Sure, she'd had private conversations with Thet before, but knowing that there were some surreal feelings at play for *both* of them, suddenly made such personal meetings that little bit trickier to navigate.

"How can I help?" Thet pressed softly and taking her hand, he calmly led her to a couple of seats, that faced out toward the runway.

Mabel focused her attention on the plane which had ceased its slow crawl and now appeared to have parked up carelessly across another runway.

"I-it's Kris," she struggled, noting from the corner of her eye that Thet turned his head away from her at the mention of Kris's name, his jaw clenched and his hand fell casually from her own and on to his lap.

"I see," he nodded; "go on."

"I dunno if news travels in the afterworld, like it does here, but Charles Valentine has been pardoned of his assault on Kris. He'll be walking the streets a free man by the time we land in the States in about nine hours' time!"

Mabel valiantly steamed ahead, as Thet stood up sharply and approached the window. Icy particles started to form on the glass pane as he breathed out on to it.

"We, that is to say, Eric and I – we thought it all seemed a bit too coincidental and I – well, I wondered if there might be something more *other-worldly* at play here?"

Mabel watched as Thet lowered his head, and slowly turned to face her. His expression was mostly unreadable, but she could tell there was something off about his demeanour. If nothing else, the amber in his eyes as burnt in to a cool green.

"So, you summoned me to check it out?" Thet nodded and sniffed. "Mab, you do know that Kris has Asmodeus to help fight his battles, why not call on the demon?"

Mabel pursed her lips, "he's too close to Valentine, you know that!" She answered curtly. It was like she'd feared, Thet was far from his usual accommodating self. Mabel had seen grown men sulk more times that she'd care to admit and in his skeletal form, he might be able to hide it, but the pouting lip, the crossed arms, the set jaw and the reluctance to meet her gaze; Mabel couldn't believe he would be so callous toward the safety of Kristoph, just to pursue personal time with her.

"Thet, do you have a problem, with Kris?" Mabel

asked, crisply.

Thet's body tensed as he quickly glanced in her direction, "no" he mumbled and shrugged.

"No?" Mabel scoffed at the moody response. "Who are you trying to fool? Don't think that moment at the Muriel between us escaped my attention! Even Eric has picked up on the notion that you might have..."

"Have what?" Thet snapped, his starting to glow an angry rouge. His voice was unnaturally sharp, like a knife; and it cut through Mabel's torrent viciously.

"Feelings," Mabel softened her tone, somewhat taken aback by her friend's turn and quietly, she added: "for me."

Thet stormed away from her and snapped his fingers, instantly, the departure lounge came back to life around them. Eric called out Thet's name and started to hurry over, but Thet turned his back on him too. As he approached the furthest side of the room, he seemed to compose himself. "I'll look into it" he said simply over his shoulder and disappeared into thin air before Mabel could catch up to grab his arm, her whole being flooded with regret for upsetting him.

Sadly, she looked down at her outreached arm, as Eric joined her. As she looked up to her friend, she felt her eyes start to well up and Eric's grim features only served to confirm that she had successfully pushed her closest friend away.

In one smooth movement, Eric had pulled her in to a comforting hold with a humourless chuckle, "men, eh? He'll be okay, we're more confusing and complicated than we like to let on!"

"Men are yes," Mabel breathed out raggedly; "what about reapers?"

The mood of the band and Mabel, as they boarded the plane, was one of stark contrast to when they had arrived at the airport. Kristoph and Mabel sat together in silence, both desperately trying to come to terms with how they felt about their own personal predicaments. Mabel had decided not to tell Kristoph about her encounter with Thet, as far as she was concerned, the Dark Omen's lead guitarist clearly had the world on his shoulders with the prospect of potentially running into Valentine again, offering the most weight to his thoughts.

Eric and Adrian had opted to sit down in the chairs in front of the two lovers. Kristoph had to bite back the urge to tell them to 'sod off' as they both started to take turns casting concerned glances back at them through the gap between their seats. He'd enjoyed the brief view of emerald green in his life at the Muriel hotel with Mabel, his friend's intermittent expressions of worry, concern, and questioning looks only served as a reminder that his life was once again on the line.

Jésús and Pete meanwhile, were lounged groggily in the seats behind Kristoph and Mabel. Occasionally, Jésús would mutter some insult under his breath about Valentine which normally wouldn't have phased Kristoph too much; however, with his nerves already on edge, the added spiel of Spanish anger, inflected with Valentine's name was enough to make Kristoph grind his teeth. Worst of all was Mabel's silence. Each time Kristoph turned to her for a comforting look, hold, or even stolen kiss; her head was glued to the window, staring out at the clouds as they lazily blew by.

With five hours of airtime left, Kristoph stood up and moved to the bathroom. Anything to get away from the frustration he felt being around everyone. Slamming the bathroom door behind him, Kristoph ran the cold water tap and splashed the cooling moisture over his face. He could feel his chest tightening and forced himself to take several deep breaths.

"Hm, this is cosy;" Asmodeus quipped over his shoulder, pressing himself purposefully close against Kristoph's back. "I didn't see you as the sort to want to join the mile high club," the demon grinned, all joviality left his face as he took in Kristoph's state; "Kris honey, you look like crap!"

"Thank you, for your observation." Kristoph sighed, as he leaned his back against the sink's counter; "what are *you* doing out here, anyway? I didn't summon you!"

Asmodeus huffed, "charming! I just thought being out here would be less crowded than your head... apparently not" he mused as he looked around the sterile interior of the airplane bathroom. "To think, you humans actually

manage to get up to antics in these spaces, eugh!"
Kristoph shook his head and decided to ignore
the demon over his shoulder as he turned around
and continued to splash cold water over his face.
Whether it was the demonic presence or his own
anger, he couldn't tell, but Kristoph could feel his
body burning up and he needed to cool down!

"Y'know, cold water won't take away what's really
bugging you;" Asmodeus smirked as he lowered
the toilet seat and perched delicately on top of it.
"Right, and you know what will?" Kristoph
scoffed at Asmodeus's dark and misty reflection
in the mirror.
"Indeed," Asmodeus shrugged, "sex. Nothing like
a good bit of angry sex to shake loose all of those
pent-up vexations."
Kristoph glowered at the demon, "maybe for you.
Bloody hell, you know, you really don't have a
clue, do you?" He snapped.
Asmodeus smirked, "don't I? Let's see, your life
may once again hang in the balance, and you
haven't stopped seeing the world through a red
lens since that news report. Your little Evey out
there is being cold with you because she's dealing

with her *own* inner turmoil, and that's not fair in your eyes, as you want to let loose. You want to forget that there's a raving lunatic with access to demonic branding, wandering around the streets of your flight's destination. You want someone to hold you, squeeze you, please you – you *want* that release. You want to feel *mighty*! *Victorious*! *Powerful*! Do please tell me if none of this is stacking up to being remotely close to how you're feeling."

Kristoph huffed, "there are other ways to gain those good feelings, other than sex."

The demon laughed, "*really*?! Well my little red target, do share with them with the class. I'm only the demon of lust after all, I know nothing outside of base, primal wants, and urges. Tell me, how else does one get to feel all those exultations all at once, outside of physical coupling, please I'm *dying* to know!"

Kristoph whirled around angrily with a host of insults lined up and ready, but a delicate knock at the door disrupted him.

"Kris?" Mabel's voice whispered, "Kris? Are you okay? You've been gone a bit of a while and..."

Her voice sounded like she was leaning close to the door as she whispered, "honestly, I'm getting a bit uncomfortable with Adrian's face regularly staring at me between the seats in front."

Kristoph turned to face Asmodeus, but the demon had gone. Feeling a tight lump in his throat, he unlocked the toilet door quietly and pulled it open.

It only took one look. Those chocolate brown eyes, wide in shock at his dishevelled appearance, the impulsive move of her hand to stroke away the water droplet trailing down the side of his face. With a speed that surprised them both, he grabbed at her hand.

"Kris!" She gasped; her eyes wide as he held her tightly.

He didn't know how long they stood like that, staring at each other, uncertain of what to do. Confused. Lost in thought. Finally, an air hostess jostling with a trolley to Mabel's right broke the spell.

"Sorry," Kristoph murmured, gently letting go of her hand; "I'll be with you soon."

Mabel nodded, disconcerted, before cautiously

making her way back to her seat. Before he shut the door, he watched her retreating and felt a pang of disappointment, why hadn't he acted? As he watched her go, Mabel looked back at him and smiled encouragingly. It was a simple gesture, but the comfort it provided coursed through his body like lava. With Mabel by his side, Valentine could never get to him!

Closing the door behind him and grabbing a few paper towels, Kristoph patted the water droplets off his forehead and took several calming breaths.

"She really has you in a chokehold, doesn't she?" Asmodeus's voice chuckled in the back of his head.

"Like you wouldn't believe!" Kristoph thought back, as two oaky brown eyes filled his memory with warmth and assurance.

Chapter 24. The Plot Thickens

Thet stormed up and down Mabel's Hall of Missed Opportunities, breathing heavily. His eyes flared violently red as he ran through their last conversation. Feelings? Where on earth did she get the notion that he would have *feelings* for her?

He was a reaper; feelings were not something he regularly entertained! If you encourage feelings, you encourage impromptu thinking. If you encourage impromptu thinking, your work gets sloppy. He was, above all, a professional. Feelings. Thet scoffed and continued his disgruntled pacing.

"Brother," a sultry and solemn voice spoke out, from the darkness.

Thet froze, "Eris?" he murmured, before adding; "sister?"

Eris stepped forward. Her slender form was resplendent in her mourning attire. Her long dark hair partially braided, fell to the nape of her back. The ancient Greeks had deemed her the Goddess of strife, Thet deemed her the sister of despair, he supposed there was little difference between the two. Regardless of her title, it was rare anything good stemmed from her appearance.

Eris smiled sweetly at him, "you seem tense." The gown she wore trailed down to the ground around her and sparkled in the dim candlelight. "I don't know what you mean," Thet held his head up, forcing himself to maintain a semblance of coolness.

Eris smirked and turned her attention to the image that was displayed in the frame next to her brother. Two large chestnut eyes, exuding sadness, warmth, despair, and worry all at once; stared dolefully back at her.

"Beautiful eyes," Eris appraised, "who is she?"

"She's... no one," Thet snapped, a little too quickly. He chose to ignore the look of growing amusement on his sister's face.

"She's mortal," Eris observed, in a bored tone. "Only mortals have those kinds of eyes. They show the weight of the world, they highlight all our flaws; and yet, they belong to a bunch of apes who lack the comprehension of our true existence."

"Hm," Thet bit back the desire to stand up for Mabel, "what do you want, Eris?"

"Me?" Eris sighed with emphasised boredom, "Nothing. That is to say, you've rather riled up mother and father. Did you know, after she met with you, Mother Dear went up top to *speak to the management?*"

She conjured up a chaise lounge and a drink before glamorously kicking back and relaxing, sipping noisily from her glass; "and has yet to return."

She cast a sideways look at her brother, hoping this update would provoke some semblance of openness from him.

Thet continued to stare at her non-plussed, "mother's been away for centuries before now, it's nothing new."

"Ah," Eris sat forward, crossing her legs, and swirling her drink, "this is different. You've heard of course about the change of management up top?"

Thet clenched his jaw, but otherwise seemed unreadable, "I don't buy into rumours, sister." Eris chuckled, it was a cold and cruel sound that made even Thet's core turn icy cold; "of course you don't. You prefer to roam these sombre corridors and perv on mortal girls from a distance;" she cast a scathing glance back at the eyes.

"I suggest you get to your point quickly, Eris;" Thet grumbled.

Eris surveyed her brother through narrowed eyes for a moment, before fluidly getting up. Her chair and drink vanished as she approached her younger brother; "very well."

She cleared her throat and smoothed down her robe, before mimicking the doleful eyes from the portrait. "Dear brother, it has come to my attention that our older sister, the trickster, Nemesis is working rather closely with the new department manager in heaven. Don't you think it rather ironic that mother would suddenly vanish after trying to determine what's happening in Limbo, with such an alliance taking place?

Also, I hear that Adam and Eve have been reunited after all these years, right in time for the change up top."

"What's that got to do with anything?" Thet asked, trying to avoid sounding too concerned with the revelations.

"It just seems interesting that those two would miraculously find themselves reunited in time for the rapture that we've all been expecting. Almost as though it was someone's plan all along to have the two people who started humanity, brought together, right at its end."

Thet cast a nervous glance toward Mabel's ever staring eyes; it was brief, but the gesture was enough for Eris to notice.

Smiling slyly, she pressed on. "So, I just thought, seeing as you were head honcho of the chaperoning business, you might have some intel on what A&E's plans are now that they're reunited. Are we likely to see the sequel to Cane and Abel's squabble, in the works any time soon?"

"What?" Thet groaned, frustratedly.

"Well, the latest on the wire is that the Demonic

lord of lust has been absent from his duties in hell for some time now, and is spending much of his life cavorting on stage in the guise of Adam, who in turn is a guitarist in a satanic band?" She smirked wickedly and cast an intense questioning look at Thet, who avoided her gaze.

Doggedly, she continued; "I'm just saying, what are the odds of those two being reunited with a lustful presence between them?"

Casually sauntering passed Thet toward the shadows of the hall, Eris uttered over her shoulder; "anyone would think there's a force out there who's determined to see the human race survive its ultimate end. Such motive would *really* upset a potentially vengeful managerial figure up top, don't you think?"

Thet watched as Eris disappeared, his eyes flaring an ice blue hue. He turned toward the still frame of Mabel's saddened soul portals. Waving his hand, the image zoomed further out, and he allowed the scene to resume playing. His shoulders slumped heavily forward as he observed Eric comforting Mabel after his earlier, rather cold, exit. Feelings...

He sighed heavily, "I suppose there might be something in the observation." He murmured to himself.

The flurry of wings settling grabbed his attention and turning around, Thet spotted a rather strained-looking Azrael, struggling with a sack by his side.
"Azrael?" Thet frowned, "dare I even ask?" Before the angel could answer, the sack he was carrying kicked out so violently that he was forced to drop it, spilling its contents. Thet stared, gobsmacked as gathering herself up, straightening her hair and pristine dress, and grumbling in a torrent of German stood:
"Miss Schneider?!" Thet stared between the young girl and the angel, both of whom looked a little uncomfortable; "explain yourselves!" He ordered.

"Mr. Grim," Helga folded her arms; "you lied to me!" Her innocent face looked so disappointed in him, that Thet felt a pang of hurt.
"Lied? I don't lie, Miss Schneider," he insisted.
"You lied!" She stamped her foot, angrily. "You

said heaven was a place of rest, of peace, of wonder and amazement and everything a child could ever possibly want!"

"And...it's...not?" Thet asked slowly, turning to face Azrael, who was busy shuffling his feet anxiously.

Helga turned her gaze toward the angel in turn and snorted, "as for *him*, he is having a crisis, of sorts."

Thet sat back and folded his arms. Evidentially, today was not going to be a peaceful one; "okay, start from the top."

* *

There was something about the oppressive heat that hit each member of the band and crew as they stepped off the plane in Orlando, that struck them with a whole new feeling of uncertainty. During the flight, Adrian had pulled out a small pocketbook for each of his fellow band members. "Fill each page with your autograph. I've covered it with management. Any fans waiting for us to land will receive a signed page and be told that we have a limited time window. I doubt Charles will be stupid enough to show his face at the airport, but I don't want to risk it," Adrian sighed dismally, as he handed Kristoph a note pad. Kristoph looked at the pad in his hand, sadly; "I hate that it's because of me that we have to do this."

"Hey!" Eric twisted around in his seat, "it's not all about you. I rugby tackled the fella remember. Can you imagine the branding he'd have in line for me?" He winked jovially, before muttering, "imagine if he branded Ade with a demon who has a god-awful singing voice! Although, I dare say it might be an improvement..." He grinned impishly at Adrian.

The Dark Omens singer stared, unimpressed at Eric; "so funny..." Turning back to Kristoph, Adrian rested a hand on his shoulder.

"Kris, all of us think the world of you and want you to be safe, simple as. Thankfully, we have an incredibly accommodating fan base who get it, y'know? Yeah, there might be some disappointment, but I think – given the latest circumstances – many of them will know and understand why we're being somewhat cautious in the States."

Kristoph had to hand credit to Adrian, his plan worked like clockwork. Courtesy of the pre-signed notes, much of their initial introduction to the humid Floridian airport went by in a blur of screaming fans waving their collected pages of signatures and wildly yelling their appreciation from behind strong barriers. By the time the band arrived at the hotel, some of the tension they had felt before, had started to lift.

* *

The lights of I-Hop on the International Drive glittered like stars in the distance from Kristoph's hotel room window. Gazing out over the splendour of the main entrance from the thirty sixth floor, one really gained a sense of how puny the human race, really was; as it milled around, like ants in a thriving nest. In the well-lit room, a figure lounged lazily on Kristoph's bed.

It was rare that she found time to be by herself and dwell on her schemes, yet when time made itself available, she found she could come up with some of the more heinous thoughts ever to have been conceived. Quietly, she waved a clawed and scabbed hand over Kristoph's pristine bedsheets. Things hadn't gone quite to plan in Germany; however, she was determined to wipe out any future for the reincarnations of the original sinners, sooner rather than later!

While Kristoph and Mabel were downstairs enjoying a delectable meal with the rest of the band and support team, the figure turned her attention toward the door, and waited. After half an hour had passed, there was a quiet knock and a soft voice uttered, "room service?"
"About time," the figure grumbled to herself. Her voice couldn't be heard by mortal ears and at the lack of response from inside the room, the figure on the other side of the door could be heard struggling excitedly with the skeleton key card.

As the room's silent occupant watched on, a small man, dressed in the smart attire of the hotel staff and hunched over a trolley, entered the room. His appearance only served to humour has as she quietly chuckled, she'd gone out of her way to stay hidden in the shadow realm, but not completely cut off from the waking world.

Completely oblivious to his spectator, the man flicked off the light switch and moved closer to the bed. Reaching beneath the trolley, he pulled out a mirror, a red candle, and some matches. With shaking hands, he ignited one of the candles, always ensuring only half of his features were reflected at him in the mirror. Sitting down on the edge of the bed, the man took several deep breaths and spoke out to the room in a surprisingly deep voice:
"I want him to notice me. I want him to want me. I want him to be with me, always."
He chanted this mantra under his breath for several minutes before finally turning to face the mirror. His features hardened with grit and determination. After a while of what looked like an intense stare-off between himself and his reflection, the man spoke aloud, again:
"Let him know me, notice me, want me, and not be afeared of me."

In the shadow realm, the figure snorted. It was pitiful really; how easily manipulated and infatuated humans could get over their peers. As the man continued to stare at his own reflection, he caught a glimpse of her shadow slinking up behind him. Slowly, he turned his head and looked into the figure's wide and delighted eyes. "It's been too long, Charles," she smiled, wickedly; "it's so good to see some obsessions never change."

"A-Asmodeus?" Charles Valentine gasped, "you came back to me? Y-you're a woman, now?"

"Of course," the she-demon grinned, lapping up the stupidity and naivety of the man, as she breathed in the smell of worship and admiration that seemed to emit from every pore of his feeble being.

"The bond between Kristoph and I is so great, that I am always by his side, providing him with the love you committed to me in your original summoning. Tell me, how was prison?"

Charles's grateful smile set into a fine line, "they mocked me. They beat me. They called me a freak! Just because I believed!" Beads of sweat had gathered on the top of Charles's top lip and his greasy black hair hung lank and close to his features.

"Yet they are still bound and shackled in place, while you are free to roam wherever you please," the she-demon licked her lips, "funny how things can work out, isn't it?"

Charles narrowed his eyes and looked closer at the demon, "it was you!" He breathed, "you helped provide the evidence that set me free!" He whispered, excitedly.

"I might have used my connections," she smiled smugly, admiring her claws. "Now then, I feel like I have earned a boon of my own, don't you?"

"Of course," Charles was practically salivating, "anything you wish! You know I would do anything for you!"

The words were like music to her ears as she leaned close to the meek little man and whispered, "I need you to create some chaos. Downstairs in the restaurant, you will see your beloved Kristoph Grayson. He is wining and dining with the rest of his friends, but there is a girl. She's nothing impressive to look at, however your *dear* Kristoph is besotted. She is a witch, you see. She has cast a bewitching charm on him and the only way to break it, is to destroy she who created it."

Charles nodded his head slowly, his eyes wide, "of course, my Lord Asmodeus. May I ask what her name is, before I conduct your wish?"

"Of course," the she-demon smiled venomously, "Mabel Marionette Weaver."

Charles swallowed hard and in a flurry, bowed at her feet, blew out the candle and restored the room to its original state; before hurrying out of the space with the trolley, panting like a dog in heat.

The she-demon looked on with ill-hidden pride, "what do you think?" She asked the empty room, "did I play my part as Asmodeus well?"

The faintest of whispers sounded from the deep, dark shadows of the room. Any human would have mistaken it as a breath of wind kissing the windowpane, but to the she-demon they were words that made her blush, "oh! You really *are* the charmer. Don't you worry, *saviour*. Germany didn't go so well, this time however, I have a feeling that this forced unity will be torn asunder in a fashion befitting the Land of the Free" she chuckled again, as she vanished into the shadows.

* *

On the ground floor of the hotel, Kristoph had finally allowed his shoulders to relax and was even beginning to enjoy the company around him. The hotel Adrian had chosen was the pricier stay out of the whole tour as it offered no end of entertainment for their guests, including a medieval act with oversized turkey legs to devour while cheering on a joust. Mabel hadn't left his side and Kristoph was silently relieved. He gained peace, serenity, and hope from her. Even an accidental brush of her hand against his, caused a rush to channel through him that he'd not felt toward anyone in his life.

The laughter from the gathered audience was intoxicating as a man dressed like a jester somersaulted around the grounds, making jokes with various audience members. In hindsight, Kristoph knew he should never have let his guard down. It wasn't until he spotted Thet and

Asmodeus talking heatedly across the room from them, that he began to suspect something was amiss. Thet's eyes rested regularly on Mabel, who was too busy laughing and joking with Eric and Peter, to notice the otherworldly company across the room.

The joust finished and the men dressed as knights steered their steeds off the show room to raucous applause. As the tails of the horses swished out of sight, the master of the show stepped out into the centre of the arena.
"Fair wenches and noblemen," he bowed deeply, "it is my greatest pleasure to introduce our next event, hand-to-hand combat. Entering the grounds, honouring the colours of his homestead from the distant lands of Dallas, Texas;" the crowd laughed at his dead-pan delivery, "Sir Daniel Sawyer!" The knight swaggered out, his cape emblazoned with the Texan coat of arms, his armour shimmering. The crowd cheered him and rallied on the announcer.
"And his opponent, he's new to our parts and a mysterious figure out of your nightmares! The Black Knight!" The crowd booed relentlessly as

the mysterious knight stepped into the limelight. He was about a foot shorter and more petite in stature than Sir Daniel Sawyer and while there were many boos, there were a few jeers and giggles as the giant from Dallas squared up against his smaller framed opponent. As the knights started to circle each other, Kristoph felt Mabel grab his wrist tightly.

Turning his attention to her, he blanched as he saw the panic and fear in her face. Breathlessly, she mouthed the word he'd been dreading, "red!" Frantically, she rubbed at her eyes, and shook her head in panic. Without another word, Kristoph took her hand, and bolted for the exit. They both needed to get to safety! Kristoph had no idea where they might find such security, but he was certain that leaving the crowded room was the best course of action. As the exit sign came into their line of sight, a scream made them stop dead in their tracks.
"SOMEONE! STOP HIM! HE'S GOT A GUN!"

Kristoph barely had time to react as the man from his nightmares; Charles Valentine, launched himself out of the crowd, raising a pistol toward them both! For the lead guitarist, it all happened so fast. One moment, he was standing upright with the exit ahead of them both, in a veil of maroon. The next, a crack like explosion echoed around him, and he watched as Mabel; now shrouded in green, let go of his hand and staggering backwards weakly, grasping at a blossoming pool of blood at her side.

"Kristoph, run!" She urged him in a strained voice, as she gasped winded at the pain.

Mabel couldn't work out what had come over her, as the image of Kristoph's wide eyed and horrified expression filled her mind. All she knew was that the deranged form of Charles Valentine had started to charge toward them both with a ferocious pace. The pain in her side burnt painfully as she moved, but there was no way she was going to allow him anywhere near Kristoph, ever again.

With a burst of adrenaline, she bowed forward and put every ounce of energy into her movement. With a force of energy, she lunged into their attacker, spearing Valentine back to the ground. In his desperation to get to his idol, Charles had carelessly thrown the gun to the ground, and while she scrabbled desperately at the whirling limbs of her aggressor, Mabel took some solace that the gun was no longer within his possession.

In a confusion of limbs, the two of them rolled around violently on the ground; clawing and kicking at one another. She caught a brief glimpse of Kristoph as he desperately tried to push and shove his way through the gathered crowds, to get to her. Amidst the chaos, she saw Eric, battling through the throngs of people to help, too. With a deranged yell, Charles Valentine punched her hard in the face. The world around her exploded into lights and stars and then, nothing.

By the time Thet and Asmodeus had battled through the crowds, Eric had hauled Charles off Mabel and had locked the fanatic's arms behind his back, while Kristoph was cradling Mabel's head sobbing her name into her hair, hoping to call her back around. Thet collapsed to his knees beside them both, the pain in his own chest unlike anything he'd experienced before. As a first aider arrived and started to conduct a range of life saving measures, Thet rested a shaking hand over Kristoph's shoulders; and the two men looked at each other, united in grief.

Chapter 25. Revelations & Assurances

The news anchor on the small television screen in the waiting room smiled happily as he reported on a series of amusing local news stories. The joy and laughter being shared between the reporter and his colleagues, however, was in stark contrast to the intense worry that each of the Dark Omens band members were experiencing. The four men sat uncomfortably on the hard benches in the sterile hospital waiting room, staring listlessly into space.

Kristoph was furious. Once again, he was in an American hospital due to the actions of the same deranged culprit. This time however, it wasn't him lying bandaged up and scared in a hospital bed but the woman who had been his soul source of optimism, hope, and support. The journey to the emergency room had been one of tense silence. Not one of his fellow band mates had known what to say to him as they followed the ambulance. Mabel had impacted on each of their lives in some small way, but not as much as she had to him.

While the rest of the group had taken their seats, Kristoph had started to pace, impatiently. With every step, every tick of the clock in the room, every grin from the news anchor, the rage inside him grew. No sooner had Mabel been carried out of the hotel on a stretcher, unconscious; Thet and Asmodeus had slipped off into a different void altogether. They claimed that they were going to monitor Mabel's progression, however they'd refused to take him *or* Eric with them.

As the seconds turned to minutes, then hours, Kristoph's minimal patience finally snapped. "I don't get it! Thet can stop time at the drop of a hat, but this one time, this *one* bloody time, he can't?" He spat out loudly.
Eric blanched, "um, Kris? Mate..." Cautiously he glanced over at the rest of the group who had looked up, pale with worry, at their friend's outburst.
"I mean it's not even like Valentine's a hitman!

He's just a deranged fan! Why the hell would he target Mab!? I swear, if Asmodeus doesn't come up with a solid explanation for this, I'm demanding I be taken to wherever Mab's being held and I'm bringing her back here myself! This whole deal of clearing out Limbo? It's off! No more!" Kristoph was blind with rage.

"Kris? Mate... time and place, n' all that" Eric tried to calm his friend down, while the rest of the band watched on with growing confusion.

Kristoph scoffed, ignoring Eric's caution. "I mean come on, Thet is a reaper, if *anyone* has any sway or control over how things go, it's him. Instead, he just stood by as Valentine paraded into a show with a firearm and just stared on gormless as that Röv shot down the one person, we *both* care about. That's it!"

Kristoph stopped his pacing suddenly and his eyes widened with horror, "he loves Mab! He allowed her to be shot in the hope that she would enter the afterlife and be with him for all eternity! I bet you *anything* that's got to be the reason why he didn't intervene. Y'know, I never trusted the guy! Sure, he might have helped with the reincarnation processes... but the only time he ever made any contribution to any of those past lives, was to ensure that I was being a good boy. Now that Mab's joined my current life cycle, he can barely go *one* day without popping in to gush over her and glower at me. Reapers Eric, they've got hidden agendas, never trust 'em!"

"Sorry to interrupt this torrent," Adrian's soft voice caused Kristoph to freeze in horror, he'd all but forgotten about the rest of the band.

Kristoph hesitantly glanced over at Eric, who simply groaned and lowered his head into his hands. Slowly, Kristoph turned around and registered for the first time that Adrian, Pete, and Jésús were all staring at him with a mix of concern, bewilderment, and confusion.

"Ade..." Kristoph croaked.

Adrian held up a hand, "I want you to be completely honest with me now, Kris. Are you under the influence of anything, right now?"

Kristoph couldn't breathe, slowly he shook his head.

"Okay..." Adrian paused, before reaffirming; "you're sure?"

Kristoph nodded his head, his face was white as a sheet.

"Right," Adrian turned to Pete and Jésús who both shrugged, "it's just, well. With everything you've just said..." Adrian smiled weakly and appraised Kristoph with an unreadable look for what seemed to be an eternity.

Finally, the lead singer of Dark Omens breathed out a long and steady breath, "it just seemed to suggest that you were referring to the grim reaper and a demon, like you're on first name terms..." Adrian watched as Eric stood up and moved to Kristoph's side, forcing his friend to sit down.

"I think we need to tell them, mate;" Eric advised softly.

Kristoph looked up at Adrian and across to the rest of his band mates and nodded sadly. The jig was up.

* *

In the shadow realm hovering in a shaded state between the waking and sleeping worlds, Thet and Asmodeus watched on, as nurses and doctors worked tirelessly to address Mabel's injuries. The setting was not unnatural for either of them. In fact, Thet liked to consider hospitals and operating theatres as his home away from home. There was something about seeing the various instruments and tubes being carefully eased into Mabel's prone form however, which triggered a reaction in the reaper, that he had not experienced before.

The two watched on in silence. Even Asmodeus found he was struggling with the scene unfolding before him. Sure, Mabel was annoyingly good and yes, the simpering and sickly-sweet feelings Kristoph felt toward her made him feel like he was bathing in a pool of roses every time he took a stroll through his host's mind; but seeing her there. Her body limp, completely dependent on machines to help her breath. The demon growled menacingly as he watched on.

"So let me get this straight," Asmodeus grumbled, a wavering calmness barely hanging on to his tone. "Nemesis and the sunspot are in cahoots. Not only that, but Azrael and Helga have forfeited their places up top as the realm of heaven has turned... what was the term again?"

"Toxic," Thet answered in a monotone, not taking his eyes off Mabel. "Mother has also gone AWOL since approaching them to determine what is happening in Limbo, if Eris is to be believed, that is."

Asmodeus's growl sounded more guttural, "Azrael quitting his post is one thing, but for Helga to feel more uncomfortable in heaven, than she ever felt in Limbo?"

"There's something else too," Thet finally broke his gaze from Mabel's form and faced the demon to his right with a piercingly intense stare. "Mabel and Kris. Adam and Eve's current reincarnations; *you* brought them together. Why? Theirs is the more well-known case of separated lovers in a perpetual state of unrest, but there are others. Why them?"

Asmodeus tensed, "why not?" He asked, somewhat defensively.

"Come on Asmo, you can do better than that" Thet murmured, "what did you know?"

Asmodeus sighed, "it's not so much what I know, it's more so what I *heard*. Yes, I sought them out specifically. I had heard whispers of a union up top, a vicious sinner palling up with someone of immeasurable power. I thought that meant an arch angel, I didn't think it meant... him. I heard rumours that the rapture had suddenly taken a great leap forward in its plans. Now, this might surprise you, but I rather like humans;" Asmodeus looked sadly at Mabel.

"There's something about them that I find inexplicably endearing. Take Mab and Kris. The original sinners, that's how they are viewed by many of our kin. For me? I see them as the original humans. They followed each other through every decision, they never parted ways. They overlooked each other's flaws. They forgave one another for their shortcomings. Believe it or not, many of the human populace are more inclined to believe in the imperfection of these beings than they are in the perfection that is the father and his son! What's not to love about that?"

The corner of Thet's mouth twitched upward, "very endearing indeed, but why?"

Asmodeus groaned, "it was a hope, more than anything. Adam and Eve were the father's playthings. His test dummies. He could never forgive them for betraying him, yet he never wanted them to rest. He wanted to keep them going, albeit separately. I'm a demon Thet, I perceive the darker, more sordid, inner workings in others better than you or any saintly angel. Think about it, the father has used my own original mindset on these two."

Thet stared, "what on earth do you mean?" He asked.

"Sarah," Asmodeus shuddered at the thought of her, "the woman I loved. Before this..." He grumbled as he gestured toward his being, "she was pure bliss to look at. Every move. Every sound. Every glance from those seductive eyes. To me, she was perfection. To her, I was abhorrent. She stole the hearts of countless men around her; she knew of her beauty and she had her own mind, but I couldn't and wouldn't let her settle with any man who wasn't me!"

"I see," Thet mused, "if you couldn't have her, no one else could, would, or should."

Asmodeus nodded, "it was a mindset that was my undoing, you see before you the results of it.

Now, think of Adam and Eve. To the father, they are just shy of perfection, he loves them and dotes on them. Then they betray him (as Sarah did to me, in my eyes – she fell for another guy, a lesser man than me). So, he punishes them. He banishes them. Yet, when they pass away, he won't let them rest in heaven, he certainly won't let them suffer in hell. Nor does he want to lose sight of them in Limbo..."

"If he can't have them..." Thet chewed on Asmodeus's words, "you're the one who wants to prevent the rapture! There's no way the father would allow it to happen, if his original creations have been reunited and are roaming the earth healthy and well and are likely to rekindle their... love;" he looked sadly at Mabel; "I never had a shot," Thet mumbled to himself.

"Hm?" Asmodeus cocked his head.

"Nothing," Thet sighed, glumly. "Well, it would appear we need to have a little chat, with Valentine."

"Why Valentine?" Asmodeus snarled, "I swear if he finds his life empty and hollow without Kris now, he has yet to see the space I have *personally*

reserved for him in my own annex down south."
"Because," Thet looked back at Mabel and he
felt the fire within him burn fiercely; "I don't
think his motives to take out Mab, were his own."

Asmodeus's eyes widened, "you don't suppose?"
"I do," Thet rumbled. "This has Nemesis's
trademarks of chaos, irony, and spite; written all
over it!"
"What's to stop her from trying to finish Mab off,
if we move away from our watch?" Asmodeus
mithered, uncertainly.
Thet smiled weakly, "We're not the only ones
looking over her right now, I have two assurances
that I will return." With a wave of his hand, the
view of Mabel shimmered, as though a viscous
bubble of light were surrounding her. Holding his
hands wide to generate the sphere of safety stood
Azrael, while Helga was sat cross-legged at the
foot of Mabel's feet, chirruping away happily.
"That should do it," Asmodeus nodded,
approvingly; "right, shall we pay Valentine a
visit?"
"Not quite yet," Thet paused, his features
breaking into a large smile, as he turned his

attention to a space unseen behind them. "If my hearing hasn't deceived me, I believe our presence is required down the hall."

* *

Adrian stared at Eric and Kristoph with a look that conveyed every spectrum of confusion and disbelief. Jésús and Peter sat by his side, both with their mouths wide open, all of them struggling to comprehend the barrage of unbelievable revelations that Eric and Kristoph had detailed. Finally, Adrian started to stutter and stammer.

"Ah, he's gearing back into life," Eric muttered into Kristoph's ear.

"So, Bo... is actually..." Adrian managed, before lapsing into silence.

"Yeah," Eric nodded. "I struggled to comprehend that one too, but we got away with it, courtesy of some other worldly magic!" He grinned broadly. Jésús's disbelieving high pitched laugh broke the soporific mood, "other-worldly magic doesn't take away from the fact that we serenaded an actual blood bath!"

"Hush!" Kristoph insisted, as a few of the late-night nurses looked up at them, puzzled; "you need to understand, they weren't technically alive to begin with! They were like me and Mab!"

"Zombies!" Pete whimpered.

"No, for the last time, we are not zombies, Pete!" Kristoph groaned; "we are flesh and blood like you, we've just been reincarnated... a lot."

Adrian shook his head, "that branding on your arm, it *actually* worked?"

"Indeed!" Asmodeus answered, stepping into the waiting room, and strutting toward the group members as though he were parading along his own personal catwalk.

Adrian, Jésus, and Pete cried out and each leapt up and backed away toward the far wall.

"SECURITY!" Pete yelled out, desperately.

Asmodeus swung down, leisurely into the seat beside Kristoph and nudged him, "Mab's critical but stable – I think is the term they used. She'll be out of action for a bit, but she's in good hands. Azrael and Helga are both looking over her."

"WHAT?!" Kristoph and Eric shouted out.

"Must you two always resort to shouting?" Thet

sighed, "just accept what's been said and move on."

"Helga, though!" Eric expressed, "she was supposed to be at rest."

"Yeah, about that..." Asmodeus grimaced, "we've a bit of an update for you both, big game changer, but we thought you could use our assistance with these three."

"NURSE, for God's sake, NURSE!" Adrian cried out, but the lady behind the counter in the corner of the room, was frozen midway between taking a bite from a bland salad sandwich.

"Adrian Smyth, *please*, compose yourself!" Thet groaned, loudly.

At hearing his name spoken out by Thet, Adrian slumped down weakly to the ground. "You're him, aren't you. The reaper... Thet?" His voice was barely a squeak, as Thet slowly approached them.

"I am," Thet confirmed.

"Please, don't kill us!" Pete reasoned, "I'm not ready!"

Asmodeus snorted loudly, as Thet looked at Pete with a look of bewilderment. "For a death metal band, you guys scare so easily at the icons you claim to sing on behalf of."

"Common misconception about us," Eric interjected. "Just because we play death metal, doesn't mean we don't have our own fears and insecurities. Pete hates flying. Jésús has very specific claustrophobia. Ade – what's yours?"

"Death," Adrian whispered in terror.

Thet nodded, "it's a clever fear, that;" He mused, "while you appreciate it will come to you eventually, you fear the unknown or being forgotten, the after effects of what might happen when you're gone."

Adrian shook his head, "Eric," he whimpered, "Thet is analysing my phobia."

"He does that a lot," Kristoph sighed.

Thet smirked at Kristoph's slight, and sat down rigidly on one of the waiting room seats, "I would dearly love to chew the cud, as they say, and wile away the time discussing the psychology of phobias; however, duty calls. Asmodeus and I are going to pay Mr Valentine a little visit, I don't suppose any of you would like to join us?" He smiled, invitingly.

Chapter 26. The Prince of Darkness

The water tank at the top of the drinking tap bubbled lazily as the host of officers standing guard outside Valentine's holding cell, mulled around uneasily. It was no secret that the satanic follower unsettled many he came in to contact with, not so much because he seemed threatening, but more so because of how peaceful and tranquil he became after being detained. Officer Danver had been the first on scene after the infamous branding ordeal in 2021, he still remembered the sanguine calmness that had taken over Valentine after he had permanently scarred Kristoph Grayson.

As Valentine hummed sweetly to himself in his holding cell, Officer Danver shuddered and approached the administrator at the desk.
"I don't get it. He gets a fresh chance of freedom and goes for Grayson again! I suppose it's true what they say about heavy metal, it is the work of

the devil."

He shuddered as a chill shiver shimmied up his spine. He couldn't quite place it, but Danver was certain that Valentine was surrounded by a host of demonic energy, and it was giving him and his team a constant feeling of uncertainty. Subtly, Danver touched his chest where a small cross pendent on a chain hung under his shirt. It was a small piece, but it provided him with a sense of courage.

Asmodeus rolled his eyes at the officer, "I like humans. I *really* do; but there are some that just... eugh." He appraised Officer Danver from the Shadow realm and murmured under his breath; "I would love to know what he would make of his Lord and Saviour's plans to obliterate him and all he knows and loves. Somehow, I don't think that small pendent he's holding would offer him much comfort, as the heavens descend upon him."

Thet shook his head, "it might not, but he's a regular attendee of his church and he volunteers at a food bank for a local charity, so he holds on to hope. It's a shame really, he'd normally be top of the list for pearl gate entry rights."

"N-N-Normally?" Kristoph shivered and blew into his hands. The shadow realm had not been designed for those with beating pulses, instead it offered the living a chance to entertain the idea of what meat must feel like when it's placed inside a refrigerator. It was like a chill blaster. It was a fascinating spectacle though, to be there in a room crowded with so many people yet be invisible to the naked eye.

"Yes, normally;" Thet smiled and conjured a robe for Kristoph and the rest of the Dark Omens band members who had reluctantly agreed to join their friend, as he faced off against Valentine. "Before we enter that cell gentlemen, there are a few things I need to bring you all up to speed on and I fear it won't make for pleasant hearing."

"Lay it on us," Eric rippled his shoulders, while wrapping the robe tighter around his broad torso, finding it was surprisingly warm. "I always find it best, if there's bad news to be shared, to have it dealt swiftly. Like ripping off a plaster. Sharp sting, but it's over and done with quickly. Sometimes I yell it out loud, just for the effect."

"Very well..." Thet grimaced as the intrigued faces of each of the grown men in front of him, looked up expectantly. Clearing his throat, Thet spread his arms wide and in a voice that thundered around them, expressed; "THE RAPTURE IS NIGH!"

The effect of these words was tremendous. Thet groaned with instant regret as Jésús whimpered and crumbled to the ground like an accordion, while Pete started to cry out and scream.

"So, we are *all* going to die?" Adrian gasped, as he stared wide-eyed at Thet, who was busy attending to Jésús.

"Not if we can help it," Asmodeus anxiously responded; as he held his hand firmly over Pete's mouth.

"Right. How exactly are you planning on stopping the grand plan and schemes of the almighty?" Eric croaked, as he shook his head in bewilderment.

"With him!" Asmodeus flourished his arm over at Kristoph, "and Mab... if she pulls through from her injuries, that is."

Kristoph blanched, "you expect Mab and I to face off against God?"

"Not God," Thet sighed, exasperatedly, as he helped Jésús back to his unsteady feet. "His son... and one of my sisters, apparently."

"Of course," Kristoph's voice had reached a whole new octave as he stared bewilderedly at the reaper; "because Mab and I did so well against a demi-god, it makes sense to match us up against the Son of God, and... a reaper's sister?"

"Nemesis," Asmodeus grumbled, as he cautiously loosened his grip on the drummer. "Her name is Nemesis. She's a trickster and focuses her every waking hour on the prospect of revenge. Thankfully, her plans usually backfire."

"They do," Thet reasoned. "However, it's only after a relentless amount of bloodshed has been caused in the process. Not that this will come to that..." he hastily added, as Pete started to whimper again.

"I don't get it," Kristoph frowned. "Why would Je..."

"Don't say his name!" Asmodeus snapped.

Calming his abrupt demeanour, the demon chuckled in a false, nonchalant tone. "Apologies Krissy-kins. Have you ever noticed that Thet and I rarely refer to the Sunspot by his given name?" Kristoph cast his mind back. Now that Asmodeus mentioned it, he'd only really heard them refer to the son of God by nicknames, insults, or titles. They had never used his given name.

Asmodeus smiled as he saw the acknowledgment dawn on his host. "You see, my little cherub, there is a reason many call on him, by his name, at times of need. He can tune in, you see. Whether he acts on requests is another matter entirely, but he is the *master* of eavesdropping. I tell you, many a sinner has made their way down to the nether realms of Hell based on a tiny tidbit of information he gleaned from a shady meeting where his name was used in vain. Of course, that was when he was behaving according to the scriptures and not scheming against them, with Nemesis;" Asmodeus snarled, devilishly.

"But why scheme, though?" Kristoph scratched his head in puzzlement, "why would he give up his role of determining a soul's final destination, to plan and scheme revenge?"

"Yeah," Eric nodded, "also, what's he seeking revenge *for*, exactly?"

"Oh, y'know, the usual;" Asmodeus drawled lazily, "man's sin and um, I don't think the whole game of '*pin the martyr to the cross*' really helped matters."

"But, that was his job or um, *destiny*, if you will!" Adrian blustered, "that was his soul purpose, wasn't it? I'm no Christian, but I remember the stories as a kid. He was created and sent by God to repent for man's sins."

"Well, ye-es..." Thet folded his arms, "but you see, that was then. Centuries have passed since, and mindsets have changed somewhat. The delightful heir to on high, has walked amongst man on multiple occasions throughout the eras, just to gain an idea of what his earlier martyrdom meant to you all. And, well... Suffice it to say, it appears he's gained a somewhat alternative mindset. That is to say, he seems to have developed something of a grudge toward mankind."

"Bugger," Pete shook his head, weakly. "We're doomed!"

"Not necessarily," Thet soothed. "If we can get a step ahead of him and my sister, we might be able to counter their next move."

Kristoph frowned, "and you think a chat with Valentine is going to get us a step ahead? The man's insane."

Asmodeus grimaced, "not as insane as you think. The man is exceptionally knowledgeable, even if he does portray the role of dimwit, well. He managed to win *me* over, which is no mean feat. Also, he appears to have won the attention of those above. It is only a matter of time before Nemesis and the *Saviour* determine that Mab is stubbornly hanging on to life. Trust me, they will be relentless in their pursuit to end her."

Kristoph's eyes narrowed, "why Mab, and not me?"

"That's a very good question," Thet mused, as his eyes darkened menacingly. "Shall we ask him?"

Charles Valentine lounged back on the bench in his cell. Sure, he would no doubt be facing time again for his actions, but not even the thought of incarceration could diminish the glow of pride he felt, burning away internally. He'd done it. He had vanquished the witch who had hexed Grayson. His beloved. Charles sighed pleasantly, everything felt right once more; and yet.

Charles closed his eyes, there was something ever so vaguely abnormal that he could sense, just out of sight and mind.
Cautiously, he leaned forward; "hello?" he asked. His voice was barely louder than a whisper, but for his onlookers in the shadow realm, it was as though he had shouted the greeting directly to their faces.
"How did he do that?" Eric shuddered, disquieted by the convict.
"Like I said," Asmodeus sighed, lazily. "The man is more knowledgeable that he would like to admit, he can communicate with the shadow realm. Granted, he doesn't always know who he's talking to, but I rather feel he's mastered the art of intrigue, don't you Thetster? I mean for a human, at least."
"Hm," Thet's eyes narrowed. Taking great care

with his footing, Thet softly stepped away from the group around him, and approached the lone figure, who's head tilted from side to side. It was as though he was trying to tune his hearing, like a skilled predator. Valentine's eyes remained closed, yet he seemed more alert, more dangerous.

"I know someone's there," Valentine spoke out; "you aren't hiding that well."

With a speed unlike anything Thet had witnessed stem from a human, Charles swiped out with his hand. Asmodeus pulled the reaper out of grabbing reach just in time, but it wasn't enough to prevent the calloused hand from tearing away part of the reaper's cloak. Thet swallowed and looked down at the hemline of his robe, which had started to repair itself, as Valentine sniffed at the frayed fabric in his hand.

"Hmm," the man mused with a dreamy expression. "Sandalwood, leather, and just a hint of fennel. Why is that scent so familiar to us?"

"Thet?" Kristoph murmured close to the reaper's side. "I don't like this. I think I preferred him as a deranged fan."

Thet smiled, "This is rather interesting."
Taking another step closer to Charles, Thet
whispered by the man's ear: "Luci?"
Charles's eyes opened wide at the sound. As Thet
stepped back, the man tilted his head so far on to
his shoulders it looked as though it had snapped!
Valentine breathed in loudly and labouredly.
Desperately, he clawed at his throat as smoke
started to dribble out of the corners of his mouth.
In mere moments, Charles Valentine started to
violently convulse; thrashing, and lashing out, his
voice barely making a sound louder than a
squeak.
The cacophony of sound made by his physical
convulsions, however, was enough to draw
Officer Danver and his crew to peer through the
door. Muffled shouts of "MEDIC! WE NEED A
MEDIC HERE!" could be heard through the
thick metal door.

From the shadow realm, the members of Dark
Omens looked on, mortified. Thet and
Asmodeus however, stepped closer together.
Asmodeus smirked.
"Two human souls and the eighth life of one cat,

says Valentine doesn't survive this," confidently, he held out his hand.

Thet weighed up the odds, before shrugging and smiling coyly at the demon, "I'll raise you; one free pass with mother dearest says he *will* survive."

Asmodeus sucked his breath in sharply, "well, how can I refuse?"

"I'm sorry..." Adrian croaked as he stared transfixed at the violent fitting from the man in front of them. "Are you seriously making bets about this man's life?"

Asmodeus raised a questioning eyebrow and turned to face the singer, "you actually sympathise with the little bugger?"

"Well, no!" Adrian folded his arms, defensively. "But can we not *do* something? He's clearly in a lot of discomfort."

Asmodeus snorted, "good!"

"Good?" Adrian whispered vaguely.

"Good!" Jésús folded his arms and glared at the spectacle, "karma is a bitch. I do not care for this Bastardo! He assaults Kris. He has caused no end of damage to our reputation as a fan-friendly

band. Now, he has left Mab fighting for her *life!*"
The bass player held his head high as he looked
down venomously at Valentines body, which had
started to slow its convulsions to sporadic spasms.
Pete, Kristoph and Eric slowly stepped closer.

"They can't open the door," Kristoph observed
as he looked away from Valentine's glazing eyes
to the steel door which was receiving a barrage of
attacks from the police officers on the other side.
"Probably for the best," Thet surmised, as with a
final guttural sigh, Charles Valentines' body fell
still. The lights in the cell flickered to an inky
darkness, and all fell silent. As Kristoph's eyes
tried to acclimatise to the sudden change of light,
two glowing pinpricks appeared at the floor and
floated up toward the ceiling. Slowly, they blinked
twice and turned their attention directly toward
the group.
In the ungodly silence that followed, a low
rumble-like chuckle grumbled about them, as the
lights flickered back on in the cell. The steel door
swung open as with an almighty crash, nearly the
entire police force spilled through the entry way,

clattering in a heap over the prone form of Charles Valentine.

"Well, that was all rather exciting." The phenomenally deep voice echoed around the Shadow Realm. It had the same charm appeal as Asmodeus's usual drawl, yet Kristoph couldn't help but shudder at the subtle acidic aftertaste that it left. Slowly, the group turned around to see a man yawning loudly and stretching his long and muscular limbs. Hair, blacker than ebony cascaded down to the base of his back. His skin was as white as snow, his features were chiselled to perfection. All of this was somewhat overshadowed by the fact that he stood before them completely naked. He blinked sleepily at the assembled men and smirked. Even Eric found his gaze drifting south of the man's waistline and a surreal thrill-like shudder ran through him.

"Oh come now," the figure rolled his eyes at the wide-eyed reception. Lazily, he twisted his ankle around on the spot. As if merging out of his follicles, a black leather like material pooled

tightly around his legs and crept up his perfectly
toned limbs, covering his modesty and fastening
neatly at his waist with serpentine lacing. Beads of
sweat glistened delicately on his pectorals.

The figure glanced boredly around the group and
groaned. "What? You really think feeble little
Valentine would be able to take out that witch on
his lonesome? *Please!*" Arrogantly, the figure
snorted and whirled around, casually sauntering
further into the darkness.

"Not so fast... if you please, sire?" Asmodeus's
voice sounded different. There was a mix of
admiration and fear in it, as he hesitantly snapped
his fingers. In the blink of an eye, the shimmering
darkness of the shadow realm gave way to the
sterile clarity of the hospital waiting room.

"Asmodeus?" The figure smiled unnaturally
sweetly; "I'm sure you didn't just force your sire
to realm hop, without permission."

Cruelly he drew closer to the demon and a faint,
guttural growl started to rumble deep in the
recesses of his throat.

"Lucifer," Thet's stern business tone cut through
the devil's taunting. "Enough, please. I think an

explanation is owed all around; but right now, a life is at risk, and I rather feel that both sides have only half a story to share."

"Ever the voice of reason, young Reaper. Very well," Lucifer threw himself down luxuriously across several of the waiting room chairs; "perhaps, an introduction would be beneficial?"

"I think we're passed all that," Kristoph's voice croaked to life, and he glared defiantly at the devil, who tilted his head uninterestedly to survey him. "The Prince of Darkness has evidentially stooped to the lowest of the low; possessed a ridiculous coward, branded me to Asmodeus, and has just tried to kill the woman I lo..."

"Ah-ba-ba-ba-ba!" Lucifer raised a finger to his lips and Kristoph gagged as he felt his mouth snap shut, outside of his control. "That's not how we address the Prince of Hell, little human," He grinned impishly, "besides, I was doing you a favour. By all accounts, she was a witch who'd cast an enchantment over you – rather medieval I grant – but it's nice to know there are some age-old traditions still at large."

"A witch?" Thet frowned, "Lucifer, that woman is no witch. This man is no *little human*. They are Adam and Eve, reincarnate!"

"Excuse me?" For the first time since his appearance, a flicker of uncertainty flashed across Lucifer's face.

"If you please, *Sire*!" Asmodeus cast a scathing look at Kristoph. "It would appear that you have just assisted in mortally wounding Eve. We are also under the impression you were doing so under the orders of Nemesis. Sire. It's been a few years, and your office below has been rather quiet. Tell me, have you been inside Valentine all this time?"

Lucifer slowly scanned the faces of the figures before him and casually glanced down at Kristoph's wrist. In a soft, murmur of a mumble, he grumbled "maybe."

Chapter 27. Purgatory

Mabel's eyes snapped open. Desperately, she tried to rub them. Not again!

Mabel had gotten so used to being back in a physical body, her mind had been all too happy to dismiss the surreal sensation that stemmed from no longer being behind the wheels of a fleshy form; but instead, a wispy thought, stuck in the ether. The space around her was pitch black. The air was still, and there was a sense of stagnation that seemed to want to gnaw at her soul's boundaries. She yearned to be able to swipe it away.

"Thet!" She tried to call, yet her soul had no form and as such, no sound came out. The surge of emotions that coursed through her were overwhelming! If she were human, Mabel had no doubt in her mind she'd be clamouring for Thet, Kristoph, Eric – heck, even Asmodeus would have gained a mention or two! The thought of shivering internally hit her, and Mabel reasoned that as a lingering soul, she had no flesh and bone diminishing the raw sting of grief that her thoughts and feelings projected.

'I need to keep calm', she cursed herself, harshly. 'Thet or Asmodeus will be around soon, this must be that hall that Thet took me to when we first met!' Ideas and inspiration came to mind as she reflected on that first meeting. There had been frames in that space. What had Thet called it? The Hall of Unlived Opportunities? Maybe, if she could get to one of those frames, she could try and gain his attention from an alternative life! The idea fizzled into nothing just as quickly as it had come into being however, plans of action meant nothing if she had no body to conduct itself in the way she wanted.

Slowly, a strong surge of despair started to build up within her. Fighting back the urge to panic, Mabel forced herself to take stock of the situation at hand. What did she know for sure? Well, she could see, which meant she must have eyes. Cautiously, Mabel tried to blink. Nothing. Okay, maybe that was a bit of an advanced thought, at this early stage.

'Why is it so dark?' Mabel mused to herself. 'If I am in the Hall of Unlived Opportunities, where are all the candle sconces that had sputtered into life when Thet took me there?' The nagging mouth that had been chewing at the back of her mind finally tore a gap large enough to break through to the forefront of her thoughts. 'What if this is limbo? The space between life and death?'

"Mother?" A deep and husky voice spoke from the shadows.

Mabel's soul froze to its core. It was like it had sensed the danger before it had made itself known. She focused on the echo around her and mulled on the after-effect of the voice's sound. It wasn't unfriendly, more so one that clearly hadn't expected anyone to swing by any time soon. Mabel's fight or flight senses were screaming at her to run, yet the physical capacity to conduct such an action was outside of her control.

'Keep it together,' she internally scolded herself; 'yes, you're at a disadvantage here. That doesn't mean you can't get an upper hand in some way, shape or... did it call me mother?'

The title stung, like a slap delivered by a
bejewelled hand that had mastered the art of
delivering a smack so vile it left a handprint and
scratches, that would last for days.
'Mother?' She mused on the word, why did it feel
so alien and yet so familiar, at once?
The sound of shackles and shuffling feet
approached her, from what direction though it
was hard to tell. Apparently, sound echoed
differently in this space. There was no up, no
down, no left and certainly no right.

"What did you do to warrant being brought here,
mother?" The voice spoke again.
Mabel felt that if she had a body, she'd been
frowning and reaching out maternally in response
to the owner of it. The question wasn't one full of
sneer and mockery, rather it was one of intrigue,
curiosity, disbelief and just a hint of concern. The
shackles clinked softly in the darkness, as though
the bounded being was uncertain of whether to
approach any further.
'How can I speak out, if I have no voice?' Mabel
groaned internally.
All she wanted was to reach out to the speaker.

She couldn't help herself. They sounded so familiar, and she could feel a distant longing and yearning, sensations she'd not experienced anything like for as long as she could recall.

The shuffling and clunk of a heavy chain drew closer, and if Mabel tuned her attention carefully, she could make out the shallow and nervous breathing of a figure just in front of her. There was a sharp intake of breath, as the figure gasped sharply.

"Who took your form?" It croaked, "is this another form of torture? To be so close to her once more, yet not have her here to hold?" The voice broke pitifully.

'I've never been a mother' Mabel thought to herself.

She and Kristoph had not yet had the chance to be physical with one another so there was no way that she could have possibly conceived... wait.

No. In the recesses of her mind a memory came to life.

Pain. So much pain. Blood. Agony. Cries of desperation and fear. Then an infant's shriek and clamour. The phantom like sense of holding a newborn in her arms, shakily, came to mind. She had been a mother, before. She'd born a beautiful baby. His eyes had burnt a fiery shade of auburn in the sunlight. His hair was the same shade of russet brown as hers. He'd smiled and his face lit up like his father's. He was her first. There was another, but he was always her firstborn. The pain from this memory burnt fiercely and with a sense of yearning stronger than anything she had experienced in her remembered lifetimes, Mabel reached out. With a rush of adrenaline, she saw her arms start to materialise. They were ethereal once more!

She had died. She must have done. She didn't care. She was with him again. She was with her boy once more.

"Cain?" Mabel tried to speak, but her voice still had no sound.

Her hands opened wide, and she stretched out her fingers into the darkness and two large, calloused, and cold fingers interlaced with hers. He tried to pull her toward him, but Mabel stood firm and pulled him to her bosom. Her arms shed some light around them both and she saw the cruel iron bonds that had been entwined around his wrists so tightly that they had cut deeply over the millennia he had been there. As he stepped back from her embrace, she looked up at the shadowed face of Cain, her boy.

The man's features were shrouded in a tangled mane of hair from the top of his head to around his face.

"M-m-mother..." He croaked, "I see you now, at last, I see you!" His shoulders heaved heavily as two pearly glints of tears trickled down from the shadowed eyes.

"My sweet son," Mabel tried to mouth, yet the words still made no sound. Cautiously, she tried to wipe the tears from his face, but they kept cascading as he shook his mop of hair.

"I killed him mother, I did it. I know you never wanted to believe that I could do it, but I did mother. I did and I was destined for this realm from the moment I dealt that final blow!" He whimpered weakly.

Mabel shook her head and felt another burning and searing sting of betrayal, disappointment and heartbreak wrack through her fibrous form. As one, she and Cain sank to their knees and held each other closely, both sobbing. One loudly, like a wounded creature desperate to have its pain taken away. The other soundlessly, suffering so silently no one could have known unless they saw the anguish in her features.

How long they stayed like that, Mabel didn't know. After some time however, Cain's shoulders finally fell still, and his arms fell to his side limply. Cautiously, Mabel pulled back and appraised the man before her. He was the epitome of defeat. Tilting her body to the side, she peered around him and noted the shackles bound to his ankles. She was no idiot, she knew the story of Cain and Abel and yet that was how she had always perceived it, a story from the bible. Two brothers who had entered a bitter, one-sided rivalry. Both tasked with bestowing the best gift to the almighty. In jealousy and spite, Cain had killed his own brother in retaliation to God's gratification being bestowed on the youngest for his offering. Not once had Mabel ever considered the ramifications of how Eve, her former self, had felt at losing both of her sons. One to murder; the other to hatred, grief, and shame.

"I'm so sorry, mother. The pain I have caused..." Cain looked up dejectedly into Mabel's face.

"I forgive you," Mabel tried to speak out, but no sound passed her lips. Frustratedly, she gestured to her mouth and Cain smiled weakly.

"I see time doesn't move forward in this realm. I have observed some changes from the land of the living, from my place in the darkness here;" he sighed and sat back, holding her hand, tightly. "Occasionally a figure passes through, I see them from my space in the recesses. I am their fear, their nightmare. I am their reflection. I am what they see when they look in the mirror in life, I am what they envision they look like when they pass through here. The men are granted voices to lash out insults at me, to berate me, to chastise and hurt me. The women remain soundless. They gesture, they tear at their silken gowns, and they silently lament. It all comes to naught in the end. It appears in the land of purgatory, where the condemned are sent to roam, and women are forevermore stripped of their right to sound their voices;" he sighed heavily, before frowning; "which begs the question mother, what did you do? Why have you been sent to purgatory?"

Mabel closed her eyes and frowned. Everything leading up to this moment was all a blur. She felt Cain stroke the back of her hand softly, just as he had done as a boy, when she had held him close to her at night. They had both struggled to sleep when the cool nights had fallen. Being cast out of paradise after being coerced and tricked by the devil left you with a haunting thought that such creatures of darkness were watching your every move, resting in wait. Lurking.

They were opportunists, desperately craving that one moment of error, that one weakness that they could jump on and pick away at until it became an oozing sore. Asmodeus's charming smile flickered to mind and Mabel suddenly realised why she had never really warmed to him; he was one of them, yet he'd changed. Just like she had. She'd sent Bo and his kin to their deaths, knowingly, not to mention the hoard of Saxons. She'd helped send a host of haunted children on to their final destination, yet she'd held Eric and

Kristoph back from preventing Pan from causing any further damage when they were in Hamelin. The countless number of children who had now passed on, because of her actions. She'd angered a demi-God, that had to account for something, regardless of how twisted his actions had been. Mabel shook her head; she was no better than Asmodeus. Sure, he lured, teased, encouraged physical urges; however, he had never killed or orchestrated deaths like she had in just a few months! Cain had killed his brother. She, Mabel, had coerced and abated the deaths of hundreds! If anyone deserved to be in shackles, living out the rest of their years in purgatory, it was her! How could she convey all of this to her son, when she had no voice, and he was looking at her like she was a deity sent from heaven?

Smiling pleasantly at her, Cain stroked Mabel's hair, comfortingly.
"Please mother, let me help;" calmly, he placed a hand against her temple and closed his eyes. Mabel closed hers and tensed as a series of flashbacks whipped through her mind. Lifetimes had passed since Eve had died. In a brief snippet,

she spotted the pearly gates and saw how her sentencing of a life with no peace had been delivered, callously, by an unknown angel. His face stern. His hair a silvery grey. He'd whipped her feet from beneath her with a golden staff and cast her back to the unknown reaper with stern orders which were transcribed into aged parchment and pressed into her chest, scorching their way inside her.

Blurrily an endless scene of reincarnations swam by. She'd passed away at various ages. The one image of her as a child in a factory in wartime England caught up in a factory blast was haunting! Various reapers had attended to her at each passing. Not one had treated her with the same level of sympathy and kindness as Thet. Instead, they had moved her along to the next lifetime, not even granting her an ethereal body to admire. Finally, there was the office. The explosion. Thet had been right, she'd rescued that cleaner without a moment's hesitation. She smiled as she witnessed her friendly reaper's kindness. When the time Kristoph had rescued her and Angel from the stranger at the bar flashed by her eyes, she felt her stomach knot. That was Cain's father! How would her son react to seeing his dad, branded, and tied to a demon? Mabel swallowed as another torrent of questions came to her mind: where was Kristoph now? Was he okay? Had she gotten to him in time to stop Valentine's attack? Cain kept his hand pressed softly against her head; his brow furrowed in concentration as he absorbed all that his mother had lived through.

With the sound of the pistol's gunfire echoing around their minds, he finally lowered his arm and breathed out a long and steady breath, shaking his head in disbelief. Mabel looked up into his unreadable face. What could he possibly think of her now?

Slowly, Cain rose to his feet and lowered his hand to help her up. He smiled at her kindly and stroked her hand.

"I call you mother and see you as Eve, but it has been so long since that lifetime. Yet you held me just, as if we were back at our old home. The lives you've lived," Cain shook his head in disbelief and chuckled, "so a life without peace was the sentence for you and father."

He mused, "I can only imagine the lives father must have lived. Thet helped find you a life to lead for passing before your time as Mabel and allowed you to carry the same name from the life before into this one. He granted you a body not dissimilar to the one I see you in now. He was the first reaper, in so long, to do so."

Slowly, Cain started to pace the space around them, deep in thought.
"Then there's the demon of lust, Asmodeus, who's tied to father. He's wary of you. Yet, he sees you as an aid to help those in Limbo...".
Slowly, Cain turned to Mabel with a look of intrigue, "The figures in heaven and hell are not adding up and the person in charge of determining souls is not conducting their job."
As his musing continued, Mabel noted a shift in Cain's mannerisms. He walked about more upright, his tone less grieving child and more businessman, weighing up the odds of an investment.
"I see you met Lilith too," he smiled wryly. "I see she hasn't changed a bit."
He snorted, as Mabel frowned. What? Did he

know Lilith?

In response to her confusion, Cain cleared his throat and offered a shaggy, sheepish look of apology. "Lilim? Be a dear, could you turn on the lights?"

The darkness around them slowly started to diminish as one by one, spots of light started to burn away at the shrouded mist and blackness they had been cloaked in. Somewhat apprehensively, a petite woman wrapped in a shawl approached them. Her hair was silken and shoulder length, shaping her small head. It shone almost blue in some lights, yet it was ebony black. Her eyes were soft yet there was something about them that seemed familiar. When she smiled Mabel was reminded of Thet's casual smirk. With a sense of unease Mabel looked questioningly at Cain who was rubbing his now free wrists, as the woman, Lilim, removed the shackles from them with a key she kept hidden between her breasts.

"Apologies for the dramatics Mother, but I have been tasked with playing a part, after all" he smiled weakly. "You see, the almighty showed me mercy for my crimes. He banished me from your lives, condemning me to be a rambler, never settling in any one place; but ensuring I was safe from the cruelties of the world and its inhabitants. This beautiful woman here was the only one who could keep pace with my moving around."

He smiled dotingly down at Lilim who rested her head on his shoulders, casting a nervous and somewhat reproachful glance at Mabel.

"Mother, or rather, Mabel;" Cain smiled warmly, "I would like you to meet my wife, Lilim, sister of Thet and daughter of Lilith."

Mabel's mouth dropped open, "mother?" She mouthed soundlessly at the slight woman.

Lilim smiled simply and nodded, "Yes, Lilith is my mother."

She sighed softly and giggled behind her hand as Mabel pointed to her mouth in shock.

Cain frowned, "you really think I would curse my own beautiful wife to be stripped of her voice? Or, rather, you really think Lilith would have allowed me to do that?"

Mabel swallowed nervously. Things had suddenly

shifted in a direction she was uncertain of.
Quietly, she reflected on what she knew of Lilith.
She'd been cast out of Eden for being too
outspoken, and head strong. Slowly, Mabel
pointed to her own mouth.
Cain smiled weakly, "yeah, about that."
He kissed the top of Lilim's head and murmured
in her ear. Lilim stepped closer to Mabel and
without warning, kissed her firmly on the lips.
Mabel tensed and tried to push the woman away,
however for a tiny little thing, Lilim held her close
with an unbreakable grip. Finally, Mabel pushed
her back with a loud grunt of effort.

"What on *EARTH* was that?" She snapped, then
gasped, and held her throat.
Lilim laughed, "a centuries long wait to meet my
mother-in-law and provide her with her voice.
Apologies, it's part of the entry requirements to
Purgatory, I take away the voice of all women to
determine if they are worthy of having it returned.
Mother warned me that there might come a time
where our paths would cross, after she paid a visit
to you all. Cain and I run this realm; you see."
Mabel turned to glance at Cain whose image had

changed to that more befitting a lumberjack.
"Paisley? Really?" Mabel raised a brow.
Cain smiled pleasantly at her and scratched at his
now combed beard and soft curls on his head, "I
had to sell the look;" He shrugged. "Again, I
apologise for the amateur dramatics, but when
Lilim said her mother had paid us a visit,
indicating that we might encounter you or father,
she didn't really elaborate further. Lilim and I
thought it might be worth our time to conduct
ourselves in such a way where we might be able to
get a full picture of what's happened and whoa
momma did you give that to us!" Cain chortled
warmly. "Oh, don't you just love karma m'dear?"
He kissed Lilim sweetly on the lips and looked
softly into her eyes.

"I beg your pardon?" Mabel snapped, confused.
"Karma?"
"Not Karma for you, Mab – if I may?" Lilim
assured her softly; "I hope you don't mind. Cain
and I are joined in mind, body, and soul. What
he sees, thinks, and feels, I do too. I understand
you're more suited to the name Mab than Eve,
these days."

Mabel waved the explanation aside, "fair enough, but who's owed karma?"

"Here come the questions," Cain murmured to Lilim jovially.

Mabel couldn't help but feel that he was enjoying being in charge and knowing more than her. Typical parent and adult child relationship she supposed, begrudgingly.

Cain smiled warmly at her; "apparently, Lilith gleaned from Thet's memories that you question just about everything these days. Honestly, it's wonderful to see, considering how long I knew you to go by life accepting everything anyone told you without querying it," he sighed. "Oh, and the karma is for the saviour. He's been a nightmare neighbour in Limbo for *centuries*. Always being holier than thou with his preaching in Limbo. You can imagine our surprise when Nemesis visited one night, drunk as usual, preening about her union with the Saviour. What did I say, m'dear?" Cain hugged Lilim's shoulders, "karma will come back to bite them both. After all, there's only one reason Nemesis makes a union with anyone."

Mabel swallowed. Nemesis, the renowned sister to Charon – Thet. The mastermind of revenge or justice. If she had teamed up with the Son of God, there was only one thing the two of them would be consorting about and it wouldn't bode well for the whole of mankind.

"I need to get back to my body!" Mabel demanded, "NOW!"

Chapter 28. Reunion

Mabel looked around her. Cain and Lilim had left her to her own mess of thoughts while they tried to find a way to reunite her soul with her physical form. Now that the lights were on around her, what she had assumed was a vast space of nothingness turned out to be a garden. It was a garden unlike anything she had ever seen before, however. The flowers that grew had a look to them that was both exotic and dangerous at once. Black petals with red tips bloomed from stems that were as thick as poles and scattered with thorns so large, she couldn't get close enough to smell the perfumed scents without feeling something stabbing her hand, leg, or throat. In a neatly presented rockery, toadstools and mushrooms of various shapes and sizes flourished proudly. Trees opened their branches wide around her, yet they seemed to be in a perpetual state of Autumn, all with leaves sporting shades of red, ochre, amber and brown. There was no grass beneath her feet, but a fine dust which had a deep orange colour to it.

Amid the turmoil in her own mind, Mabel couldn't help but smile at the surreal beauty of it all.

"It's his pride and joy, you know," Lilim had silently approached her while she'd been busy marvelling at her surroundings. "He never gave up hope that he would one day see you; his father; maybe even Abel – although that ship sailed many millennia ago. So, he worked on creating beauty where originally, there was none."

Mabel frowned, "how come?"

"Well," Lilim stroked at a flower head as though it were a pet cat, reaching its head up to be petted. "Everyone remembers him for the murder of his brother, they seem to forget he was a master at growing things. His gift to the Almighty were shafts of wheat which he had grown from his own farm. I don't know whether you've tried to grow wheat in the desert. It's a phenomenal achievement. When he eventually passed away in life, he learned that he would never be allowed past the gates of Heaven. It had been ordained by the powers that be. So, he assumed if that was to be *his* fate, the fate of his parents would be just as restricted for their original sin. He wanted to create a space where you could all stay together once more, should your paths ever cross. It would be your own paradise away from paradise."

Mabel looked around her once more and felt an ache in her chest. Had she hurt Cain's feelings by suddenly wanting to vanish away from the world he'd created for them all?

As if in answer to her thoughts, Lilim chuckled softly; "I see where he gets it from now."

"I'm not sure I follow," Mabel smiled back.

"Cain's head is always buzzing with questions, theories, conspiracies. I only have to say or ask something, and I can see a trail of thoughts flit across his features before he responds with maybe one or two words," Lilim chuckled. "You both have very expressive faces."

Mabel sighed, "this space is truly beautiful. It's not like any purgatory I'd ever envisioned, if I'd envisioned it at all, while living."

She rubbed at her arms, feeling a phantom chill stroking at them.

"I hope I haven't caused any offence at wanting to leave it so quickly?" There, she'd said it. She needed to know that everything was alright between them all.

Lilim shook her head with a soft laugh, "Mab, you especially, could never do wrong in your son's eyes. Ever! We, that is to say, Cain and I, both know you don't belong here; not right now at least - if you ever will."

"How so?" Mabel frowned.

"Well, for one," Lilim smirked as she watched Mabel continue to rub at her arms. "You feel how cold it is here. You are still connected above, you have not yet died in life, you are only lingering here. We're both terming this as a surprise, sweeping visit."

Mabel considered this and mused on the implications of what her absence might be causing in the waking world. She watched Lilim continue to stroke the heads of the plants. There was no doubt in her mind that Cain had sent his wife out to keep her company, while he focused on only heaven knew what, out of her sight.

Mabel returned to her thoughts. The son of God had teamed with Nemesis. The concept of such a union was beyond her comprehension; if anything, it was a clash of cultures! Mabel couldn't help but marvel at just how close the various religions through the aeons had been to getting it all right! Quietly, she wondered if other religions out there were experiencing just as complicated a circumstance as this. Every faith in the world had its own story of the beginning, it stood to reason that they all had their own questionable personalities who would be up to causing mischief. She smiled inwardly at the thought of Bo and Loki hashing out schemes against Anglo Saxons. Absent mindedly, she sat down and started to doodle in the sand, lost in thought.

"I recognise him," Lilim's voice cut through Mabel's thoughts, her tone one of concern. Mabel looked down and realised she had drawn the branding of Asmodeus into the sand, she frowned. Why had she done that? She'd not been thinking of Asmodeus.

"And *him*!" Lilim hurried across to the other sketch in the ground that Mabel had done of Thet.

The two women frowned at each other. How long had Mabel been sat there, drawing? She was surrounded by a host of sand art. Cain approached his wife and looked down.

"Drawing in the sand, my love?" He kissed her cheek, affectionately.

"No. Your mother, or rather, Mab has;" Lilim wrapped her arm around his waist. "There's something unsettling about it all though."

"In what way?" Mabel asked. She was surprised to see Helga's face looking balefully up at her through the sand. When she turned to her side, there was Kristoph's look of worry; ahead of her, Eric's nervous expressive eyes. She could even make out the vague trace of the rest of the Dark Omen's band members.

Cain laughed loudly, "they're calling for you. You see them in your mind's eye;" he rested his hand on Mabel's shoulder. "We just need to get you back there somehow..." his voice trailed off as his eyes rested on a portrait of someone Mabel didn't recognise.

"Cain, my love?" Lilim's voice was laced with concern, "what's wrong?"

Cain silently pointed at the portrait and Lilim glanced down and gasped, "I'm sure there's a reasonable explanation."

Cain's body had tensed, and his eyes burnt with a fury that Mabel had only seen once before when Kristoph had worked out Pan's vile actions in Hamelin.

"I don't understand, who is he? I've never seen him before," Mabel struggled to hide the nervousness from her voice as she stared at the cunning eyes that leered up at her from the sand.

"Lucifer," Cain clenched his jaw, angrily. "As if he hasn't caused enough problems for our family!"

Before anyone could say anything more, the air around them grew thick. The ground started to rumble. Mabel wondered if there was an earthquake happening, could that happen on another plain of existence? Without warning, the sand by their feet started to sink into a cavernous hole. With a cry, Cain grabbed both Lilim and Mabel around the waist and lifted them up, skirting backward to avoid their all sliding down into the sink hole that had greedily devoured the portraits. Protectively, he pushed the two women behind his back and readied his fists as a mix of coughing, spluttering, and complaining echoed upward from the hole. Finally, a series of hands scrabbled for grip over the lip of the gap.

"Whose bright idea was this?" Spluttered a familiar Welsh accent, as Eric's heavily tattooed arm waved frantically in the air before finding purchase on one of the thorned plants; "ARGH! Ooo, you little bugger! Whoa, watch it Kris, there's something with knives up there!"
"Dear Stable boy," came Asmodeus's drawl; "there are no knives in Purgatory, unless you count Lilim's sharp wit as one? Takes after her mother of course;" he grumbled unhappily from somewhere in the darkness below.
"Remind me again Thet," Kristoph's voice was laboured as his branded arm reached up and sank into the soft ground, desperately searching

for something sturdy to hold on to; "why you thought Mab would be in Purgatory?"

"Because," Thet's voice sighed heavily as he gracefully rose up out of the ground as if he were being carried by invisible wings, and stepped on to the sand and smiled with a look of relief at Mabel; "I knew I would hear her from the Hall of Unlived Opportunities, smashing valuable frames, if she were dead. The only other place *they* would have sent her, would be here."

In just a couple of long strides, Thet stood before Cain with an outstretched hand.

"Cain," Thet bowed his head and shook the man's hand. "I assure you we mean none of you any harm. All I ask is this... please could I give your mother, a hug?"

Cain mouthed wordlessly as Mabel squealed excitedly and rushed at Thet, hugging him tightly; she'd never been happier to see her old chaperone! She beamed as she loosened her hands from around his waist and looked into his dark eyes which had never glowed warmer. Thet smiled softly back, loosening his hold around her before gesturing behind him, "I think there's some folk back there who want to see you too," he smirked.

Without hesitation, Mabel offered a brief apologetic look to Cain and hurried over to help Kristoph, Eric and the rest of the Dark Omen's members. It wasn't long until everyone was brushing sand from their bodies and the gaping chasm that had opened up for them, had sealed itself closed. Kristoph and Mabel held each other closely, not daring to let the other go. Mabel couldn't believe how much she'd missed him in so short a space of time. Feeling her cold arms, Kristoph wrapped the robe that Thet had conjured up for him in the shadow realm, around them both and stroked her hair.

"It's so good to see you on your feet again," he glowed.

"Easy lover boy," Asmodeus gently teased; "she's not completely back to rights after all."

"No thanks to you," Kristoph's tone changed maliciously, as he snapped at the giant of a man who's back was hunched over Cain's flower bed. "If it weren't for you, Mab wouldn't be stuck here with... with..." something in Kristoph's demeanour changed completely as he caught a glimpse of Cain and Lilim talking to Thet. His arms instinctively reached out and he stumbled forward with an involuntary gasp, and he clutched at his chest.

"Kris? KRIS?!" Eric and the rest of the band members lunged forward.

"what's happening mate?" Eric asked cautiously.

"S-s-son?" Kristoph managed to croak; his eyes glazed over as he stared unblinkingly at Cain. Cain turned his attention toward the sound and numbly pushed Thet aside, before rushing toward Mabel and Kristoph, who were hunched on the ground. The three of them embraced tightly, finally reunited after an endless age of years apart.

"Well, isn't this all so delightful," Lucifer wrinkled his nose at the scene. "Mama, papa! It's me, y'boy, Caine, the bane!" He snorted in a falsetto voice.

"Just because you never had a father who loved you completely," Lilim snapped, venomously. Lucifer glowered at Lilim and fell silent.

"I see, and how are your family ties dear Lilim?"

He growled, menacingly. "How's your mother doing these days?"

"Missing," Thet and Asmodeus cut in together. Lilim's eyes widened in shock, while Lucifer simply raised a questioning brow, "abandoning her children again, I see?" he sighed, in mock frustration.

The hue of Thet's eyes turned a menacingly cool blue and with forced calm, he explained all that Eris had shared with him about Lilith's absence, and Asmodeus's hopeful intent to reunite Adam and Eve to prevent the rapture. Finally, he hissed viciously at Lucifer.

"And now, it appears as though the son of *your* father, Lucifer, is collaborating and unionising with my other sister Nemesis. Resulting in even the Prince of Hell being hoodwinked by the offspring of Lilith and Samael!" By the time he'd finished, even Lucifer couldn't hide his concern.

The silence that followed Thet's deluge of information was stifling. As Mabel worked on processing the information, a thought gnawed at the back of her mind. It chowed down relentlessly until she built up the confidence to break the silence. "Samael?" She asked, hesitantly.

"Yes, my father," Thet nodded; "Lilim's stepfather."

"Your actual father being?" Kristoph cautiously asked, already anticipating the answer.

"Me," Lucifer grinned. "Hello, daddy."

"Eugh," Kristopher groaned. "All the women in the world Cain..."

"Leave him alone," Mabel chastised; "Lilim is wonderful, and I couldn't be happier for them... " She shook her head at Kristoph's reproachful look, then turned her attention to the rest of the Dark Omens band members.

Mabel had been surprised to see Jésús, Pete and Adrian emerge from the cavernous hole into Purgatory too, but she couldn't help but feel a sense of relief at the thought that she, Kristoph and Eric would no longer have to disguise any afterlife matters as unique personal quirks. Mabel composed herself and returned her eye contact with Thet, "so, your father, Samael. What's his role, remind me?"

Thet cleared his throat awkwardly, "well, he's the

Angel of Death. Much of my kin and I chaperone, while he issues the orders and determines the life span of each human out there. He can make it as long or as short as he pleases. Why?"

Mabel mused, "does he have a steed?"

"A what?" Thet blinked, perplexed.

"A steed," Kristoph snapped his fingers as he clocked on to Mabel's thoughts, "as in the four horsemen?"

Thet groaned and pinched the bridge of his nose, "the four horsemen were a concept. They don't exist, physically!"

"Funny," Mabel smirked, "barely half a year ago, I would have said the same about you, Asmodeus, Lucifer, and Lilith! Now look, I'm surrounded by you all!"

"What are you trying to say, Eve?" Lucifer yawned, stretching out his long limbs in the sand; "I do have places to be you know."

Mabel glared at the Prince of Hell, "really? Where have you been all this time? I remember what Asmodeus said to Lilith, things have been awfully quiet down south, apparently."

Lucifer grimaced and shuffled his feet uncharacteristically awkwardly and mumbled something under his breath.

"Sorry?" Mabel scorned, "I didn't quite catch that!"

"I was trapped inside Valentine's husk, okay? The little bugger charmed and ensnared me and well, I was *bored* in Hell, okay? Happy?" Lucifer thundered.

Mabel smiled wickedly at him, "I see. So, it was you who tried to kill me. It was you, who branded Kris. In your *boredom* you have caused no end of pain and suffering to us all, resulting in Cain's torment here. Kris and I will *NEVER* be able to find peace after death, all because of *YOU.* And you ask if I'm "happy" that you've confessed to being bored in Hell?" Before anyone could stop, she stormed over to Lucifer and slapped him so hard across the face, the sound echoed around the vast expanse of the garden around them.

Everyone stared in shock at the duo as they stared each other down. Lucifer's dark and malicious eyes were wide as he delicately touched the side of his snow-white face that now sported a bright pink handprint. Slowly, he stood up straight and tall, leering over Mabel's petite frame. Mabel was livid however and refused to back down. Instead, she rested her hands on her hips and stared defiantly back at the ruler of Hell. Kristoph and Cain hastily got to their feet and made a move to hurry toward her, but Lucifer raised his hand and the sand around their feet gripped them tightly in place. Slowly, calmly, and not leaving eye contact with the woman in front of him, he offered her his hand.

"Truce, Mab?" He asked simply.

Mabel smirked, confidently and held the Devil's hand firmly in her own and shook it, one singular time; "on one proviso," she hissed, refusing to let go of the bear paw sized palm she was holding. "You help us to clear up this mess and play your role to perfection!"

"Um, I'm sorry..." Asmodeus cleared his throat and hurried over to be by his master's side, "role?"

Mabel grinned impishly, "yes, role. It strikes me, much needed maternal words of wisdom, are lacking both in heaven and hell. The little sunspot needs to be reprimanded by his parents. Seeing as his dad isn't all too active these days, and I don't doubt Mary is condemned to an afterlife of being a mute, I think Lilith could provide the rebellious son with the mother of all hidings; don't you? If nothing else, I reckon she'd certainly put Nemesis back in her place too, if we're lucky."

Mabel looked around the collection of perplexed faces on the men in her life and sighed; "I propose that someone break into heaven and free Lillith, while you fine gents provide an apocalyptic distraction. Besides, who's to say the four horsemen don't exist? No one ever thought a union between the Son of God and Nemesis would be a thing, yet here we are. Lucifer is the king of Hell and is renowned for waging war against the heavenly host. Asmo, you've proven you have the chops to act, and let's face it – you're all about conquests. Thet's father Samael will no doubt want to aid Lilith, so he will play his role as the angel of Death."

"That's three," Lucifer smiled, dangerously; "who'll be the fourth of this quartet?"

"I will," Cain snapped. "I grew produce while living. Purgatory is not a realm that promotes healthy growth in plants, I will represent famine."

"Delightful," Lucifer tilted his head. "Now you, dear Eve, what will your role be in all of this?"

Mabel grinned, "well, I'm going to seek some divine intervention with Azrael, with the aid of Thet, of course. I aim to head up top, finally; and find Lilith."

Turning her head slowly to Asmodeus, she smirked, "genius, really."

"Well, this is all very well and good," Asmodeus scoffed. "I don't know whether you've taken into consideration how colossal the four of us will be in our true form, little Mabby-boo. Where on earth do you think we will find four steeds powerful enough to carry us into battle with the saviour's host of minions?"

Slowly, Mabel let go of Lucifer's hand and turned sheepishly to look at the Dark Omens members who froze in shock and stared at her wide eyed.

Eric shook his head, "no! They can't transform us! It's not in their, you know... spell book repertoire... is it?"

Asmodeus's cackle rang around them, gleefully, for the first time since arriving in Purgatory, "looks like I get to ride you after all, Stable-Boy!"

Chapter 29. Plotting & Scheming

"I am not being turned into a horse! Mab, please, don't encourage this," Adrian whined for the umpteenth time.

It wasn't exactly an ideal situation, Mabel had to agree, but Asmodeus had a point. Up until now, she had only ever seen Thet, Asmodeus and their brethren in relatively tame and shrunken down versions of their true forms. These were other-worldly beings, though! They had been conjured into being in order to terrify and to inspire awe. It stood to reason that there would be no standard steed in the living world that would come close to accommodating such beings on their backs.

"I'm sorry Adrian, but I don't see any other way," she chewed at her lip. "These are deities, angels, and demons. They simply do not ride into battle on regular horseback."

"Hold on now, Ade. Let's think about this for a moment," Pete mused quietly, stunning everyone.

"You've been complaining for weeks now that your well of inspiration has run dry. Since Mab and Kris teamed up with these guys, mate, you've created a hit record while serenading a hoard of Vikings!"

"Who happened to be bludgeoning a bunch of Saxons to death," Adrian sulked.

Pete waved away the comment and continued. "Minor details. Look, you've got to admit, the energy of the group has rocketed from feeling stuck in a rut to feeling emboldened in a very short space of time. We've all noticed it in some way. If we truly work out the dates, it's a no-brainer that this surge of good vibes stem from their interaction. We've always looked out for each other, haven't we?" Pete looked around at the assembled band members.

Eric and Kristoph glanced suspiciously at Asmodeus who held up his hands innocently, "don't look at me laddies, this one's all on the Aussie!"

Pete snorted, "Kris, remember your stage fright? Ade, Hey-hey, Eric and even you were unsure if it would be better for your health, if you went your own way! I mean, sure, Valentine-or Lucifer here, screwed you over, but with Asmodeus's help you come to life on the stage mate!"

"Not to mention in the bedroom," Asmodeus winked impishly at Mabel, who rolled her eyes.

"All I'm trying to say is," Pete sighed. "We owe these guys, Thet and Asmodeus at least."

"Charming," Lucifer scoffed bitterly.

"And well, if nothing else... we've got the hair for it" Pete grinned weakly, as he ruffled his matted mess of shoulder length, hair. The few dark blonde dreadlock tangles he had, flopped messily in with the rest of his crop.

Adrian groaned, "*fine!* Fine. I'll do it. What's to say we won't just be normal sized steeds though?"

"You won't," Thet smiled. "Your heights, added to a standard height of a full-grown stallion, I reckon it should work out to a suitable size."

With the horse debate settled, Mabel returned to mithering on the finer details of her scheme. Kristoph knew better than to interrupt her trail of thought when he saw her brow furrow in deep concentration. Instead, he looked over at Cain, barely comprehending that the man standing before them was not only a religious icon on multiple negative grounds, but also his own son from a life so far removed from his current role. Aside from their embrace, Cain had barely said a word to him, and Kristoph couldn't help but wonder if he was a disappointment in the man's eyes.

How long had he been in purgatory now? Surely Cain, like any child separated from their family for so long, would have developed an idealised imagining of what a family reunion would be like. Kristoph considered all the various lifetimes he'd led. Some he recalled; others were barely more than a long-forgotten dream. He'd all but forgotten what it had been like to be Adam, only the paternal instinct seemed to have lingered and that had only shown itself when he'd first seen Cain. In contrast, Cain had spent all this time with only his wife for company, no children of his own to entertain. Only his garden and a host of memories stemming back to a time that no one outside of the minds of other-worldly beings and deities could recall, to keep his mind occupied. What a lonely life! Kristoph couldn't help but think that he and Mabel had gotten off lightly in comparison to the man who was more of a stranger than a son to him now.

Eric's impatient voice interrupted Kristoph's thoughts as with a loud groan, the rhythm guitarist turned to Mabel.
"So, what's the ultimate plan here?" Eric asked, "I'm still in the dark, Mab."
Mabel cleared her throat and cautiously addressed the idea she'd been hashing out in her mind.
"Well, Nemesis and Mr. Holier than Thou are in cahoots, yes? They want to bring fire and brimstone down on humanity," she looked hesitantly at Thet, hoping he'd lessen the horrific imagery that kept filling her mind. Thet however, casually nodded in agreement and didn't say a word. So comforting, Mabel thought to herself, drearily.
"I propose we hoodwink the daring duo, but it is going to be a group effort and I'm unsure if we can even pull it all off." Slowly, she turned to Thet and smiled nervously; "Thet, can you create a pocket world within our waking life, full of

empty human husks? Like a sandbox world? One where, if there are any casualties, it's going to be us or them; no innocents?"

"Or, y'know, just them," Adrian interjected, hurriedly. The lead singer quickly shut his mouth and looked ashamedly at his shoes, as the rest of his band members cast stern glances his way.

Thet pondered on the idea for a while, "I suppose a pocket world could be done. I can't create life though Mab. I use pre-made husks, so to speak, from those who have just departed; and I've been somewhat off duty, recently." He bobbed his knees anxiously in the same way he had when they'd first met. Mabel couldn't help but smile, despite the setback. Disappointedly however, her shoulders sagged. She couldn't afford to risk the lives of an entire populace on her plan, far too many would be at risk, and it just didn't seem fair.

"If I might interject?" Kristoph's voice piped up quietly, from Mabel's side. "I have an idea?" The whole group turned expectantly toward him and, without Asmodeus's overly confident energy surging through him, Kristoph felt the familiar nauseating sting of stage fright twist in his gut. Swallowing his nerves he offered, "what about the mullions of souls in Limbo? Pardon the phrasing, but we could kill a few birds with one stone here. Instead of husks, Thet, do what you did with Bo and the Saxons, but to the entirety of Limbo!"

"Yes Kris!" Mabel breathed, marvelling at him. "Fill the sandbox world with the populace of Limbo, maybe ensure they are dressed to more modern-day standards to avoid suspicion? That way, should they find themselves on the wrong end of the powers that be, they can finally move on!"

Thet nodded, "that I *can* do," he grinned broadly, "a Limbo away from Limbo. Now then, where do the apocalyptic horse riders come into this scheme?"

Mabel grimaced, "I want to be wrong in my assumptions, I *really* do. However," she sighed helplessly. "To wipe out the entirety of the human race, even by the Son of God's standards, that's going to take some doing. I can't help but think he's gained sympathisers. We know of Nemesis, however, there could be a small host of followers rallying behind him. We need to match fire with fire, so to speak. Meet him and his army face to face, hinder their movements. Draw them out somehow. I propose our acting horsemen of the apocalypse serve as distractions while I go hunting for Lilith. We just need their attention drawn elsewhere, so that all eyes are on what's happening in the sandbox world; and not on me, one of heaven's most wanted, scurrying around the lesser-known areas of Heaven."

Jésús snorted, "I like the idea Mab, but I think you've overlooked a slight um, how do you say? *Kink*? In your plan."

Mabel turned slowly to face the bass player who was smiling so sweetly and warmly at her, that she couldn't help but feel a pang of regret that he would be transformed into a horse and charge headlong in to battle in just a short space of time.

"What's that Hey-hey, I mean, Jésús?" She asked, nervously, Pete's nickname was surprisingly catchy.

"Well, don't you have to die, to enter heaven?" Jésús's voice was barely a whisper, as he allowed his worry to seep into his voice.

Mabel nodded slowly, "I'd hoped you would overlook that," she sighed.

Swallowing hard, Mabel turned to Kristoph, "I need to find Lilith, and I think the only way to do that would be if I were to..." She looked around at the assembled members of Dark Omens who were all looking mortified at what she was proposing. "I mean, I'm in Purgatory, I'm half-way there anyway. The only thing keeping me connected to life are a few pipes and strong medicine."

"NO!" Eric and Kristoph yelled in unison, before she could finish her sentence.

"I'm not having any of that talk," Eric shook his head defiantly.

"Agreed," Kristoph grumbled, angrily. "I am not on board with *any* of this, unless you can ensure that no one here, snuffs it!" The two men folded their arms, stubbornly and glowered at her.

Mabel sighed, "Kris! Look, I have been dead for some time now, so have *you*. It's just a simple clause or rule that determines my soul continues to be reincarnated. Kris, once I'm gone, no one will remember me. Eric, you won't have to worry about the pain or grief that stems from losing a *normal* person in your life. Kris, you can continue playing in the band without me; you more than anyone here knows that I'm just a spirit, passing by in your lives."

Eric snorted derisively, "don't care. I'm not joining in with this plan unless one of *them...*" he jabbed his finger angrily at Thet and Asmodeus, "can guarantee the safety of you."

Mabel sighed heavily, so much for that idea. She loved Eric dearly, but the Welshman was being as uncooperative as a toddler in a toy shop. Desperately, she looked at Thet and Asmodeus for assistance, but they were both discussing matters so quietly with their heads close together that she didn't think they'd taken on board any of the man's frustrations.

She looked around at the peacefulness of Cain's Garden. At the very least, if she passed away, she would be able to spend her time here. Cautiously, she looked up into Kristoph's eyes. They looked so sad and full of pain at the thought of her leaving her life behind. She hated that her plan risked losing everyone and everything she loved and those who loved her in return. The Dark Omen's group drew closer to Eric and folded their arms, mimicking his stance.

"If you're insistent on doing this Mab, I won't let you do it alone," Kristoph sighed, heavily. Slowly he turned to his fellow band members.
"Come on guys, you'd find another guitarist, a better one! There are hundreds of them out there!" He reasoned.
"Only one Kris though!" Adrian sniffed, as he shrugged away Kristoph's assurances.
"Kris," Mabel whispered softly, "maybe you should listen to them. You don't have to join me, I can do this alone!"
"Nope," Eric shook his head, aggressively. "Don't play the martyr Mab, you're just as valuable to us as Kris is."
"But," Mabel felt like pulling her hair out. "I'm just the set manager! I play no key part in your lives other than painting and erecting a backdrop and..."
"Being a wonderful and nurturing person in our lives," Jésus finished her sentence. "The world might end for mankind if Nemesis and God's son

wins. The world will end for *us* if we lose you and/or Kris."

"Oh please! Someone pass me the spew bucket," Lucifer demanded.

The Prince of Hell's baritone voice dripped with displeasure as he looked down his nose at the band and Mabel. Up until his sarcastic moan, he'd been sat to the side surveying the actions of those around him with mounting displeasure. Even Hell was more excitable than this plotting and scheming malarky. Impatiently, he started to kick at the sand in the ground, creating dust clouds that irritated everyone's eyes.

"Luci, enough!" Thet snapped. "Asmodeus and I have an idea, of sorts. It's risky, but if we pull it off, there's every chance Mab and Kris will live to see another day. It just means that Kris at least, will need to enter a similar state, physically, as Mab."

"Comatose?" Kristoph shuddered, "how do you propose I do that?" he asked, with a voice laced with concern as he eyed Asmodeus's wicked smile spreading widely across his face.

"Leave that to me, my little moon beam," The

demon purred.

Thet shook his head and rubbed his temples, "Mab is neither here, nor there. We are all addressing her spirit right now. Her physical body is wired up to machinery in the waking world, however she is being protected by two heavenly beings. One is a host; the other is a lost, found, then purposefully lost again, soul. It's going to take some convincing on their part, but I propose Mab and Kris, as spirits, request that they serve as your vessels and take you to heaven!"

"Wouldn't that leave our physical bodies open to the forces of good *and* evil?" Kristoph frowned, it was difficult for him to determine who was truly a figure of good or bad right now.

Thet nodded, "it would, if it weren't for the fact that I will be staying behind to protect you both from any threat. I might not be able to hold everyone off forever, but I can certainly stall them. Which means, you both need to be quick with your task at hand."

Mabel chewed at the inside of her cheek, "can a spirit possess a spirit?"

Thet shook his head, "it's not a common

practice, but angels can certainly serve as vessels to those they deem worthy. Lost souls on the other hand, well, I believe they can offer a cloak of sorts. Consider it an aura like fog. Most angels will see right through it, but I'm inclined to believe that the vast majority of the hoard above will be paying close attention to what their department manager is up to" He smiled, faintly. "We're basing this plan on a lot of assumptions, but I struggle to imagine a version of this where there isn't a huge risk factor at play. We are all going to be putting our lives on the line to save humanity and mankind."

The idea Thet and Asmodeus had briefly mashed together seemed to soothe some of the concerns expressed by the Dark Omen's members and, after what seemed like an eternity, the conversation finally turned around to who would offer their back as a steed to which rider. Asmodeus draped his arm lazily over a very uncomfortable looking Eric before anyone else could say otherwise. Mabel could only look apologetically at her friend who offered a weak smile of acceptance in response. Cain cautiously extended his hand in friendship to Pete, who nervously accepted it. There was very little difference in height between the two in this realm, however, Mabel had felt the energy Cain had exuded when she'd entered his world and knew he would be able to stand his own ground in a battle against a hoard of divine and damned beings. Finally, Lucifer eyed up Adrian and Jésús as though he were at an all you can eat buffet. Tauntingly, he circled the two men, enjoying each flinch and recoil they made as he drew close to them. Finally, he cupped Jésús's chin firmly in his hand.

"Silky black hair smelling of roses, handsome, delightfully sculpted frame, and pert buttocks. Not to mention a name that mimics our foe's. What better steed for the Prince of Darkness" He preened.

Adrian breathed out a long sigh of relief, but one glance from Thet caused him to tense up.

"That leaves you, Ade, as the steed for my father – Samael" Thet mused.

"If we can get the angel on board, that is," Asmodeus folded his arms. "No offence Thet, but your father isn't exactly the most engaging member of our order of beings."

"In what way?" Adrian croaked, weakly.

"In that he's boring!" Lucifer yawned. "In his defence, I tolerate his presence in my realm once in a while, as he is more accommodating of our more questionable mannerisms in Hell, and he's Lilith's beloved; but my goodness is he a bore!" Lucifer flourished his hand dramatically and in a pompous voice started to mock the angel of Death, "Tis I, Samael, purveyor of the dearly departed. The author of your last rites. The father of your chaperone. Mine is a tortured soul, torn between good and evil...".

"We get the idea," Thet clenched his jaw. "He's also my father and as such, I will not tolerate you taking the proverbial piss out of him."

"Well, you have some balls for a reaper," Lucifer grinned. "Thet, the reaper who doesn't play by the rules set by his father and adhered to by his siblings. The reaper who has a God-complex. Yes, I've heard your parents discussing your antics. Tell me, do you *yearn* to be human, like them? Experience relations? Have a family of your own? I'm sure I could make it happen you know. Just say the word and you could be a real boy, no strings to hold you up. Or are you happy to play God and toy with their lives, like my father?" Lucifer's mockery had such an acidic sting that even Thet seemed somewhat taken aback by the taunting.

Eric cleared his throat, and the two figures broke their thunderous eye contact and cast a sideways glance at the rhythm guitarist.

"I'm just throwing this out there," the Welshman rippled his shoulders.

"Eric, shut up," Pete murmured into his friend's ear.

"I don't tolerate anyone I like being bullied," Eric snapped. "I'm more inclined to believe in and worship a God like Thet, then a devil like you." He held his head high as everyone around him stared, gobsmacked.

"You allowed yourself to be used, abused, and trapped in a tiny runt of a man. I tackled that same runt, Valentine, to the ground after he branded Kris. Thet pulled you out of the bugger, by just saying your name. It strikes me, you're not

as almighty as you like to think. You're just a
spoilt little brat, who clamoured for his father's
attention and affection. The cast away, chucked
on the dog heap like the rest of your fellow
demons."

"Eric," Kristoph hissed, as Lucifer's eyes blazed
dangerously.

"No, enough. He calls himself a Prince, he's not
even a King in his own domain!" Eric shouted,
gesturing flippantly to the now raging Lucifer.
"Tell you what, I'll start respecting you more
when you start by following the rules you set out
for your *own* followers!"

Lucifer's raging force stalled in his slow advance,
and he blinked curiously, "I have rules?"

"Your followers do," Eric nodded. He turned
accusingly to Asmodeus, "as a duke of Hell, it
never fails to amaze me, how little *you* adhere to
these same rules too. You know, they say never
meet your idols or heroes. I see why now. Unlike
the rest of these guys, I've followed the Satanic
practices for so long now, and I've got to say, I'm
disappointed. I tell you, it's no wonder there are
so many stuck in Limbo when the goalposts to

Heaven are being moved and the rules and regulations of Hell aren't even adhered to by their leadership!"

Chapter 30. Father & Son

As Eric addressed the laws of the Satanic religion to its founder, Thet gestured to Asmodeus, Kristoph, and Mabel. While the rest of their party seemed to be hanging on to the Welshman's every word, the four of them slipped away to a more secluded space where an outcrop of evergreen trees filled their senses with the homely smell of pine. The collection of fallen pine needles at their feet carpeted the sandy earth, muting their footsteps from the soft crunch. Once again, Mabel found herself marvelling at the beauty and serenity in Cain's garden.

Thet smiled at both Mabel and Kristoph and spread his arms wide.
"I thought I would call you all aside as we need to determine how to get Kris to enter into a spiritual state," he hastily whispered.
Asmodeus chuckled, excitedly, "ah yes, would you like me to do that now?"
Mabel and Kristoph exchanged a nervous look, "how?" They asked, cautiously.

"Like this," Asmodeus said, and taking a swift step toward Kristoph, he lashed out and delivered the most intense right hook to the right temple of the man's head.

Mabel yelped and covered her mouth, as Kristoph's body fell limply into Thet's outstretched arms. Mabel watched on in horror, as her lover's physical body slipped gracefully through Thet's grip and sank into the ground, out of sight; leaving behind his unconscious spirit, draped like a large ragdoll across the reaper's arms.

"You killed him!" Mabel squeaked accusingly at Asmodeus, "you killed Kris!"

Asmodeus scoffed as he wrung his right hand, wincing "nonsense. It would take more than *the Duke of Hell's upper-cut* to kill your little sweetheart."

Mabel stared at the demon in disgust, "the Duke of Hell's uppercut?" She asked.

"Before Kristle here, I had a brief stint inside a wrestler," the Demon sighed. "No where near as snug as your beloved's slender frame. Ah, he was lavishly roomy, yet as dainty and gentle as they come. Weakest handshake I've ever had," he shuddered. "He made a deal with me and next thing he knew, he had the finisher *the Duke of Hell's upper cut.* He climbed to fame, only for his life to be cut short during a DIY job with his home's electrics. In my defence, I did warn him that live electrics and wet, sweaty hands would never end well. Long story short, he saw a flash of light, and I found myself thrown back into my Dukedom – rather unceremoniously, I might add," Asmodeus sniffed, disapprovingly.

Thet snickered, "I remember Tony 'the demon' Jonson, he did have a rather limp handshake, didn't he? Even gave me the heebie-jeebies," he wiggled his slender fingers under Kristoph's prone soul, as if trying to rid them of the ghostly touch of the deceased wrestler's weak grip.

"Anyway," Thet rippled his shoulders. "Asmo' if you could, I believe you still have some life essence?"

"Just enough for half a day's worth of reimagined life," the demon grinned, as he pulled the same pouch he'd presented to Helga, out from under his robe.

The fabric of the bag was impossibly black. Mabel stared at it, puzzled. All around her was darkness, yet even in Purgatory there was light, albeit dim. The pouch that Asmodeus held seemed to ignore this point, however. It was like a black void was dangling on the end of a silken pull string. As Mabel watched on, Asmodeus weighed the bag in his hand, and made a show of calculating the weight of its contents before he upturned the entirety of the fine powder over Kristoph's soul. The effect was not unlike watching cast offs from brushed away golden leaf, scattering, and floating through the air.

Within moments, Kristoph's soul was upright and patting itself down.
"I don't think I'll ever get used to being in this state," Kristoph murmured, disconcertedly. "I want to breath, I feel like I need to breath, and yet my form is telling me 'nah, it's cool'."
"All things considered," Mabel mused; "I've got to say, that one's at the top of my list too."
Thet smiled warmly at them both and shook his head, "I don't think I will ever get tired of the adorable pat downs you humans give yourselves

whenever I give your souls a sense of form."
Asmodeus nodded, "mmm, it is rather endearing,
isn't it? I particularly love the range of
expressions. Wonder, euphoria, betrayal,
confusion, denial;" the demon duke looked
wistfully off into space.
"That escalated," Mabel frowned.
"Well," Asmodeus shrugged, "the betrayal sets in
when they see me or one of my kin loping over to
say 'heyo, tar muchly m'lord, I'll take it from
here!'"

Kristoph rolled his eyes, "okay, we don't have
that much time. How are you going to transform
the guys over there? Also, what's happened to my
body, exactly?"
"Ah, yes;" Thet jumped as if stung by a bee and
grabbed Mabel and Kristoph's ethereal arms.
Hastily, he dragged them over to the rest of the
assembled group.
"Now then Luci, you know what to do; out of all
of us, your powers of transformation are
unparalleled," Thet explained in a hurry.
Lucifer smirked coldly and stared long and hard
at Thet, "yes, well – as much as I would *love* to

get the proverbial ball rolling, I think we're overlooking a crucial matter here."

"Yes?" Thet asked, impatiently.

"We're a rider down. How do you think your dearest papa is going to handle this little arrangement?" Lucifer smiled smugly at Thet and the tension around the group grew so chilled that even Cain found himself rubbing his arms, uncomfortably.

"You really think I wouldn't inform him?" Thet growled, between his teeth.

"Forgive me reaper, I fail to see how you could have passed on the memo to daddy dearest that he's to saddle up and be ready for battle," Lucifer's face was ecstatic, his tone full of gloat.

The Devil's features suddenly turned sour however, as his gaze drifted to a point over Thet's shoulder.

"Dear Father,

While I appreciate this might be somewhat uncouth, could you perhaps meet me and a few of my comrades in Purgatory? Please bring your horse-riding gear, Fate's Shard –

aka your sword, and this body with you. All will be made clear when you get here.
Hope you are well.
Reaper Thirteen, Thanatoscharonanubis Erebusyamabaldr Tartarus (aka Thet)

P.s. I found Lucifer.
P.P.S. I have news of mother.
P.P.P.S. The body is the reincarnation of Adam, yes, *that* Adam. Treat with care."

The dulcet, dry, and unimpressed tone sent chills through everyone gathered. Slowly and deliberately, the assembled group turned to face the owner of the voice. Mabel's jaw dropped. With a wingspan that glistened in the dim light and trailed silently behind him, the figure gliding gracefully toward them, with a look of ill-disguised fury, was of a phenomenal stature. Draped unceremoniously over his left shoulder, was the pale and almost lifeless form of Kristoph. Over his right shoulder was an elegant and beautifully crafted saddle and reigns. Around his waist and across his torso were the straps to a sheath which accommodated a great sword, the pommel of which rested against Kristoph's body. In his hand, he held a phantomized note that shimmered and shone.

"Thet," Mabel whispered, "is that..."
"You will no longer address Reaper Thirteen as Thet. You will no longer address him as anything other than your chaperone, human girl!" The figure snapped.
"Father, please..." Thet rested his hand on Mabel's shoulder.
"Don't. You. *Dare*. Father, please... Me!" The figure fumed. "I have been hunting high and low for your mother ever since she went in search of *you*! And now," the figure's furious stare rolled over to Lucifer, who for once looked unnerved. "I find you in Purgatory, coercing with the ghosts of the condemned? *Humans*? Spirits? Angels? And *you,* Lucifer. The Prince of Darkness who has allowed his own thrown to grow dusty and cold in the bowels of Hell."
"Please, sir..." Mabel's voice was barely a squeak in comparison to the thunderous tone of the figure who, now he was near them, towered over even Lucifer!

The figure looked down at her and his eyes burnt with a ferocity that made her ethereal legs shake, nervously.

"You dare to address me?" He scoffed, "one so puny, should not step above their station. Something *you* have been lectured about on multiple occasions Reaper Thirteen," He glowered venomously at Thet.

Thet sighed and the sound echoed around the expanse of space around them.

He looked at his father, unimpressed and held out his hands, "can I have the body back please? If this is just going to turn into another argument, I'd rather just rehash plans with my friends here and you can carry on *searching* for mother, if that *is* what you've been doing."

"You forget your place, *Reaper Thirteen*. You have gone against the code of our realm, time and time again. This time you have gone *too* far! You have played GOD with these people. Coercing with the *Devil*? Now you're in cahoots with Cain, the *murderous* sinner? I have *never* been more disappointed to call you, my spawn!" The figure spat.

Mabel watched heartbroken as Thet's shoulders slumped, dejectedly. Even though she knew these deities were aeons old, it never failed to surprise her just how human and infantile they could be in turn. Sure, Thet wasn't perfect, but who was? As far as she was concerned, there was no need for this figure, regardless of his paternal status, to speak to Thet in such a way.

Surprising herself, Mabel quietly seethed; "your son has moved mountains to help the helpless! He has gone against everything he stands for, to help humanity. He has been a staunch aid, companion, friend and confident and the *best* chaperone I have ever encountered. He has defended me, protected me, dared to defy those more powerful, in order to ensure the best for the lives of those who have entrusted their souls with him. He has conducted himself with a professionalism that is *sorely* lacking from *ANYONE* I have encountered so far in this after-life. He calls you *father.* He addresses you with the role you were assigned when you sired him. You address him as spawn, you give him a codename as opposed to a unique, singular name;" Mabel could feel the eyes of her friends boring into her back. She could see the rage bursting from the angel before her; but she didn't care. He could vaporize her to dust if he wanted to, she was not going to tolerate the sight of Thet be bullied by his father, in front of her.

"If *anyone* in this other realm has forgotten how to address someone properly here, it is the likes of Lucifer and *YOU!*" She spat out viciously, "this figure, this deity, this man," hastily, she gripped Thet's hand tightly; "is my friend. He is the closest I have had to a true and meaningful friendship in any life I have ever lived and by all accounts, I've lived a lot of them. So, Samael, angel of Death, husband of Lilith; I ask you now to set aside your superfluous anger and listen to the reasoning that comes from his mouth and for all that is holy! Address your *SON* by his preferred name, THET!"

While the ground was covered in the sands of time, one could have heard a pin drop as Samael stared angrily down at Mabel. He glared at Thet who stared up at his father; the Angel of Death was still hovering just above the gathering of demons and humans.

The subtle movement of Thet stroking Mabel's hand comfortingly offered Samael pause for thought. He looked hard into the girl's eyes and saw not just tears of rage, but passion and protection too. Despite himself, a small smile kissed the corner of Samael's mouth and slowly he settled his feet on to the ground and bowed his head.

"You know," he said, his voice soft now and calming. "I remember a time when your mother spoke to the almighty that way, about me. I remember her defending her choice to be by my side to the ends of time. I remember ensuring her protection by binding her to me, after she'd sired you, Lilim. By *him*..." Samael offered a deathly glare at Lucifer. "I promised her that her voice would always be heard, valued, and honoured. Reap..." The angel cleared his throat awkwardly, "Thet, my apologies. I have been somewhat out of sorts without your mother being near and not responding to my summons."

"Your summons?" Thet frowned.

"I summon her, she comes," Samael shrugged;

"it's how it's always been."

"Are you sure about that?" Mabel smirked.

The angel looked lost, "what are you trying to say?"

"I'm saying," Mabel rolled her eyes; "men do not summon Lilith, she summons men. Besides, Lilith rarely goes out of her way to abide by someone else's command unless there's something in it for her."

"So, you're saying," Samael's brow furrowed in confusion.

"She's ignoring you," Lucifer scoffed.

"No," Samael shook his head, "not Lilith. She is her own independent woman, but she would never ignore me."

"That much is true, father," Thet assured him; "you have both regaled your tales of lust and love to my siblings and I over the eons of time. You come to her aid, she is always there to answer your call, we all know it's to humour you, but she knows it makes you feel good. So, why would she go out of her way to ignore your call now?"

Samael looked concerned, "when she knows danger is near and she doesn't want to lure me toward it; or *it* toward me."

Thet nodded, "father, I'm afraid I'm going against mother's wishes... again. I don't want to *lure* you toward the danger that we're facing, I want you to race toward it on a magnificent steed alongside Luci, Cain, and Asmodeus. I want you to charge toward our foe as the harbinger of Death and one of the four horsemen of the Apocalypse."

Calmly and meticulously, the assembled group inundated Samael with everything. Thet openly reintroduced him to the group and informed his father of how the unlikely friendships between them all had begun. When Mabel, Kristoph and Thet informed him of all they had learned about the son of the almighty's plan to rid the world of humanity, the angel of death's jaw dropped and his eyes boggled.

"So, this is why you have created the plan for the four of us to charge into battle?" He asked, cautiously.

"I'm afraid so," Mabel sighed, "Kristoph and I believe Lilith is being held against her will somewhere in Heaven, unable to get word back to you or Thet. We aim to get up there and free her, but we can't do that with all the heavenly host being on high alert."

"You need a distraction," Samael nodded. "So, as the horsemen were a human myth, I don't suppose you have a steed that would accommodate me in my full form? Also, how are the human populace not going to notice an otherworldly battle?"

Mabel grinned as she filled him in on the particulars of the plan. When she mentioned Adrian's somewhat hesitant acceptance to serve as his steed, Samael looked over at him.

"I assure you Mr Smyth, and your kin, I have seen your deaths. They are all, many moons from now and in human form. None of you will come to any harm as you carry us forward;" he smiled the same warm smile that Mabel had seen Thet present her with on more than one occasion.

"Can you really see their deaths?" She whispered, as Eric, Pete and Jésus all slumped to the ground with a united sigh of relief and laughter.

"In a manner," the angel shrugged. "I see a bed for Mr. Smyth; I hear an ocean for Mr. Payne; I feel the wind roaring by my ears for Mr. Campbell and I taste metal for Mr. Guerrero. I sense laboured breathing for all, as though they are aged and weary. I just cannot say for when this will happen specifically, as life is made up of choices. All I can say is that it is highly unlikely that those events are likely to occur in this plan, I therefore made the assumption that each instance must be moons from now;" he smiled charmingly at Mabel; however, the gesture did not instil any confidence in her.

"If I may?" Lucifer's drawl sounded above the crowd who were chattering pleasantly with each other. "I think we've dallied here long enough, don't you? Are we all ready to pursue our allotted tasks and goals?"
"Wait," Samael held up his hand. "How do you know the son will fall for such a scheme?"
"Are you kidding? That's easiest part of this plan," Kristoph looked around at the staring faces, "you're going to call him. His name is a summoning of its own, after all."

Chapter 31.
Transformations

"Any further annoying questions?" Lucifer's frustrated drawl carried out over the murmuring babble of voices all speaking at once. At the sound of it, the gathered group fell quiet and looked at him expectantly. Adrian, Pete, Eric and Jésus all swallowed hard as their soon to be riders stretched their joints and allowed the façade of their diminished statures to fall by the wayside. As the beings rippled their shoulders, reached out their limbs and flexed their muscles to the accompaniment of creaks, cracks and unending clicks; their bodies grew, upward and outward.

Kristoph's jaw dropped as a pair of leathery, batlike wings erupted out of Asmodeus's back. Two horns that reached up and around to the nape of Lucifer's skull erupted out the front of the Devil's head. Samael's already impressive frame dazzled them all, as his lean physique filled out to reveal a surprisingly muscular figure with remarkably chiselled features. Finally, Caine, who had seemed so unassuming, grew in stature to a height that rivalled the Angel of Death. His whole body was shrouded in a fine, powdery mist which Mabel could only assume was a culmination of the sand they were standing in, mixing with his own ominous aura.

The four riders had only just settled into their true forms when Lucifer started to twist, hook, writhe, and stretch his long, taloned fingers. Electric flashes of blue light sparked between his claws. His eyes, which were a naturally violent red, glowed with an evil delight as he channelled the energy into four floating orbs that drifted lazily in the air, stopping in front of their destined targets.

"Gentle deities, if you would be so kind," Lucifer spoke in an authoritative voice, excitement rippling through his entire being. "Reach out your left hand, declare your preferred appearance and consume the orb, whole. Do not fight it, do not recoil from its burn or else your final figure will show the scars of your regret. Have an image of your desired alias in your mind's eye and

NEVER let it slip from your imagination."

"Is that why your father created the tiny water basilisk?" Thet smirked, at Lucifer, "a lizard that runs on water with a surreal horned crown?"

Lucifer growled menacingly, "How was I supposed to know he saw my beleaguered attempts to transform into a snake? Have *you* ever tried to transform into something that has no legs? It's a truly surreal feeling and I have no shame in saying I panicked a tad."

Samael snickered, "I remember the fury he had in the aftermath of your revolt and the casting out. He kept such a close watch on you from thereon. When he saw your first abysmal attempt at transformation, he laughed himself to tears. He created the little lizard as a miniature reminder of it and kept one as a pet. When you corrupted the minds of those two," he nodded at Kristoph and Mabel. "He cast it out of his office and left it to fend for itself. Ironic really, he hadn't realised the little devils could run on water. You can imagine his frustration when the humans he loved started to call it the Je..."

"HUSH you idiot!" Snapped Lucifer, "we don't want to alert *him*, just yet!"

Rolling his shoulders and taking a deep breath, Lucifer closed his eyes and furrowed his brow in concentration. Purposefully, he reached out his left hand and gripped the orb.
"The apocalyptic horseman, War," he said, in a clear, concise, and deadly voice.
Gripping the ball of energy that floated before him, in both his large monstrous hands, Lucifer crammed the orb into his mouth and tensed his frame as an internal battle ensued.
Mabel saw the strain it took for the devil to not spit the thing out. In her mind, she envisioned a gobstopper, bigger than any sweet she'd ever seen, and they were to swallow it whole! She cast a nervous glance at her friends, the soon-to-be steeds, and hated the look of fear and nervousness adorning their faces. Would they even consider her to be a friend after this debacle?

Finally, with a loud gasp of air, Lucifer successfully knocked back the ball of energy.

Everyone watched on, transfixed, as his lean torso bulked out into one of immense power and strength. His arms stretched outwardly as muscle piled upon muscle. His long, silken, raven-black hair receded to a short buzz cut. Scars and lacerations split across his arms, torso, and face and two tremendous slashes tore across his abdomen.

Lucifer bared his teeth and the straight pearly white tombstones, started to shift, and became crooked. Blood oozed from his canines as they grew in length. His lips went from pale to purple. His snow-white skin turned to charcoal, rippling with red lights of energy. His violently red eyes turned to black with no white to be seen. As a final afterthought, a shredded cloth made up of what looked to be skin, sewn crudely together, wrapped itself around Lucifer's thick neck and trailed down his back like a grotesque cloak. His trousers tore and ripped. With a final crack, the horns from his head snapped off, close to the skin, and fell down his back. As they tumbled down heavily, the cloak seemed to embrace them and pinned them to his shoulders and before everyone's eyes, the two impressive demonic horns moulded together to create the deadliest looking battle axe they had ever seen.

The Devil doubled over, panting as his transformation came to a close. No one knew quite what to say. Taking a final steadying breath, Lucifer stood upright and roared out in anguish, allowing himself to express all the pain he had pent up inside throughout the gruelling process. The sound reverberated around them and the sand at their feet rumbled in fear at it. With a rare, pitying glance, Lucifer turned to the rest of his fellow riders and gestured to the orbs. "Who's next?" He croaked simply, in a gruff, husky, and shredded voice that was a far cry from his usual smooth, baritone delivery.

"Y'know, I'm actually on a bit of a diet right now," Asmodeus grimaced, as he eyed the orb floating listlessly in front of his face. "I mean this thing is *full* of carbs, surely..."
"As your master, I implore you - do not make me order you, Asmodeus," Lucifer grumbled.
Asmodeus sighed, dejectedly; "Mab, Kris," he

smiled weakly at them both; "remember me as the handsome demon I once was."

"You have three gory heads, a tail, and fangs, and you wear the smallest toga that barely covers anything at all;" Kristoph stated, plainly.

"Your point being?" Asmodeus smirked.

Taking a deep breath, he stated clearly, "The apocalyptic rider, Conquest," and with a great amount of force, the Duke of Hell smashed the orb into his mouth.

Cain followed suit, stating in a plain and simple tone "The apocalyptic rider, Famine."

Finally, Samael sighed and grabbing his allocated orb with his left hand, he nodded to Thet before stating "the apocalyptic horseman, Death."

The transformation for each of the deities looked immeasurably painful. Asmodeus's three heads whirled around on their necks with strained looks, desperately diminishing the agony they were experiencing. Cain's large and cumbersome figure, meanwhile, seemed to suck itself inward as though a vacuum were devouring his physical mass. His skin turned an unwholesome shade of ochre as his bones and sinew became more and more apparent. Samael's masterful wingspan turned from a shimmering fibre optic glow to a pair of skeletal scythes, resting criss-crossed against his back.

After what felt like an eternity, watching the three figures suffer in painful silence, the transformations ended. Asmodeus no longer looked like a demon from hell but rather an impossibly tall and upright gentleman, straight from a cliché romantic chick lit' front cover, wearing flouncy shirt and tight trousers. Wrapped around his torso was a holster with two large blunderbuss guns tucked away inside it. His hair fell in blonde ringlets. He could have just stepped off a Hollywood set, were it not for his face. There was something truly haunting about Asmodeus's new features. It was like the ghost of battle had scarred it and his eyes were scratched bloody, as though he'd tried to gauge them out. His fingers were unnaturally long owing to the impressive growth of his nails.

Cain meanwhile was like a wraith! Mabel couldn't help but feel disgusted at the physical interpretation he had envisioned for the rider Famine. She'd seen clips of starving children in far-off countries on television, and Cain's appearance wasn't far from how they looked. As he offered her a consoling look of comfort, she shivered. All things considered, she felt like the worst person in the world.

Samael slowly approached Mabel. In his guise as the horseman Death, he was as far removed from the handsome and angelic being they knew him to be. His frame had yo-yoed in so short a space of time between his arrival, that he seemed to stagger with the new, lean physique he had attributed to his persona. The scythes clattered hollowly against each other with each step. Mabel shuddered, he looked like a shaman from a third-world country, his teeth yellowed and crooked. His eyes were almost hollow, and his body was covered in a range of tribal and magical symbols. Adorning his neck and arms were a series of trinkets carved from bones, Mabel was too scared to ask if they were animal or human.

"What do you think?" He asked her, and his voice crackled and snapped.

"Y-you're all truly terrifying," Mabel barely managed to muster.

"Of course, we are," grumbled Lucifer, "you think the masters of disguise would settle for sub-par attire for such a ruse as this? Honestly Ev-el, you do us a disservice if you think we wouldn't sell your little charade."

Through his gritted teeth and spasms of lingering pain, he grinned wickedly at her. Satisfied with Mabel's discomfort, he turned to the four members of Dark Omens and clicked the back of his tongue, encouragingly.

"So, who's first?" He raised an inquisitive brow.

"Do we have to eat one of those ball things too?" Pete croaked.

Lucifer snorted and shook his head, "believe me drummer boy, if you were to devour one of those things as a human, your insides would become your outsides and you'd die an unimaginably painful death. No, you get the next best thing, you get to allow me to consume your thoughts and transform you with just a little touch, nothing more, nothing less."

"It won't be permanent?" Adrian whimpered.

"Oh for the love of Thet," Eric groaned, "enough of your jibing, I'll go first."

"Atta boy!" Asmodeus wheezed. His charming melodic voice had completely transformed, and Kristoph couldn't help but feel a pang of regret for the demon upon hearing it. It just didn't sound right.

Lucifer smiled, "in all my years, I don't think I've come across a satanic worshipping Welshman, so eager to engage with demons and the devil." He chuckled, tunelessly, "very well Mr. Eric Payne, stand before your rider. Observe his attire. Recall his persona. Imagine his new alias's requirements. Now, in your mind's eye, envision the kind of steed you believe would be worthy enough to bare its back to such a being."

Eric swallowed and stood as close to Asmodeus as he dared. The demon smiled affectionately at him, and the rhythm guitarist did something that caught the group off guard and extended his hand.

"He's a rider who has chosen to remove his

ability to see in an attempt to escape the memories of his conquests. He's damaged. He's hurting. He needs a friend," Eric simply shrugged and closed his eyes as Asmodeus, his lip betraying a subtle wobble, clasped the man's hands and closed his own clawed fingers around Eric's broad palm.

Lucifer rolled his eyes, "very well, although for the life of me, I never thought I'd see the day when Asmodeus would create a *bromance* with a human. Mr. Payne, focus on the idea you have in mind, so that I might bring it to life, through you."

With the softest of touches, the Devil stroked up Eric's spine, sinking his dexterous fingers into the shock of messy, dark hair. With both his hands, Lucifer clasped Eric's face on either side, and pulled downward as though trying to stretch the man's face.

Asmodeus opened his palm and Eric's hand fell limply to his side as he groaned out in discomfort. Lurching forward, he heaved, wretched, and collapsed on to all fours. Kristoph tried to rush over to help his friend, but Thet held him back.

"Thet! Let me go, he's in pain, I need to be there for him!" Kristoph blinked back tears of rage, but Thet maintained his grip.

"The pain is only envisioned and imagined. The transformative spell causes no physical pain, contrary to what you see. Imagine it as a skintight one-piece suit being drawn up and sticking awkwardly to him. It's not the greatest feeling in the world, but it's far from painful," Thet reassured Kristoph, who looked up at the reaper in doubt.

"Kris, I'm fine mate, it's just the wieeeeeeeeeehurhurhurghhum," Eric's voice started to whinny and blare out a range of equestrian sounds, before finally, with a flourish the bulky Welshman transformed before their very eyes in to a horse, unlike any other they had seen. His mane, tail and body were rippling hue of midnight black, a white diamond shone on his forehead. He was taller than any horse Mabel had ever seen, and his whinny even had a Welsh undertone.

"Well I'll be damned," Lucifer raised a brow,

"your friend here is rather poetic, a stunning Black Beauty."

Thet nodded, "poetic indeed, Welsh Cob if I'm not mistaken. Very gentle disposition, much like the man within the guise. Very apt breed for the traumatised horseman Conquest."

Asmodeus stroked Eric's cheek, "we've seen some stuff, ol' par'ner," he smirked, as Eric the horse snorted and pawed at the ground impatiently, turning his head round to look at his fellow band members.

Slowly and nervously, the men took up their positions in front of their assigned riders and proceeded to undergo the unnatural transformation. Mabel and Kristoph could only watch on, speechless; as Jésus transformed into another handsome, ebony stallion, reeling aggressively on his hind legs. Adrian shimmered into a pale gold horse whose coat appeared almost like liquid metal, his steel blue eyes looking around wildly. Finally, Pete all but exploded into a wild brumby, forcing Cain to wrangle him into a close, soothing embrace, both breathing heavily.

Hurriedly, Mabel and Kris approached each of the steeds and held them tightly, one by one. Mabel couldn't stop her phantom tears from trickling down her cheeks as she buried her face into Eric's mane.

"For goodness's sake, stay safe!" She pleaded him. The muzzle of Eric's equestrian form, stroked against her head and when she looked up into his face, she was certain she saw a couple of pearly tears hastily blinked away by tremendous lashes.

All transformations over, each of the riders mounted their steeds and nodded to Thet.
"Ready when you are, reaper," Cain nodded, "Kris, Mab – please stay safe up there."
"Thank you, Cain, and Lilim!" Mabel's voice was barely a whisper as a painful lump formed in her throat. She didn't want to see him or any of her friends ride off in to the distance out of sight, with no clear knowledge that they would survive.
"Kris," Asmodeus wheezed, as he looked around sightlessly; "if I survive this encounter, I propose we part ways, I'm beginning to think this is more than what I signed up for, originally."

Kris snorted, "I was thinking the exact same, Asmo."

The demon grinned, "great minds eh?"

"Son," Samael turned to Thet, "when you're ready."

Thet nodded, "stay safe and true, father," he murmured, as with a flourish of his hand, a wide portal opened before them. Mabel briefly saw a world comprised of a barren wasteland, crumbling buildings, and deserted streets.

"Where on earth did you get the inspiration for that place, Thet?" Mabel asked in awe.

Thet sighed, "you would not believe the number of warzones I have traversed, Mab. I have never known a time when mankind was ever, truly, at peace. So, it seemed fitting to create a world where your friends can charge toward an unknown foe, safe in the knowledge that they are in a pocket world that has been specifically designed to accommodate such volatility and will remain ever the same. Derelict and abandoned, long after the conflict has ended;" he looked down at his feet sadly, his smart black shoes were covered in dust from the sand and now rubble

that had gently blown through the portal.
Slowly, he looked at Mab, her face torn with grief and concern for her friends and he nudged her gently, "nothing will happen to your friends Mab, their riders and I will assure that. I will head over to Limbo now and will return to take you to your assurances up top. Be ready, we only have a brief window for all of this to take place."

As the portal closed behind Eric's tail, Thet bowed to Kristoph and Mabel and disappeared through the ground. Crushed by the knowledge that any prayer for his friend's safety would give away their plan, as their very foe was the one who was supposed to provide their sanctuary. Kristoph wrapped his arms tightly around Mabel and in the brief window of privacy, they both held each other and wept silently for the safety of their friends.

Chapter 32. Stairway to Heaven

"Have they all gone?" Lilim asked.

Mabel and Kristoph jumped at the subtle sound of her voice. The daughter of Lucifer and Lilim had remained resolutely silent throughout the duration of the group's scheming that they had all but forgotten about her being there. Lilim smiled affectionately as she moved closer to the couple.

"I figured you two might benefit from some inside knowledge," Lilim said, as she pulled out a series of rolled up pieces of parchment from behind her back. She knelt down gracefully in the sand and smoothed out the ancient looking material before them.

"When you enter heaven, there are two things you need to keep in mind. Number one, nothing is as it seems. Number two, security is tight. Every door you encounter will be closed to you. Not only that, but it will also look uniform. Every corridor, hallway, entryway, it all looks the same.

So, I while you guys were plotting, I dug up these blueprints for you," Lilim explained.

"Where and *how* did you get these?" Kristoph asked as he marvelled at the detailed illustrations that Lilim had presented them with.

"Mother," Lilim blushed. "She's never trusted the space up top and has made it her mission to conduct regular visits up there in different guises. She's been up there more times than normal, recently. She never spends longer than intended, to avoid being discovered. Believe me when I say, if she doesn't want to be found, there's no way you will locate her."

Mabel groaned, "are we embarking on a fool's errand?"

Lilim simply grimaced, "you could be, but this feels different from her usual recon visits. She claims she goes to speak to the management, but there's no one up top ever readily available to talk to when she visits."

Mabel frowned, "or so she says;" she murmured. "Lilim, does none of this seem suspicious, to you? You're trying to tell me that the all-seeing, all-knowing father, has no idea that the first woman he ever created, and queen of Hell, is roaming the hallways of heaven? Not to mention reconning the area in enough detail to create blueprints?"

Lilim paused and chewed at her lip, "when you say it out loud like that..." She mused.

"What's this darkened square?" Kristoph pointed to a miniscule blotch of ink that seemed to leak from the main central corridor from the gates.

Lilim shrugged, "I'm not sure. I asked mother on multiple occasions, but she always shuddered and shook her head. My theory is, if mother reacted like that to it, it can't be good."

"Then, that will be our first point to check," Kristoph folded his arms and looked grimly at Mabel, who nodded.

"Why?" Lilim puzzled, "I've just said that..."

"Your mother really puts on a performance that the place is not good," Mabel nodded. "Lilim, you said it yourself; nothing is as it seems. I think your mother was dropping hints."

"Hints?" Lilim frowned.

Kristoph smirked, "speaking to the management. How do you know there was no one up there to talk to?"

Lilim shrugged, "because mother said so."

Mabel and Kristoph looked at each other knowingly, just as Thet pulled himself up from the ground beside them coughing and spluttering, while brushing sand particles off his t shirt and khaki trousers.

"Well, that's the pocket world warzone filled with most of Limbo's populace, now. Not sure whether I should be pleased or concerned as to how many jumped at the opportunity to see the apocalypse," he sighed as he straightened up. Skirting around the opening in the ground, he peered over their shoulders and observed the area of intrigue that Kristoph's finger was still pointing to.

"Ah, the main vantage point. I would start there if I were you," he suggested, nonchalantly.

As the trio kneeling on the ground stared aghast at each other, Thet looked between them and faltered, "was it something I said?" He asked.

* *

The journey back to the hospital was surreal. As Thet explained to them both, there was a surprising number of souls who found their way into Purgatory, very few made a return journey. Lilim hugged and kissed them both before they departed, wishing them every luck in every world. As Thet stood between Mabel and Kristoph, holding their hands tightly, they sank down through the sandy ground.

Mabel fought the desire to panic as the sand rose first about her mouth, then nose and finally eyes. The darkness that obscured her vision caused her to tighten her grip on Thet's hand. Amid the vacuous silence, she vaguely heard her friend's voice humming softly to her left, and his thumb brushed comfortingly against the side of her hand. Just as Mabel thought she couldn't bite back the urge to scream any more, the sharp, sterile light from the hospital blinded her and there, lying on a hospital bed, pale and unresponsive, was her physical body. She noted that Kristoph's prone form had been draped rather unceremoniously across a couple of visitor's chairs to the side of the room. The right side of his face sported an impressive welt from Asmodeus's earlier assault.

The shock of realising she was having an out of body experience, however, was nothing to the shock of seeing Helga Schneider squealing and clapping at the foot of the hospital bed.

"Miss Weaver! You're here! Oh, it's so good to see you again!" The young girl was borderline ecstatic.

Azrael, the angel, looked at her and Kristoph with pursed lips, "so, not content with committing the first sin, you're adding breaking and entering on to the list now?" He sniffed.

Thet sighed, "I see you received Asmodeus's note with Kristoph's body?"

"Note?" Mabel asked. "I didn't see Asmodeus write any notes while we were in Purgatory."

"Not a physical note," Azrael sighed. "Demons and reapers have the capability to pass on memos through bodies."

"I'm sorry, what?" Kristoph blinked in confusion.

Helga chuckled, "your body sort of flopped out of nowhere across those two chairs, sat upright, said *you and Miss Schneider are to accompany*

Kris and Mab to Heaven, then fell backward into a sleep," she grinned, as if this was a normal occurrence that happened every day. "So, when do we go?"

"Now, ideally;" Mabel said, glancing at Thet who nodded encouragingly.

"I suppose you will fill us in on the task at hand, on the way?" Azrael asked, "after all, one does not simply walk into heaven unannounced and then know the way around."

"We have plans," Kristoph grinned, waving the rolled-up blueprints.

The angel's face turned a sickening shade of green and he looked at Thet, "are you quite sure about this? I mean, what is there to gain from their going up there anyway, Charon?"

Thet's eyes narrowed briefly at the angel, "it matters not to you. Your role in this is to guide them through the gates, then return here to help me protect their physical forms, understood?"

"I can only carry one," Azrael sniffed, looking between Mabel and Kristoph.

"That's okay Mr. Angel," Helga beamed, "Miss

Weaver and I will go together, you can take Mr. Greyson."

Mabel didn't even get a chance to query exactly *how* she and Helga would be heading up to Heaven. The young girl simply held out her hand and grabbed Mabel's wrist, with a surprising amount of strength and dragged her down to eye level.

"Let me hug you!" Helga whispered, excitedly. Mabel nodded, and Helga Schneider embraced her tightly. The result of the connection was something Mabel quickly concluded was by far the most unnatural experience to date. She could feel her soul, merge into that of the young girl's. Being buried in the sands of time had nothing on being absorbed into someone else's soul and looking out the back of their head. Mabel couldn't help but feel like her head was projecting out of the back of Helga's transparent back, like a surreal rucksack.

"Mab, Kris;" Thet addressed them both, "you don't have much time. Once you are gone, I will maintain the shield Azrael and Helga have created for you both, here. Azrael, Helga, once you have arrived at the gates, let them in. Helga, you return to me. Azrael, join the rest of the heavenly host, turn their attention to the pocket realm I created inside this one, you'll spot the signs from a mile off!"

"How?" The angel asked, suspiciously.

Thet grinned mischievously, "it has your name written all over it."

With one final nod to them all, Azrael snatched Kristoph's hand and Helga held on to the hemline of his robe. In a single beat of his wings, the four of them rose up above the hospital. Another two beats and they found themselves skirting above the clouds. Mabel felt the urge to vomit as she hovered in the sky so precariously, the ground slowly but surely disappearing to nothingness. Bursting through the vaporous clouds the angel paused and looked about before strolling casually through the air.

Cautiously, Azrael looked about, as if he was anticipating running into someone in the airy atmosphere. Hesitantly he scuffed his sandaled feet at a couple of wispy cotton strands of cloud, then stopped, his eyes flashing angrily.

"Of course," He grumbled, quietly to himself. With one wave of his hand, the skyline around them shimmered from baby blue to a starlit stairwell. Mabel stared, wide-eyed, from the position out the back of Helga as the sight of sandy coloured steps rolled down before her. The memory of the stairway slapped her across the face. She recalled the myriad of images she'd witnessed during her time in Purgatory, the stairway to heaven hadn't changed one bit from the image she had witnessed of her being hurled down those very steps, with orders to never be allowed entry to paradise.

Azrael dropped Kristoph's hand as though it burnt and wiped his own on his robes in disgust, the angel then hurried around and gripped both sides of Mabel's face. With a sharp tug, she felt her body break free from their Helga Schneider confines. Mabel hurried over to Kristoph and grabbed his arm for support. The man was unresponsive however, gaping at something ahead of them. Confused, she turned to see what he had gained his attention, and her jaw dropped. There before them were the infamous gates. Awe soon gave way to confusion however.

"I thought they were supposed to be golden," Kristoph murmured in Mabel's ear.

"*I* thought they were supposed to be pearly," she affirmed.

The gates before them however were a dull, unpolished bronze, shrouded in a coating that had taken on a muddy brown appearance.

Mabel turned to the angel to get some answers, but Azrael was too busy peering over the edge of the stairwell and grumbling to himself.

"Um, Azrael?" Mabel hesitantly tapped the angel's shoulder, "everything okay?"

"Yes, yes!" Azrael snapped, the angel waved his hands in the air animatedly and the world below them vanished completely.

"Right," he finally said. "I will open the gates and let you in, but that's it! You two are on your own from there to do whatever it is you need to do! I... have to join the rest of the host and see what their plans are and see if they have any... plans of their own! Helga? I don't suppose you could..."

The three of them turned around and noted that

Helga had vanished. The angel sighed and shook his head.

"I swear that spirit will be the death of me," he murmured.

Without another word, the angel pressed his palm against the dull, rusty gates that stood before them. Immediately, the metal ornate entry started to vibrate and the coating that had shrouded the awnings in a thick layer of dust and grime fell away to reveal the shimmering beauty that only mother of pearl can offer. With a dramatic creak, the gates opened wide, dazzling both Mabel and Kristoph with a bright, iridescent light.

"Go, go, go!" Azrael hissed, "I... I will see you soon" he sighed, almost defeatedly.

Blinded, Mabel and Kristoph staggered through the gates as Azrael rushed past them in a blur, leaving them completely and utterly alone, lost in paradise.

Chapter 33. A Tale Retold

The first thing that struck Mabel was just how sterile everything around them seemed to be. She was unclear as to what she had expected to reside behind heaven's gates, but whatever imagery she might have conjured in her younger years, the actual entryway of heaven was nothing short of disappointing. The floor was laid with burgundy corded carpet tiles. In the decorator's defence, they were plush carpet tiles, yet Mabel sensed it was mostly down to the spiritual footsteps that didn't bear down on it the same way a physical tread would. The walls were a paisley green colour which would have clashed sickeningly with the carpet, were it not for the fact that every inch of surface space was adorned with frames depicting unique symbology.

"What do you suppose they all mean?" Kristoph murmured, puzzling over the intricate designs displayed behind each frame.

Mabel looked up toward the vast ceiling above her, as she searched for a clue. The frames were endless and so high up that it was impossible to determine what symbols were depicted in the frames that adorned the alcoves.

"Here," Kristoph whispered, pointing above the gates. Faded paint flaked down from the arch detailing a cursive transcript; "Angeli et Sancti anni Recognitione? Tell me that's not saying what I *think* it is."

"Angel and Saint of the year recognition. You have got to be joking," Mabel snorted.

"I suppose even heaven needs an employee of the year award, but I don't get why," Kristoph shook his head in bewilderment, at the countless number of frames around them.

Mabel shrugged and reviewed the framed symbology again, "so these must be the symbols assigned to all angels and saints who serve under heaven's lore. That's why they're so small and line each of these walls, time is never-ending up here and they never forget," she mused quietly to herself. "I suspect, our horseman War..." Mabel caught herself before saying Lucifer's name. If

Jesus used his own as a summoning card, only heaven knew what saying the almighty's greatest foe's name would do. She squinted her eyes as she strained to look higher up, but it was no good.

"I suspect *War's* symbol would be in one of those older looking frames up there. Remember the story of the great rebellion? When so many were cast out?"

Kristoph nodded, "sure."

"Well, legend said it was because... *War...* was an advocate for freedom of speech and he was not ashamed to promote that mindset against his father. He refused to bow down to mankind and having a lust to sit on his father's thrown, he naturally disagreed with much of what the almighty did. *War* is the anti-everything when it comes to Heaven and its lore. Remember what Asmodeus said to Azrael back in Germany? In Hell, freedom of speech is welcome, but somewhat prohibited up here. That was why he coaxed my original self to eat the apple and gain full knowledge. He wanted to provide to his father that his rule was weak, and his creations were just as pathetic," Mabel explained. "That being said, I'm starting to question much of that original story."

"How come?" Kristoph asked.

"Well, if that were the case, why do this? Every deity receives worship on earth in some small way, even *War*, so why would they need recognition awards up here?" She queried.

"They do seem like a bunch of pompous pri..." Kristoph started to reason, however a clatter further up the corridor caused them both to stop their discussion and pin their backs against the wall.

Slowly, they shuffled along the long corridor and approached a closed doorway where muffled clattering could be heard coming from within. Hesitantly, Kristoph unwrapped the blueprints he'd kept tucked under his arm and pointed to the spot that Thet had termed the vantage point. Mabel nodded, and frowned, the door had no handle. Cautiously, she reached out to touch the metallic barrier. With a soft but firm grip, Kristoph grabbed her wrist and pulled her back. "We don't know who or *what* is in there," he hissed. "What if it's a trapped demon?"

"In Heaven?" Mabel frowned, "it's rather unlikely, Kris."

"Regardless, it could be a trap;" Kristoph reasoned, "the son spot might have left something in there to..."

"Kill us?" Mabel finished Kristoph's sentence with a smirk, "Kris, we're already in a death like state on earth. We are two souls in heaven. We've just swung by our estranged son in Purgatory. We are friends with a child from Limbo. We're also friends with a Duke of Hell. What could they possibly do to us, that would deter anyone of our allies from coming to our aid?"

Kristoph considered Mabel's point and smiled, despite himself; her confidence was unquestionably infectious.

Refusing to let go of her wrist however, Kristoph gently pushed Mabel's hand against the door. With a soft click it moved smoothly away from the doorframe, slowly swinging inward.

"Ah, *finally*! Thank you both, so much," came a soft, exhausted, and tired man's voice from within. Before Mabel and Kristoph had a chance to react, two aged and purple blotched hands, reached out to clasp theirs and gently pulled them in to the room.

"F-father... do you think this... wise?" Another delicate, exasperated, yet younger man's voice spoke from the shadows of the room.

Mabel and Kristoph looked around. The space they were in was adorned on both sides with bookshelves that reached up to the vast expanse of space above them. There was no ceiling, just a starlit night's sky delicately lighting the room. The door behind them had dissolved into a small puddle of liquid mercury which slid about merrily on a path of its own choosing. Steps led down in front of them to a grand vantage point with a golden railing bordering the perimeter. Just ahead of it the Earth could be seen stretched out, far below them. Had they not got a job to do, Mabel felt she could have easily made a snug home here, devouring all the books hungrily for the knowledge they would provide; eager to learn all the mysteries of the universe. As she gaped at the majesty before her, the older man chuckled.

"You were also so inquisitive Eve. Sorry, it's Mabel now isn't it," the man beamed.

He reminded her of the Christmas card depictions of St Nicholas, his frame was slenderer; however, and frail, as though age had finally caught up with him.

Mabel slowly turned to him and frowned. How did he know her name? Aside from Azrael, neither she nor Kristoph had spoken to anyone. As impossible as it was, there was only one explanation she could conceive.

"God?" Mabel asked, uncertainly.

Kristoph's jaw dropped open as the figure of the almighty started to chuckle. The man embraced Mabel as though she were his long-lost daughter and knocked the wind out of Kristoph as, with a surprising amount of strength, he drew the two of them in for a bone breaking hug.

"Oh, my children! I knew you'd find me," the man beamed. "I admit, it took a little longer than I'd anticipated, but you're here. Oh, I've missed you both!" He grinned.

"Father?" The young man behind them shook his head, "you cast them out, remember? They disobeyed you. They were the original sinners, the sole purpose behind my going down there and sacrificing myself..."

"Yes, yes, yes," God waved away the man's frustrations. "It was an *act* my dear boy!"

"O...kay," Kristoph croaked. "So, you're God?" He asked the beaming man who refused to release his grip. In response, the figure nodded, enthusiastically.

"And... you're...?" He turned to face the young man

"Er... his son, yes..." The younger man seemed to look just as bemused at the overwhelmingly positive reaction of his father, too.

Kristoph looked at Mabel, "so this changes things a bit," he said uncertainly and chewed at his lip.

"A bit?" The son of the almighty snapped, "you've broken into heaven and set off the apocalypse!"

Mabel stared dumbfounded between God and his son, barely able to comprehend that notion that she was stood in their presence. She felt like her voice had been sucked out from her all over again, upon seeing the almighty; and found

herself wondering if Lilim might be too far away
to be called upon, to kiss her voice back.

"I think..." she managed in a faint squeak of a
voice, "that Kris and I could do with an
explanation."

"I hear you, I appreciate you, and I value you,"
God nodded. "I concur, this is a good call."
Graciously, he ushered the shell-shocked Mabel
and Kristoph on to a comfortable sofa suite which
looked out over the grand expanse of earth. Two
meteors blazed a trail by the room as they sat
down; the sheer energy from their fiery tails,
roared and filled the room with a warm glow. The
comforting light glinted off the almighty's thinning
crop of snow-white hair and the hint of gold in his
son's shoulder length mop.

"So," God lifted a table that lay on its side with a
missing leg. Waving his hand over it, the wooden
appendix vanished from its resting place on the
other side of the room and reattached itself
snugly to the underbelly of the oaken surface.
Mabel quietly admired the artistic carpentry of
the ornate piece. Following her gaze, the
Almighty chuckled, "I see you're admiring the

craftsmanship. It's a small token of thanks from the greatest carpenter I have ever met."

Mabel quickly looked across at the almighty's son, who rolled his eyes, "not me. He means Noah!"

"Noah was a farmer though, wasn't he?" Kristoph's brow was furrowed so much, his eyebrows were almost touching.

"He was," God smiled. "But he whittled on the side, hence why I got him to build an arc. The man was a genius with woodwork!"

"Oh," Kristoph said weakly and, realising he was sounding a little aloof he added, "that's... cool."

"It is, isn't it," God smiled. "But those discussions can wait. You are both in need of an explanation, not Noah's back-story. So, as you know, we arranged that I would allow you, Eve, to eat the apple and cast you out of..."

"Whoa!" Mabel jumped up, "first up, not the explanation we were looking for. Secondly, you, I, *we*... agreed, that I would eat the apple?"

The son groaned, "apologies Mabel. He might be all seeing, but sometimes he is rather all-forgetting. Father, *remember...* it was arranged that Eve's memory would have that point in her history, erased?"

"Ah," God looked guiltily at his feet. "Of course, well... Mab, if I may... When I created Eden, I required a large host of angels to manage and maintain various elements of the job. I admit, Eden was a passion project of mine, and I might have become a tad over-zealous in my ambition..."

"He means," the son couldn't himself as he stared vexedly at his father, "that he was a proverbial ball-buster."

"Quite," God nodded, "although I wouldn't use such language..." he offered a warning look at his son who rolled his eyes and continued to stare out at the earth below them.

Mabel and Kristoph looked at each other hesitantly, wondering whether it was best to skip to the end of the world part, and why God and his son had found themselves on the observation deck outside of either a heavenly death bed in one instance; or riding in to battle below them, in another's. Opting for patience, however, they both remained quiet.

"Suffice it to say, there were a few characters in my work force who felt rather put out, misused, undervalued, underappreciated, if you will;" the Almighty continued.

"Three guesses as to who the main ringleader to that was," scoffed the son, who was now bouncing his knee, impatiently.

"*Anyway*," God pressed on, with the smallest hint of irritation. "Said ringleader, created a union, of sorts. They were of the belief that there should be equal recognition for all parties involved in the building of Eden. In my youth and arrogance, I waved them off and focused my attention on my goal, you, Adam. Well, Kristoph. Sorry, um, Kris," he fumbled. "I wanted to make you in my image. Pure, gentle, honest; maybe not as omnipotent, but with enough knowledge to know how to get by in life, comfortably."

"No freedom of speech though," Mabel couldn't help but grumble.

The Almighty's smile faltered and dropped a fraction, "alas. In my youth, I was arrogant enough to think that it would be easier to manage and control a subservient human species. It was to be my downfall somewhat. You see those who were already conspiring against me saw you, Kris, in your earliest form, as a target, an insult, and an abomination. I had to protect you in some small way and so I created the female of your species... Lilith."

Mabel sat up at the sound of the Queen of Hell's name, "that's why we're here, Lord," she tried to explain, however God held up his hand, sadly.

"I know why you are both here, but I need you to know this information, as it is crucial to your future actions," he calmly explained. "You see, in Lilith, I thought I could try to accommodate some of the frustrations of the heavenly host who stood against me and offered her the ability to see clarity and have reasoning. She would be the one who would stay your blade, Kris, from the beast who might bite you out of fear. She would have provided an opposing side to a frustration on your part. She would have been (if you will), the yin to your yang; however, when I introduced you both I forgot one key and crucial thing."

"What was that?" Kristoph asked, cautiously.

"Chemistry," the Almighty shrugged. "You were

both so incompatible. She thought herself superior to you. You tried to abide by her every whim, she thought you were a push over and weak for doing so. She favoured nature and was rather promiscuous to say the least when it came to trying to procreate. In turn you found yourself trying to keep up with an insatiable appetite, because you see without chemistry, there is no love. Lilith favoured the more feminine creatures I had created. You, Kristoph, as Adam, adored her; but you could see that her affections were never yours. She had seen clarity in her mind and had reasoned that her life was not meant to be with you, it was to be with another, like herself."

"So," Mabel smiled, "the first woman you created, turned out to be..."
"I termed the phrase *homosexual*," God nodded, smiling. "It was a small play on words from my creation *homo sapiens.* Yes, Lilith is what most humans refer to these days as bi-sexual, more in favour of a feminine touch, but not averse to those of a man's – hence her union with Samael who can be both, pending Lilith's desires."
"But," Kristoph shook his head, "those who

worship you devoutly claim that the path of homosexuality, is an outright sin against you!"

"They do say that," The Almighty mused, sadly; "humans have an interesting ability to analyse words put before them in a book and take on board a meaning that can be rather different from what the might have originally author intended. One could almost say that every time a piece of written work is put out into the world, the author, figuratively, dies; as any intentions, messages, or moral to their writing is stripped apart by enthusiastic readers. In turn, the reader develops their own idea of what the author intended. If an author is lucky, the ideas match with theirs. If unlucky, they can face debates at best, witch hunts, at worst."

"Apologies, I digressed..." God sighed. "Kristoph, you were the first to note Lilith's sway of affections and brought it to my attention."

"So, you banished her;" Mabel concluded.

"Far from!" The father shook his head, his white hair seemed to glitter in the light with the movement. "I spoke to her and highlighted Adam's words. Unfortunately, I hadn't realised that the leader of the rebellion had spoken to her first. The angel in question, twisted Adam's words. He tricked Lilith into believing that Adam thought her to be a crude mistake, that she was too much of a woman for him; that he required someone meek, someone mild. In short, someone who could please him the way *he* preferred. I think we can all agree Mab, that you are far from meek and mild."

He paused and turned to look down sadly at the earth below them; "I could say nothing to change her mind. She was eager to punish Adam for a crime he hadn't committed. So, to protect him, I offered her an alternative life where she could be free to pursue her interests. I created, if you will, a pocket world."

The term triggered Mabel and she looked at the Almighty with a scrutinizing glance.

"I only know of one person who creates such worlds," she murmured, uncertainly.

"Thet, Charon, The Grim Reaper; he has many names it is true," the almighty smiled fondly.

"Personally, I call him *friend*. He's certainly the more down to earth of his brethren. He rather likes you too, I know."

Kristoph shuffled uncomfortably and felt his shoulders tense.

"You needn't worry Kris," God smiled, warmly. "I happen to have an idea in mind for our young Thet that will draw his wandering gaze further afield..." His smile wavered with those words and his gaze trailed off briefly, before snapping back to the moment.

"Lilith's decisions, lead us to where we find ourselves today," God clapped his hands, and the dimming light in the room burned brightly.

"You see, Lilith ignored the option for a pocket world to reign as her own. She instead chose to loiter in the chaos of the world outside of Eden. What was once a pure and beautiful mind, turned bitter, twisted, unpleasant. It corrupted. For you see," the Almighty sighed heavily.

"She felt scorned and, well, you know the phrase; Hell, hath no fury... so, she started to make a home, a hovel of sorts, really. She entertained the less than perfect beings who eventually started to spread out around the globe after you were banished from Eden. She enticed; she acted out her craven fantasies. She corrupted minds. She built her own group of followers, for she had reason to believe that the clash of opinions between myself and my angelic kin, would result in her gaining powerful sympathisers. For you see, she had a plan, a scheme."

Mabel groaned, "I think I can see where this is going."
"You were always the quickest of the two," God beamed at her, proudly. "Yes, she wanted to teach a lesson to the men in her life, that women could not and *should* not be controlled by men."
"Here, here," Mabel nodded.
"The world she lived in however, was filled with men who did just that. She has watched it evolve over the eons of time and even I'm ashamed to say that while progress is being made, it's slower than a snail's pace – and even *I* had to speed up the snail as I thought it was slow. The poor things are regularly going at breakneck speeds now; yet human minds are just that little bit too ill-advanced to comprehend it. *Anyway*, rather than rally the masses and raise awareness, she decided to rid the world of man;" God groaned, and

slumped back, tiredly, into a chair on the observation deck.

"Won't that wipe out women too?" Kristoph shook his head, how could they have been so wrong?

"Nope," the almighty's son grimaced. "She intends to wipe out men in general – including your horsemen and their male steeds. There's only one man she's gotten on board for the job and I'm ashamed to say, I considered him a friend. I even brought him up to Paradise with me when the Romans hung me up on that cross which your demonic friend used in your faux battle."

"Stirling job with that, by the way," God nodded approvingly.

"Your friend?" Mabel asked, cautiously, disregarding the holy praise she'd received.

"Yes. Dismas. We were crucified together. He was a lowly thief who showed penitence," the son sighed; "I was duped. He's Lilith's mole in heaven. He's the reason we were locked tight in here and have been for far longer than I would like to admit. I know Limbo must be teaming with souls, now."

Chapter 34. Nothing is as it Seems

Mabel looked between the two men, speechlessly. She'd been so certain, based on everything she had heard, that the young man attending to his father before her, was the mastermind behind everything. To learn that the very person they had both come to save, had successfully tricked *everyone...*

Slowly and steadily, she approached the vantage point and looked down at the earth. The overwhelming feeling of being above everything and hovering in space caused a surreal sense of vertigo and she gripped tightly to the sturdy railing support structure for security. She'd left Kristoph to discuss crucial elements of a revised idea to call off the charge and save their friends, with God. While she felt peace and comfort in the room she was in, joined by the company; something gnawed at the back of her mind and Lilim's cautionary advice 'nothing is as it seems' kept rolling around her head, as if on loop.

Mabel turned around to survey the room from a different angle. In her prior life, when she'd worked in that office space, if she'd been faced with data that had been hard to pull apart, she'd found looking at things from a different angle sometimes helped. Admittedly, back then the angle hadn't been a holy vantage point, and the data hadn't been to do with the creation and destruction of mankind, but the premise remained the same.

There was the almighty's son, his face strained, his presence unsettled. Whenever he sat down, his knee would bob impatiently. Throughout his father's discussion, Mabel had seen his eyes flit nervously between her, then the door, then back to her. Mabel couldn't help but think that now they were free, God would be able to miraculously stop all of this with just the click of his hand if he wanted to, so why was his son looking so impatient, nervous, and shifty? Kristoph laughed loudly at a joke shared by the almighty and a slight frown furrowed her brow. She was missing something, she was certain. Things seemed to be going too smoothly. How on earth could the Almighty have allowed himself to be trapped behind a simple door, which both she and Kristoph had only needed to rest their hands against to open; why had he resorted to throwing furnishings?

"Hey, Mab?" Kristoph laughed out, snapping her out of her musings. "The Lord's asked if you fancy seeing how Eden is doing?"
Mabel forced a pleasant smile, "shouldn't we be doing something to help our friends, first?" She fixed her eyes on Kristoph's, but his gaze was dopey, with a glazed sheen to his eyes.
"Besides," she continued. "I didn't think the clause signed, after our initial deaths, allowed us anywhere near Paradise."
Kristoph snorted and huddled closer to God and they both started giggling like school children. Something was not right. Mabel glanced hesitantly toward the doorway, and pondered on whether she could make a run for it and find Azrael, but something caught her attention. On a plinth, by the door, was a golden ball of the largest and juiciest looking apples, she had ever seen.

Mabel looked around the room. All the knowledge in the world was written and stored in there. Immediately, her classics knowledge kicked in and her mind entered a whirlwind of pondering. What had the Almighty said earlier? "So, as you know, we arranged that I would allow you, Eve, to eat the apple…"

There was a reason behind the shock revelation, it had stalled them, encouraging time for lingering with back stories. Another thought came to her mind, she'd interrupted him. She, Mabel, a lowly human woman, had interrupted The Lord. No sooner had this thought come to the forefront of her reflections, another one swiftly took its place: his son had referred to him as the all-forgetting. Mabel felt a sense of panic slowly start to creep through her soul.

"How do we know you're him?" Mabel heard her voice project the words and felt the shock of their delivery silence the room. She certainly couldn't recall having given the words permission to air, but the reaction from the man who claimed to be God was all the validation she needed to have queried it.

"What do you mean Eve? Um, Mabel? I-I mean, Mab?" The man smiled sweetly and innocently, but there was something else there, something forced, unsettled, mistrusting.

Kristoph continued to giggle impishly, as his luminescent cheeks turned a faint pink, he looked drunk.

"I thought it was a simple question, my Lord;" Mabel forced herself to continue. "How do we know you're God?"

"Is this not proof enough?" The man stretched out his arms to emphasise the grandeur of the room they were in, then pointed toward the now pale and uncertain form of his son who seemed to be glowing with sweat, which had gathered above his top lip.

"I'm sorry, no;" Mabel held her head high.

"Mab," The Almighty figure slowly stood up and pressed his hands together; "how could you possibly doubt me?"

"Because you never showed yourself to us when we were Adam and Eve. We only ever spoke through prayer and your angelic host," Mabel loosened her grip on the banister while the man looked down smiling at his hands.

"What miracle would you like to see, that would convince you that I am *he*?" The man smiled, confidently.

"Um, I think father's a tad tired," the son suddenly piped up. "Perhaps we should go and rest, Mab and Kris you have been a great blessing, you can leave now."

Kristoph hiccupped loudly and giggled before slumping forward in his seat.

"What have you done to him?" Mabel asked, nervously.

"Nothing at all, he's just happy to see his father again, aren't you laddy?" The man slapped his hand heavily on Kristoph's shoulders and that's when Mabel saw it. There on the back of the man's hand, an ugly welt of a circular scar, pale and shining in the light of the room. Another meteor filled the space with light, and a glint of gold by the man's feet showed a golden chalice, encrusted with lavish gems. How had she not seen it before?

"He's drunk," Mabel blinked, "how have you..." Then it hit her, the faint, sweet aroma of honey and ambrosia. It had been dulled by the sweet smell of apple that had filled her senses as she'd walked in, but it was there.

"Who are you?" Mabel's voice shook with ill-suppressed anger.

"My dear, I honestly have no idea what you... ah, hehe, hmmm;" the man's innocent smile gave way to one of evil cunning. "Nicely played Mab. Make the omnipotent father sound clueless – not easily done."

"That's because you're not him," Mabel snapped. "Who are you?"

"F-father, I really must protest..." The man who was playing the son of God jumped to his feet, nervously.

"Ahh, give it up Az', the jig's up;" the man sighed frustratedly and with a flourish of his hand, his form shifted from that of the jolly Santa Claus form to a lean, and smartly dressed thug. His hair was slicked back neatly, and a golden cap covered his right incisor, the metal sheen glinted in the dim lighting as he sneered. Sniffing, he straightened his collar and turned to his friend. Mabel's stomach would have turned, had she have been in her physical form.

"Azrael?" She gasped, in shock; "but how? *Why*?" Before she could ask anymore, the thug crossed the room in an uncanny speed and leered at her.

"Enough, with the questioning Mab. I had enough of that last time I encountered a human. Didn't really work out for me then, determined to not let history repeat itself, now!" His breath smelt sickeningly sweet.

"The name is Gestas. You might remember me from such roles as the impenitent thief?" He smirked smugly and flopped down next to Kristoph; "I must say, he is such a lightweight! I suppose it's a given, what with not having that leech of a duke loitering around inside of him, selfishly sucking in all the good vibes, and filtering out the smell, only."

Mabel turned to Azrael, "you promised those children safety, paradise, security. What did you do with them?"

"I assure you Mab..." The angel whimpered weakly.

"Mabel..." Mabel snapped, "only *friends* call me

Mab."

The angel swallowed, "the children are safe...
Mabel."

"Even Helga?" Mabel growled, "Or was that
another one of..."

"Gee Miss Weaver, I shall carry you on my back
like a satchel to heaven," Gestas mocked the
Germanic twang of Helga's voice, before scoffing
and jumping off the sofa.

"Too *easy*!" He gloated, as he swaggered to
Azrael's side.

Mabel hurried to Kristoph and tried to kick the
chalice away from him, however, her foot sailed
straight through the golden cup. She stared down
at her feet in startled shock.

"Looks like you're running out of physical juice,
now you're in heaven," Gestas cackled. "Anyway;
love to chat an' all that, but we've got an
apocalypse to oversee. Chow for now! Azz, get
your ass into gear and carry me down, will ye?"

As Azrael miserably slunk after the impenitent
thief, he looked over his shoulder at her sadly.

"I just wanted to be recognised, y'know? To be
seen? All those names on the wall, not one of

them was me! I-I didn't mean for it to go this far, Mabel. No one was supposed to get hurt..." His eyes were wide and tearful, "please, forgive me?"

"I'm in a holy place Azrael," Mabel hissed viciously; "I can't tell lies. Just know that you might find forgiveness from someone in authority one day; but you will never find solace and forgiveness from me!"

With one final, miserable look, the angel followed Gestas out of the doorway and with a dejected flourish of his hand, the small pool of mercury formed a solid metal seal in the doorway, shutting him out of sight.

Mabel rushed to the door immediately. She reasoned that if she was losing any sense of physicality, she would be able to pass right through it. THUD! She staggered backward, dazed. She hadn't run into the door, but she'd certainly run into some form of shield, barring her exit. Desperately, she hurried back to Kristoph, who was quietly snoring with his head forward on his chest.

"Kris? Oh, for goodness's sake, KRIS?" She tried to poke him, shove him, even hit him; but it was no use. No matter what she did, her arm would only pass through him.

'Looks like you're on your own with this one Mab," she murmured to herself.

She stared angrily at the chalice by Kristoph's feet and grumbled angrily, if only there were a way in which it could be kicked. Quietly, she longed for Asmodeus to show himself right now and offer his possessive services. The thought struck her like a slap across the face.

Hesitantly, she approached the almost comatose Kristoph.

"Kris?" She whispered, timidly; "I've had a thought, but I don't think you're going to like it much – I know I won't. Please don't be too angry with me."

Lining her feet up with his and resting her hands limply at her side, Mabel slouched down onto, then into, Kristoph. Nothing happened.

Out of sheer frustration, Mabel screamed out: "IN THE NAME OF ALL THAT IS HOLY, KRIS! WAKE UP!"

The sound of her scream caused Kristoph to jolt awake. In that moment two things happened. The first thing that happened was the pain that seared through Kristoph's head. The force of it caused him to grip his ghostly temples in agony. The second thing that happened stemmed from Kristoph's alterness to the room around him. Being awake and in a state of vulnerable pain Mabel was surprised that such weakness allowed for her to easily sink into his being. In mere moments, Mabel found herself looking through the eyes of Kristoph Greyson.

There was a moment of confused silence.
"Kris, you need to get yourself to an optician's, your eyesight is really awful!" Mabel spoke out of Kristoph's mouth, then squeaked. In a kneejerk reaction, she went to clasp her hands to her mouth, only to feel the heavy hit of Kristoph's large palms colliding with his own face.
"Mab?! Damn your eyes, I suppose there's a logical reason as to why you're hitchhiking inside of me?" Kristoph's thoughts echoed around her, and the colours inside his mind shimmered in a hazy sea blue.
"Kris, you were drugged into a stupor by Gestas," Mabel explained, desperately.

"He was the impenitent thief who was crucified next to Jesus. No one really knew what happened to him, but we've just been witness to him acting as God. It was all a ruse! We need to find Lilith along with all the children and potentially Bo. We're locked in here and they're descending down to earth to revel in the apocalypse which *we've* enabled. I dread to think how long it will be, before they clock on that it's just a small pocket world and not the *actual* world." Mabel started to wring Kristoph's hands in panic.

"Uh-huh," Kristoph's mind turned to a violent hue of red, and Mabel felt the heat of his anger. "That's some of it making more sense. What doesn't add up is how you're in such a loose state that you have been able to possess me?"
Mabel felt a hint of grief hit her hard and she felt the pain creep through into Kristoph's chest, "I can't be sure Kris;" she sighed. "But I think I might be dying in the world below. Heaven is pulling me further away from my physical being. Why it's not affecting you is, I can only assume, because you weren't already on a near deathbed when you entered this state."

Kristoph reached out and softly placed his hand over his heart and gripped at his chest. The pain was indescribable, and it felt like his legs would buckle from it.

"What do you need me to do?" He asked, his voice sounded as though it were speaking right next to her.

"I don't know," Mabel sighed. "Azrael found a way to somehow loop around us into this space and take on the role of the son spot, without us noticing. If we could work out how he did it, we might be able to find a way out of here."

"You've always been the brains, Mab;" Kristoph murmured softly to her, "take full control and look around, let me be your vessel."

Mabel felt the space behind Kristoph's eyes shift and become roomier as she took full control of his barely physical form. Hastily, she hurried across to the main entrance and rested Kristoph's palm against the door; nothing. Not that she'd expected anything. Looking around her, Mabel spied the table that Gestas had reassembled. Rushing toward it, she tried to pick it up and throw it, but the weight of the surface was too heavy, it came as no surprise that only an other-worldly being could have hauled it across the room... across the room.

Feeling the tension rise inside Kristoph's body, Mabel hurried to the banister by the vantage point and peered over the rail.

Peering over the precipice, she quickly realised what had caused Azrael's earlier discomfort at the gates of heaven. Thet's pocket world could just about be seen running adjacent to a bustling city. The grand expanse of the conjured warzone spread out from the initial crumbling and decaying glimpse Mabel had spied earlier through the portal in Purgatory and reached out into a barren wasteland of nothingness. At an initial glance however, the world twisted, turned, and swept in a subtle yet obvious attempt of joined handwriting.

TRAITOR

"Azrael called Thet, Charon, before we left the hospital;" Mabel thought to Kristoph, "there's no love lost between the two of them, but we all know how Thet feels about his name."

"Even Azrael had started to call him Thet, while we were looking for Eric's nephew," Kristoph recalled. "God bless Thet and his quick thinking," they both thought together.

"No wonder Azrael was nervous in his son-spot form," Mabel reasoned, "he realised he'd messed up as soon as he saw that message! What did Thet say before we left for heaven? Azrael would know where to send all help, as the pocket world would have his 'name written all over it', Thet knew if he let on to the Angel that he knew, we'd have been in for it."

"He could have booted us off the stairway there and then, though;" Kristoph mused, "why didn't he?"

"Azrael didn't want anyone to get hurt with his pursuit of recognition," Mabel considered. "He might be an idiot, but he's not an out-right killer, I think he hurried off to warn Gestas who had slipped off as Helga without any of us noticing, an argument ensued, a table thrown in rage against a sealed door maybe? They must have heard us debating whether to enter the room or not and had to think of something on the spot to stall us.

All thieves are opportunists after all, Gestas learned to think on his feet to avoid getting caught, while in life."

"He wasn't very good at it though, seeing as he got tried and crucified for his crimes," Kristoph reasoned.

"Exactly, the worst thief ever!" Mabel agreed, "whether he knew I would soon see through his guise, I dunno. Either way, he knew that the shock of seeing them as the almighty and the son-spot and through curve ball alternative explanations to the story of creation would stall us."

"So, what do we do now?" Kristoph asked. "With the door shut, there's no way out."

Mabel tapped at the railing Kristoph's hands were leaning on and smiled to herself awkwardly, "Not necessarily,"

"You can't be serious!" Kristoph's mind drowned in a pale blue light of terror.

Fighting back his inner fear of falling from great heights, Mabel swung one of Kristoph's legs over the railing. Ensuring that his grip was tight, she leaned backward, over the vast expanse of space and surveyed the adjacent room.

The neighbouring space was dark and unaccommodatingly cold and gloomy, to look at. Nothing stirred and there was an unsettling amount of silence stemming from it. Feeling Kristoph's grip waning, Mabel eased his body back to the top of the railing to carefully clamber back over into the vantage point, when the sound of a small throat being cleared pierced the silence like a knife.

"Herr Greyson?"

The sound of Helga's voice coming from the darkness caused Mabel to freeze, clutching the railing with all of Kristoph's might. Carefully, she inched his body over the expanse again.

"Helga?" Kristoph's voice called out toward the darkness

"Careful Miss Schneider," came an all too familiar woman's voice. "The body might be here, but I can see there's someone else behind the steering wheel."

"LILITH?" Mabel called out, excitedly, as she encouraged Kristoph to shimmy across the railing closer toward the adjacent room.

As he reached the joining wall and tried to reach around to grip the other side, Mabel felt Kristoph balance slip. The world looped around them both and they cried out in terror as his body fell back. Their fall was stalled as a strong hand clasped Kristoph's ankle with an unnatural strength.

"I sincerely hope there is going to be a decent explanation behind all of this. One that would explain why I am surrounded by a sea of children and, I'm sorry dear, what was your name again?"
"BO!"
"Ah, yes. Adam, Greyson, Kristoph, Kris... Mabel? Whatever you prefer to be called these days. Would you care to shed some light on this infernal darkness we have all found ourselves in?" Lilith asked, the smallest hint of humour tickling at the tone in her voice.

Chapter 35. Convincing the Masses

Mabel felt certain that Lilith had just stood Kristoph's form upright. Furthermore, there was little doubt in her mind that they were both on the receiving end of a deeply disapproving look. The room they were in was so incredibly dark however, that there was no way she could be completely sure of either of these things. She felt Kristoph's ears twitch like a dog's at the slightest sound of shuffling bodies around the room. Whispers and confused murmurs drew closer, yet when she reached Kristoph's arms out, his hands sailed through the air, uncompromised.

There was however, one thing that Mabel was completely certain of. Kristoph's form was growing weaker by the minute and with a gut-wrenching thought, she remembered that his form was only there based on a limited amount of life essence. If either of them stayed in heaven much longer, they would both fade into nothingness, their physical body's useless husks, lying lifeless in the hospital back down on earth. The thought of Kristoph dying, without any full sense of knowing it, while she was in control of his own soul in heaven, sparked a fury inside her.

"Lilith?" Mabel asked. Everything was a mess in her mind, and she needed clarification. "I need you to be brutally honest with me."
The Queen of Hell's voice played by Kristoph's right ear, "only if you tell me who I'm speaking to right now. I hear the voice of a man, yet I sense the vague hint of someone else there, and it's certainly not a hitchhiking Duke."
"It's Mabel, as you well know;" Mabel fought the urge to be frustrated with the woman, time was of the essence. "Lilith, why have you been frequenting heaven, so often?"

Even in the darkness, Mabel sensed Lilith's form tense, as a deep intake of breath sounded in front of her.
"The Almighty is sick;" Lilith responded, coolly. "He has left matters up to his son to handle. In turn, he sent me a message, a sign if you will. It

was an hourglass, filled with the sands gained from my daughter Lilim's domain. It had ceased falling and was instead pooling in the air, unable to fall."

"He was holding on," Mabel understood the imagery and pressed on. "So, you've been frequenting here to... do what, exactly?"

"Assist with his ailment," Lilith's voice was curt, and Mabel couldn't help but detect a note of sadness to it. "I was created to be by Adam's side, to nurture him and provide clarity and reason. I hadn't realised that much of what I said to my betrothed at the time, offered the same level of solace for my creator, in turn. He too, is repentant, Mab. He sees his folly from his younger years. The lives he has created and ended, the wars mankind wage on his behalf, not to mention the gluttony he has thrived upon from his follower's beliefs; all of which keep him strong... He asked me to visit him frequently so that I might be by his side, so he can reflect on matters while he rests in a prone state."

Mabel swallowed hard. The idea was almost unimaginable. What if the father of all creation succumbed to this mystery illness? Could that even happen?

"Where would he go?" Mabel wondered out loud.

Lilith breathed out a steadying breath, "The Lord will not *go* anywhere. He is not like a human. He's mighty. He does not pass away from illnesses; he knows every ailment out there and *creates* antidotes for them. Death would only come when there is not a single soul left on earth who believes in him. The faith of his human pets keeps him holding on. That being said..." The Queen of Hell sighed, loudly. "He is gravely ill."

Mabel grimaced, there were so many questions and so little time, "how can we make him better?" was all she could ask.

"We cannot. He is the superior deity, Mab;" Lilith's voice wavered. "His being ill, is unheard of."

"So, what's caused it? What symptoms is he showing?" Mabel struggled to hide the desperation in her voice.

The faintest brush of air against Kristoph's ears

sent chills through his spine; as Lilith whispered "love."

"Love?" Mabel snapped.
All this time, the Almighty had been wallowing in bed because he wasn't loved enough? It was utter madness. What more could he want? People were dying with his name on their lips. Religious leaders praised him and sang out to him, they devoted their lives to worship him...
"You cannot be serious!" Mabel snapped, "he has love in an immeasurable abundance! He only needs to look down on earth to see someone call out his name in praise, valuing him. What does he want the whole world to do? Unite as one, call out his name and beg him to accept their devotion? Because, Lilith, that's not going to happen!" Mabel shook her head. "What *love* could measure more than that?"
There were a few quiet murmurings of agreement in the darkness around her, and Mabel was glad that she wasn't the only one to show some sense of frustration, even if it did potentially stem from what she could only assume was a small hoard of religious Saxons.

"Not just any love, you insufferable creature! His Son's love," Lilith snapped in desperation. "He has lost the respect and love of his son, because of his love for you humans."

Mabel's mouth shut tightly. In just that one sentence, Lilith had provided all the evidence Mabel had needed to know that the Queen of Hell was not at fault for any of this. Silently and in the dark, she nodded Kristoph's head in quiet acceptance.

Still Mabel's thoughts were flitting through Kristoph's mind like a whirlwind. If Lilith had been in heaven all this time, watching over the Lord, how had she ended up in this room of darkness, surrounded by children and heaven only knew who else.

"Lilith?" Mabel asked, as nothing seemed to be adding up. "Why are you here? In this room I mean. You're right next to the vantage point, you could see where I, we, were about to fall," Mabel turned around to face the vast expanse of Space, but it was gone. "Wait..."

The phenomenal view of the stars, meteors, and the planet earth, had gone; only darkness remained all around them. "Where did it all go?" Lilith's chuckle caressed Kristoph's ears again, and Mabel hated the feeling of the electric thrill his body felt in reaction to it. Jealousy, it wasn't the greatest of looks or feelings to have at so crucial a time.

"You mean, you can't see it? It is rather glaringly obvious. Why do you think Miss Schneider here called out your host's name?" Lilith's jabs and mocking were far from helpful.

"The Lord is omnipotent, Mab. While his powers are somewhat hibernating, he sensed danger and advised that I hide. I just happened to run into Azrael on my way home as he was leading a host of children. I advised the angel of the trouble his father had predicted; and in turn, he suggested I duck in here with the children. We did just that, and I cast a light out charm to ensure that we couldn't be seen, even by my fellow deities."

Azrael! The angel's name stoked a fire within Mabel and Kristoph.

"I don't believe this," Mabel snapped, "Lilith, we need to go!"

"Belief is an interesting concept, don't you think?" Lilith jeered, mockingly. "Even when you find yourself in the glorious world of Heaven, Mab; you still find yourself barely able to believe in things?"

"I tell you what, Lilith;" Mabel snapped. "When you're faced with trying to avoid an untimely demise for yourself, all your loved ones, your best friend (who happens to be a reaper), and a small host of Hell bound fiends - *you* try and keep you head firmly in the *belief* game."

"Mr Grim is in danger?" Helga's voice quivered by Kristoph's arm.

Mabel sighed, sadly. "Yes, Miss Schneider. Thet is in danger, my friends are in danger! Lucifer, Asmodeus, Cain, even Samael are in danger..."

"What?" Lilith's voice snapped like a stick in the silence of a woodland, and all fell quiet. "Mabel Weaver, you will tell me everything, *NOW!*"

With a groan more in keeping with a rebellious teenager, Mabel hastily explained the plot to obliterate mankind, which Nemesis and the son had concocted. She detailed the recent encounter with Gestas and Azrael along with the concocted stories they had designed to dupe both of them, in the observation deck.

"Azrael desired more recognition but seemed repentant. I've no idea what would Gestas would gain from this," she admitted.

"Fame, glory, a right-hand seat to dethrone St. Dismas no doubt;" Lilith growled, menacingly.

Mabel hurried on to detail the apocalyptic plan with the horsemen in one of Thet's pocket worlds and finally, she got to the point she'd been working up.

"Lilith, we came up here in the hope of finding you, as we thought you were being held captive. We intended to set you free so that you might reason with the son-spot; even better, maybe give him the hiding of a lifetime. We hoped you might be able to make him see that what he is doing isn't God's work, but his own!"

Mabel shook her head. "He's jealous, that much is evident, so he is doing this to claim his father's affections. While I would love to think his *vengeance on mankind* will fail, any hope is dashed when I consider that *your* daughter, Nemesis, has helped to fuel this uprising!"

Kristoph's voice was yelling Mabel's words in anger. "So, Lilith. Either you help us and in turn save the ones we both love and hold dear. Or you continue with this twisted little game of verbal sparring and keep me in the dark!"

Mabel wished she could see Lilith's reaction to the multitude of revelations she had just divulged. All she heard however, was a small click. From the deep recesses of the room, small floating orbs of light sparked into life. As Mabel watched on, the orbs would shudder, then duplicate themselves, moving slowly out and bathing the space in a warm, amber glow. Very soon, Mabel was able to see the walls that were lined with illustrations of creatures in all shapes and sizes. Dioramas lined the wall in front of her, depicting majestic creatures that she'd only ever seen in fairy stories. Taxidermy animals stood on plinths, positioned in a range of stances. Her gaze fell on a taxidermized centaur. His face looked as though it had been stretched in the same way she had seen Lucifer stretch the Dark Omen's member's. However, rather than having had a full equestrian transformation, it still maintained the human features and torso, which was covered in short, silken strands of fur. The style of the creature's hair was that of a horse's mane and trailed in a singular line from the furthermost point of his head, like a Mohican, all the way down his back and horse-like hind, merging in with the tail. Mabel struggled to tear Kristoph's eyes away from the surreal sight.

Aside from the multitude of mythical creatures, the room was also full of spirits, ghosts, and angelic beings. There in the centre of them all, was Lilith. Her arms were folded, and her lips were pursed. Her face was an image of white-hot fury, and for a moment, Mabel thought she'd gone too far with ordering the Queen of Hell around. Swivelling on one heel however, the Demon Queen stormed to the balcony and peered over the edge. After a moment's observation and an unimpressed sniff, she spun around and returned to her original spot, standing in front of Mabel.

"Miss Schneider," Lilith spoke softly. "Could you and your friends follow me, please."

Helga and the children that had been promised redemption, gathered closer together and followed Lilith to the only bookshelf in the room. With a stroke of her hand, Lilith caused the woodwork to burn to cinders and ash. Through the opening, Mabel heard a machine beeping, faintly, weakly. The smell of a sterile hospital room stung at Kristoph's senses.

"Please, Helga;" Lilith spoke softly to the head of the Piper's friends. "I think there are a few folk in there who would appreciate some company and maybe some childish mischievous assistance." Helga grinned and gestured her head to the rest of her gang of youngsters. With a final impish wink at Kristoph's form, she hurried through the doorway.

No sooner had they gone, Lilith called out, "Bo?" The Viking leader hurried over, excitedly. As he passed by Kristoph, he pointed happily and performed a surreal air guitar tribute to him.

"Hella?" He asked, staring up, wide eyed; at Lilith's amused expression.

"Hm. Please be a darling;" she cooed. "You and your kin, protect those children at all costs, understood?" As Bo nodded a gruff agreement and headed through the doorway, Lilith added, "Saxons, you go too!"

Mabel felt Kristoph's jaw drop in shock as the Vikings and Saxons shuffled through the doorway after Helga and her friends.

In the back of his mind, Mabel heard Kristoph's surprised tone 'was it me? Or was there no language barrier there? How did she do that?'

Finally, Lilith turned to the lingering deities from Heaven.

"You have all heard of the plot the Almighty's son-spot has concocted?" She looked sternly around at the angelic host, who were all shuffling their feet, awkwardly.

"Angels, will you now fight to save the humans that your father loves?" Her stern delivery fell flat, however. Much of the angels simply looked at her in confusion.

"What?" Lilith sighed, impatiently. "What could possibly be your reason for not jumping over that balcony? Fear? Disinterest?"

One of the six angels, who had been resting with his back against the wall next to a bizarre diorama of what Mabel could only presume was a cross between a hedgehog, bumblebee, and a squirrel; stepped forward.

"Madam Lilith. It is neither fear nor disinterest that holds us back. We would gladly charge into battle to protect those that our father loves," he spoke with such eloquence and with a soft harmonious charm to his voice.

"Michael," Lilith's impatience was biting. "Pray tell me *why* you choose to stay put, then?"

"There are multiple reasons," Michael looked almost sorry; "however, I will stick with the top two. Number one, based on Miss Weaver's revelations, we would be charging toward the one figure our father loves more than the humans, his *son*. Number two, as the Queen of Hell, you have no authority over us."

Lilith's eyes flared as Mabel felt Kristoph's form stagger. The life essence was wearing thin. They didn't have time for this!

"Arch-angel Michael?" Mabel hated that her words caused Kristoph to strain his voice as his form desperately clung to the final traces of life essence.

"Lilith might not hold authority over any of you, it's true. I don't expect the voices of the former Adam and Eve would offer any sway either." Michael's perfect, blemish free brow furrowed at her words, however she persevered. "Consider this though. The Lord loves his son, above all. It is an unrequited familial love and there is nothing more painful, however it can be rectified with the right support. Imagine if that love were to be cruelly cut away, should his son fall in battle!" In the back of his mind, Kristoph gasped painfully, 'Mab, I can't hold on much longer, think through your words. Don't pit the archangels against us, too!'

His form breathed in raggedly and sank to its knees as Mabel used the last of their form's energy and gasped out; "the son has turned to those who care not if he fails this selfish pursuit... he needs your help to see that. No one wants to see him fall..." One last ragged breath, Kristoph's eyes started to close, "stand by Lilith and her kin... help us to convince him of that!" With a desperate struggle, Kristoph's form fell on its side.

From the gap in the wall, where the machine had been softly beeping away, the pauses between each beep grew longer, and longer. Thet's voice broke through, drowning in indescribable pain and anguish.

"NO, MAB! KRIS! PLEASE... COME BACK TO ME! NEMISIS, STAY AWAY FROM THEM!" With a scream like a banshee, the blurred form of Lilith thundered through the light. Kristoph feebly reached out his hand. "Wait..." the two entwined souls whispered. Before darkness descended upon them, Mabel felt Kristoph's form rise. As his ethereal form's eyes closed, Mabel heard his weak voice speak out to her in his mind, 'we're finally ascending Mab! Joined together, as one, in heart and mind.'

Chapter 36. The Words of a Humbled Father

"Mabel Marionnette Weaver and Kristoph Greyson, hear me now.

Every story in life has a beginning, a middle, and an end. Does that make it a good story though? What about those that start at the middle and end at the beginning? What about those tales that are never-ending, that seem to traverse through the ages, picked up by a different voice and tweaked to accommodate a new lease of life, a new beginning?

Mabel Weaver, you were born from the rib of Adam and granted the name, Eve. Even your name hinted toward the imminence of an end. The eventide of a story that I was too blind with pride to consider, as being the downfall to all I loved and held dear. Eve.
As Eve, you broke the norm. The norm that was to obey and not question. The norm that was to allay temptation and protect Adam at all costs. As

Eve, you were designed to bring about the birth of new life. I was too blind to consider what that new life would look like, I knew of it, I chose to ignore it.

Because why? Why would I have reason to believe that the creatures I had created would stray so far from my rules?

The tree of knowledge - do not eat from it. Why were you so easily swayed? Of course, I ask the question with the knowledge I had then because it is in your human design to er. It is the perfection of human beings, to be imperfect. I created you in my image and yet what you created was in your own images and was harboured by the cruelties of the world around you, but also the beauty. You bore two sons. One a shepherd, one a farmer; both deserving of my affections. Yet, jealousy and anger tainted the first born, resulting in the murder of his younger sibling. Again, I knew this would happen, I could have stopped it. I chose not to intervene, for I knew that Cain would one day see the folly of his ways. I knew one day, I would create a son who would repent for the sins of *all* of the mankind that you, Eve, had helped to sire.

I see all. I know all. I am omnipotent. The Almighty. Yet I am guilty too, of pride.

What I once created out of love and care, I harboured jealously. I fell victim to my own vices. It is human to have faults, but what is it to be almighty? I cannot afford to make such luxuries as an error. I make an error; I am cast out of someone's life. My mere existence is questioned. As a result, I feel my form chipped away. But where one might question their faith in me, millions more will fill in those chips, rebuild me, help me back up again. Such is the majesty of human belief.

So, Eve, mother of human sin, how is it that the love you had with Adam never ended? How is it the love you had from Cain never wavered, even after his death? How is it that the creator of all sin, is surrounded by love, care, and affection – while the father of all creation, has lost the love of his own kin and his sired son?

Dear Eve, I hurt, I ache. My heart feels torn. My son turns his back to me, while yours waits in Purgatory, ever hopeful to be reunited with you. My son's mother cowers and bows to my needs, yet there is no love, for she believes her purpose in life was to bear him, her love goes to another, Joseph. I kept you and Adam apart, all those years. I knew one day you would reunite, and the eons of time apart would mean naught, with the desire and love that you once had for each other burning through the range of lifetimes.

Now, I look down and I see the folly I created. My affections, my efforts, my time was invested in creating life and abundance. I called upon Lilith for clarity and reason, both of which I already had, I just could not accept to hear it from myself. I needed to hear it from her, as while she condemned herself to Hell, she speaks on behalf of you, Eve. She speaks on behalf of all women, of all men, of all my children. She loved all, I would have kept her safe in Eden; were it not for the words of my own kin, poisoning her core. I offered her an alternative realm, but she chose pain and suffering, she told me that someone needed to be there for those who felt rejected by me.

I knew this would happen. I knew she felt this way. I knew the consequences of her actions. My pride, however, prevented me from accepting it and in turn, preventing it.

Right now, my son charges in to battle, in a world of make-believe and conjuring. He too, is blinded by his own ambition and greed. He is united with Nemesis, and she has turned on her own brother, Charon, Thet. Once again, I see siblings fighting to the death. I see my own creation falling foul of sin. I see perfection tainted and I question, is history always doomed to repeat itself?

There is a difference in what I see now, though. The suffering sibling does not have my name on his lips, it's yours. My son charges into conflict full of justification and bliss, he is far from repentant or filled with rage. I see Lucifer and his brethren, racing on the backs of human men, fighting for the existence of humans. None of this, did I perceive as *ever* happening. I had faith in my son, now I question it.

Eve, you bore human sin to this world, yet you bore something else. Something so powerful and strong that time and distance cannot touch it. You bore human love. This is something I cannot comprehend. I am the Almighty one, I love as a father to all living, breathing creatures. I have not known the intricacies of the love humans bestow on each other. I separated you and Adam as punishment, not daring to see my creations die; however, I ensured that you would both live on endlessly. I see now that the love of humans is greater in strength, than my own punishment's brutality.

I see you now Mabel, as the battle draws near, resting in state. Kristoph rests peacefully, by your side. Your friends gallop into battle blindly, unknowing of their fate, but united in their belief in you. You are surrounded by the ghosts of children, failed by my kin and me. Those infants are in turn defended by those deemed heathens, who chose to follow a different path. Those brave men are joined at the hip by their mortal foes, who vowed to defend my honour to the death. My kin, my sired son, and I - we have failed them all. We have failed you and Kristoph, Adam and Eve. I see all those figures who chose to leave their state in Limbo and populate the imagined world of Thet, rallying on Lucifer; all strong in their belief that the side of my once greatest enemy, is the one that will see ensure that they are greeted warmly at the gates to my halls. They are right to think so, Eve. They will be greeted with open arms. I see those lingering in Limbo still, uncertain, scared, anxious – I might not have foreseen all these current events, but I do know that you will help them.

Mabel Marionnette Weaver, you are stronger and greater than even I. Both you and Kristoph have done things in the space of a few brief moons, that I could not in the space of millions of years. Allow me to grant you and your partner a gift. I grant to you life, unending. To be united, until the ends of time. Allow me, to apologise for my past ignorance; and for all the pain and suffering I have caused you in my blind fury and hurt pride. I bless you both for your past repentance and I grant you immunity from the sting of any blade or weapon that would harm you. In turn, I ask you to do the impossible. Please, return my son to me. Let me have the chance to apologise to him in much the same way as I have apologised to you.

As a final offering, as I watch Lilith fall and cry out in agony from a blade that would have pierced her son's heart, by her own daughter; I grant you and Kristoph, with the power to conjure and wield a power of your own design. Know that this power will be with you until you choose to relinquish its hold when you eventually choose to submit to that everlasting sleep and meet me, like an old friend. Farewell for now, Mabel and Kristoph, I know we will meet again in Paradise, one day.

Praise be with you, both.

Chapter 37. Nemesis

Mabel opened her eyes, blearily. The light from the hospital room burned at her retinas, and the heat that surrounded her was almost unbearable. Was the place on fire?

Sounds of screaming and tortured cries of agony sliced at her ears. The scent of sterile hospital and sulphur insulted her nose, and she wanted nothing more than to pull the sheets over her head and hide away from the mess that surrounded her.

"YOU WILL NOT TOUCH HER!" Thet's voice yelled in an unfamiliar strained tone. He was in pain, in agony.

No. Mabel thought to herself. Not Thet, not my beautiful friend.

"STAY AWAY FROM HERR GREYSON, YOU LIAR!" Screamed Helga, powerfully; "BO! ATTACK!"

"VIKINGR! AROO!" Further chants echoed around her head and the sound of wooden shields being clattered, thundered by her head.

"I just want peace," she heard Kristoph murmur sleepily beside her. "Gerroff, don't touch me!" He snapped.

Mabel felt a sudden movement, as though Kristoph had just swatted a fly. The distinctive sound of a slap echoed across the room and a stunned cry of astonishment, followed by; "I'M BURNING!" caused Mabel to force herself to sit upright.

The sight that slowly came into focus was one of surreal chaos! Thet was slumped weakly by the main doorway to the room, cradling Lilith's prone body, his hands coated in a dark pool of blood which stemmed from the wound in her chest that he was desperately applying pressure to.

Helga and the gang of children were nothing more than orbs of light, whirling madly around the room, screaming, and screeching at Gestas and Nemesis, who were both desperately trying to lunge toward her; their attempts being thwarted by, what Mabel could only presume were Saxon and Viking muscular, phantom arms, throwing them around the room. Azrael, meanwhile, was staring flabbergasted at his own arm, which was blistering and burning before his eyes.

Seeing the angel looking murderously at Kristoph and hearing Thet's tortured pleas to Lilith to stay with him, caused Mabel to burn with fury. She turned to face the two foes reaching out toward her. Nemesis, her silver blonde hair, plaited back tightly, jet black eyes cold and venomous; sneered maliciously and swiped at an orb, sending it careening into the wall. With a faint groan, Helga's spiritual form slumped down to the ground, dazed. At the sight of the fallen child, Nemesis cackled with triumph.

"HA!" She cried out, ecstatic.

With a deranged look on her face, Lilith's daughter pointed a taloned finger at the child; "don't think for one second that a Demonic spawn can't make contact with a pathetic, lousy orb! You are nothing more, than a worthless waste of air-born ener..."

Nemesis's insult was cut off as a blast of light sliced through the air. Spatters of black blood splashed against the wall, and all fell deathly silent.

Nemesis looked down at where her outstretched arm had been and where it now fell, on the floor, rolling toward her mother's leg. Mabel slowly turned to glance at where the source of light had stemmed from and was gobsmacked to see Kristoph, standing tall, shaking with pure, unrivalled rage.

"Take another step toward the child, Nemesis, and it will be more than just your arm that will be rolling on the ground," he snarled.

Mabel gaped. Kristoph's voice had a calmness to it, but it was evident he was anything but. His hands were glowing. Asmodeus's branded scar on his wrist was burning away before her very eyes. His golden flecked hair shimmered, and he stood with a confidence and certainty she'd never seen him portray before. He looked every bit the protective hero she'd read about in the Grecian legends. He stood as tall as Eric, how had she never appreciated this gentle giant's height before?

"NO!" Azrael's whiney protest shattered the stunned quiet, in the room. "Father granted *the male human* powers, and bestowed nothing to *me*?" With a sudden burst of volatility, the angel lunged toward Kristoph.

"AZ! YOU IDIOT!" Yelled Gestas, "DON'T..." There was an almighty burst of light, fire and a blood curdling scream as Azrael was vaporized into ethereal dust.

Kristoph, slowly panned around and looked down in shock at Mabel who was kneeling on the bed, staring in wonder at her outstretched hands.

"Well... that was different," she croaked.

Lilith coughed as she chuckled weakly in her son's arms, "You thought that the Almighty would let you both face this bunch of otherworldly beings, without giving you some powers for self-defense?"

Soundlessly, Kristoph mouthed 'the Almighty?' to Mabel, who shook her head in disbelief. How? When had that happened?

"Nemesis, Gestas..." Thet's voice was hoarse; "please, cease this madness. You cannot win. Even as I speak, mother has convinced the rest of the angelic host to charge against the usurper. Your fight here, is lost. Surrender! Sister," he pleaded to Nemesis. "Mother is injured! Help us, please!"

Nemesis glared evilly at her brother, "you were always the favourite son. Next to Reaper Thirteen, not one of us ever stood up to the mark. *I* provided conscience. *I* provided mankind with moral compasses, so that when they died, they could pass on knowing they did right or recognise where they did wrong, but *you...*" She spat, furiously. "You, brother, bastardized that. *You* granted them alternative lives if you determined they'd died *too soon*. You manipulated my skills and gave them some flashing light system so that they would always do right! You made me SUPERFLUOUS!" She screeched.

"No," Thet's eyes were wide, his cheeks streaked with tears. "Sister, I hadn't intended...".

"ENOUGH!" Nemesis staggered as she grasped at her bleeding stump. Panting wildly she continued. "Reaper Thirteen, you are the bane of your ENTIRE family's existence. You were a mistake. The result of a one-night fling between that bitch in your arms and the sorry excuse of a father who spends his life in the closet. You were destined to be alone. Unloved. I swore a vow when I united with the Lord's son, that we would see perfection in his time of rule. The imperfect human race, swiped from the land. It was to be his gift... from me."

"A gift?" Thet's voice was weak, with grief and confusion.

Mabel's eyes widened, as she watched Nemesis stare forlornly at the disembodied arm. As she looked down at the taloned, pale hand; formed into a tight fist.

"You love him," Mabel gasped. "You are in love with the almighty's son!"

Lilith choked and coughed as she breathed in sharply. "You *love* the son-spot? Daughter, you, who were the product of reason and clarity... you have been blinded by a mad man who has no love for you, my sweet dear."

"NO!" Nemesis screamed, "it is you and Reaper Thirteen who surround yourselves with mad men, mother. It matters not," her voice became cool and calculating; "I suppose you can hear the cries from the battlefield too, don't you mother dearest? The son and I are united in mind, and I hear him calling my name in exultation. I hear the thunder of hooves. I perceive his glorious victory. He. Will. Win." With one last vicious look, she turned to Mabel and Kristoph, "and your friends will fall, one... by... one."

With a final murderous look at her brother and mother, Nemesis hastily retreated from the room; Gestas, stared wildly around at them all before hurrying after her.

Lilith groaned loudly as she tried to prop herself up.

"Mother, no. You're weak," Thet mithered, however his mother simply waved his protests away.

"I will be fine, Thet;" she gasped weakly, wincing in pain. "Your sister is a bona fide idiot. I need to return to Hell. I need to heal, rest, and speak to the rest of the family. Hopefully, she's not been successful in convincing the others."

"Others?" Mabel swallowed hard.

Lilith chuckled, "don't play dumb now, Miss Weaver. You know my history; you know the siblings of Charon, sorry, Thet - you read about them in your ancient texts."

She smiled knowingly at Mabel's confusion, "yes, I know all about your education. The Almighty made it his mission to keep an eye on you, both. Incidentally, he's rather a fan of Dark Omens, Mr Greyson, he has a few posters and rare singles dotted around his halls;" swallowing hard, Lilith sighed.

"Thanatos, Hypnos, Eris, and Keres. Not to mention the large number of reapers and demons. What can I say?" She winked impishly at Thet; "it was cold in Hell, once upon a time."

"Mother," Thet slowly stood up and reached down to help Lilith stand, but she tutted and brushed his hand away.

"Ahhh Thet," she sighed. "Think not on what Nemesis has said. Sam and I have loved you all dearly, equally. We just focused on you more, as you *never* played by the rules. No one writes a guidebook for parents, least of all for deities and their offspring. I'll be fine. Go! Help your friends. When all this is over, help me find your siblings before Nemesis does. Something tells me this infatuation she has is going to crumble apart rather messily, and we need to do some damage control."

Shakily, the Demon Queen rose to her feet, "Mab, Kris... I'd like to say it's been a pleasure..." shaking her head weakly, and holding at the wound in her chest, Lilith closed her eyes and allowed the ground to swallow her up.

Mabel slowly pulled at the wires and cords attached to her. Most of the electronics had burnt and frayed away in the chaotic battle that had ensued around her while she'd been unconscious and were now serving no purpose, other than tethering her to the bed.

"Thet?" She sighed, as she pushed herself up, her side aching but miraculously healed from Valentine's bullet wound. "Are you alright?"

Thet looked over at her and smiled weakly, "I'm fine Mab. Do you think you're strong enough to move?"

Mabel grinned, "let me get dressed, and I'll be ready when you are;" she smirked as she wrapped the blankets closer around her, aware of the hospital gown's limited coverage around her back and the floating orbs of children and Vikings loitering behind her.

Thet nodded, "very well. Miss Schneider?"
Slowly, he helped the child up as she rubbed her
head, "how are you?"

Helga grinned, "Mr Grim, I have bumped my
head. Pain is a feeling I haven't felt in a long time.
It's still as unpleasant as how I remember it. I am
fine though."

Thet nodded and sighed with relief. "Listen, Miss
Schneider. While Miss Weaver, Herr Greyson
and I go to help our friends, I cannot return you
back to heaven. Will you be alright returning to
Limbo? Just for the interim?"

Helga grinned childishly, "Mr Grim, normally I
would say yes."

"Normally?" Thet raised a questioning brow.

"Ja, but you see... there is a portal of light behind
you that is beckoning to us all," she pointed.

Everyone turned around. Sure enough, where the
door to the hospital room should have been, a
splendid white light had started to grow and
expand. One by one, the orbs of children,
Vikings, and Saxons passed through the portal.
Mabel smiled as the faint sound of a deep, warm,

jovial voice that seemed almost vaguely familiar; as if from a dream, spoke from beyond. "Welcome, to you all. It has been too long. Please, pass through and welcome to your new Paradise."

As the light dimmed behind Mabel's waving hand, Thet turned to her and Kristoph.

"So, new powers?" He rubbed his hands together, his face anxious yet clearly excited.

"It would seem so," Kristoph wiggled his fingers; "not quite sure how they work yet, but um, ready to give them a go." He frowned, "so much for getting your mother to deliver the hiding of a lifetime, though."

Thet shook his head, "I think in this instance, seeing you and Mabel wielding weapons gifted by his own Father, might just be enough of a deterrent, for now at least" Thet hurriedly reached out and pulled the curtains around Mabel's bed, for her privacy.

Mabel snorted, the fabric was barely holding on to the railings and she could just about see the top of Kristoph's head when she stood up. Hastily, she pulled on her old clothes, wrinkling her nose

at the dried blood on her once favourite blouse.
As she pulled on her shoes, she tugged at the
curtains, pulling them down to the ground by
accident in the process.

"Oops," she grimaced; "sorry."

Kristoph snickered, "I think if we survive this,
you shouldn't have to apologise to *anyone*, ever
again, Mab."

"Well, it's always good to practise humility;" she
grinned as she grabbed Kristoph's hand and
kissed him on the cheek.

"Right, well..." Thet brushed down his attire, "I
do hate leaving this room in such a state, though.
That equipment is not as affordable as it should
be for such a service this place provides."

With a flourish of his hand, the disarray in the
room vanished into thin air. The machinery and
wiring mended itself miraculously and the bed
and curtains neatly cleaned, pressed, and folded
themselves up for the next occupant. With a final
nod at Mabel's clothing, the crusty stain of dried
blood crumbled away to leave a pristine, soft
fabric behind, without a bullet hole to be seen.

"So, shall we?" He grimaced, and without another word, Thet clicked his fingers.

Chapter 38. Casualties of War

The trio stepped out on to a crumbling, flat rooftop and surveyed the immediate scene around them. The first thing that hit Mabel about the realm Thet had created, was the scent of decay. The smell was acrid and upon breathing it in, Mabel started to choke. Her eyes started to burn.

"Where is that smell coming from?" Mabel wheezed.

"It is rather potent, isn't it," Thet considered. "You wanted me to set the scene Mab, so, I conjured a warzone, with all the delightful scents that come with it."

"Delightful?" Kristoph choked, "I never thought I'd find myself saying this, but I prefer the scents of the rat-infested Hamelin to this."

The trio looked about them with wrinkled noses, trying to ascertain where their friends had based themselves. It was silent as the grave however, and Mabel couldn't help but shake off an ominous feeling that they were too late. Only Samael's reassurance of her friend's demises being 'moons from now' kept her from worrying too much about the Dark Omens members.

"You don't suppose we're too late?" Kristoph asked, as though reading Mabel's mind.
"No," Thet answered. "Can you both feel that? It's acceptance. This world was designed to host a fight, it's accepted and welcomed that conflict." Mabel and Kristoph nodded, the air was thick with an oppressive anticipation. How much time had passed since their visit to heaven? They'd only secured an hour's worth of life essence, which had since worn away. How long did it normally take for soldiers to rally the troops, get into position, and meet their foe, head on?
As they surveyed the crumbling ruins of the buildings around them, Mabel shivered as she saw the haunted forms of a few lost souls who had made the journey from Limbo, flit across the potholed streets and disappear.
"Thet, you've created a literal ghost town;" Mabel's voice quivered as the unnatural feeling of being surrounded by the unknown supernatural

world, played at her subconscious.

"I agree," Thet clenched his jaw, and looked quickly over his shoulder as some rubble crumbled away from a tall building behind them and clattered noisily to the ground. "I think I might have outdone myself with this place."

Cautiously, the three friends made their way down the flimsy fire escape that was barely clinging to the front of the building they'd stepped out on. As soon as Mabel's foot touched the ground, the shriek of a horse's call rang out, loudly. The sound reverberated through the streets and alleyways. It echoed around them to such an extent that it was impossible to determine where it had originated.

"Would it be worth splitting up?" Kristoph considered, chewing at his lip.

"Have you ever watched a horror movie, Kris?" Mabel hissed, "never split up! We'd be much easier pickings for the likes of..."

Another piercing shriek filled the air, and Thet's head snapped sharply to face an alleyway to his left.

"Down here!" He murmured, as he hurried

down the unevenly paved gulley. Kristoph and
Mabel desperately ran after him.

Laboured panting and grunting grew louder with
every step they took. Mabel looked between
Kristoph and Thet, wondering, and almost
hoping that it stemmed from them! No. Thet
couldn't breathe and Kristoph, despite having
abused his lungs from years of smoking, was
surprisingly fit and agile. Mabel swallowed a lump
in her throat, anticipating her worst nightmare as
they rounded a corner and there, with a cruel
barbed lance penetrating its haunches, lay a jet-
black steed.

"Jésús," Mabel felt tears begin to fall down her
cheek, as she hurried toward the struggling
creature. "It's okay, we're here. You're alright!"
Softly she cradled the steed's head in her lap.
The horse tried to shift its front legs around and
lift itself up from the ground, but the foul weapon
had lamed him by skewering him cruelly to the
ground. The pain her friend was in looked
unbearable and beads of sweat mixed with bright
red blood mingled together around his strong
haunches.

"Thet?" Mabel choked back a loud sob, "can't you do something?"

Thet looked sadly down at the horse, who's bloodshot eyes looked up at his with an acceptance of fate that only such noble creatures can exude.

"I'm sorry Mab," he sighed, "this is beyond my skill."

"No," Mabel shook her head, "I refuse to believe that."

Jésús buried his long muzzle into Mabel's hands. Blood had congealed around his mouth and with a thought that felt like a blade, piercing her own heart, Mabel recalled Samael's words "I taste metal for Mr. Guerrero."

Thet knelt beside Mabel and wrapped a comforting arm around her, "Mab, there's very little any of us can do for him right now. We need to move on. *War* would have fallen with him, so we need to find him quickly."

"I'm not *leaving* Jésús!" Mabel gasped, incredulously. "We can't just abandon him here like this, can we Kris?"

Kristoph grimaced as he looked closer at the

lance which had pierced through their friend.
"Who wields a spear like this?" He asked, as he
surveyed the cruel blade. The long wooden shaft
was jagged, twisted and splintered with age. The
wood was burnt black and seemed to smoke
acridly.

Thet looked up and narrowed his eyes
"Longinus," he said through gritted teeth; "I
should have known he'd have rallied with the
son."

"That's poetic," Mabel wiped her eyes. "The
Roman who pierced the side of the Son-Spot,
pierces our friend Jésús. No one really knew what
happened to him."

Thet nodded, "I heard lions would maul at him
in a cave. I think that would be enough for
anyone to develop feelings of resentment. Not to
mention he's a Roman, and they were always a
weird bunch. Full of spite and mistrust. So eager
to incorporate a conquered people's religion, just
in case theirs wasn't quite right."

"Can you not remove it?" Mabel asked the two
men, "at the very least we can offer him *some*
relief!"

Thet and Kristoph shared a brief look of
uncertainty, before they both cautiously
approached the protruding handle.

"I'm so sorry mate," Kristoph murmured,
sincerely; "this is going to hurt."

Jésús closed his eyes tightly, and nuzzled his face
into Mabel's stomach, his hind shivering and
spasming with pain and sadness.

As the two men set to work, grunting and
groaning with effort, they tried to manipulate the
weapon out of the wound, the black stallion
stayed as silent as possible. On occasion, he
would flinch, and the spear would slip from his
friend's grip; but overall, Jésús was the perfect
patient.

With one final yank, Thet and Kristoph pulled
the blade out from their friend who shivered all
over with a sense of relief, as blood started to
gush freely from the open wound. Mabel looked
down into her friend's eyes and saw them look up
at her lovingly and sleepily. As his laboured
breathing started to quieten, Mabel felt a tickle of
inspiration caress her mind. Gently as she could,
she lifted the horse's head up to her face.

As Thet and Kristoph looked on perplexed, Mabel rested her lips on the velvety ones of the horse's and softly blew into its mouth. All the while, her eyes remained closed as she focused on a mantra that had started to churn through her mind.

'I am Eve. As I bore life into this world, so I breathe life back into you. Restore. Heal. Live.' She kept her eyes tightly shut as she strained her mind to focus. She didn't care that the light around her was starting to get uncomfortably warm. She ignored the murmurs of uncertainty from Kristoph and Thet. She ignored the change of texture of the horse's lips. Only when a gentle hand brushed the hair away from her face and a soft chuckle vibrated against her mouth, did she open her eyes and pull back.

"I think," Jésús's tired, Spanish tone spoke huskily. "We had best stop, before Kris spears me to the ground again."

Mabel beamed as her friend and the bass player of Dark Omens sat back on his bent knees and patted himself down.

"I'm not even going to ask, at this point;"

Kristoph shook his head, bewilderedly, with a wide grin spreading across his face. Chucking the spear to the ground, he fell to his knees and the two men embraced each other tightly. "You had us so bloody worried for a moment there." He spoke into the crook of his friend's neck.

"Ah, it was a flesh wound," Jésus joked. "Listen guys, we were outnumbered from the start. The um, enemy, has a number of beings by his side. That man you said, the one with the lanza, when he saw me fall, he grabbed Luci... I mean, War. I don't know where he took them, but we were scattered. I was trying to call out to the rest of the guys, but only you three came." He looked around at the trio almost adoringly.

"And not a moment too soon. Do you think you can stand?" Thet asked cautiously.

No sooner had their friend steadied himself and assured them that he was tired, but well; the group began the laborious task of racing up and down the streets, trying to listen out for any sounds of their friends. The search seemed to take a lifetime, but there was still no sign of anyone. Aside from the obvious scenery, it was as though the battle had long ago moved on to another time and place. As they gathered in the main town square, feeling completely defeated, Cain's voice roared from the distant treeline.

"MAB! LOOK OUT!"

As the man raced toward them with long strides, the group looked around as the faintest of whinnies suddenly cried out. Kristoph looked at Cain whose head was tilted upright as he pointed to the sky above them.

"OH! BLOODY HELL!" Kristoph cried, pointing up.

The group craned their necks and cried out in horror as Pete the Shire Horse twisted and turned in distress as he free fell from the sky.

"I don't think you'll be able to kiss life back into strawberry jam," Kristoph yelped next to Mabel who could only watch on, speechless.

With a blast of light, an angel swooped gracefully through the air and caught the huge form of the grand steed as if it were nothing more than a bag of sugar. No sooner had the angel wrapped his arms around the horse's flank, the transformation spell lifted and soon they were watching Pete scream wildly, while clinging tightly to the angel's neck.

As the angel landed and struggled to loosen the drummer's grip from around him, Mabel broke free from the group.

"Pete, oh thank goodness!" Mabel hurried toward the angel and the drummer, who slumped weakly to the ground.

"Pleased to see you too, Mab;" Pete whimpered weakly, before falling back on to the ground, breathing heavily.

The angel surveyed Mabel and nodded, "I'm glad to see I got you and My Greyson back to your bodies in time. You were nearly nothing more than a memory."

Not allowing Mabel to answer, he turned to Thet. "Reaper, the battle has become more equal in number since our arrival. It seems our father's son had managed to successfully rally quite a few of our number, not to mention some of the lesser-known deities from the other realms. Nemesis seemed to have successfully gather some of the more demonic and condemned hoard. Suffice it to say, your friends stood little chance on their own;" the angel turned to look at Pete who was being helped up and patted down, by Cain.

"As soon as he saw my brethren and I join your friends however, the son bolted," the angel continued. "We know not where to. I was searching for him when I spotted Cain and your friend charge toward Satan. The Demonic lord threw Cain off the back of your friend, with a blast of hellfire. Your... horse... friend here, valiantly served as a blockade while Cain withdrew. I watched as Satan hurled this giant horse into the air in his wrath to reach Cain. He didn't see my blade swipe down to smite him back to his damnable abyss below. So, well played master Peter Campbell, you are a self-less warrior. I am honoured to have saved your life."

"Um... Cheers?" Pete smiled weakly. "Who are you?"

The angel snorted, "Michael," he answered simply.

Michael turned to Mabel and Kristoph and folded his arms, "I must head back to help your allies. Asmodeus and Samael continue to ride, they gave chase to the son. I can't be certain where they are, but I would say the treeline is your safest bet, it offers shelter and places to hide."

"Thank you, Michael!" Thet nodded, and with barely a second glance, the group of friends hurried to the treeline they had seen Cain race from, the sound of blades crashing and rebellious cries, growing louder with every step.

As they ran, Kristoph couldn't help himself, "so, Lucifer and Satan *aren't* one and the same?"

"Not now, Kris!" Thet groaned and pushed forward.

Chapter 39. God's given Powers

Mabel couldn't help but feel a foreboding sense of dread as they ran through the forest. The last time she'd been in this kind of scenario, she'd had a demigod chasing her. Through the vague spattering of trees to her right, she could see the skirmish between the archangels and the son's followers. Michael and Jésús hadn't been lying when they'd shared their remarks of being outnumbered. Still, Michael and his impressively skilled team of archangels, were providing more than enough cover while they raced through the woodland; tuning every sense to the sound of hoof fall and conflict ahead.

As they hopped over fallen branches and rocks, Kristoph suddenly skidded to halt with confusion etched across his face, "I'm sorry, but there are some things I am really struggling to understand." "Like what?" Thet asked, impatiently. He looked around him, anxiously, as the sounds of war cries echoed around them.

"Well, think about it. Gestas and Azrael. They were the masterminds behind the trip to Heaven. If they didn't want us to get involved, why did they tell you about the plot?" He panted, bending double with his hands on his knees. "Not to mention, Mab and I have powers that can both destroy and heal, apparently. What's that all about?"

Mabel shook her head, "Kris, those are both very valid questions, but can we hash out the reasonings of mad men when we're not in the middle of a war zone?"

"Gestas?" Cain asked. Even *his* cheeks were flushed with the exertion. "The impenitent thief? He's involved in this?"

Kristoph and Mabel nodded at Cain's stunned response.

"That makes no sense!" Cain shook his head. "Gestas is, for all intents and purposes, a friend of mine. He hates the Son of the Lord. His feelings never changed, hence his condemnation to Purgatory. He's a neighbour if you will."

At the look of confusion on Mabel's face, Cain

hastily explained: "there are multiple recesses in each realm. Hell has its echelons; Heaven has its collection of halls. Purgatory has, well, neighbourhoods. Homes for the homeless. Purgatory isn't a place of unending suffering... well, it *was*, before we added some semblance of order to it. Now, it's a place where we can take our time to decide whether to make peace with our actions, accept our fate, or repent for our crimes."

"No offence mate," Pete said, as beads of sweat shimmered across his brow. "But with the amount of time you've been there, I'd have thought you'd have made a decision by now, either way?"

"I did," Cain said. "Lilim and I chose to accept our fate but agreed to a life outside of politics between heaven and hell. Neither of us can stand the constant bickering between the two forces. So, we created a home. Gestas followed suit. Although, he's far from repentant, he isn't altogether keen on spending eternity in Hell, so he opted for Purgatory. Life in darkness. He was once a thief after all, he's no stranger to the dark."

"But..." Mabel's voice trailed off uncertainly as over Thet's shoulder she spotted something that made her blood run cold.

Walking toward the group was the son. His smile was cruel, and he looked exhausted, but victorious.

"Who's that he's dragging?" Kristoph grimaced, turning around to follow Mabel's mortified gaze. As if in answer to his question, with a display of venomous hatred, the son hurled the figure he'd been pulling along the ground, toward the group. There was a moment of terror as the limp form of Eric landed heavily, like a rag doll, at Thet's feet.

"I believe," the almighty's son cried out, "that *disgrace* belongs to you!" He spat angrily and stayed his ground, his eyes looked deranged and wild.

Mabel crouched by the rhythm guitarist and tried to shake him, but it was no use. Eric lay on the ground, white as a sheet and unresponsive. "WHAT HAVE YOU DONE TO HIM?" She screeched, her voice drowning out the battle behind them.

The figure simply cackled, "I have done what I intend to do with all the useless flesh sacks that overpopulate this world. I will create husks from their bodies, fill them with the souls of my brethren, my kin. Not to mention all the powerful deities who clamour for the graces of the Lord and who are owed recognition, honour, respect. That is but one casualty of war *Eve*," he sneered wickedly, as Mabel clung to Eric's frozen hand. "Get used to seeing billions more!"

Kristoph lunged forward with a cry of anger, however Thet held him back. The son continued to laugh in a deranged way.
"I almost forgot about *you* Adam, father of Sin and Hate!" He scoffed, "maybe if you'd controlled that woman of yours better, we wouldn't be in this situation."
Cruelly he pointed at Eric's body. "You only have yourself to blame for *that!*"
Arrogantly, the figure strode confidently toward the group. Cain charged forward with violence in his eyes, but with a wave of his hand, the son simply sent the small giant, careening back, felling a tree in the process.

"Not one of you can touch me," he snarled, maniacally. "I have power and dominion over you all. *I* stand in my father's feet, ready to bestow the glorious death on his creations that he never could. *I AM THE ALMIGHTY!*"

"Let me tell you something, Mr. Almighty;" Lucifer's deep voice caused everyone to whirl around to see him nonchalantly resting, in his War guise, against a tree with a bored and unimpressed look on his face.
"Part of the job is to be omnipotent," he drawled, lazily.
The son scoffed, "I *am* omnipotent, Devil. Your foolish charade of the horseman War had no one fooled. I saw you and your demonic kin sat on the backs of those flesh sacks from the start. You were doomed to fail the moment you saw me."
"Is that so?" Lucifer yawned and slung his battle axe made from his devil horns, lazily by his side.
"How'd you explain that then?" He smirked and pointed over the figure's shoulder.
The Son of God turned around confused, staring questioningly out to the empty space of land

between the forest and the crumbling town. As he did so, Lucifer silently approached him.

"You really think I would allow someone to creep up on me, from that crumbling heap of rubble over there?" The son snorted.

"No," Lucifer reasoned, silently raising his axe in the air, "I had hoped you'd fall for the 'what's that over your shoulder trick' though."

He grinned wildly, as he arced his axe through the air with tremendous force. The son barely stood a chance, as the weapon took him completely unawares, knocking the wind out of him and sending him souring back through the trees.

"NOW, SAM!" Lucifer yelled.

To everyone's surprise, Samael charged out of the shadows on the back of Adrian the horse who looked resplendent in the dim light. With a tremendous leap, Adrian launched himself over the group of bewildered humans and galloped wildly toward the stunned figure of the son. With a rebel yell that deafened everyone, Samael raised his sword in the air and pointed it directly toward the lone figure ahead of them.

Quick to overcome the startling change of events, Mabel found herself racing after Samael, screaming at him and begging him to stop. Behind her, she heard Kristoph and Thet thundering behind her, calling her back but she was faster. Much faster. Quickly she charged, a phantom voice ringing in her ears: *please return my son to me.*

Finally, the powers made sense. The almighty had granted them both powers so that they could be a force of protection, not of violence and menace! She and Kristoph had the power to restore mankind. Lilith might have been created to provide clarity and reason; yet she, Eve, had been created to bring life into the world around her. She would be damned if she was about to allow it to be snuffed out under her watch.

In a burst of speed, she found herself matching the pace of Adrian's incredible steed's form.

"Adrian," she panted, impressing herself with the renewed vigour she'd been granted; "cease your charge. Trust me!"

"MAB!" Kristoph yelled behind her, "what in God's name are you doing?"

His question made her laugh out loud, as she overtook the slowing horse and stood between the angel of Death, and the son.

"Don't you see Kris?" She grinned, "we were granted these powers for a reason. It was to ensure that *we* were used to protect *ALL* of mankind, *not* just our friends."

"Father granted you powers?" The son scoffed, "he must be more weak-minded than I thought." Mabel turned to face the so-called saviour and smiled sweetly at him. "I didn't always live this life you know. I was once an administrative assistant who dealt with people who thought they knew better than me and spoke to me as though I was beneath them. I always saw it as a reflection on them and what they were going through, more so than a reflection on my own capabilities," she said, her chest heaving from the exertion of her sprint. "Just like I see you for what you are now;" she laughed, confidently.

"Well Eve, I'm sure we're all waiting on bated breath to hear your thoughts.;" the son rolled his eyes, tauntingly.

"You're a boy who wants his daddy's affection.

You clamour for it," Mabel grinned.

"And?" the figure wrinkled his nose in disgust.

"I'm just saying, it's typical behaviour... of a human;" Mabel said. "Any one of us humans gathered here could have told you that. Yes, you have a unique family, but the premise remains. You were born to a human woman and were brought up in a human way. You have spent so long in the clouds with your father however, you've forgotten what it was like before you developed a God-complex."

"How dare you!" the figure of the saviour raised his hand and aimed a vicious swipe at Mabel's face, however his hand stalled midway through its arc.

"You will not touch her," Kristoph glowered, his body ablaze with resplendent light as it had been in the hospital room.

"I don't understand! How are you both..." the son struggled.

"It's only human to er," Mabel smiled, as her own body started to glow brilliantly; "but you see, Adam and Eve; that is to say, Kris and I, we were not born human. Nor are we human now. We were created from your father's own hands, just like his angels. While they are bound for heaven though, we were grounded on earth to ensure the life of mankind will *never* die. You might try and wage your trivial wargames, but it will not work. Not while Kris and I are here!"

"Well, I'll just have to kill you both first then, won't I," the figure glowered at her, dangerously. Mabel's eyes burnt brightly as she laughed, whole-heartedly; "how do you kill something which is already dead?" She asked. "How do you destroy those who are blessed with ever-lasting life, who will only rest in the earth when we feel our time is up? How do you aim to convince the angel of Death who has chosen to ride in opposition to you, to take us away? How do you aim to chaperone Kris and I to the afterlife, when we have the best in the reaper business, by our side?"

For the first time since he'd appeared to them, the son's smug look waned.

"Face it," Mabel spoke coolly, "you have lost today's fight. Your allies have been thwarted. Your prized fighter, Satan, has been cast back down to Hell. The archangels are currently rallying up your loose cannons and you can be sure that Kris and I will ensure that any who escape today, will always be looking over their shoulders."

The son of God shifted uncomfortably away from the two figures before him.

"You cannot stop this," he hissed. "I've only just begun. Sure, I might have lost this battle, but the war will continue to wage on, so long as I have followers."

"Then we have some convincing to do," Kris smiled softly, as he held Mabel's hand.

"You don't even know who I have on my side," the son laughed. "I will watch all of humanity burn and crumble to the ground before you will find the last of my followers. What could your diminutive powers as Adam and Eve do, which those bestowed on me by my father, will not?"

"Well, for one;" Mabel closed her eyes as she focused on the ruins and destructions that rested on one side of the forest. She felt the pain of the fallen lying on the ground, suffering, on the battlefield to the other side. Her thoughts reached out to Eric who lay unconscious behind her, and she smiled inwardly as she smelt the familiar scent of ambrosia stemming from him, keeping him safe in state.

With a surge that ran through her, she allowed the energy she'd been building up, to burst out from her, reaching out to every inch of Thet's pocket world. She heard the gasps of relief as the souls who'd left limbo to fight by Lucifer's side, were lifted to new heavenly heights with peace in their spirits. She felt the ground thunder as the ruined town restored itself to a grandeur that had never existed before.

Finally, she calmed down her power and allowed the burning light within her to subdue itself.

"My name is Mabel in this form;" she said. "I was created as Eve, and I have lived countless lifetimes where I have ensured lives could continue to live. I might have been living in the dark then, but I live enlightened now. My name may have changed, but my powers are the same. My bond to this earth is stronger than that of any creature, be they spiritual or earth-bound. As such, I grant you one chance, and I encourage you to consider it, carefully."

The son's body shook with unbridled rage as he clenched his jaw and fists and glared between Kristoph and Mabel.

"Return to your father," Mabel advised. "He calls for you. He has promised you his attention and his undying affection. Return to your father and open up to him about your grievances. He will listen, he has promised me this. Do not let the negative influences of Nemesis blind you from the love of your own kin!"

"If I refuse?" The son asked through clenched teeth.

"Should you refuse," Kristoph answered smoothly. "You will invoke the wrath of your father, channelled through us! You see what he has offered us today." He spread his arms wide, creating a splendid forcefield of energy between the son in front of them, and the gathered group of deities and humans behind them. "It might be worth imagining what his wrath might take the form of. Because I assure you, while Mab will continue to breathe life into those deserving. I will ensure that all life will be protected, at... all... costs!"

The son growled under his breath and went to lunge toward him, but his movement was stalled by a disembodied voice.

"My love," Nemesis's cooing voice spoke out to the glade. "Return to me! Our allies have retreated, we need to reconvene. Return to me!" Her voice pleaded.

"STOP HIM!" Lucifer cried from behind them, but it was too late. Before anyone could do anything, the son's smug sneering form disappeared.

Chapter 40. Dark Omens

Kristoph and Mabel stared blankly at the space where the almighty's had disappeared. The very idea that they had allowed the mastermind of all the grief and turmoil they had been facing, to slip away in front of them was incomprehensible. Footsteps hurried up behind them as a pair of hands firmly twisted them around. Thet's eyes blazed with a fierce blue flame and his face was twisted in an array of emotions.

"Mab! Kris! Speak to me, are you both alright?" His voice sounded desperate.

"He got away," Kristoph finally managed, his chest aching with anger and regret.

Thet shook his head, "for now;" he assured them. "We will catch up with him, but he has left an almighty mess to clean up. The main thing is, you're both safe!"

Mabel swallowed hard, "Thet... we failed."

"No!" Thet snapped, "Neither of you have failed. It is we, the very deities you entrusted your souls with, who have failed *you!*"

The rest of the group slowly approached them. Eric's arms were slumped drunkenly over both Pete and Jésús's shoulders, while his legs dragged lazily behind him.

"Eric!" Mabel cried and hurried toward him. "Is he...?"

"No," Samael answered, grimly. "Your friends were noble, valiant, and loyal throughout. That said, I think we can all agree that Eric went above and beyond. Perhaps a little too far."

"Where's Asmodeus?" Kristoph asked suddenly, looking around. "Eric carried him, where is Asmodeus? He made a promise that Eric wouldn't come to any harm!"

"A promise, Kris," Lucifer smirked and folded his arms. "That he is working on keeping. I see your awful scar has healed..."

Kristoph looked down at the smooth skin of his wrist and his brow furrowed. "It must have been my powers."

"Really?" Lucifer asked, sarcastically. "Forgive me. You said your role as Adam reincarnate, was to protect; while Mab illustrated that she could restore those on the brink of death. I didn't realise you were on Death's door, Kris?"

Kristoph looked at Mabel who shook her head. Cautiously, she brushed away the strands of dark hair from Eric's face. His skin was getting warmer, but it was still clammy. She could hear his laboured breathing, his chest heaving and struggling under his black shirt.
"Oh Eric, what happened to you? Guys, I don't think I can heal him, right now;" Mabel confessed. "What I did back there, I don't think I have anything left as back up."
Samael chuckled softly, "Rest Miss Mabel. You projected a force of life across this expanse of land that has revitalised a lot of fallen comrades, you have allowed those who fought alongside us from Limbo, to ascend. You are, how would you humans say? Spent. I promise you; that Mr. Payne will be fine. We just need to get you all to safety. All will be made clear, let's just get you out of here."

Everything seemed to happen in a blur. Before she knew it, Mabel found herself back in the

familiar surroundings of the tour bus that had
been parked up in the basement carpark of the
Hotel on International Drive, Florida. She was
surrounded by the Dark Omens members.
Adrian, now back in human form was excitedly
writing his experiences down in lyrical form, his
hand a mere blur as it scribbled across a note
pad. Samael, Thet, and Lucifer sank leisurely on
to the bus's couch that seemed to magically
extend to allow for the other-worldly derrieres.
Cain, Pete, and Eric collapsed, exhaustedly,
around the table where Adrian was hastily
scrawling away. Jésús walked to the back of the
bus and flopped heavily on to his old bed,
ignoring his claustrophobia, and started to snore
softly within moments of his head hitting the
pillow. Kristoph and Mabel, however, sank
sleepily to the floor, still holding each other's
hands, tightly.

"Cain?" Mabel asked, "what happened back
there? What did we miss?"
"I think you need sleep, more than answers right
now, Mab," Cain smiled softly, but Mabel shook
her head.

"That's the problem, I want to sleep, but I need answers," she insisted. "Is the battle still ongoing? What on earth happened to Eric and Asmodeus?"

"Hush," Cain soothed gently. "Once you are all fully rested, we will tell you."

Somewhat reluctantly, Mabel and Kristoph stiffly rose from the ground staggered into the bunk room, and collapsed on one of the bunks, holding each other close.

As Mabel felt the tiredness come crashing down on her, she heard the dull murmur of Lucifer's voice, "I wonder how much luck Asmodeus is having with healing that man's wounds? It was a rather brutal hit from an elephant."

"Not sure," Cain answered quietly, "what I *do* know is that my father is now free of his possession and Asmodeus has a life debt to a human man. I don't know about you, but I'm inclined to think that such a selfless act warrants a reward."

As much as she tried to strain her ears to hear more, Kristoph draped his arm over her and pulled her in closer to him. The warmth of his body against her back, offered more comfort and security than she had felt since being injected into her new life. With a soft and contented sigh, Mabel allowed herself to slip into a deep sleep.

* *

Several weeks had passed since Mabel and Kristoph had sneaked into Heaven and the son and Nemesis's host had faced the wrath of Lucifer and his horsemen.

"I could do with a drink. What about you?" Thet asked as he leaned against the support barrier at the front of the stage, next to Mabel.

Mabel grinned, and stroked at the course fabric of the VIP lanyard around her neck as Dark Omens performed their last show in the US. While Kristoph and Eric whirled around each other playfully on the stage, performing to the screams of the crowd; she and Thet threaded their way through the mass of people, to the bar.

"I don't think I've ever seen you eat or drink," Mabel said, as she nodded her head in rhythm to the beat Pete played on the drums.

"I'm a reaper and undead, Mab – I don't need to.

You on the other hand look like you're overheating and could do with a drink," Thet smirked. "You might be one of the miraculous creations of God, but you still need your sustenance."

Perched on an ornate bar stool, Mabel enjoyed a mocktail in a plastic cup, while Thet sat next to her. It was amazing how much had changed since her initial resurrection into this life. Even now as she watched Kristoph lose himself in the rhythm of the music and the intoxicating cheering of the crowd, she still couldn't quite believe he was no longer sharing his body with a demonic entity. Eric, on the other hand, was in full swing and seemed to be throwing himself into the experience more and more. His energy, combined with Asmodeus's lust for life, reminded her of a red squirrel high on caffeine.

"Thet?" Mabel asked, "how are things in Limbo now?"

Thet smirked, "well, it has a new caretaker, in the form of Azrael. Admittedly, his mouth has been fused shut courtesy of Michael, so he can't spread any unpleasant rhetoric; but the place looks homelier than ever, now;" he folded his arms and snorted as Eric and Kristoph mimicked charging horses at each other.

"And the populace?" Mabel asked.

"Michael and his brethren have taken on the son's duties while he's otherwise outside of our radar, so the populace is far more manageable in number and not overrun;" Thet nodded.

Mabel's shoulders sagged. It wasn't that she was saddened to hear that the souls in Limbo were finally being moved on, it was more the feeling of emptiness she felt at having not completed her job with Kristoph.

"What's the matter?" Thet asked, seeing Mabel's frown. There was something about seeing her mouth tilted downward that he felt would always trigger a protective instinct within him.

"Well, it's just... Nemesis and the son are now awol. There were some of his followers who were caught and have had their punishments handled swiftly, but there are so many still at large. I just feel like we failed;" she sighed, heavily.

"Failed?" Thet shook his head in disbelief;

"Mabel Marionette Weaver... you helped to shed

light on the fate of so many children who had been trapped in Limbo for eons! You stopped a demigod from pursuing his sordid scheme and hurting other young souls in the process. You not only helped two opposing armies to live out the fight they were forever doomed to have, but you helped in enabling them to look past their differences and fight together for the future of mankind! You helped free my mother from her entrapment in Heaven and cleared her name of any wrongdoing;" Thet smiled sweetly at her. "Mab; you, Kris, and Eric have done so much! I don't think I need even mention the fact that Eric put his life on the line, along with the rest of your friends on that stage, and charged straight toward the enemy, while you and Kris risked your own very souls in Heaven."

"Yes, about that;" Mabel frowned. "I'm still not overly sure how Eric is standing and dancing up there. By all accounts, he should be six feet under! Lucifer said he was booted across the battleground by an elephant. I've also heard that Cain and Asmodeus had to tackle him away from a small army of demons who were happily bludgeoning him with..." her voice trailed off. The thought of Eric being attacked so cruelly and viciously was too much.

Thet bowed his head grimly, "yes, I think the battle scars Eric sustained will take some time to heal. Asmodeus only has energy spare to leave the man's body of an evening time as he spends the daytime healing his *noble steed* from the inside out. No one, other than those two, will ever really know how he feels about what happened. We'll just have to wait for him to divulge all, in his own time."

Mabel nodded and fell silent. Quietly, she sighed and felt a thrill run through her as Kristoph subtly winked in her direction. The opening chords of their latest hit, written in honour of Bo and his kin started to jar around the hall. The audience lapped up the chants and threw their fists in the air at the stomping beat.

"This one goes out to all you heathens out there," Adrian called out to the crowd, raising his own fist. "Friends, I want to hear you singing so loud that even Odin himself will hear! This is, *HEATHENS... OF... OLD!*"

Screams and cries from the crowd erupted as everyone found themselves swept up in the euphoria of the moment. The lights turned down to a deep red that pulsed around them. As Adrian started to growl out the lyrics, a thought crossed Mabel's mind.

"I still don't get what happened with Gestas, though;" she puzzled. "According to Cain there is little to no love lost between him and the son. He's still unrepentant yet wasn't sold on the idea of being sent to Hell, either. Why would he and Azrael come down to earth, reveal their plans, take Kris and I to heaven, only to betray us? It all seemed a lot of effort for no real gain. I mean look at Azrael, he wanted recognition, now he's stuck in Limbo as a caretaker."

Thet nodded along to the rhythm of the song for a while before answering, "Azrael shared some insight into their motivations, prior to being silenced by Michael. It would appear that at the last minute, he had a change of heart after his time spent in Limbo, with the Piper's Friends."

"That may be so," Mabel said. "But what of Gestas?"

"Gestas has always been closed off to all parties of the afterlife, and now he too is awol, so, it's difficult to discern his motivations. That being said, Cain visited his neighbour's house as soon as he returned to Purgatory. By all accounts, it's been ransacked. Whether that means there's been a struggle or, Gestas left in a hurry, we've yet to determine;" Thet shook his head grimly. "I fear that this isn't the last we've heard of the impenitent thief."

The show continued late into the night and by the time the final chords had been struck, Mabel and Thet's voices were croaky and tired from their cheering. As the last of the crowds drove away from the car park, their rear headlights burning red in the distance; the Dark Omen's group staggered tiredly out to their tour bus, sucking water greedily from flasks and wiping sweat from their faces on aged hand towels.
"You have the voice of an angel Thet," Adrian laughed, as he embraced the reaper with open arms.
Thet laughed loudly, "I don't know about that, maybe an angel falling from the heavens."

Adrian winked mischievously, "your words, not mine!"

Eric winced as he stretched his arms wide, and grasped his shoulder; "I tell you Mab, I'll be glad when these hurts heal. Nothing worse than having a black and blue shoulder to rest your guitar on for over an hour;" his eyes glazed over, and he stared off into space before groaning. "Yes, I know you're doing the best you can with the energy you have... No, I will not be getting the caterer's number for you... Oh, please, I don't need to see those images!"

He looked around sheepishly as the rest of his friends watched on amused, "Asmo's feeling a little jaded;" he explained. "Even Kris secured a few numbers for his demonic appetite once in a while."

"What?" Kristoph scolded, "I did not! The lying little..." he stopped short at Eric's laugh.

"We're joking mate! Honestly, having Asmo chilling about inside the ol' noggin' is a bit of a hoot. He's really opened up to me, I think this is going to be a new bromance in the making, no offence!" He added, as Kristoph looked at him, put out.

"So, Thet..." Peter draped his arms lazily over Jésús and Adrian who wrinkled their noses at the ripe smell of sweat and body odour stemming from his underarms. "Mab said you have some news you wanted to share with us all?"

"Ah, yes..." Thet pressed his hands together. "So, courtesy of your efforts and assistance, I have received word from on high that you are to be rewarded when your times come."

"Well, that's a little ominous and grim;" Adrian's smile faltered. "Should we be worried?"

Thet blanched, "Heaven's no! It's just an FYI, if you will, for future reference. See it as a permanent VIP pass to any after life location. You will all have free reign to slip between them as and when you eventually... move on. So that's one bit of news."

"The second bit of news?" Kristoph asked, as he patted his towel at his temples and rested his elbow on Mabel's shoulder.

Thet grimaced, and Mabel tensed as she spied his typical nervous knee bob.

"So, there's a room up top;" Thet explained, hesitantly. "It's called the room of planning. It's where the Almighty used to work on potential projects to add to the human world below. Some of them made it, others didn't and remained in little realms adjacent to those of yours, like alternative realms if you will."

"Right...?" Mabel narrowed her eyes, suspiciously.

"Well, that room happened to be where you and Kris found Mother, the archangels, and the spirits. When Mother opened the portal for you all to slip through, she did it in a mad rush to protect me; and well... she might have forgotten to close the portal behind her."

"So?" Eric frowned.

"So, some creatures got loose, and we could use some help shepherding them back;" Thet winced.

"That's not possible," Mabel frowned, "I didn't see any creatures there other than taxidermized imaginings."

Thet bobbed his knees again, "These creatures are used to being hunted, killed, even imprisoned by the likes of humans and us deities. As such, they've mastered the art of hiding in plain sight." Mabel recalled the image of the centaur and how large and menacing it had looked, and her thoughts inadvertently recalled the tales of creatures from the ancient myths and legends of different cultures that she'd read about, during her studies.

Swallowing heavily, she asked; "when you say creatures, you mean..."

"Creatures of great power from your myths, legends, dreams, and nightmares;" Thet grimaced, as Mabel, Kristoph, and Eric groaned and staggered on the spot in disbelief.

Adrian, Pete, and Jésús however, simply laughed loudly; "well, that's the inspiration for our next album guaranteed!" Adrian grinned.

Printed in Great Britain
by Amazon

37278689R00370